9/8

DORR TOWNSHIP LIBRARY (DOR)

3 1341 00070 2481

P9-BTM-921

Premier
Selection

DATE DUE

AP 16 '00

DE 03 '01

JY 12 '11

AP 10 '12

MY 25 '12

AUG 0 1 2018

JUL 1 7 2019

WITHDRAWN

Demco, Inc. 38-293

:01

First Second

New York & London

Dorr Township Library

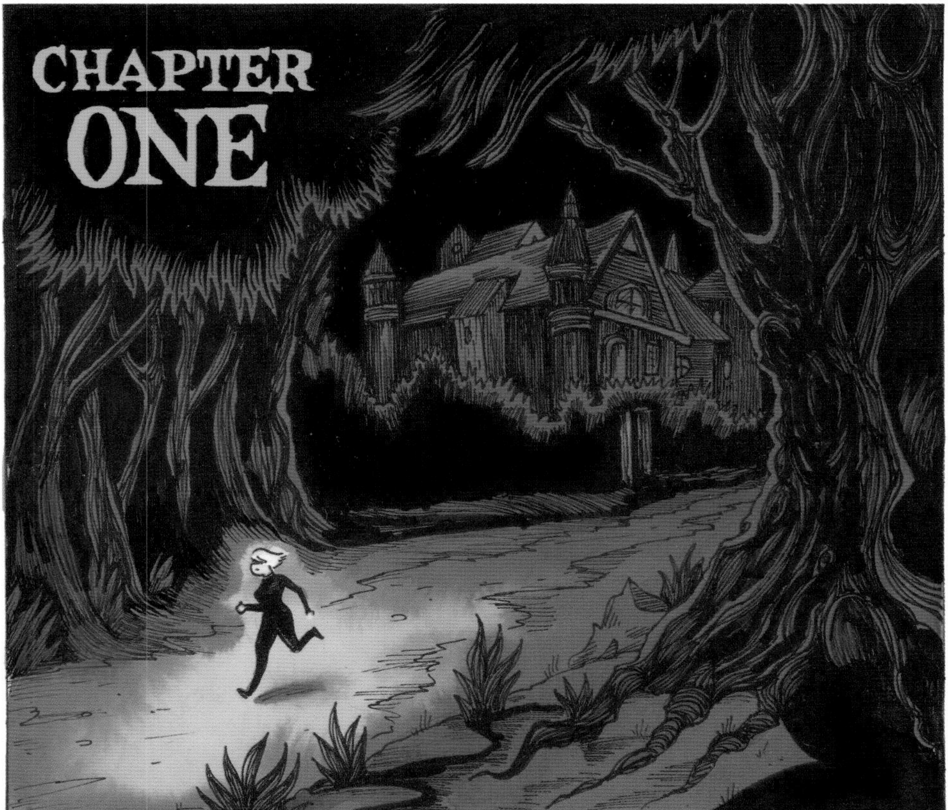
CHAPTER
ONE

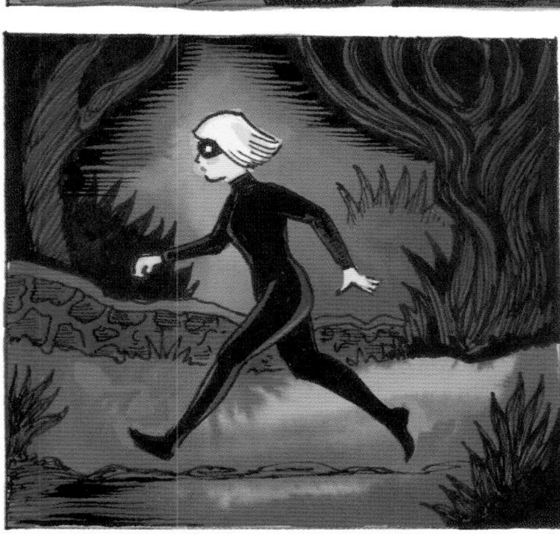

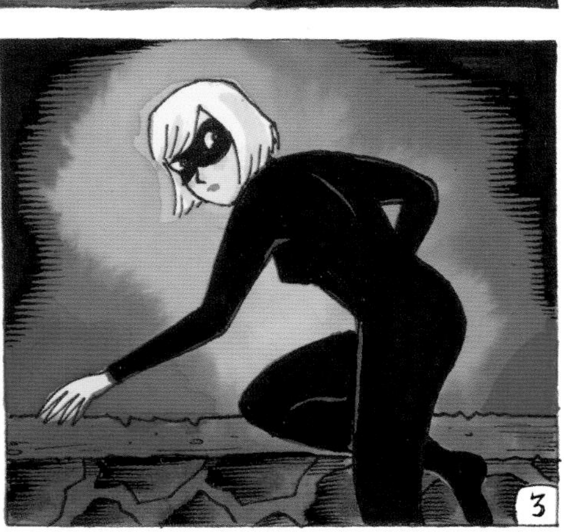
3

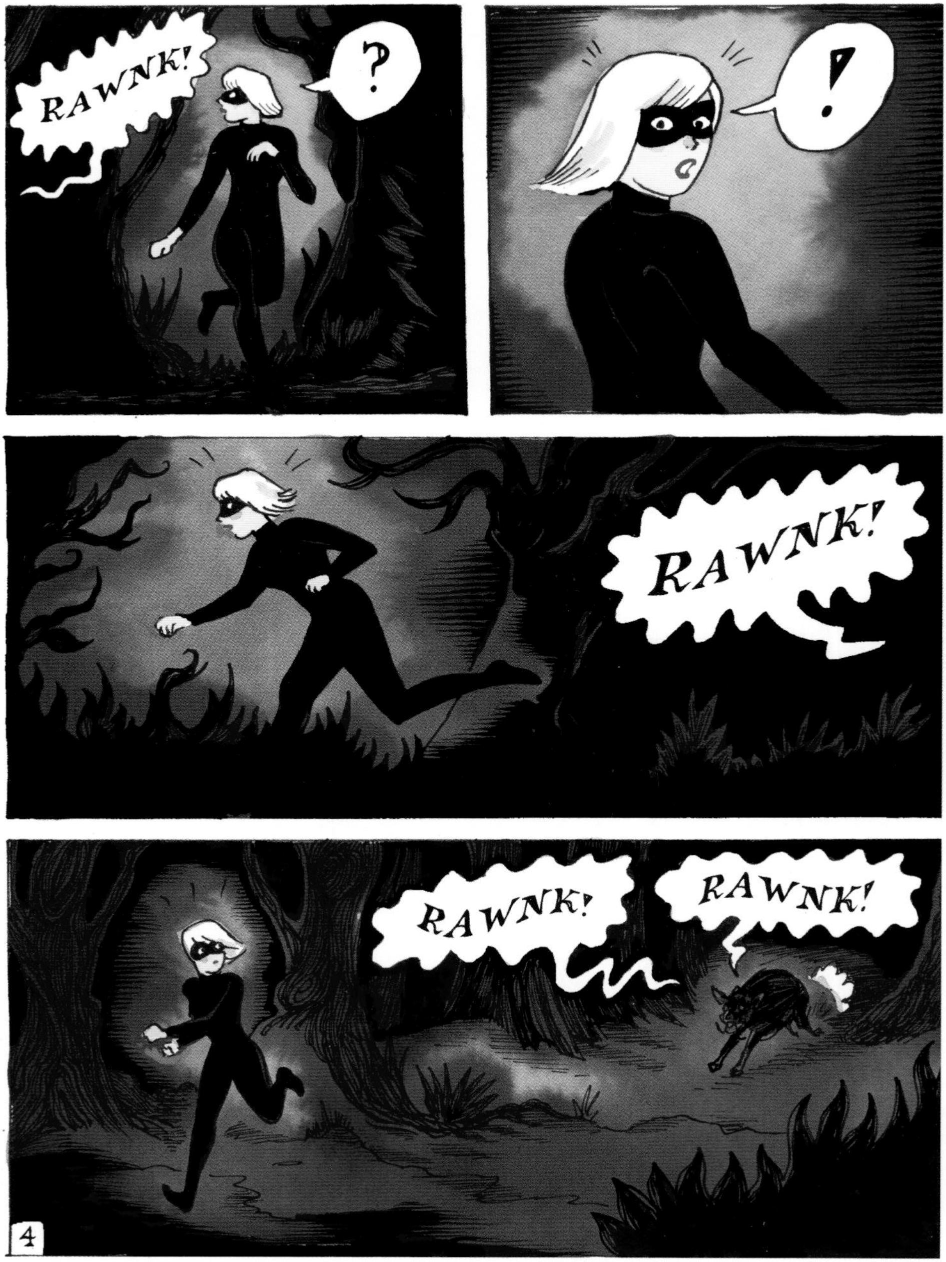
RAWNK!
?
!
RAWNK!
RAWNK!
RAWNK!

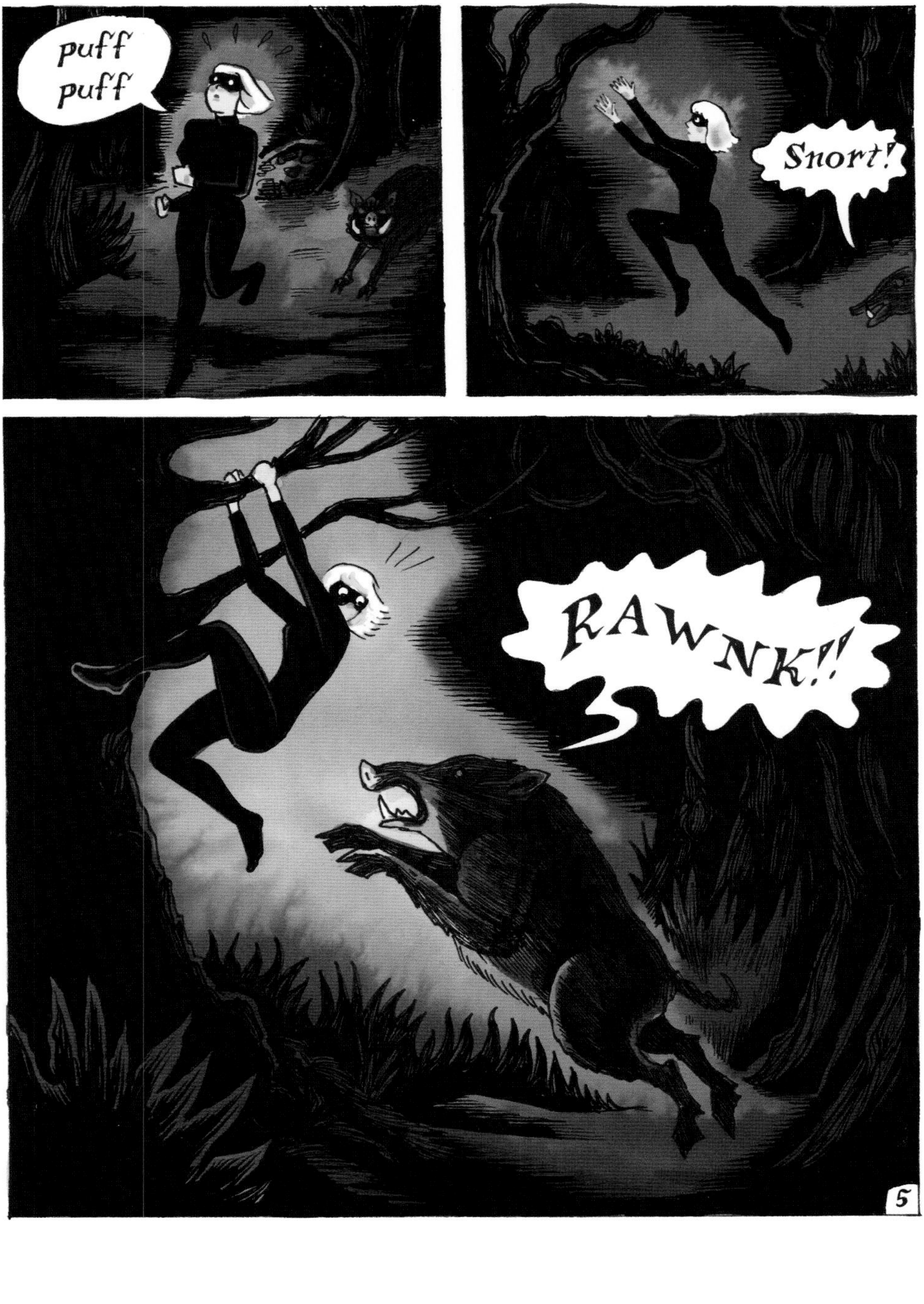

puff
puff
Snort!
RAWNK!!

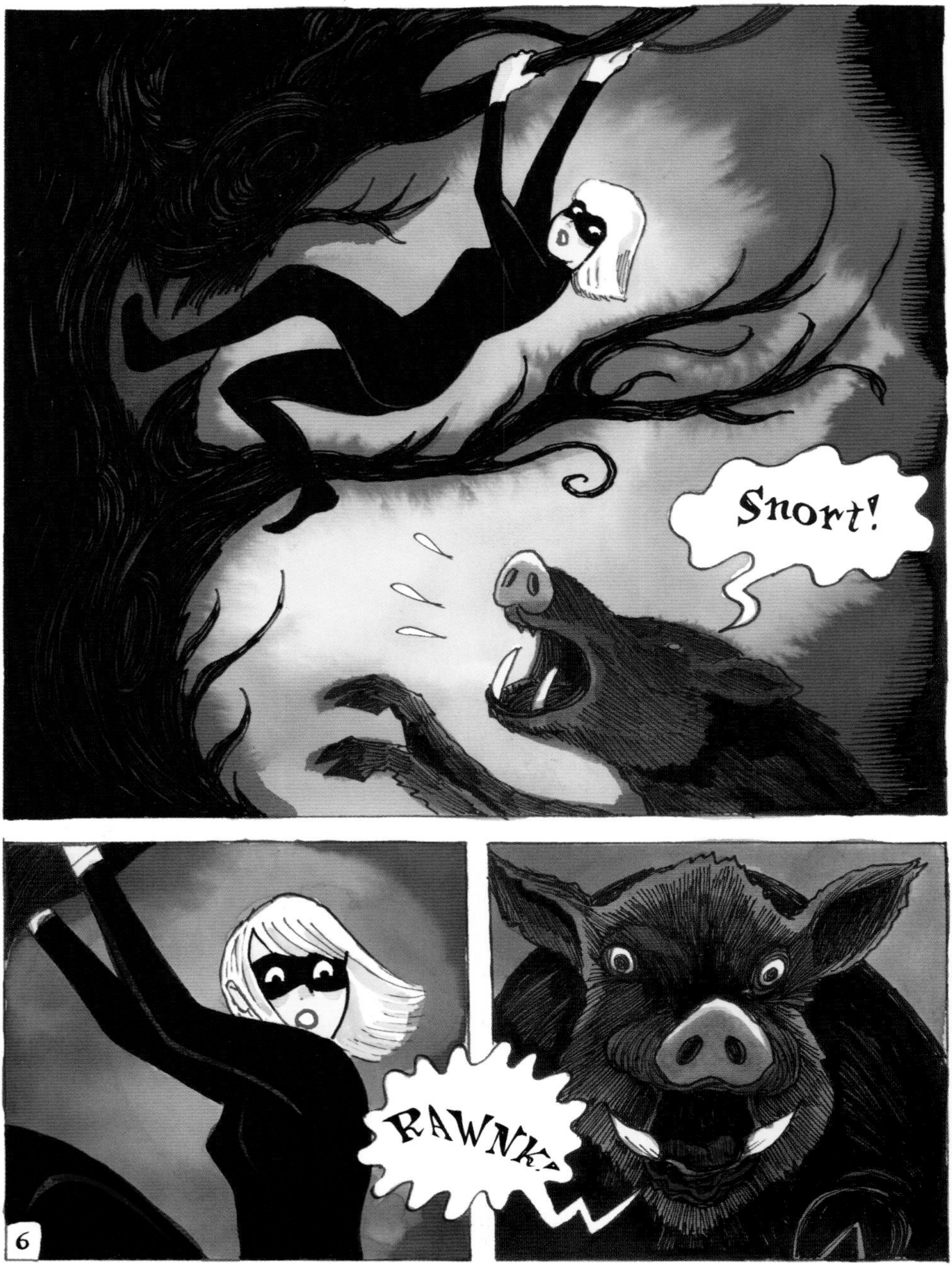
Snort!
RAWNK!

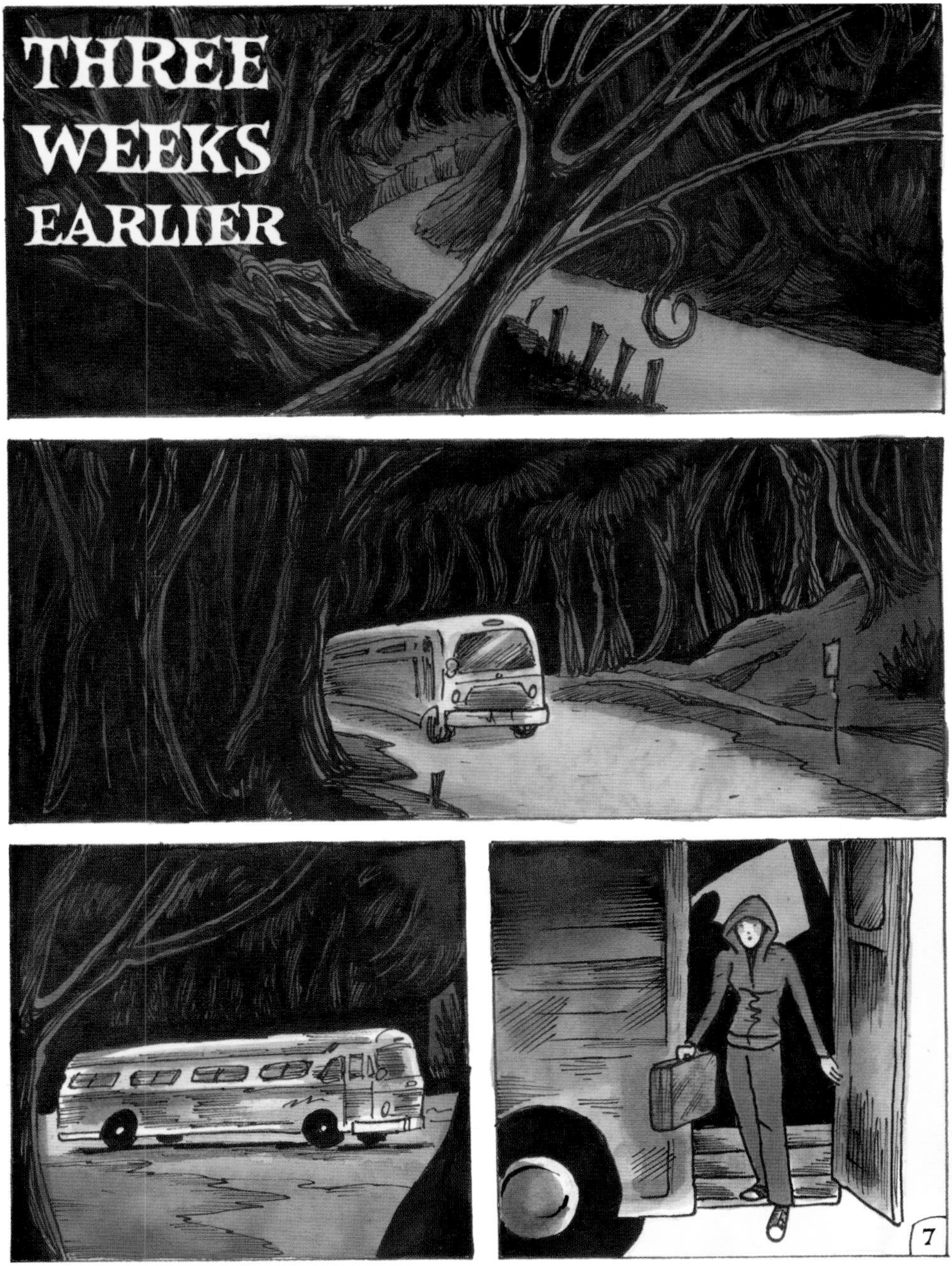
THREE WEEKS EARLIER

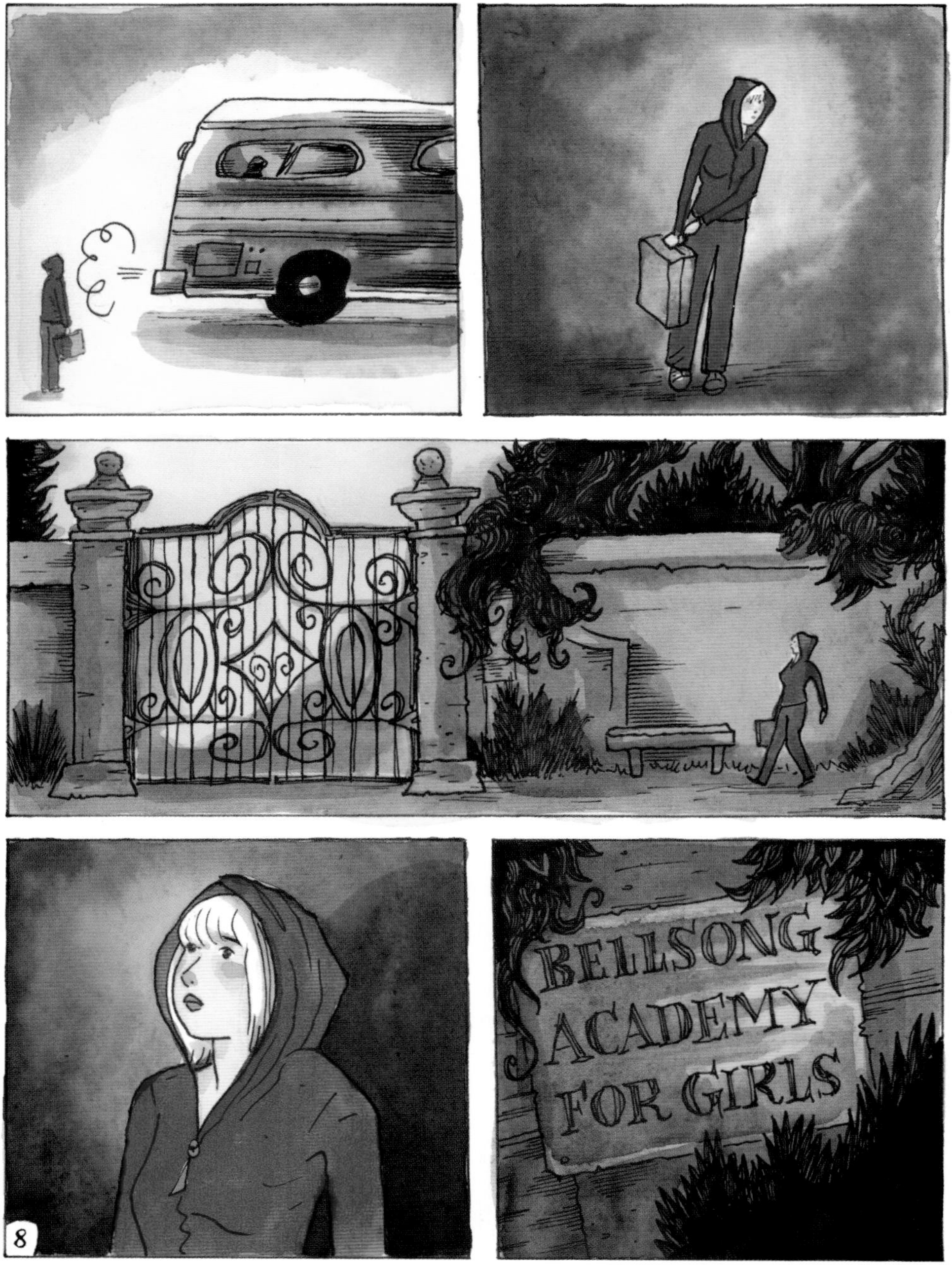
BELLSONG ACADEMY FOR GIRLS

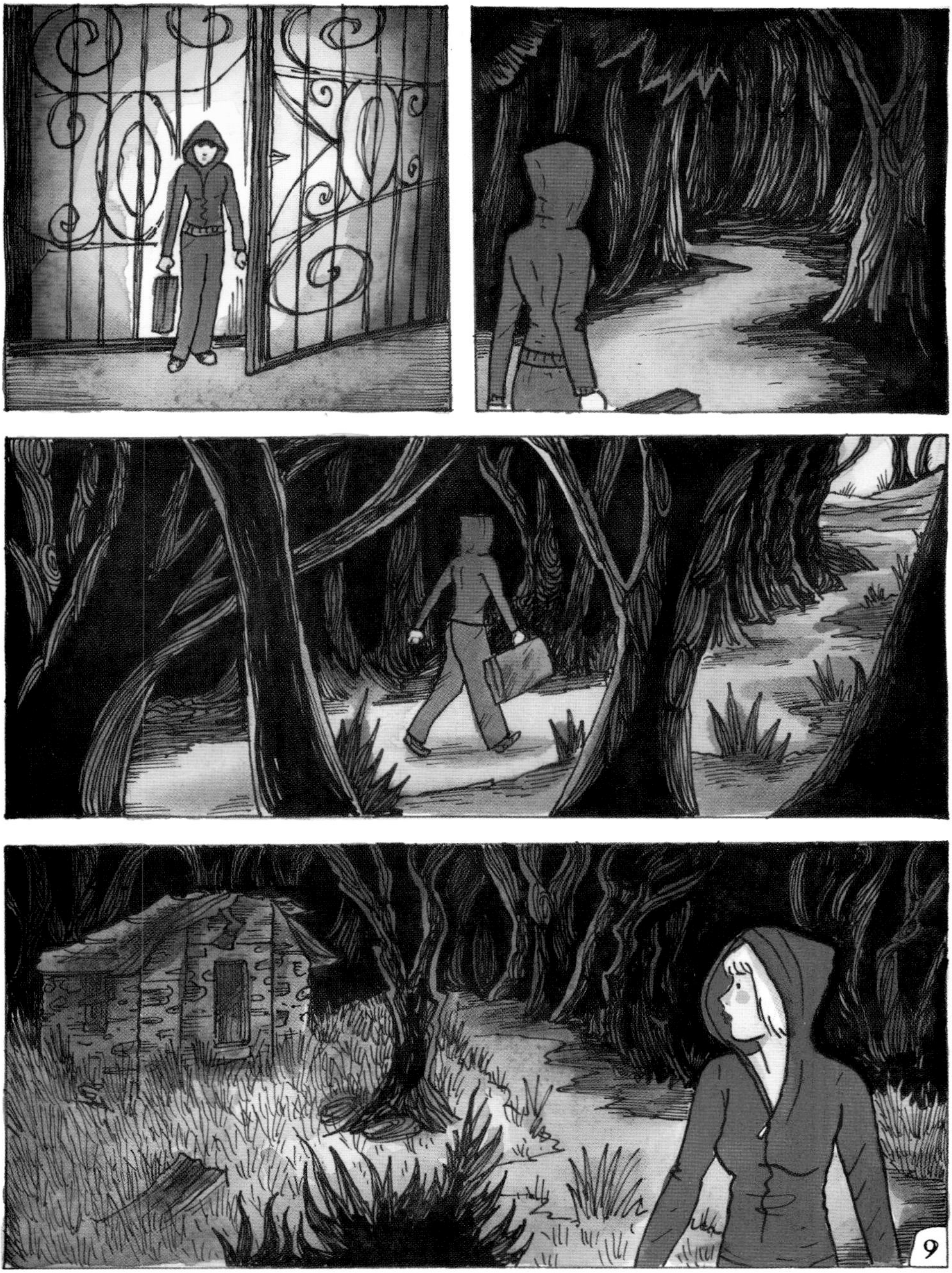
9

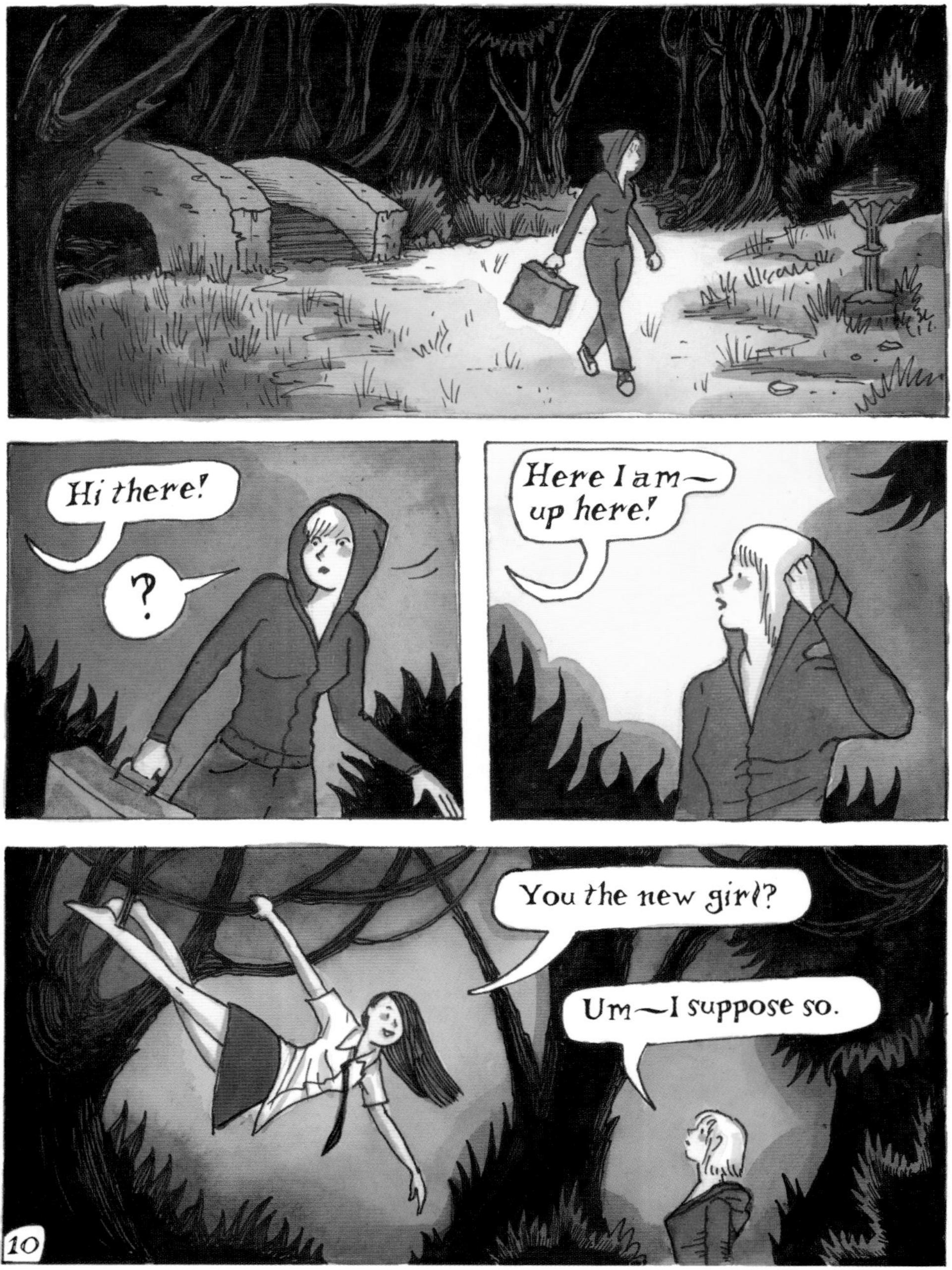
Hi there!
?
Here I am— up here!
You the new girl?
Um—I suppose so.

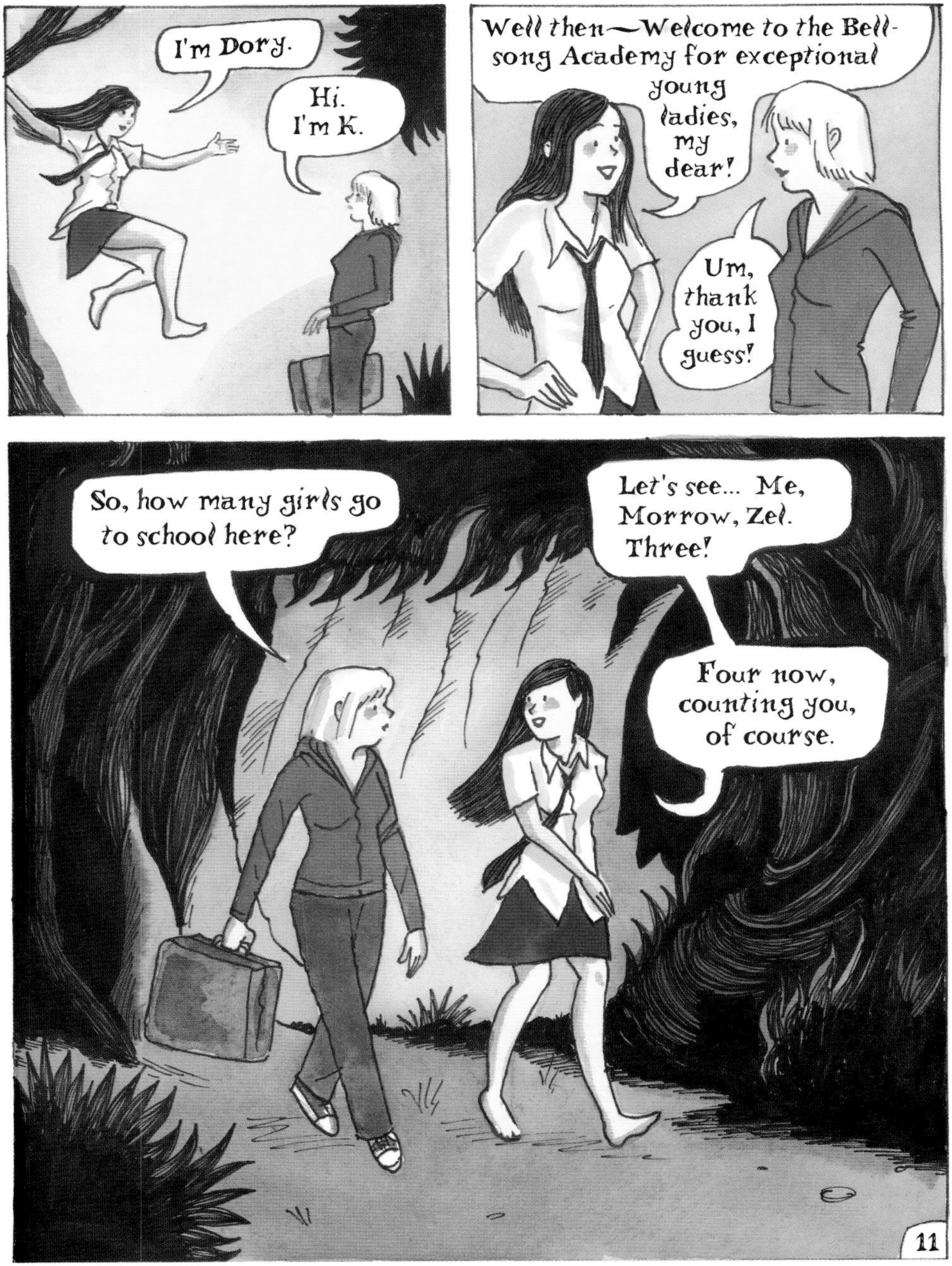
I'm Dory.
Hi. I'm K.
Well then—Welcome to the Bell-song Academy for exceptional young ladies, my dear!
Um, thank you, I guess!
So, how many girls go to school here?
Let's see... Me, Morrow, Zel. Three!
Four now, counting you, of course.

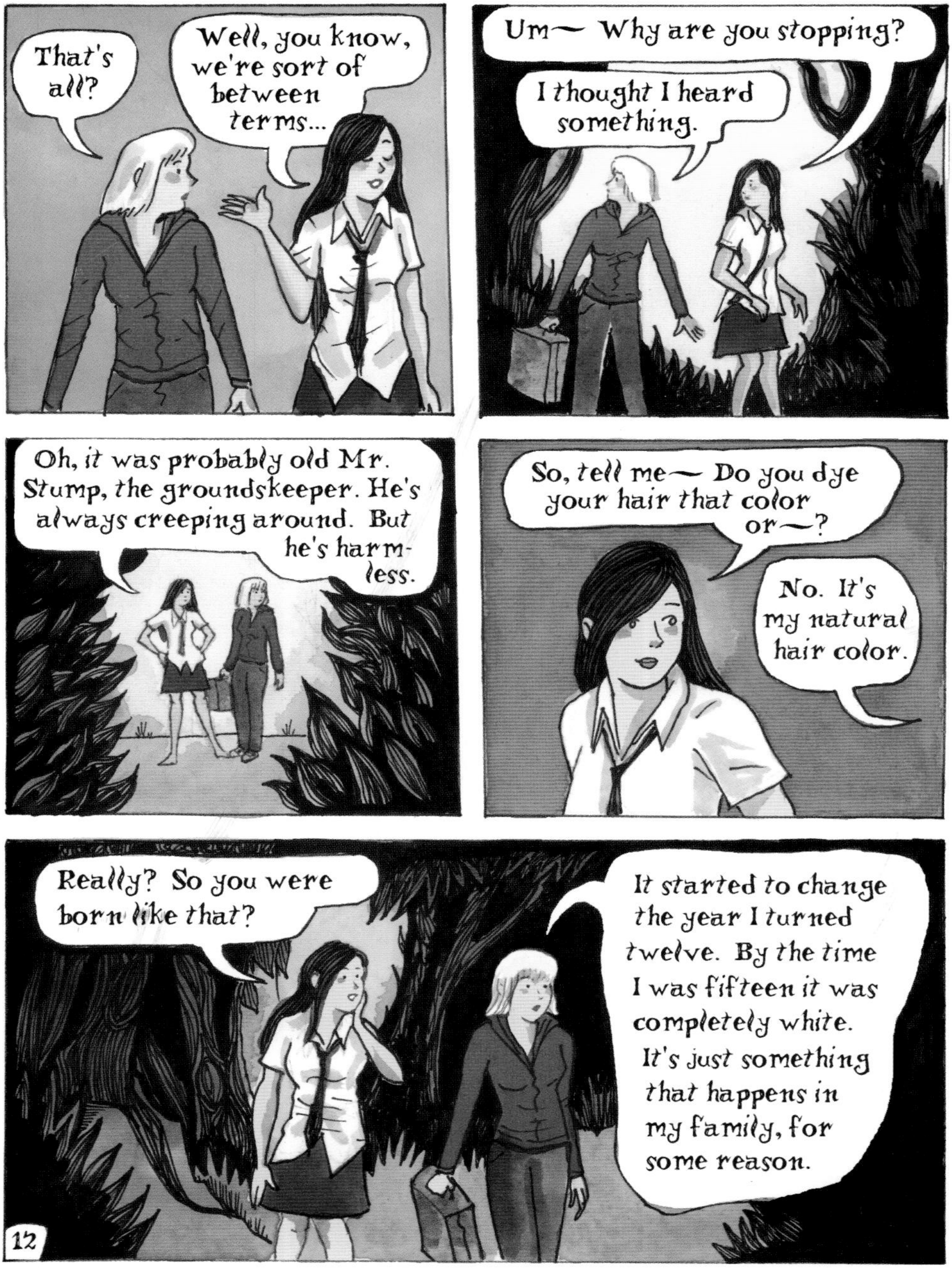
That's all?
Well, you know, we're sort of between terms...
Um— Why are you stopping?
I thought I heard something.
Oh, it was probably old Mr. Stump, the groundskeeper. He's always creeping around. But he's harm-less.
So, tell me— Do you dye your hair that color or—?
No. It's my natural hair color.
Really? So you were born like that?
It started to change the year I turned twelve. By the time I was fifteen it was completely white. It's just something that happens in my family, for some reason.

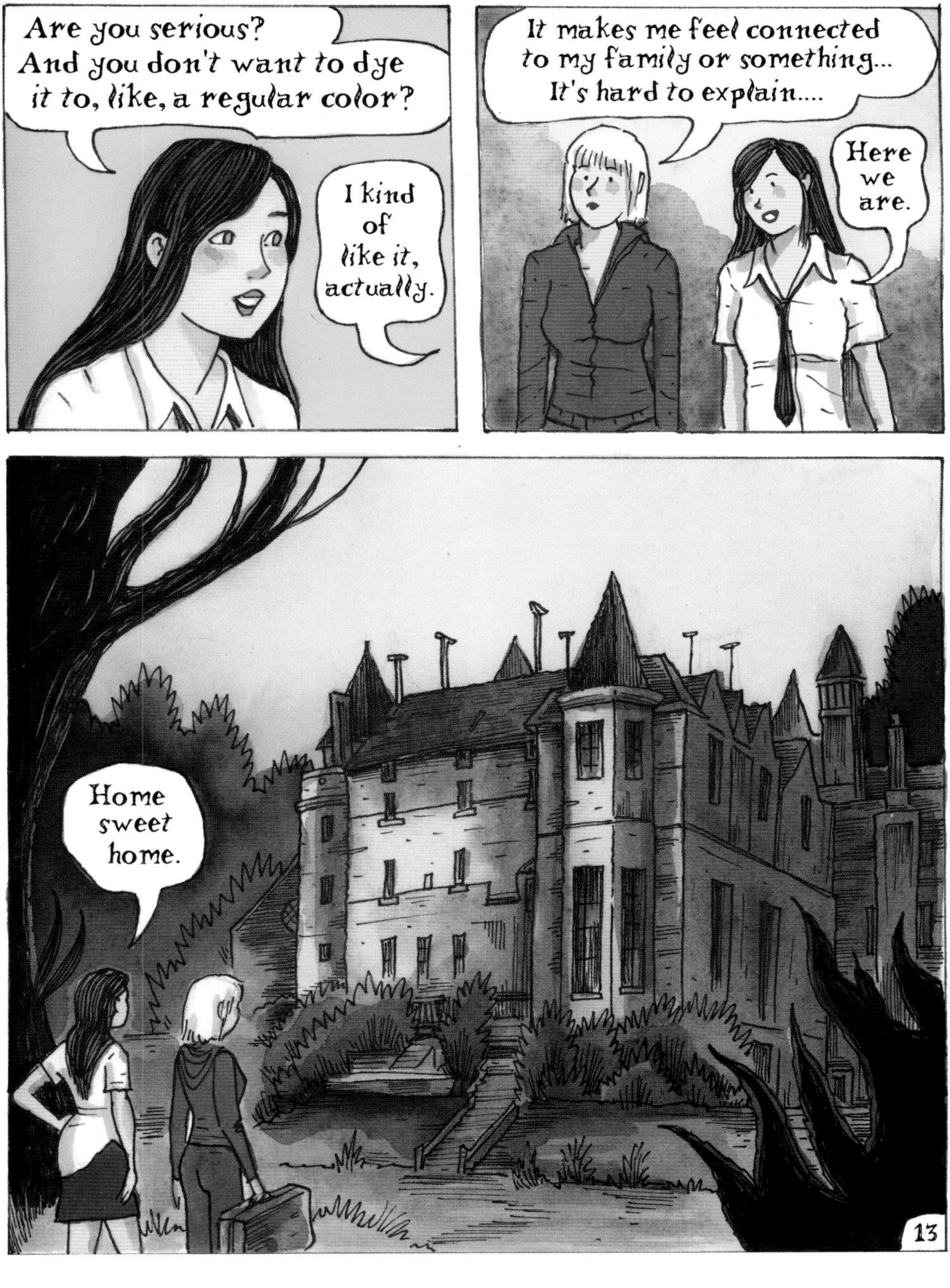
Are you serious? And you don't want to dye it to, like, a regular color?
I kind of like it, actually.
It makes me feel connected to my family or something... It's hard to explain....
Here we are.
Home sweet home.

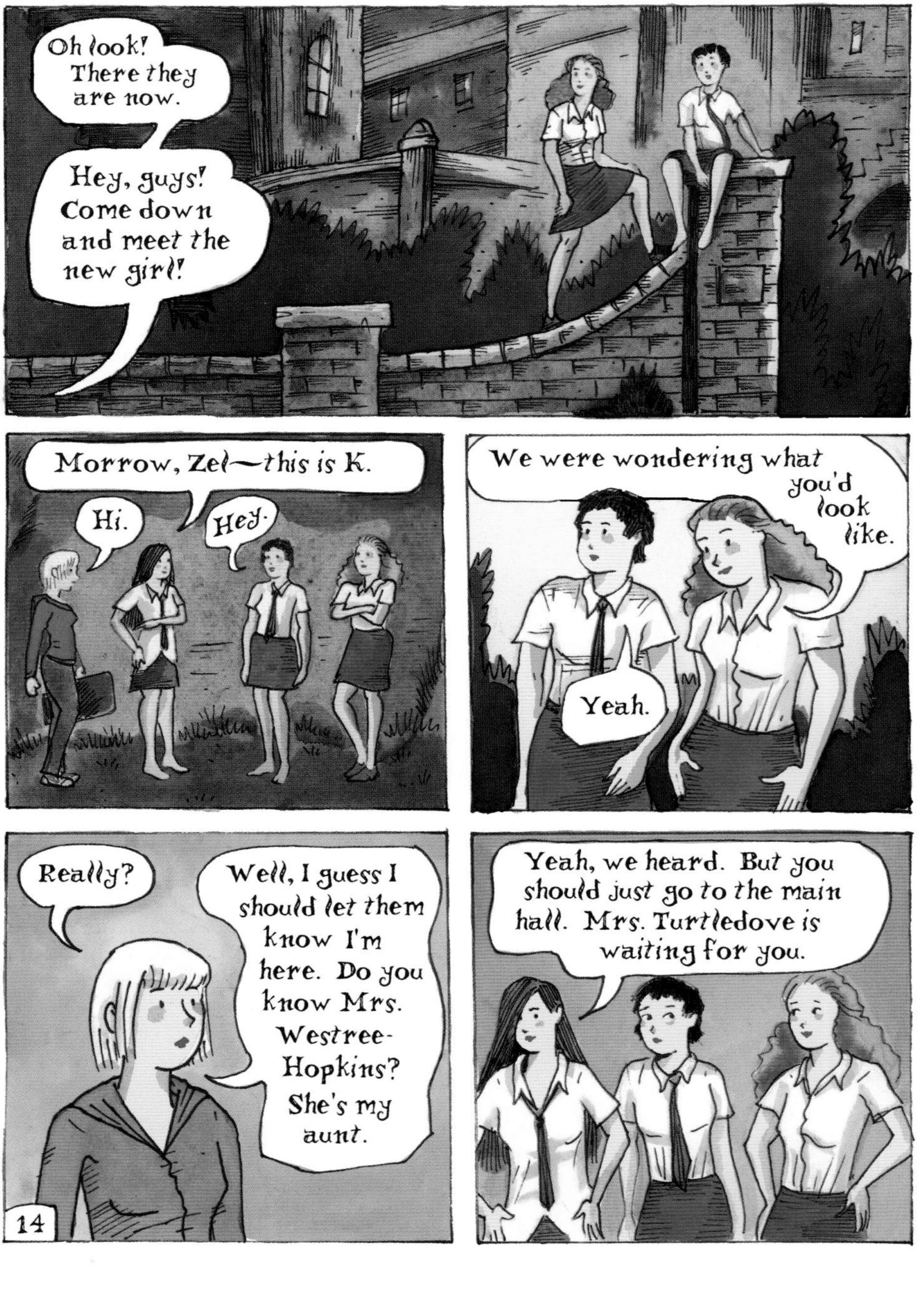
Oh look! There they are now.
Hey, guys! Come down and meet the new girl!
Morrow, Zel—this is K.
Hi.
Hey.
We were wondering what you'd look like.
Yeah.
Really?
Well, I guess I should let them know I'm here. Do you know Mrs. Westree-Hopkins? She's my aunt.
Yeah, we heard. But you should just go to the main hall. Mrs. Turtledove is waiting for you.

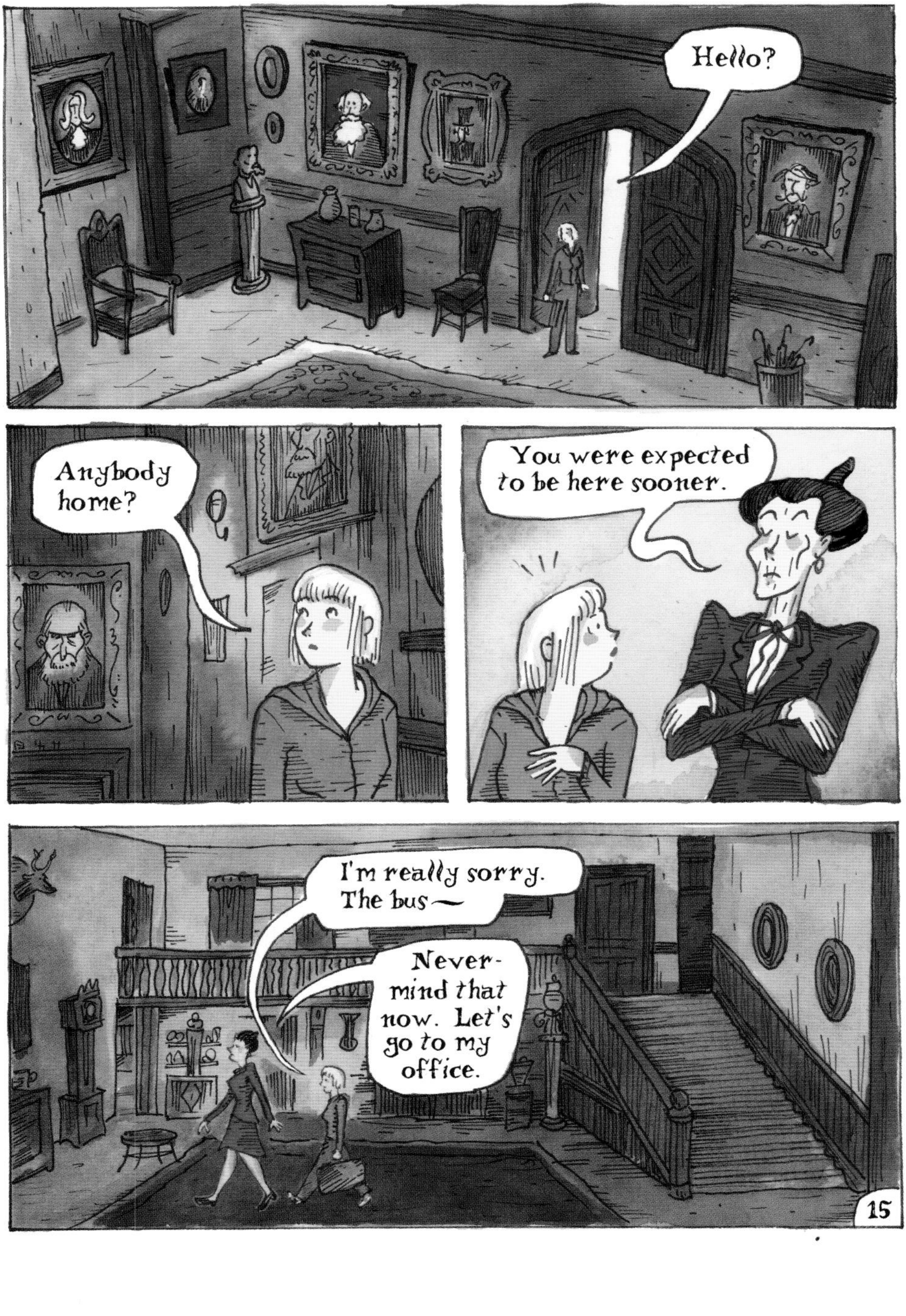
Hello?
Anybody home?
You were expected to be here sooner.
I'm really sorry. The bus—
Never-mind that now. Let's go to my office.

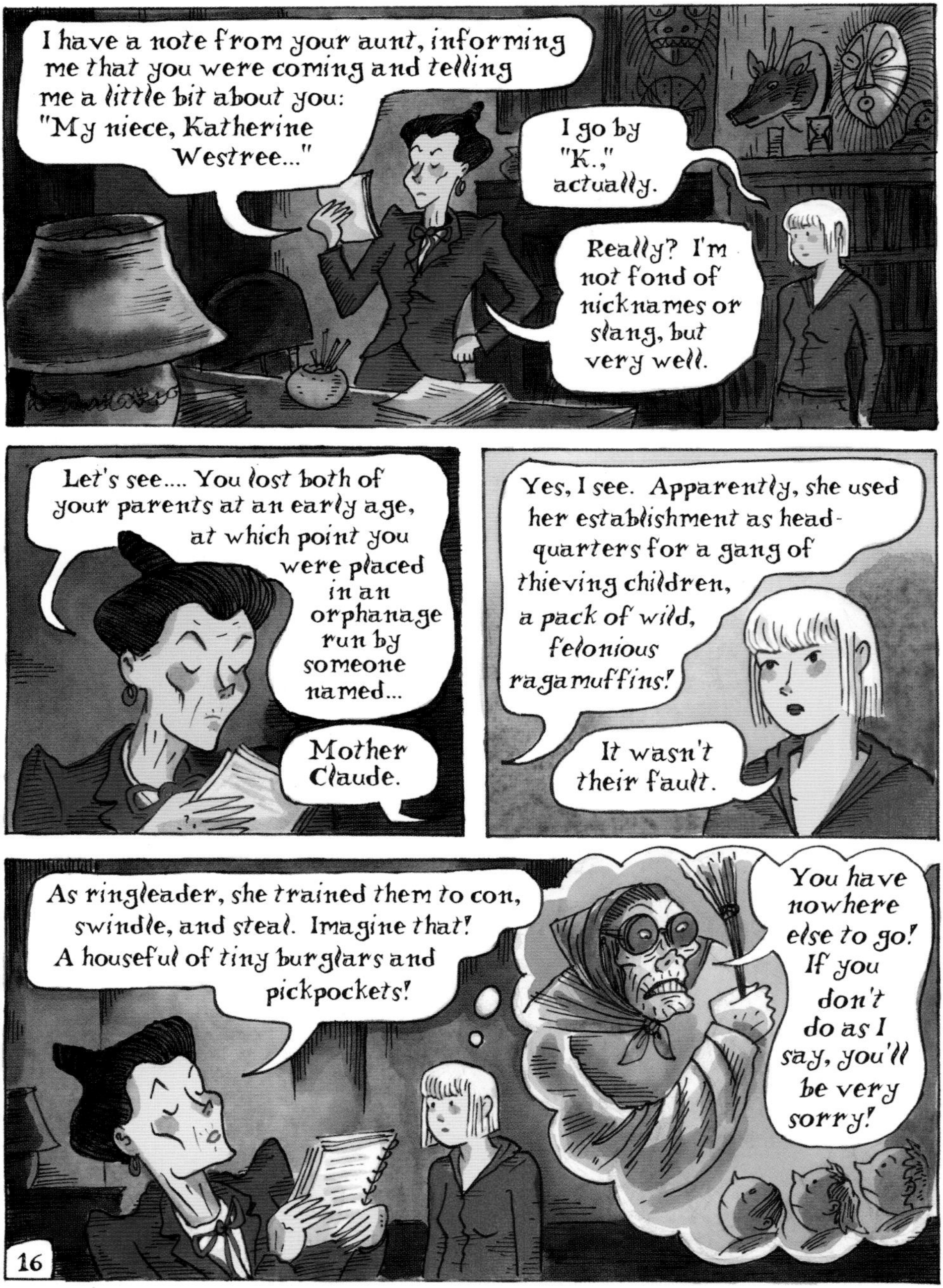
I have a note from your aunt, informing me that you were coming and telling me a little bit about you: "My niece, Katherine Westree..."
I go by "K.," actually.
Really? I'm not fond of nicknames or slang, but very well.
Let's see.... You lost both of your parents at an early age, at which point you were placed in an orphanage run by someone named...
Mother Claude.
Yes, I see. Apparently, she used her establishment as head-quarters for a gang of thieving children, a pack of wild, felonious ragamuffins!
It wasn't their fault.
As ringleader, she trained them to con, swindle, and steal. Imagine that! A houseful of tiny burglars and pickpockets!
You have nowhere else to go! If you don't do as I say, you'll be very sorry!

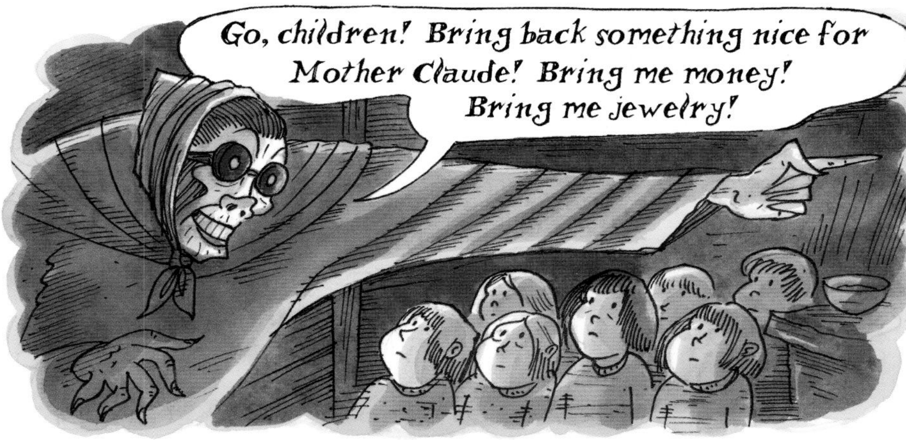
Go, children! Bring back something nice for Mother Claude! Bring me money! Bring me jewelry!

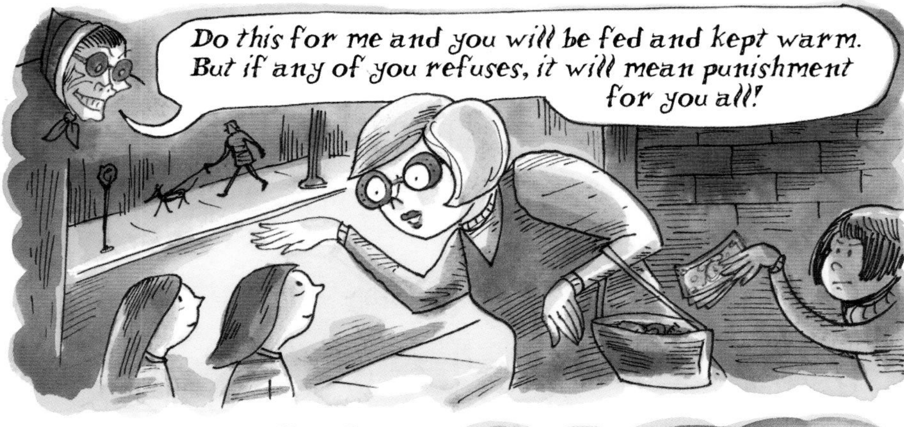
Do this for me and you will be fed and kept warm. But if any of you refuses, it will mean punishment for you all!

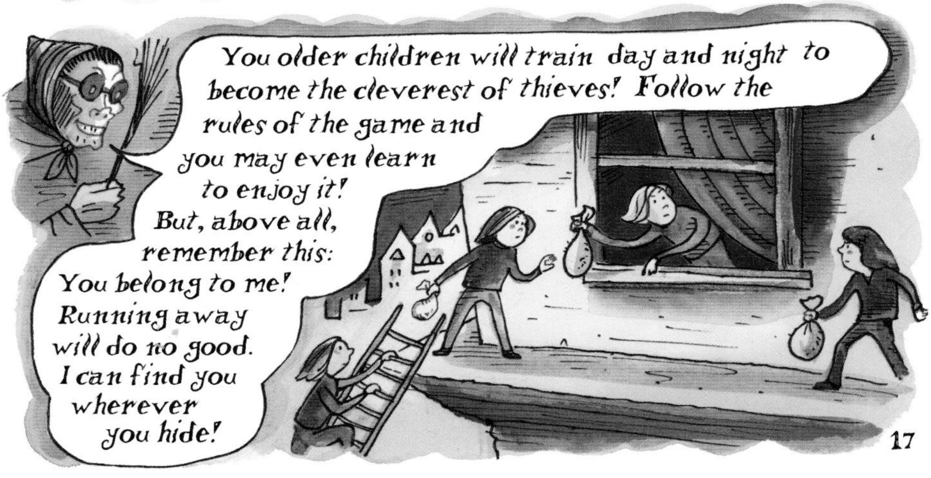
You older children will train day and night to become the cleverest of thieves! Follow the rules of the game and you may even learn to enjoy it! But, above all, remember this: You belong to me! Running away will do no good. I can find you wherever you hide!

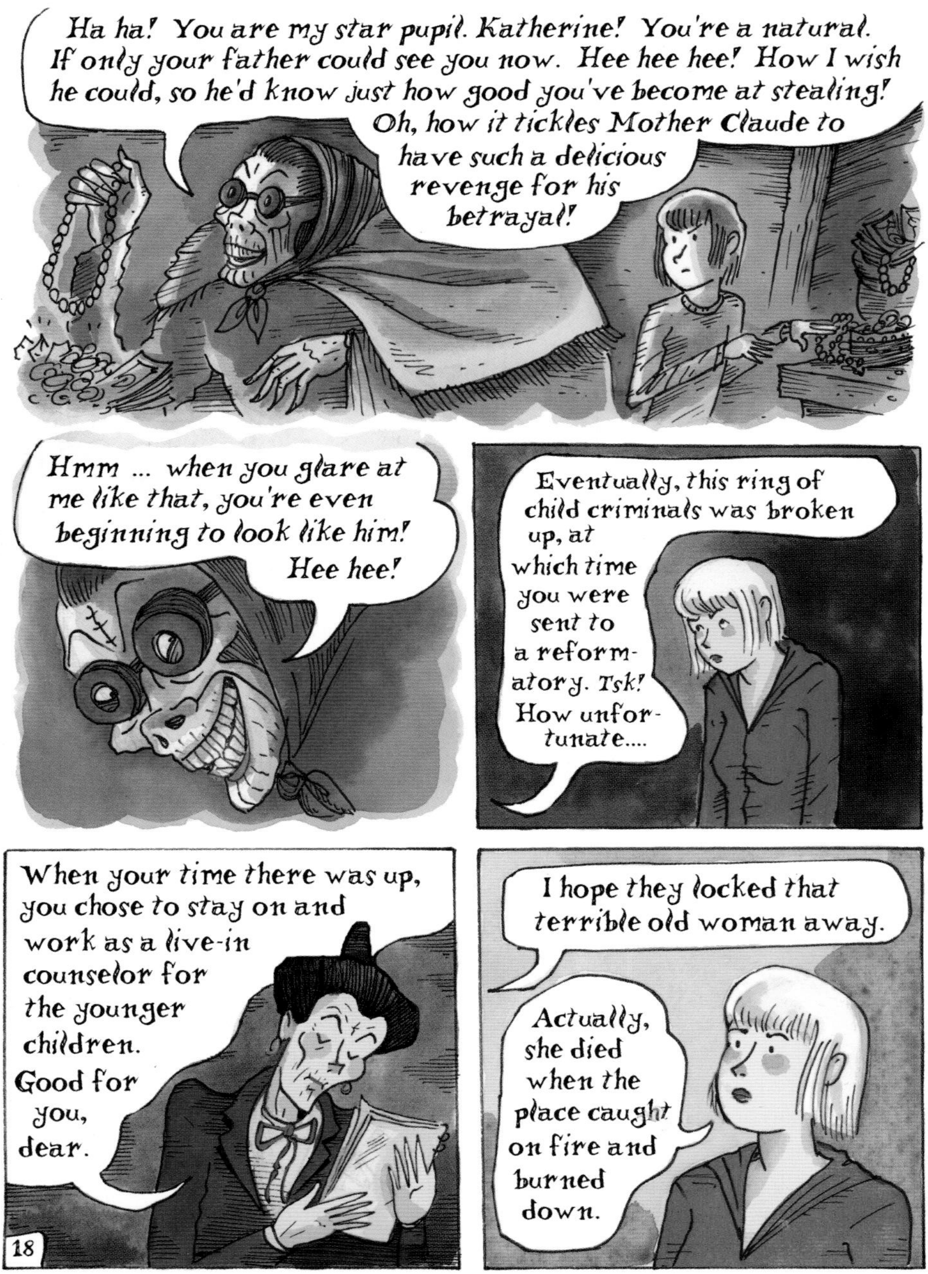
Ha ha! You are my star pupil, Katherine! You're a natural. If only your father could see you now. Hee hee hee! How I wish he could, so he'd know just how good you've become at stealing!
Oh, how it tickles Mother Claude to have such a delicious revenge for his betrayal!
Hmm ... when you glare at me like that, you're even beginning to look like him! Hee hee!
Eventually, this ring of child criminals was broken up, at which time you were sent to a reformatory. Tsk! How unfortunate....
When your time there was up, you chose to stay on and work as a live-in counselor for the younger children. Good for you, dear.
I hope they locked that terrible old woman away.
Actually, she died when the place caught on fire and burned down.

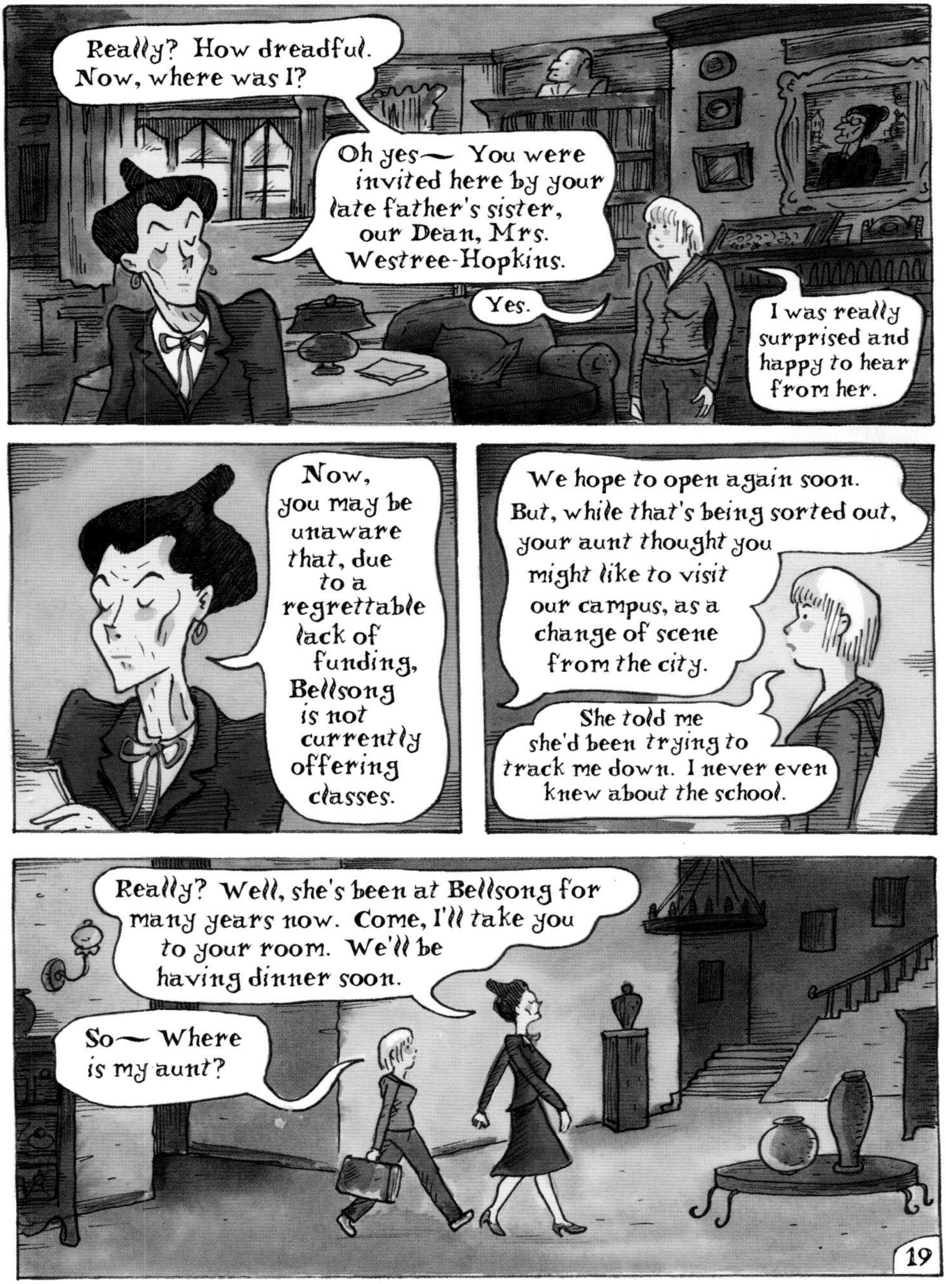
Really? How dreadful. Now, where was I?
Oh yes— You were invited here by your late father's sister, our Dean, Mrs. Westree-Hopkins.
Yes.
I was really surprised and happy to hear from her.
Now, you may be unaware that, due to a regrettable lack of funding, Bellsong is not currently offering classes.
We hope to open again soon. But, while that's being sorted out, your aunt thought you might like to visit our campus, as a change of scene from the city.
She told me she'd been trying to track me down. I never even knew about the school.
Really? Well, she's been at Bellsong for many years now. Come, I'll take you to your room. We'll be having dinner soon.
So— Where is my aunt?

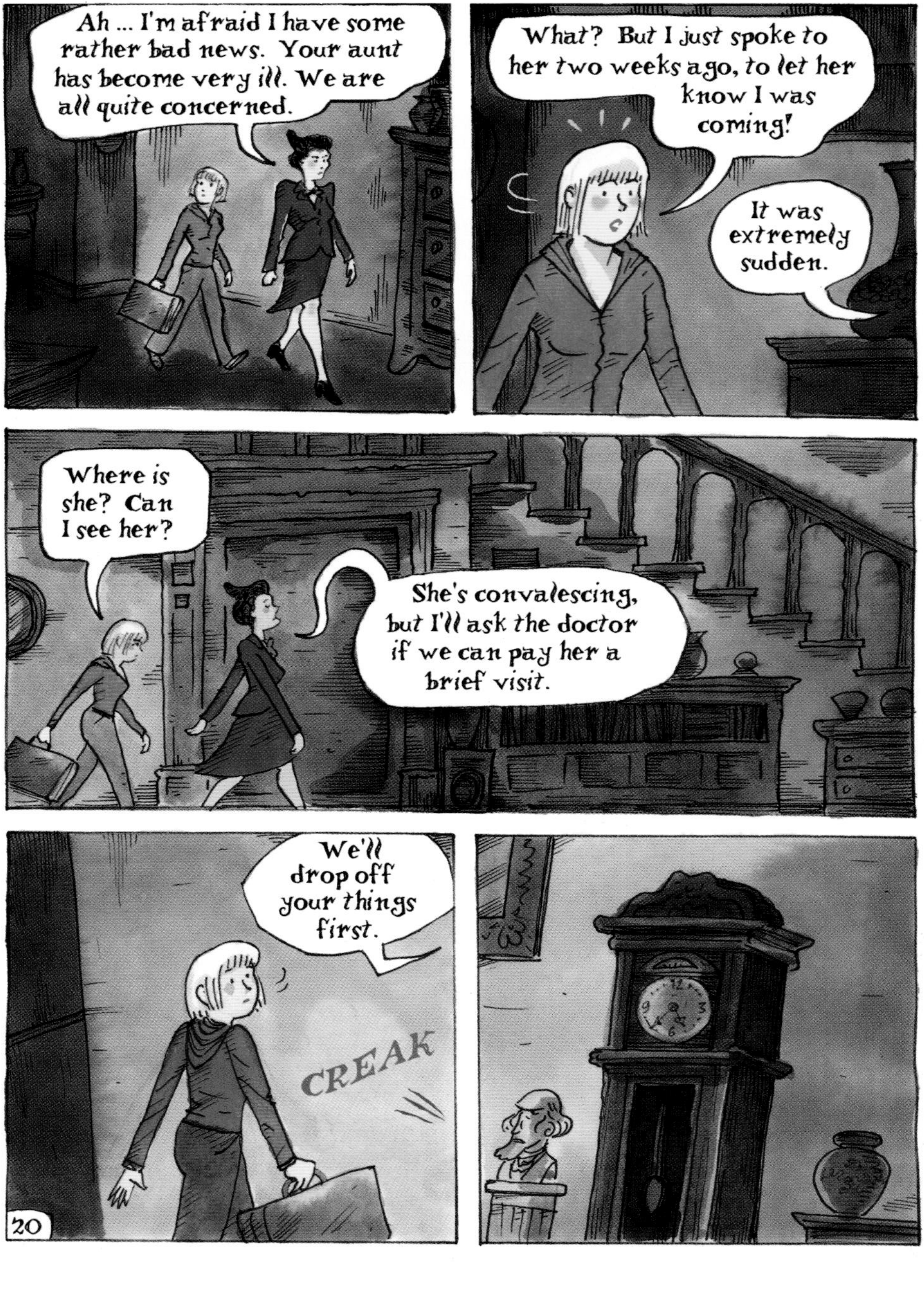
Ah ... I'm afraid I have some rather bad news. Your aunt has become very ill. We are all quite concerned.
What? But I just spoke to her two weeks ago, to let her know I was coming!
It was extremely sudden.
Where is she? Can I see her?
She's convalescing, but I'll ask the doctor if we can pay her a brief visit.
We'll drop off your things first.
CREAK

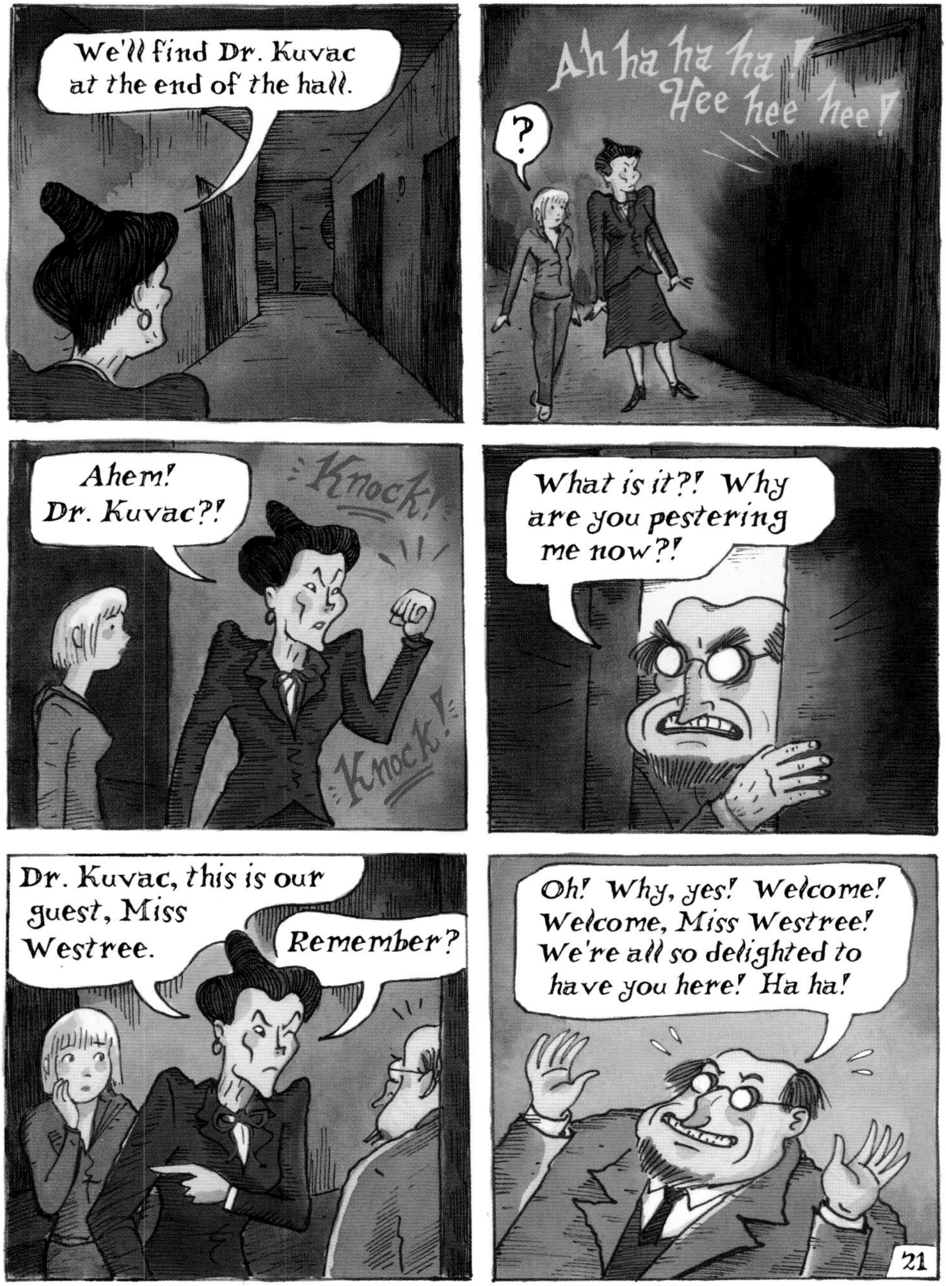
We'll find Dr. Kuvac at the end of the hall.
Ah ha ha ha! Hee hee hee!
?
Ahem! Dr. Kuvac?!
Knock!
Knock!
What is it?! Why are you pestering me now?!
Dr. Kuvac, this is our guest, Miss Westree.
Remember?
Oh! Why, yes! Welcome! Welcome, Miss Westree! We're all so delighted to have you here! Ha ha!

We mustn't stay long. She needs her rest.

What's wrong with her?

Wrong?

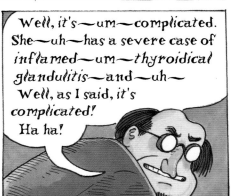

Well, it's —um—complicated. She—uh—has a severe case of inflamed—um—thyroidical glandulitis—and—uh— Well, as I said, it's complicated! Ha ha!

Hello! Are we decent? Ha ha! Dr. Kuvac here! We're coming in, ready or not!

Ha ha!

Knock Knock

Ah! There she is! There's my patient!

Getting plenty of rest, are we? Ha ha! Splendid! Delightful!

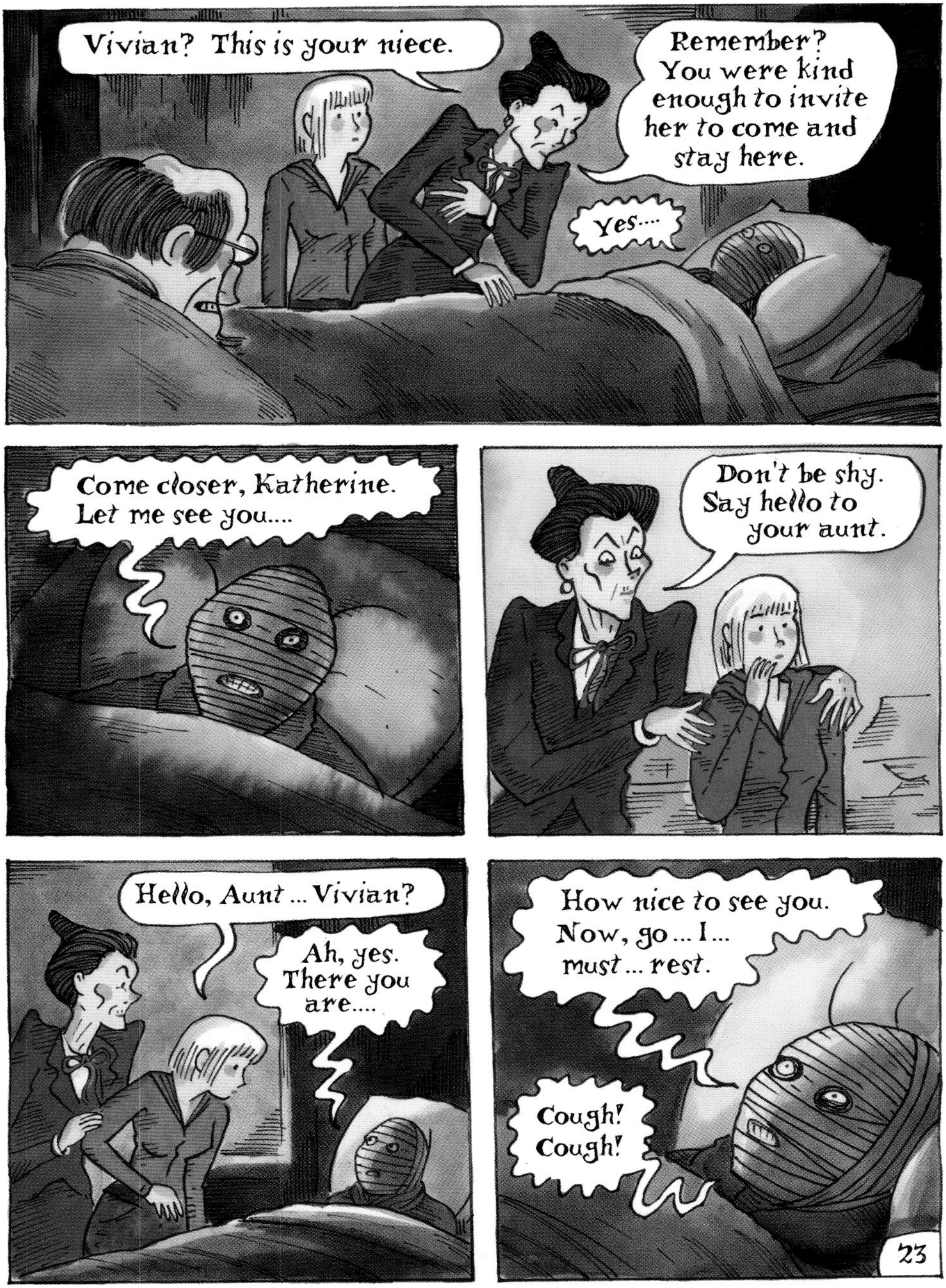
Vivian? This is your niece.
Remember? You were kind enough to invite her to come and stay here.
Yes....
Come closer, Katherine. Let me see you....
Don't be shy. Say hello to your aunt.
Hello, Aunt ... Vivian?
Ah, yes. There you are....
How nice to see you. Now, go ... I ... must ... rest.
Cough! Cough!

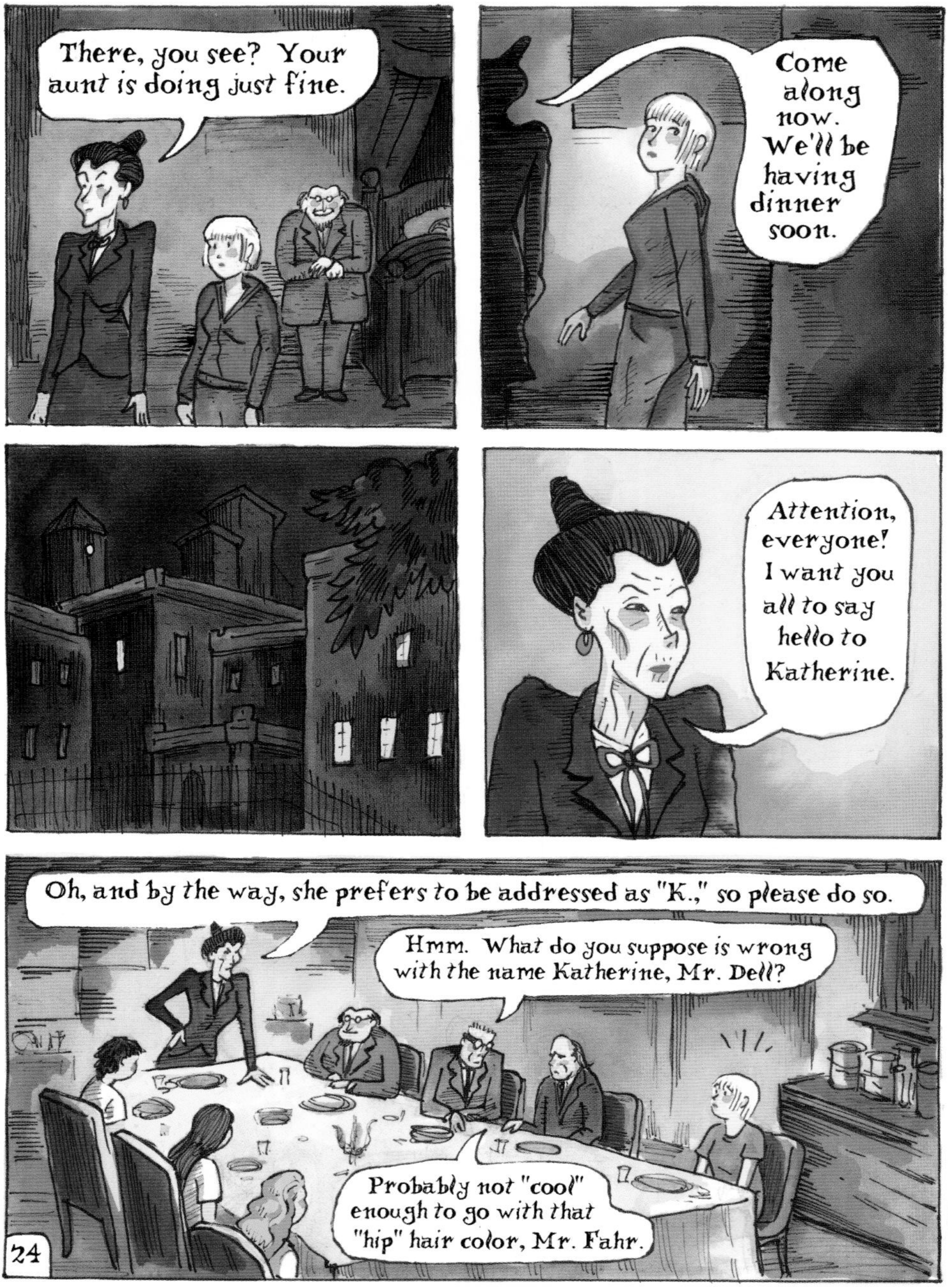
There, you see? Your aunt is doing just fine.
Come along now. We'll be having dinner soon.
Attention, everyone! I want you all to say hello to Katherine.
Oh, and by the way, she prefers to be addressed as "K.," so please do so.
Hmm. What do you suppose is wrong with the name Katherine, Mr. Dell?
Probably not "cool" enough to go with that "hip" hair color, Mr. Fahr.

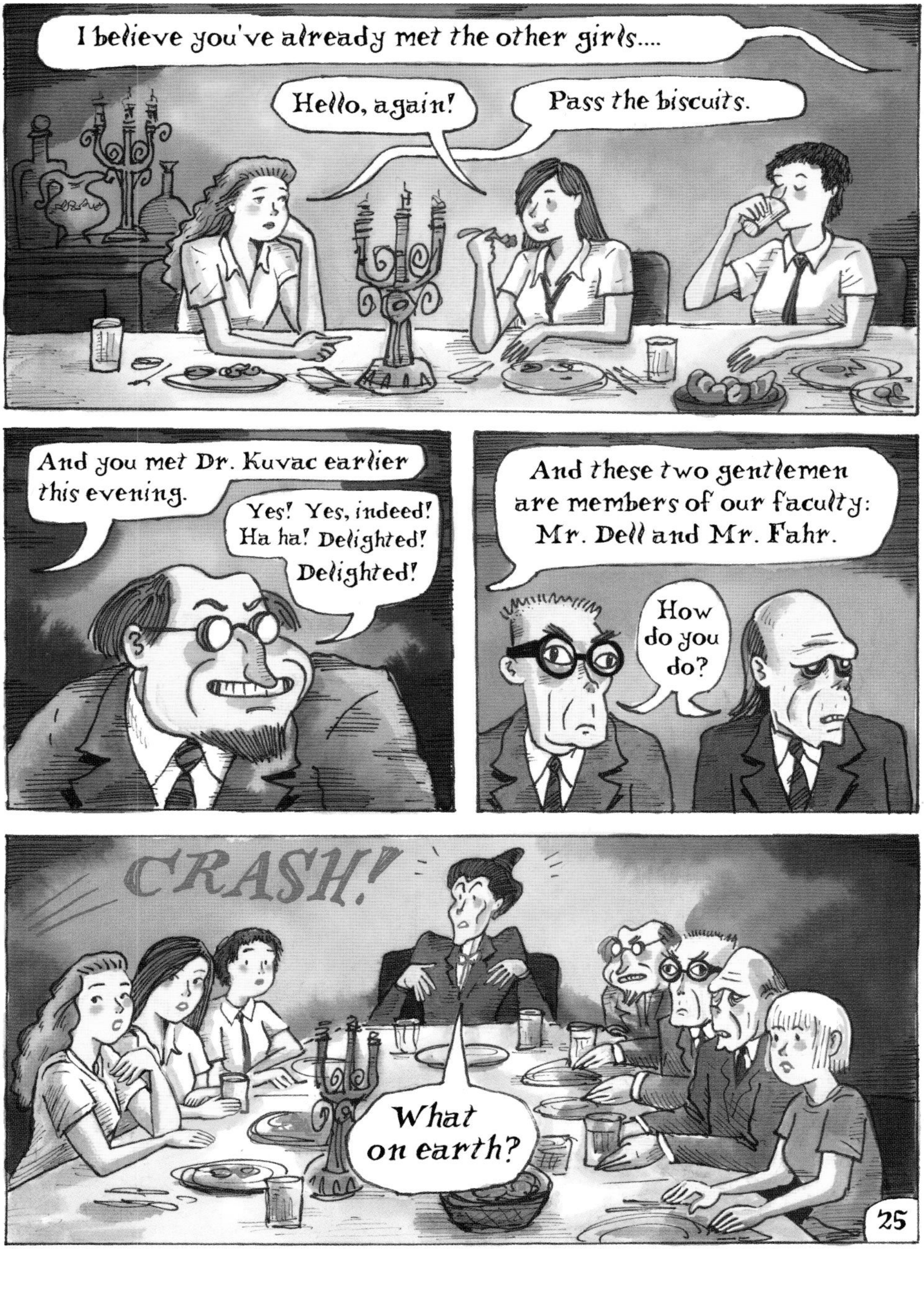
I believe you've already met the other girls....
Hello, again!
Pass the biscuits.
And you met Dr. Kuvac earlier this evening.
Yes! Yes, indeed! Ha ha! Delighted! Delighted!
And these two gentlemen are members of our faculty: Mr. Dell and Mr. Fahr.
How do you do?
CRASH!
What on earth?

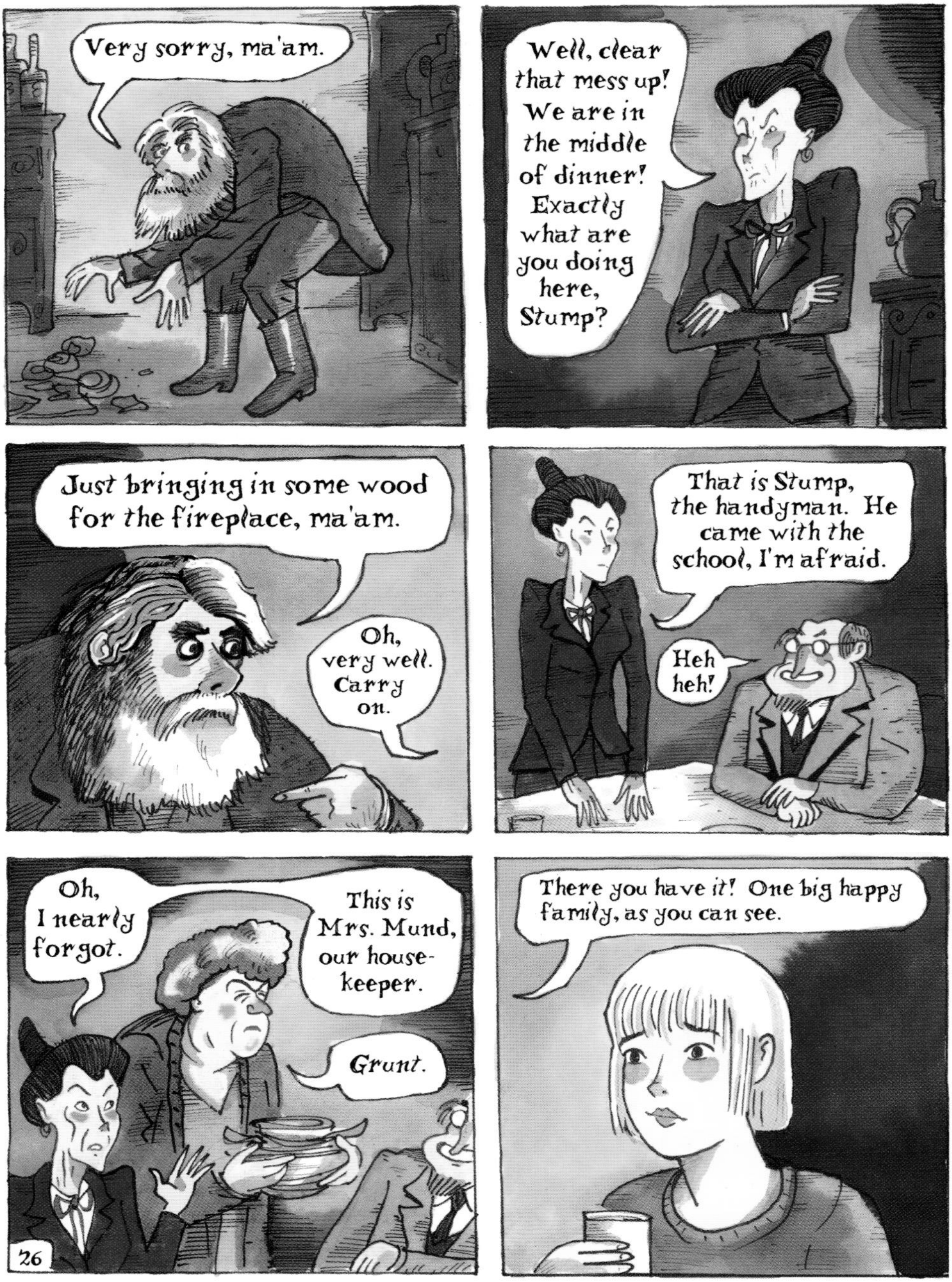

Very sorry, ma'am.
Well, clear that mess up! We are in the middle of dinner! Exactly what are you doing here, Stump?
Just bringing in some wood for the fireplace, ma'am.
Oh, very well. Carry on.
That is Stump, the handyman. He came with the school, I'm afraid.
Heh heh!
Oh, I nearly forgot.
This is Mrs. Mund, our housekeeper.
Grunt.
There you have it! One big happy family, as you can see.

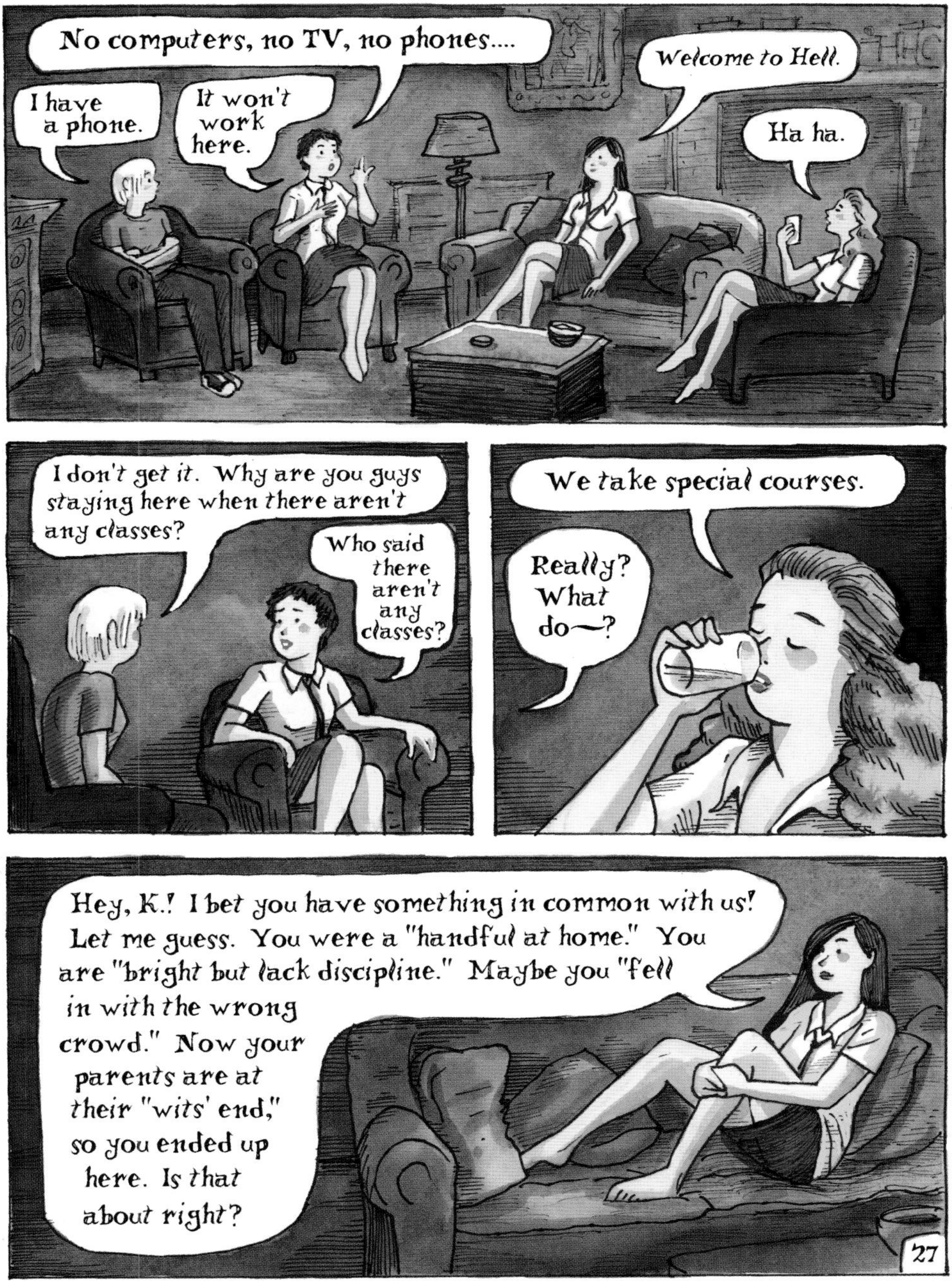
No computers, no TV, no phones....
I have a phone.
It won't work here.
Welcome to Hell.
Ha ha.
I don't get it. Why are you guys staying here when there aren't any classes?
Who said there aren't any classes?
We take special courses.
Really? What do—?
Hey, K.! I bet you have something in common with us! Let me guess. You were a "handful at home." You are "bright but lack discipline." Maybe you "fell in with the wrong crowd." Now your parents are at their "wits' end," so you ended up here. Is that about right?

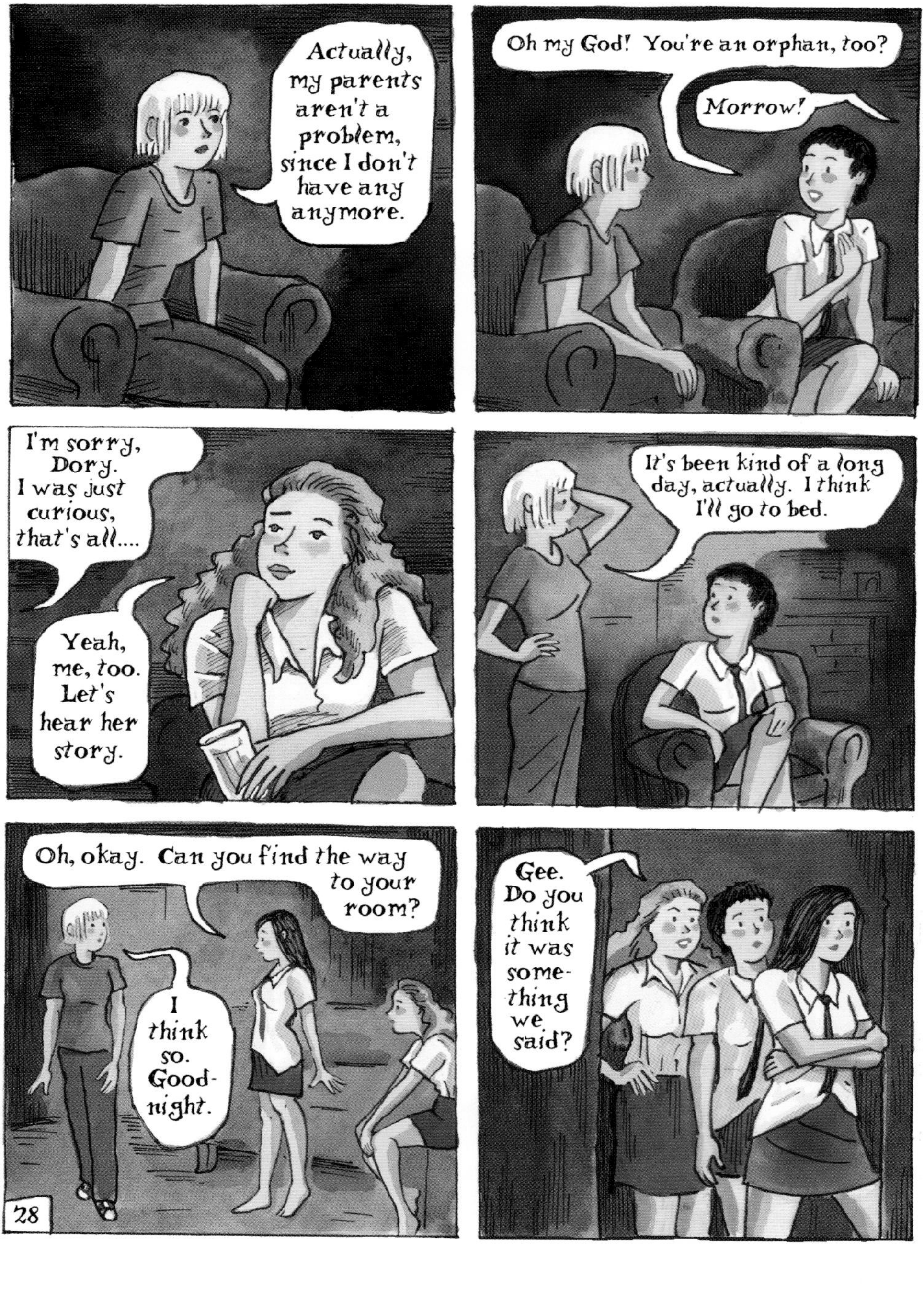

Actually, my parents aren't a problem, since I don't have any anymore.
Oh my God! You're an orphan, too?
Morrow!
I'm sorry, Dory. I was just curious, that's all....
Yeah, me, too. Let's hear her story.
It's been kind of a long day, actually. I think I'll go to bed.
Oh, okay. Can you find the way to your room?
I think so. Good-night.
Gee. Do you think it was some-thing we said?

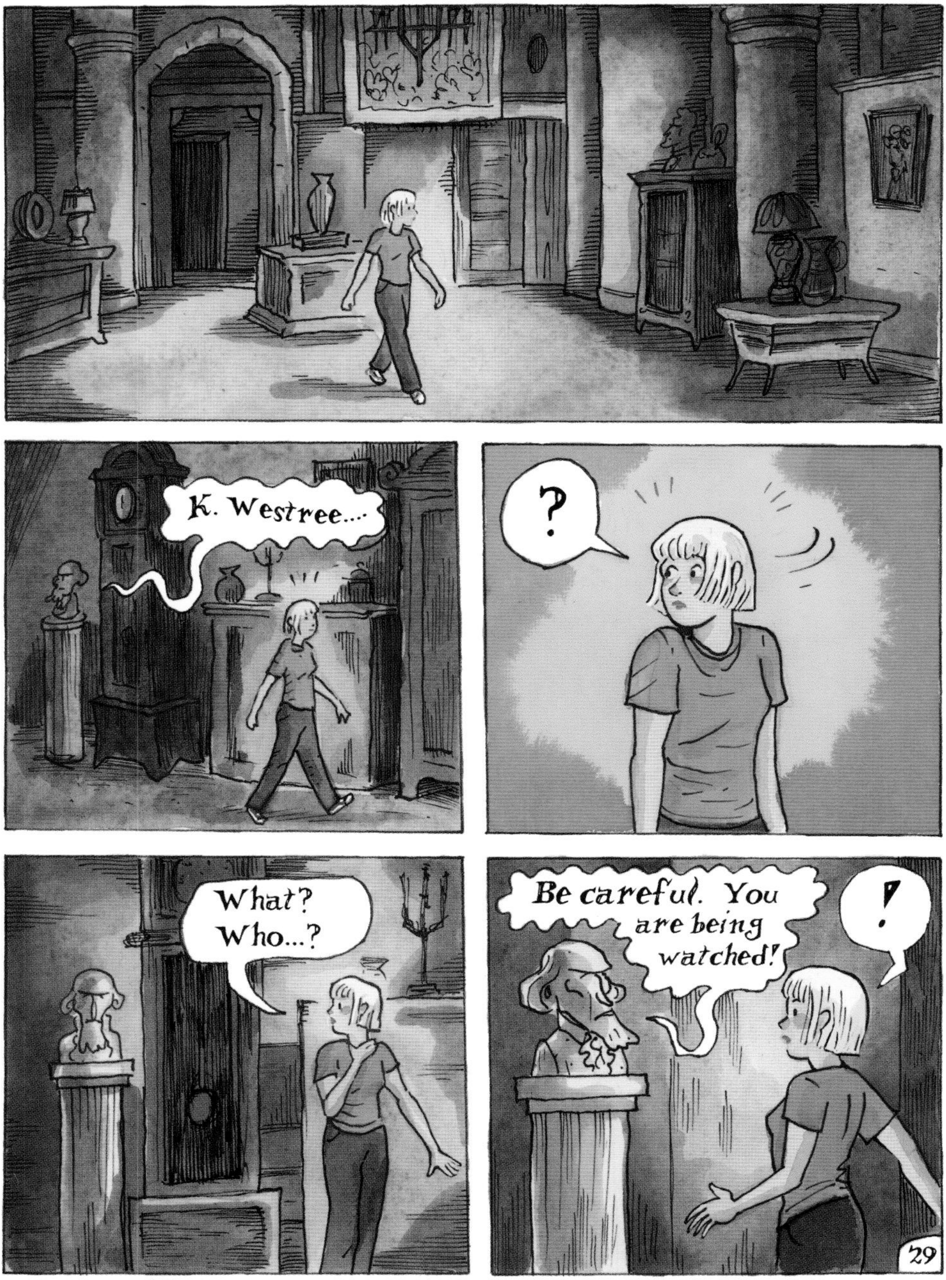
K. Westree....
?
What?
Who...?
Be careful. You are being watched!
!

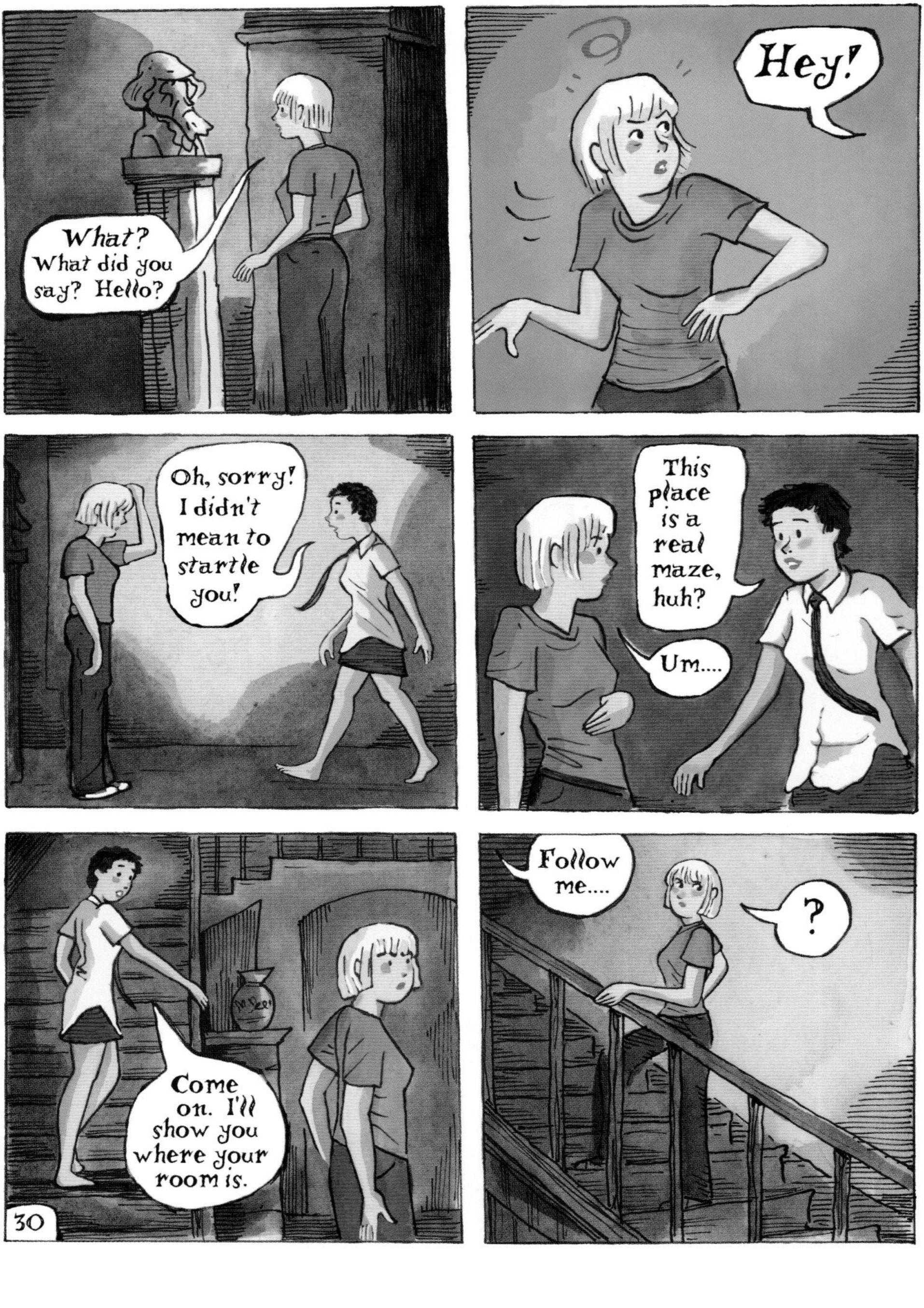

What? What did you say? Hello?
Hey!
Oh, sorry! I didn't mean to startle you!
This place is a real maze, huh?
Um....
Come on. I'll show you where your room is.
Follow me....
?

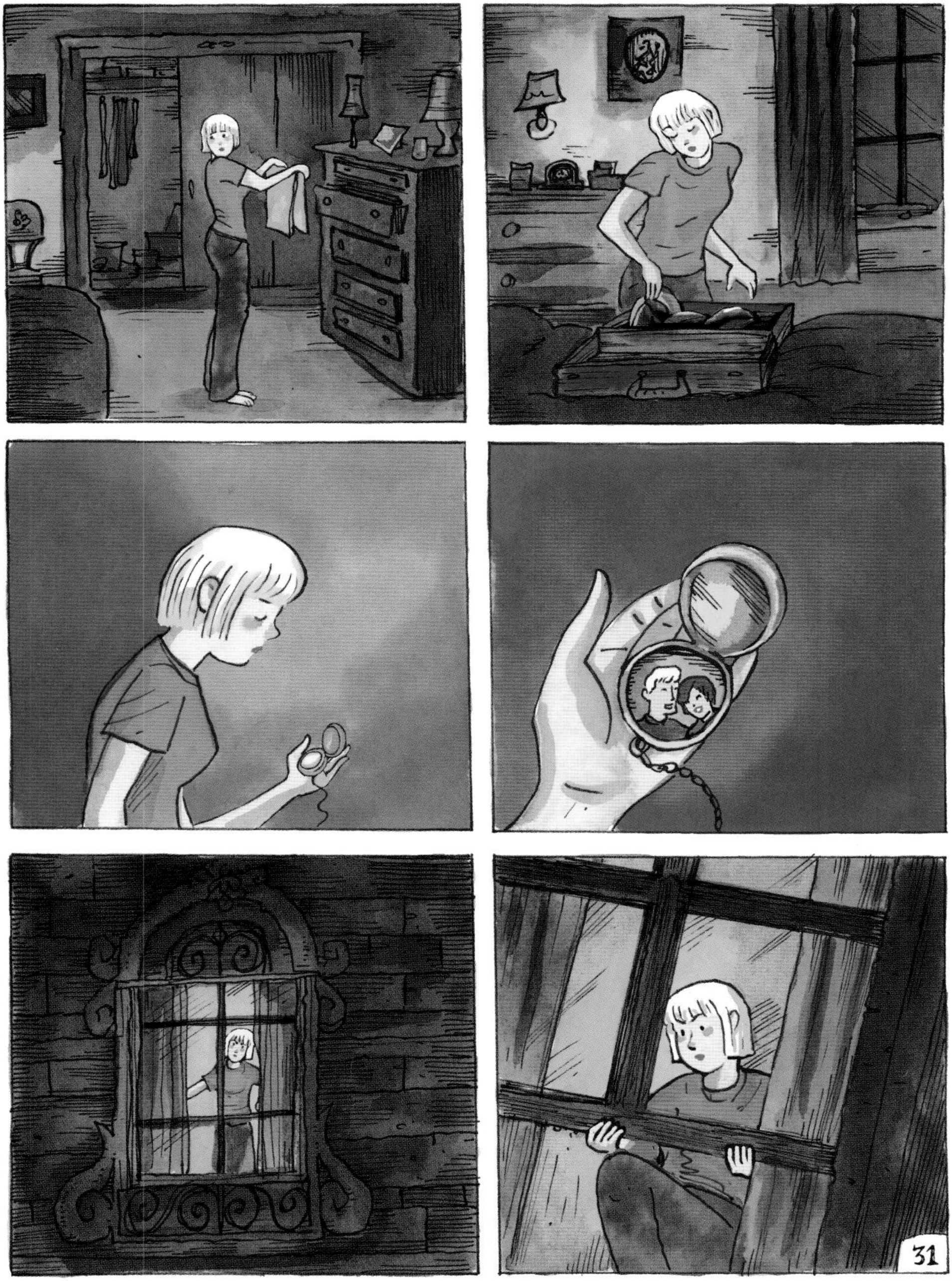

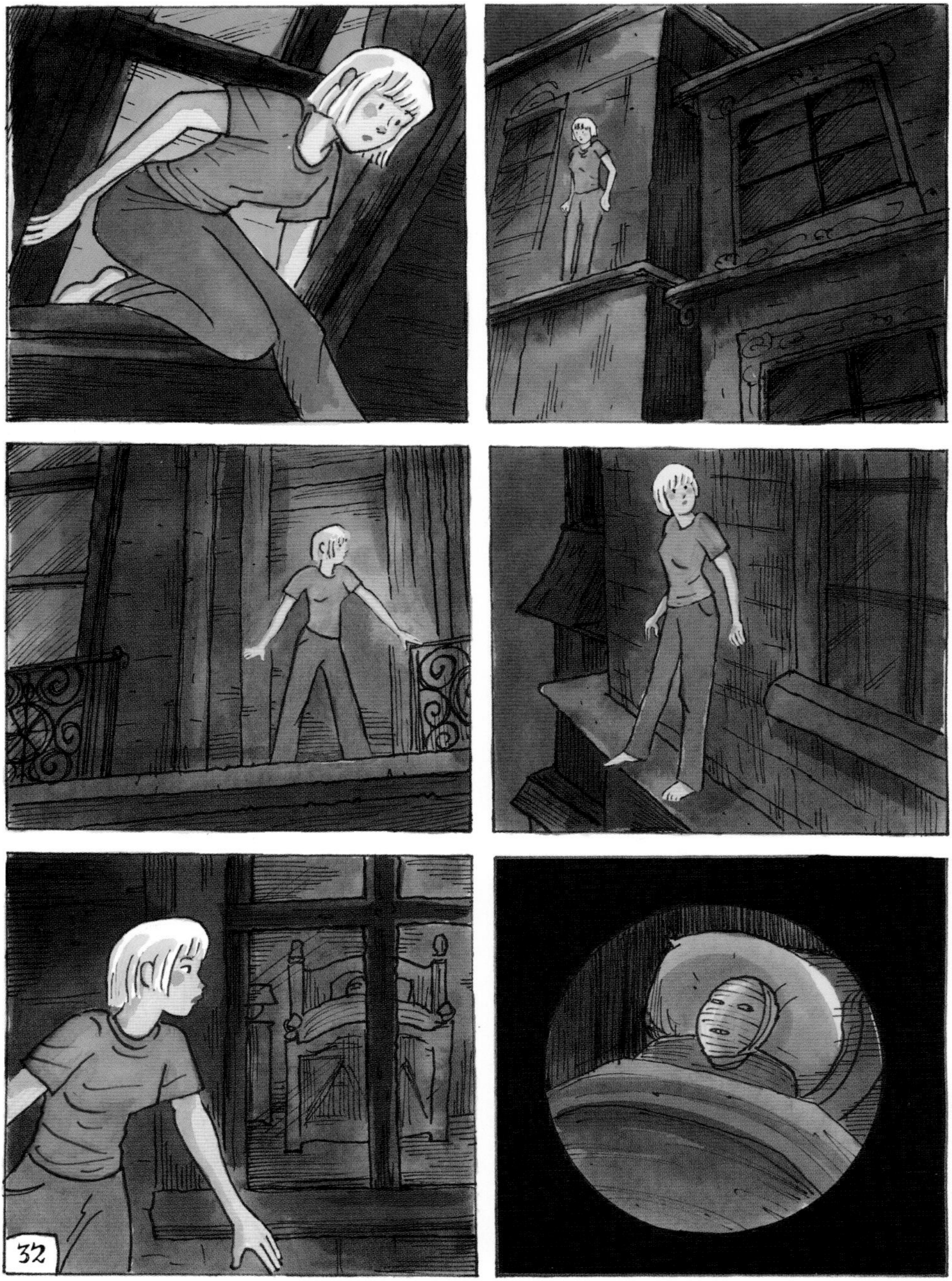

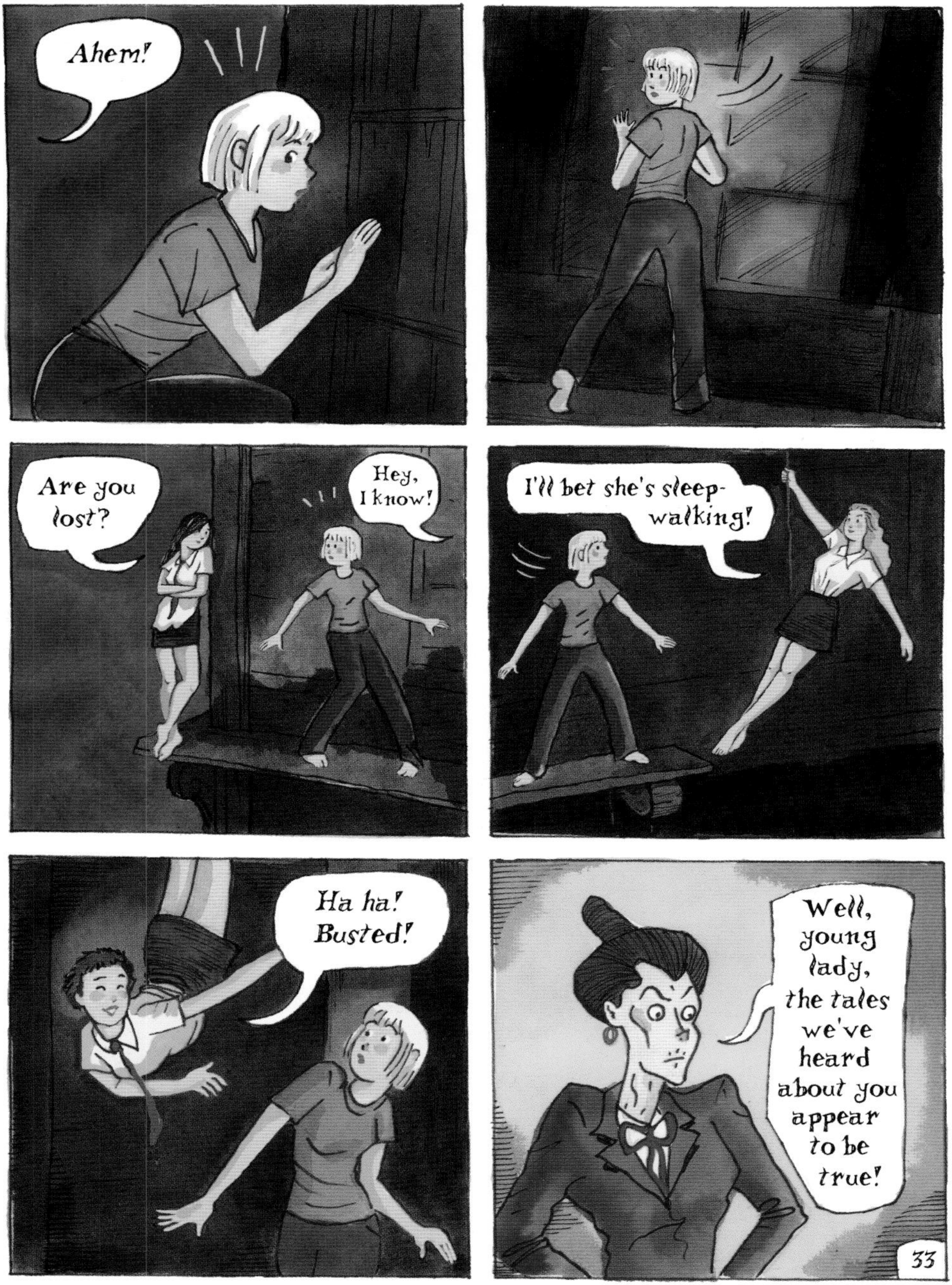

Ahem!
Are you lost?
Hey, I know!
I'll bet she's sleep-walking!
Ha ha! Busted!
Well, young lady, the tales we've heard about you appear to be true!

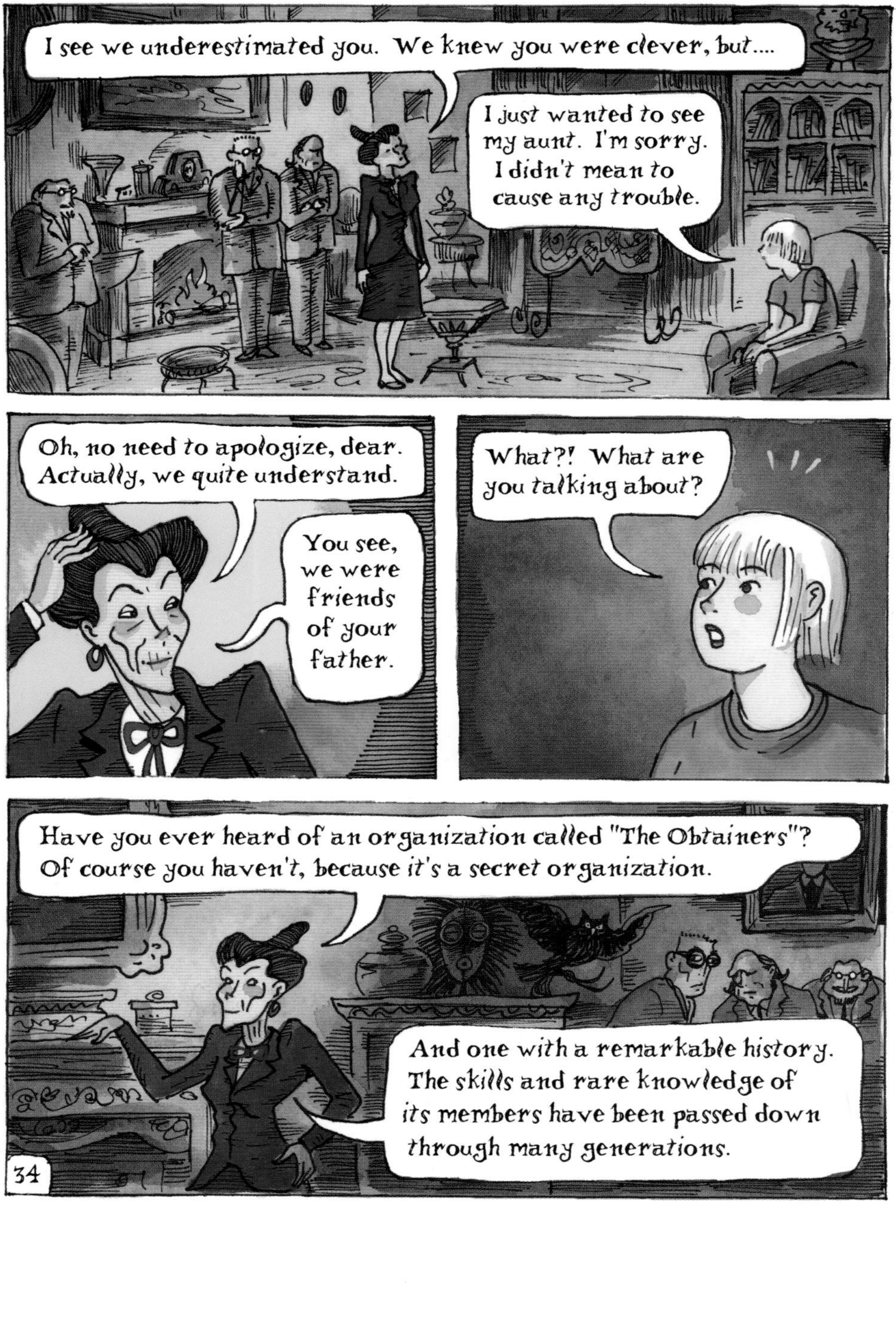
I see we underestimated you. We knew you were clever, but....
I just wanted to see my aunt. I'm sorry. I didn't mean to cause any trouble.
Oh, no need to apologize, dear. Actually, we quite understand.
You see, we were friends of your father.
What?! What are you talking about?
Have you ever heard of an organization called "The Obtainers"? Of course you haven't, because it's a secret organization.
And one with a remarkable history. The skills and rare knowledge of its members have been passed down through many generations.

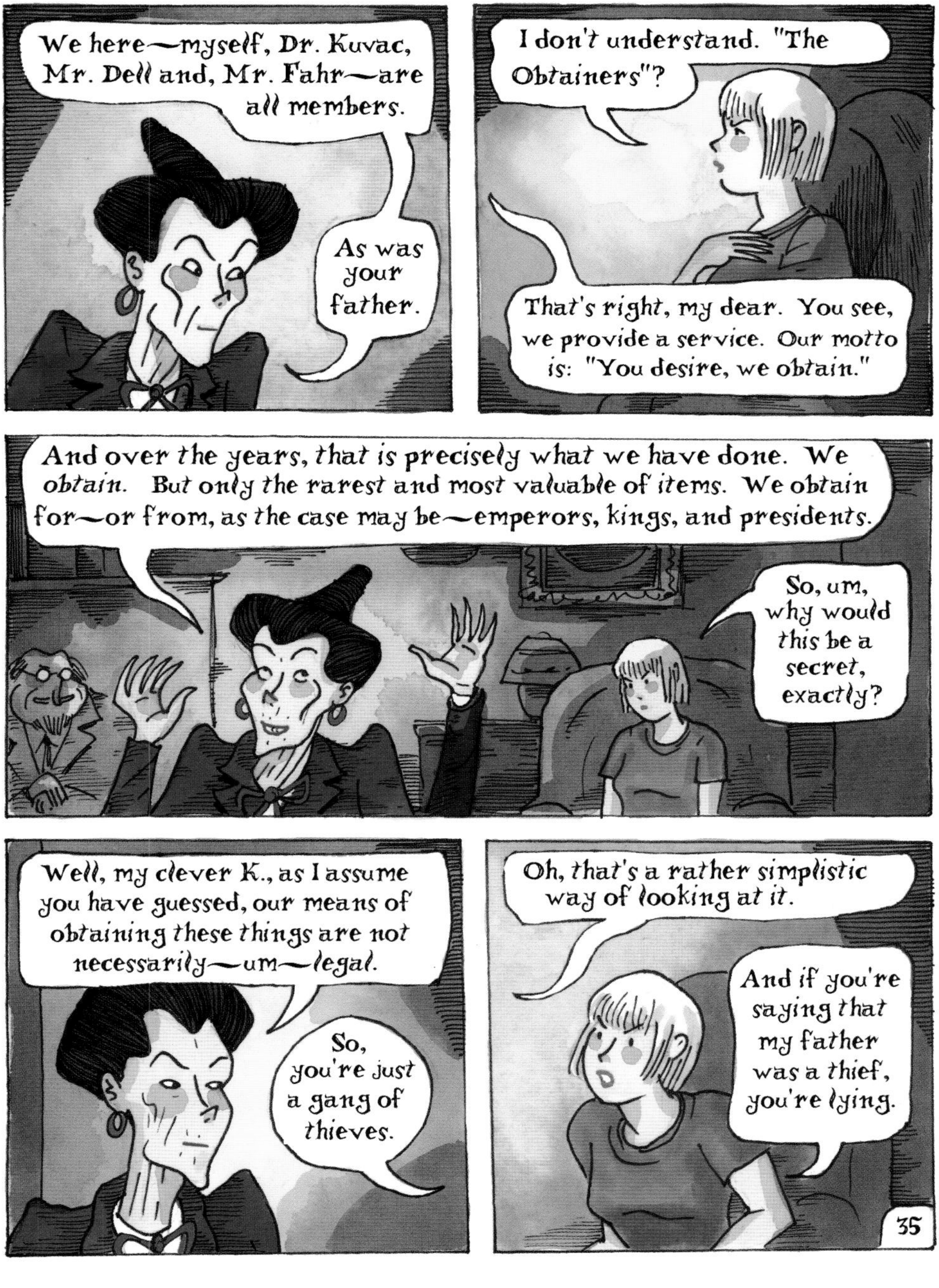
We here—myself, Dr. Kuvac, Mr. Dell and, Mr. Fahr—are all members.
As was your father.
I don't understand. "The Obtainers"?
That's right, my dear. You see, we provide a service. Our motto is: "You desire, we obtain."
And over the years, that is precisely what we have done. We obtain. But only the rarest and most valuable of items. We obtain for—or from, as the case may be—emperors, kings, and presidents.
So, um, why would this be a secret, exactly?
Well, my clever K., as I assume you have guessed, our means of obtaining these things are not necessarily—um—legal.
So, you're just a gang of thieves.
Oh, that's a rather simplistic way of looking at it.
And if you're saying that my father was a thief, you're lying.
35

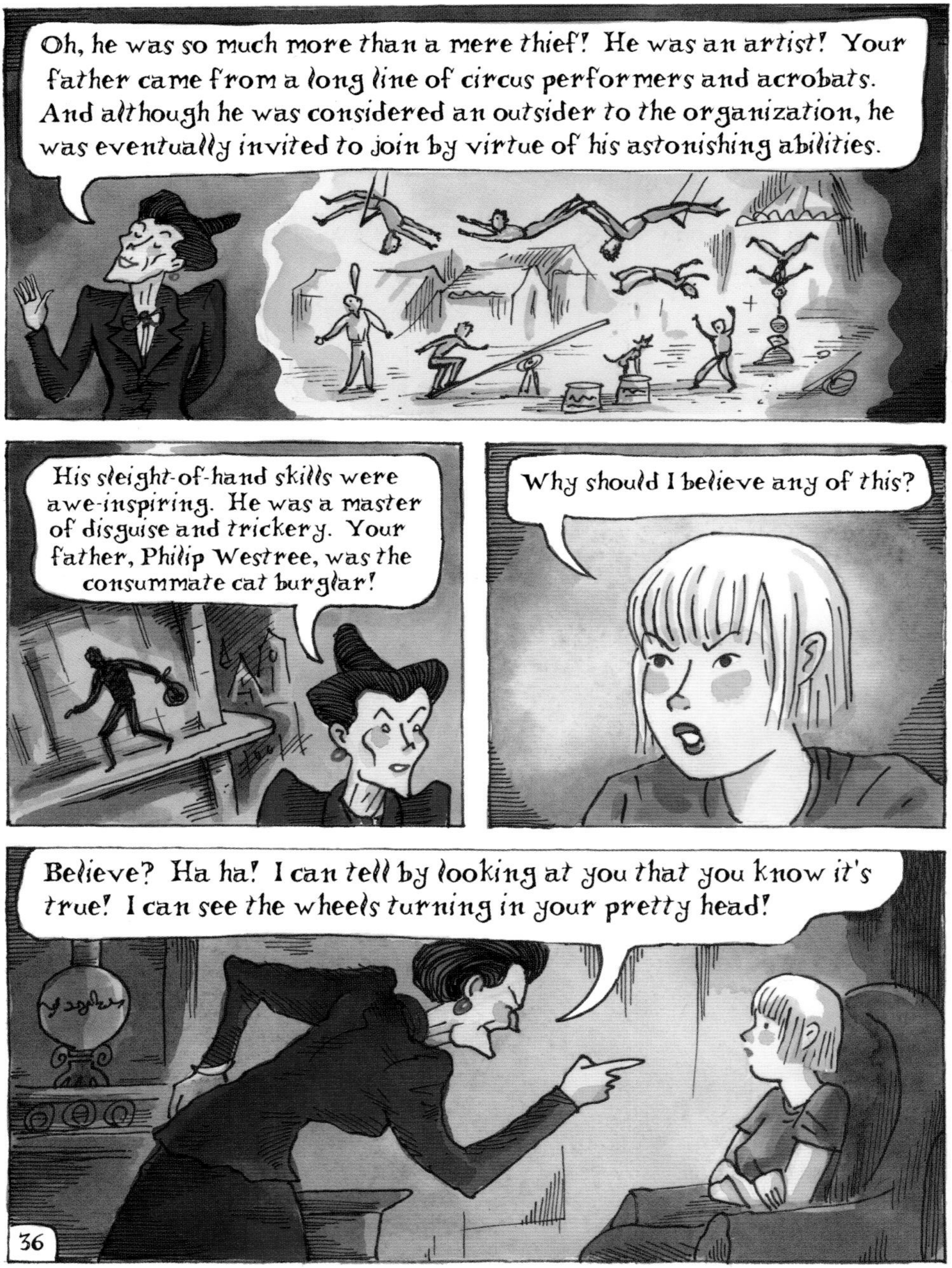
Oh, he was so much more than a mere thief! He was an artist! Your father came from a long line of circus performers and acrobats. And although he was considered an outsider to the organization, he was eventually invited to join by virtue of his astonishing abilities.
His sleight-of-hand skills were awe-inspiring. He was a master of disguise and trickery. Your father, Philip Westree, was the consummate cat burglar!
Why should I believe any of this?
Believe? Ha ha! I can tell by looking at you that you know it's true! I can see the wheels turning in your pretty head!

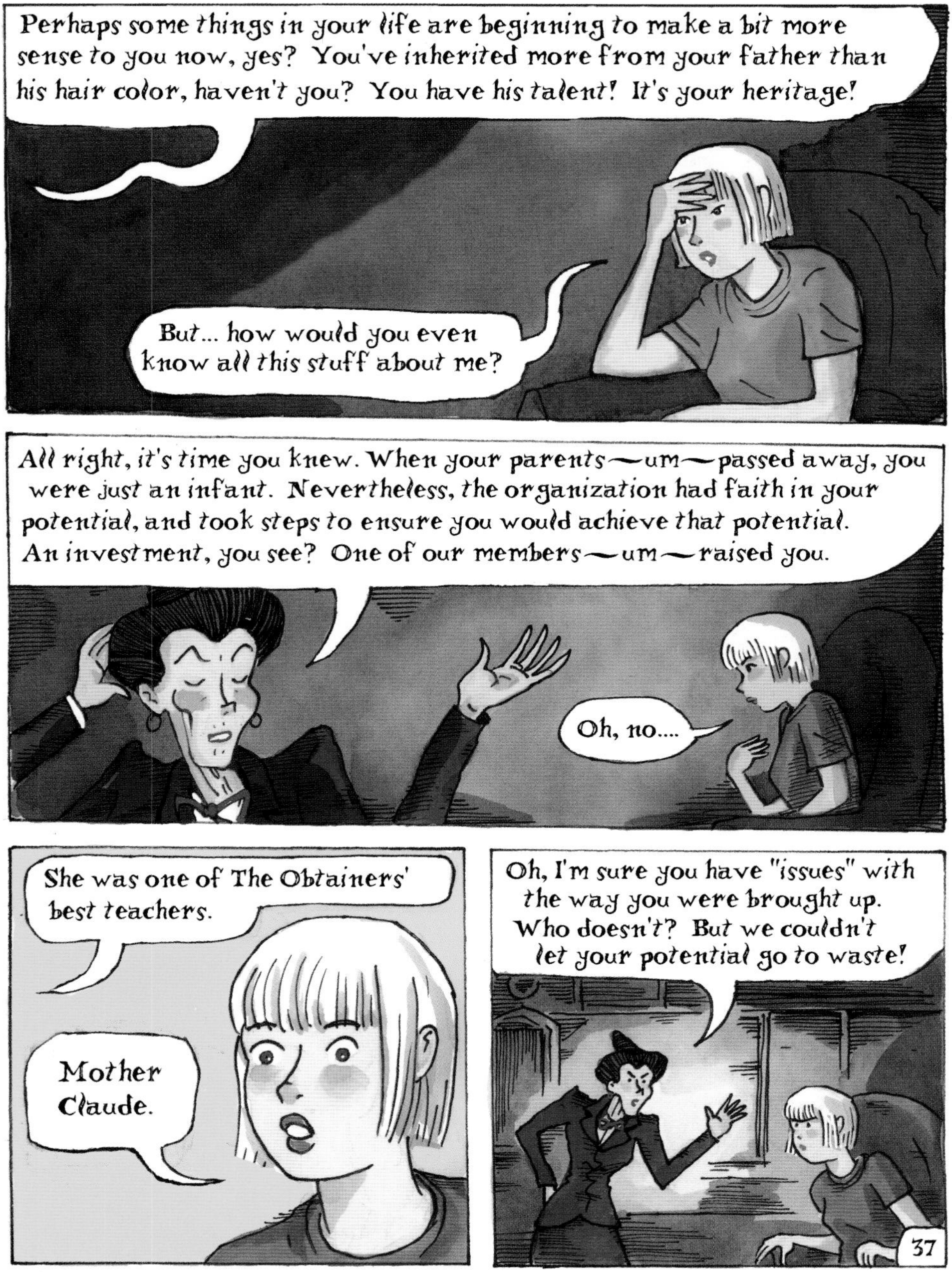
Perhaps some things in your life are beginning to make a bit more sense to you now, yes? You've inherited more from your father than his hair color, haven't you? You have his talent! It's your heritage!
But... how would you even know all this stuff about me?
All right, it's time you knew. When your parents—um—passed away, you were just an infant. Nevertheless, the organization had faith in your potential, and took steps to ensure you would achieve that potential. An investment, you see? One of our members—um—raised you.
Oh, no....
She was one of The Obtainers' best teachers.
Mother Claude.
Oh, I'm sure you have "issues" with the way you were brought up. Who doesn't? But we couldn't let your potential go to waste!

Oh my. You're speechless. You're in shock. Well, I'm sorry, but it is time you learned the facts. My dear, be happy! You are one of us! We are your family! I'll bet anything that despite your attempt to "reform," you miss those thrills of your childhood!

It's true that, much like you now, your father was ambivalent about his talent. He had only joined The Obtainers as a lark, and as a way to provide for his parents, who were in financial distress. He thought he could leave any time!

When your mother became pregnant with you, your father thought he could "settle down" and lead a normal, boring life. Well, that's not the way it works, and there were those in the organization who strongly objected, I'm afraid.

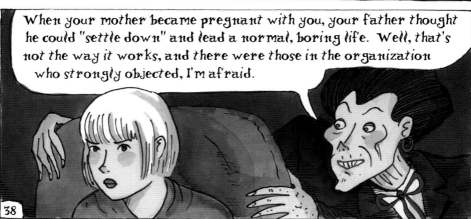

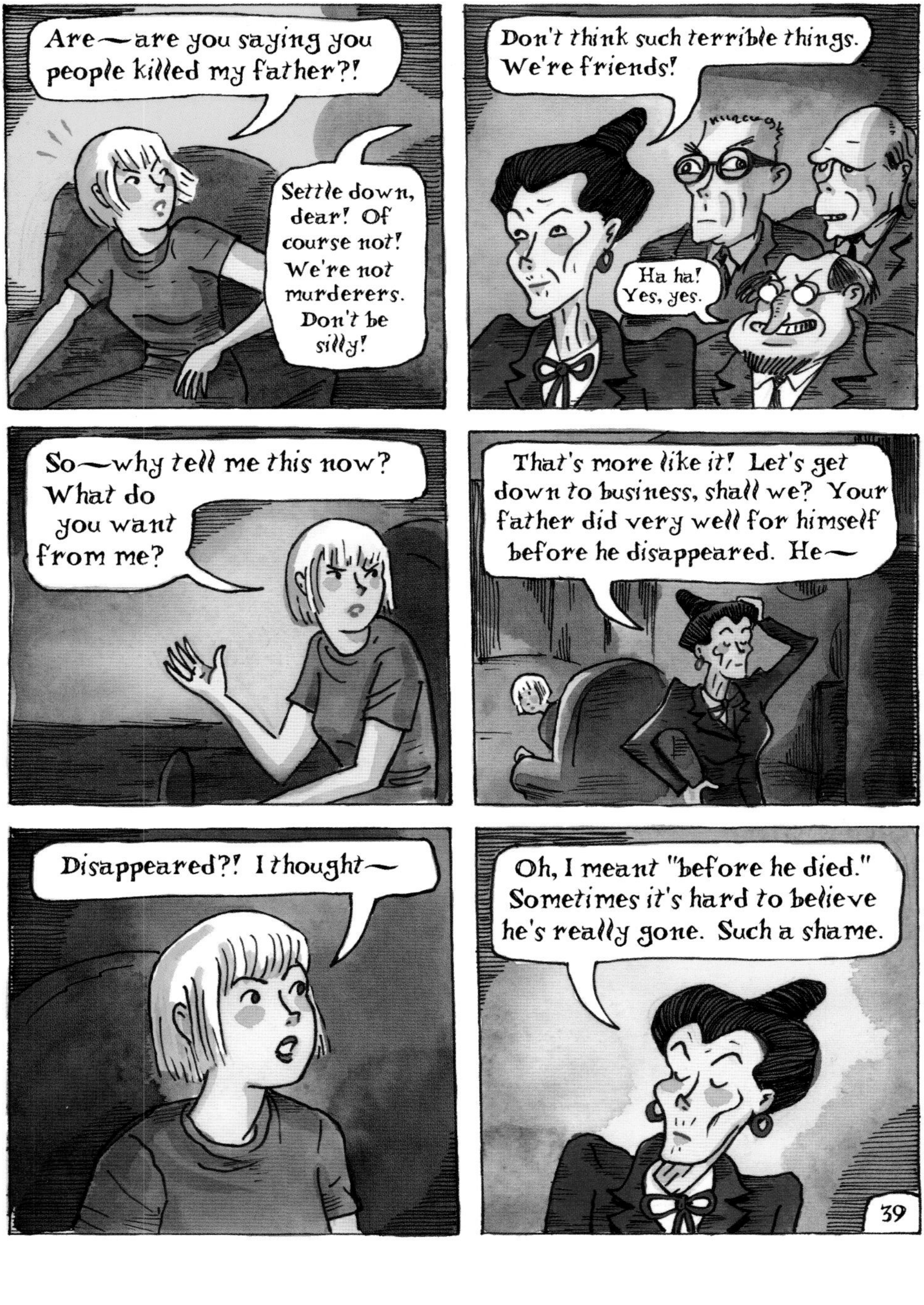
Are—are you saying you people killed my father?!
Settle down, dear! Of course not! We're not murderers. Don't be silly!
Don't think such terrible things. We're friends!
Ha ha! Yes, yes.
So—why tell me this now? What do you want from me?
That's more like it! Let's get down to business, shall we? Your father did very well for himself before he disappeared. He—
Disappeared?! I thought—
Oh, I meant "before he died." Sometimes it's hard to believe he's really gone. Such a shame.

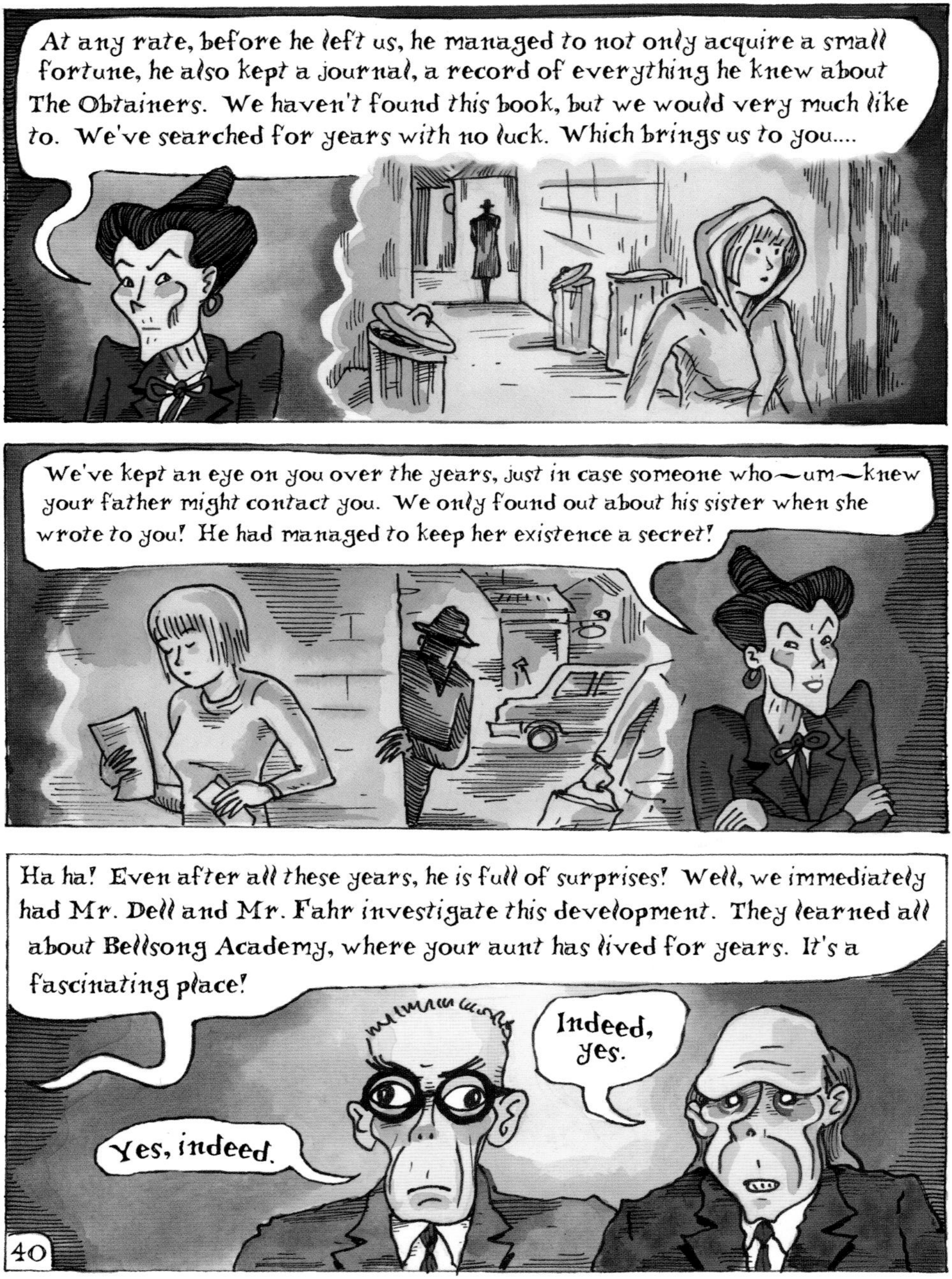
At any rate, before he left us, he managed to not only acquire a small fortune, he also kept a journal, a record of everything he knew about The Obtainers. We haven't found this book, but we would very much like to. We've searched for years with no luck. Which brings us to you....
We've kept an eye on you over the years, just in case someone who—um—knew your father might contact you. We only found out about his sister when she wrote to you! He had managed to keep her existence a secret!
Ha ha! Even after all these years, he is full of surprises! Well, we immediately had Mr. Dell and Mr. Fahr investigate this development. They learned all about Bellsong Academy, where your aunt has lived for years. It's a fascinating place!
Indeed, yes.
Yes, indeed.

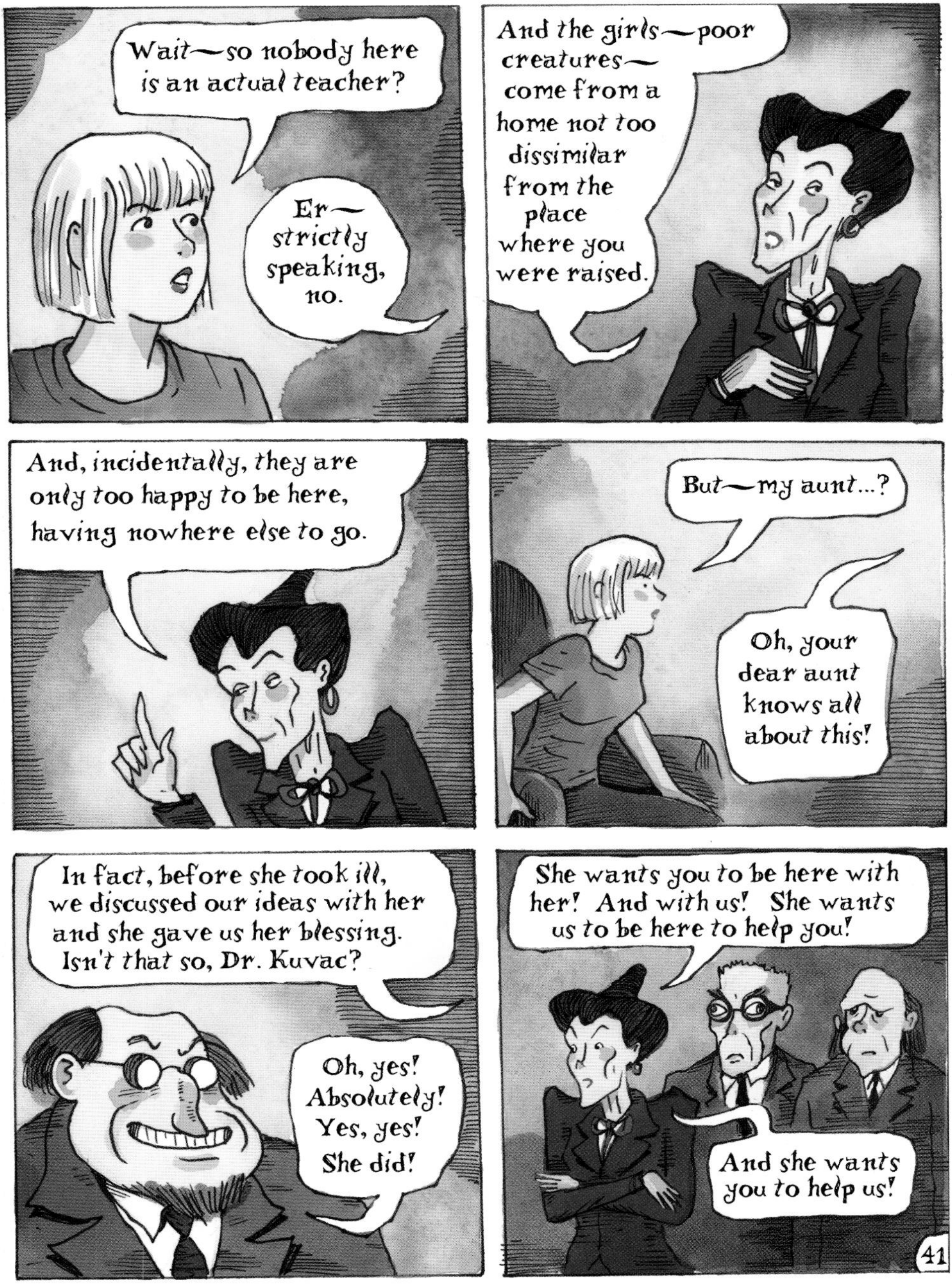
Wait—so nobody here is an actual teacher?
Er—strictly speaking, no.
And the girls—poor creatures—come from a home not too dissimilar from the place where you were raised.
And, incidentally, they are only too happy to be here, having nowhere else to go.
But—my aunt...?
Oh, your dear aunt knows all about this!
In fact, before she took ill, we discussed our ideas with her and she gave us her blessing. Isn't that so, Dr. Kuvac?
Oh, yes! Absolutely! Yes, yes! She did!
She wants you to be here with her! And with us! She wants us to be here to help you!
And she wants you to help us!
41

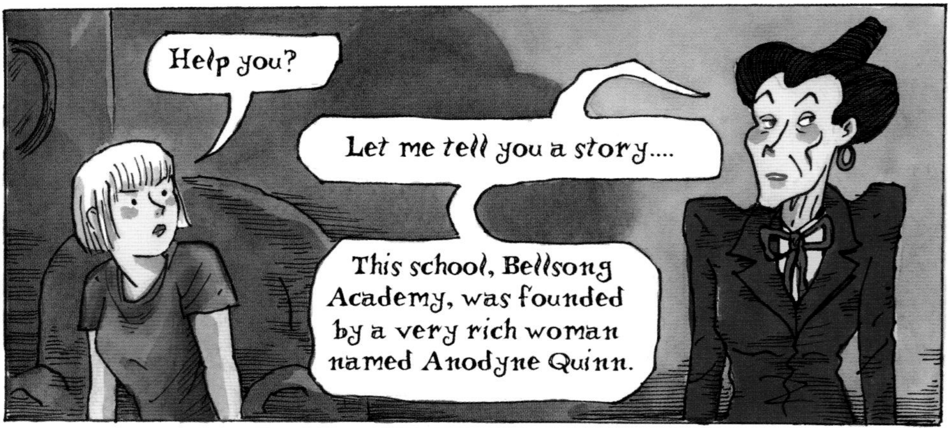
Help you?
Let me tell you a story....
This school, Bellsong Academy, was founded by a very rich woman named Anodyne Quinn.

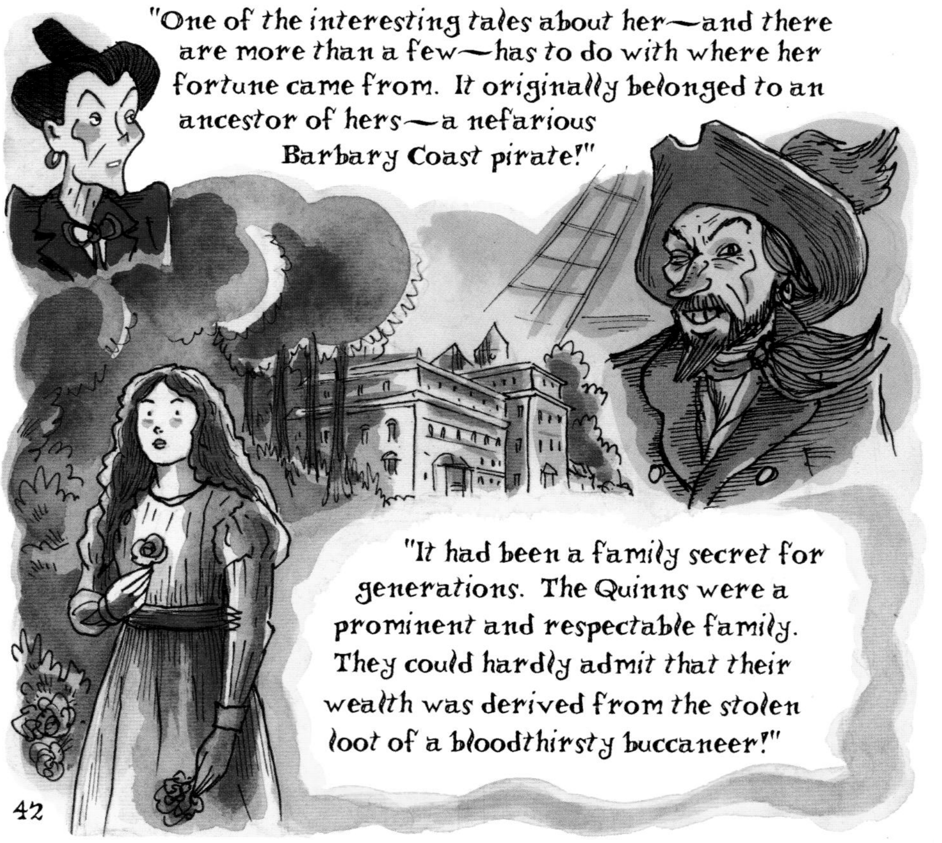
"One of the interesting tales about her—and there are more than a few—has to do with where her fortune came from. It originally belonged to an ancestor of hers—a nefarious Barbary Coast pirate!"
"It had been a family secret for generations. The Quinns were a prominent and respectable family. They could hardly admit that their wealth was derived from the stolen loot of a bloodthirsty buccaneer!"

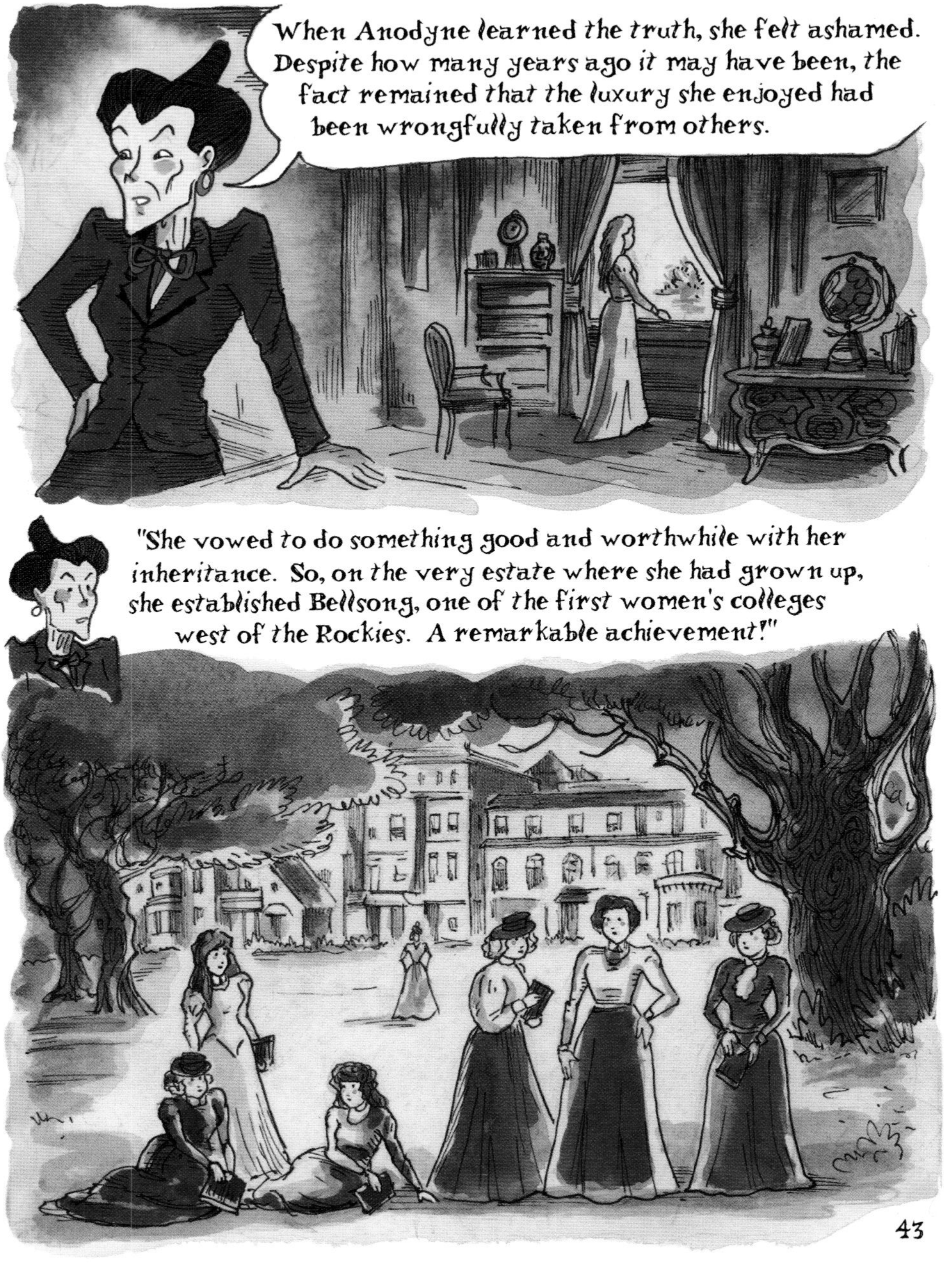
When Anodyne learned the truth, she felt ashamed. Despite how many years ago it may have been, the fact remained that the luxury she enjoyed had been wrongfully taken from others.
"She vowed to do something good and worthwhile with her inheritance. So, on the very estate where she had grown up, she established Bellsong, one of the first women's colleges west of the Rockies. A remarkable achievement!"

"Anodyne made provisions for the school to carry on after she died. And it has, for many years. Yet there were some who wondered about that pirate treasure. Anodyne had described seeing it with her own eyes— a secret room filled with glittering gold and jewels."

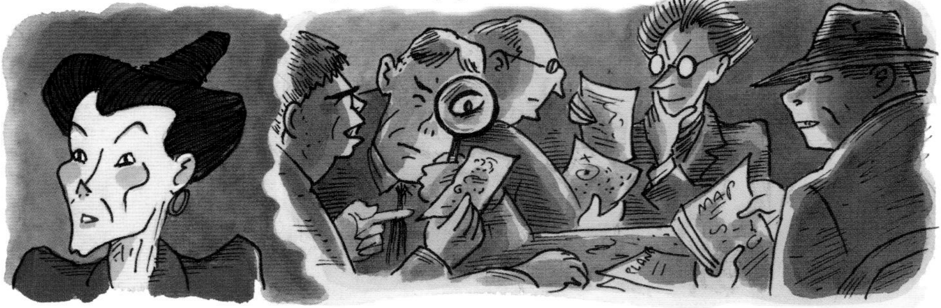
MAP

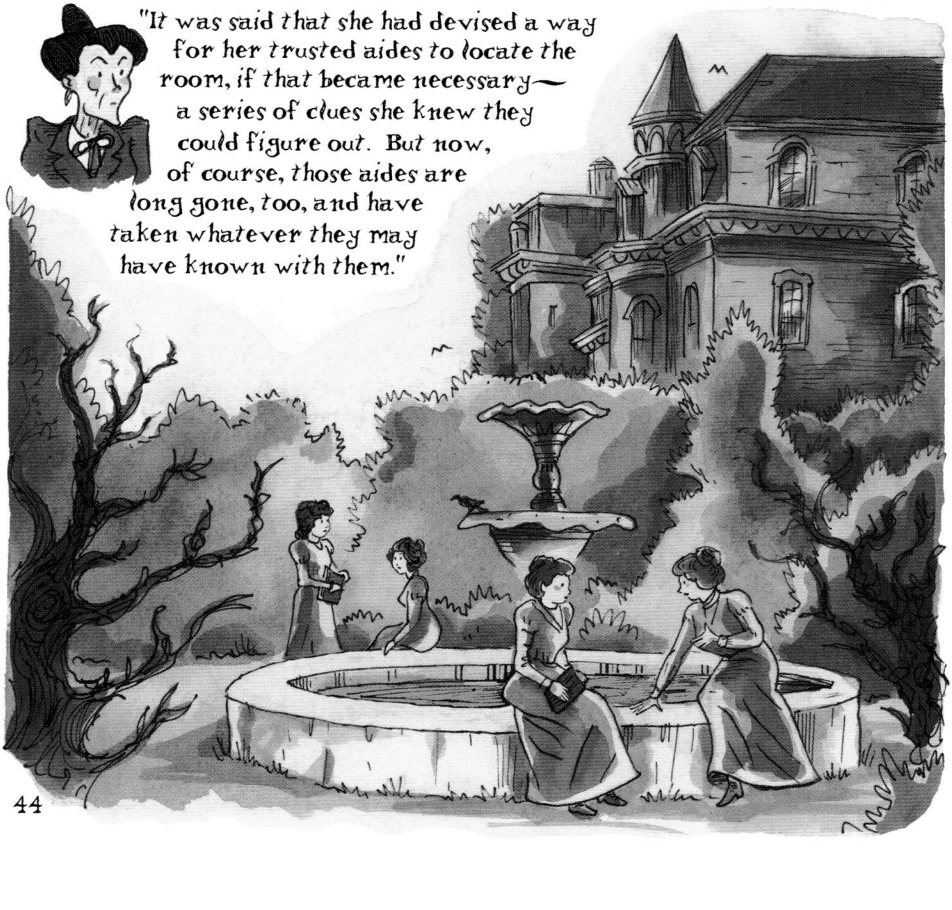
"It was said that she had devised a way for her trusted aides to locate the room, if that became necessary— a series of clues she knew they could figure out. But now, of course, those aides are long gone, too, and have taken whatever they may have known with them."

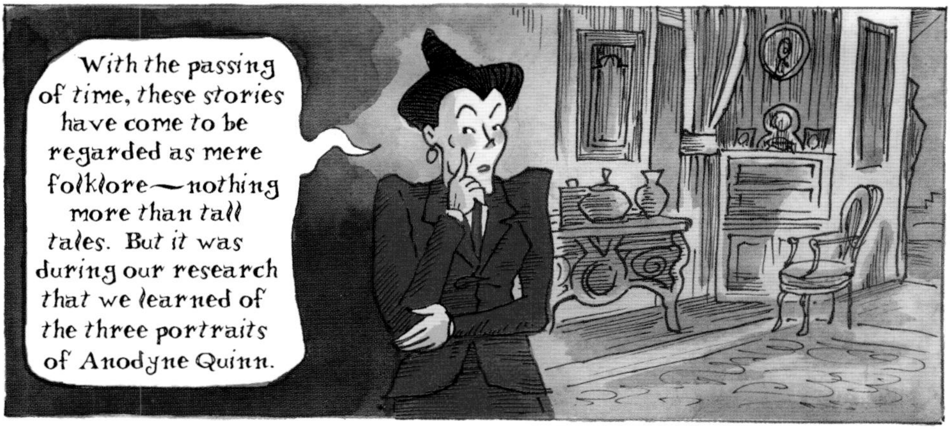
With the passing of time, these stories have come to be regarded as mere folklore—nothing more than tall tales. But it was during our research that we learned of the three portraits of Anodyne Quinn.

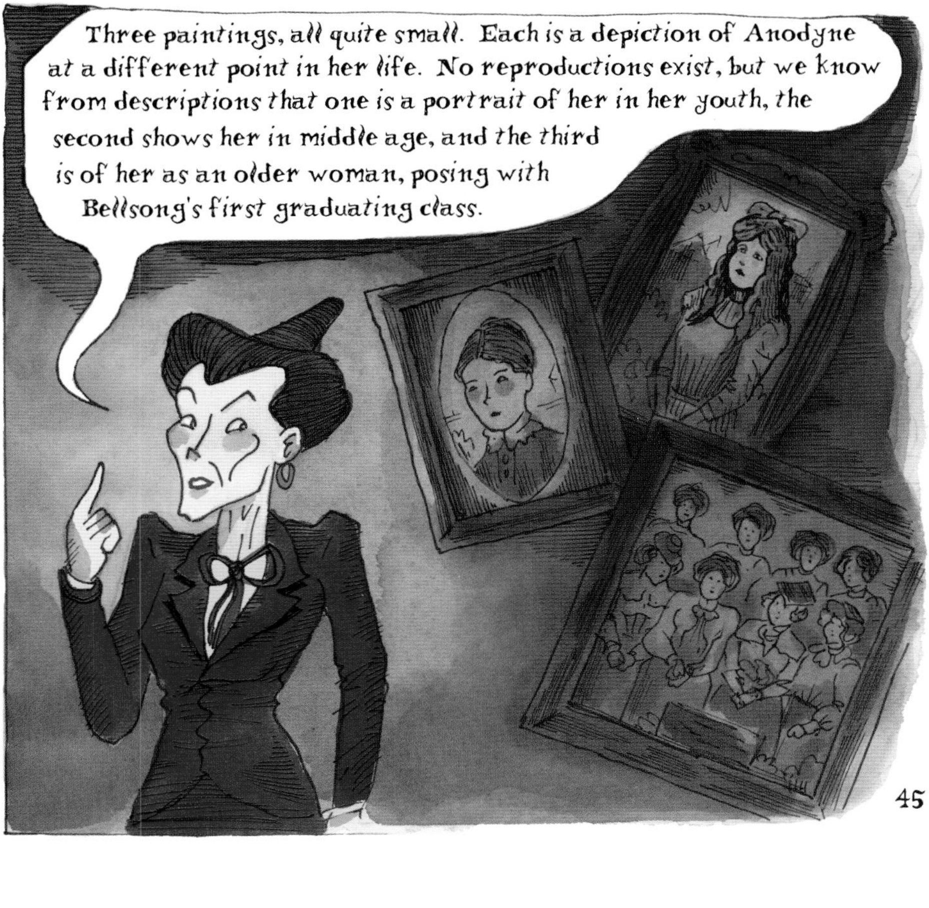
Three paintings, all quite small. Each is a depiction of Anodyne at a different point in her life. No reproductions exist, but we know from descriptions that one is a portrait of her in her youth, the second shows her in middle age, and the third is of her as an older woman, posing with Bellsong's first graduating class.

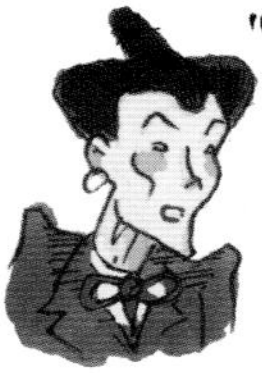

"What makes these paintings of interest to us is this odd fact: Each one was given to a family in the nearby village of Moorlock's Gate, and each family was promised a generous annual payment from the Quinn estate, as long as they kept the paintings on display in their homes."

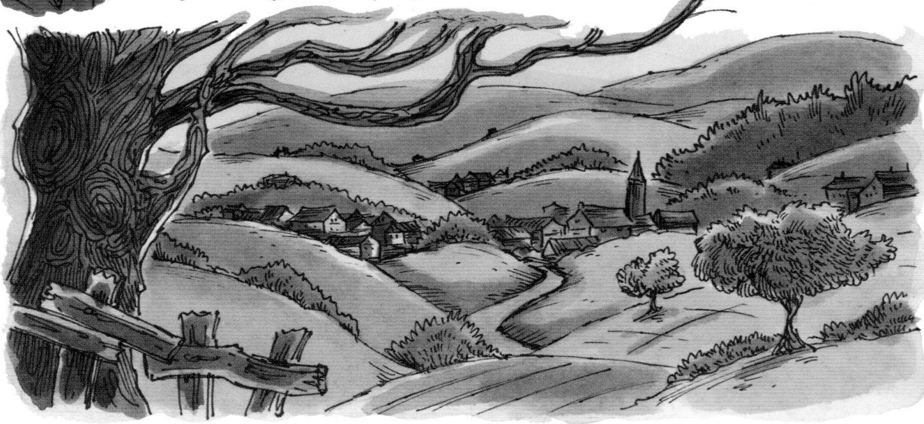

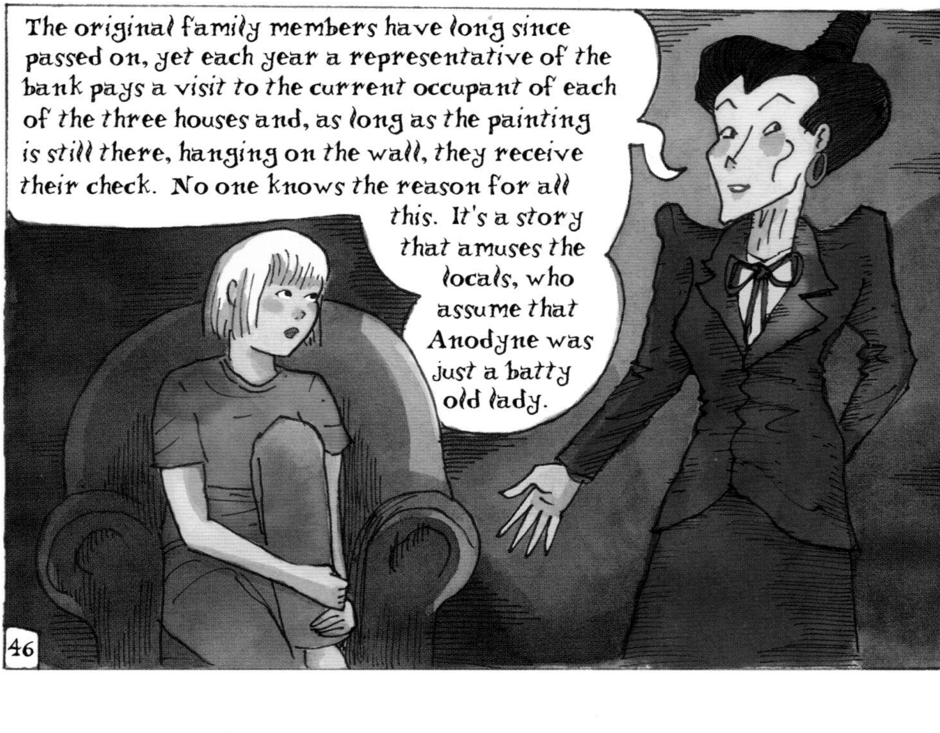
The original family members have long since passed on, yet each year a representative of the bank pays a visit to the current occupant of each of the three houses and, as long as the painting is still there, hanging on the wall, they receive their check. No one knows the reason for all this. It's a story that amuses the locals, who assume that Anodyne was just a batty old lady.

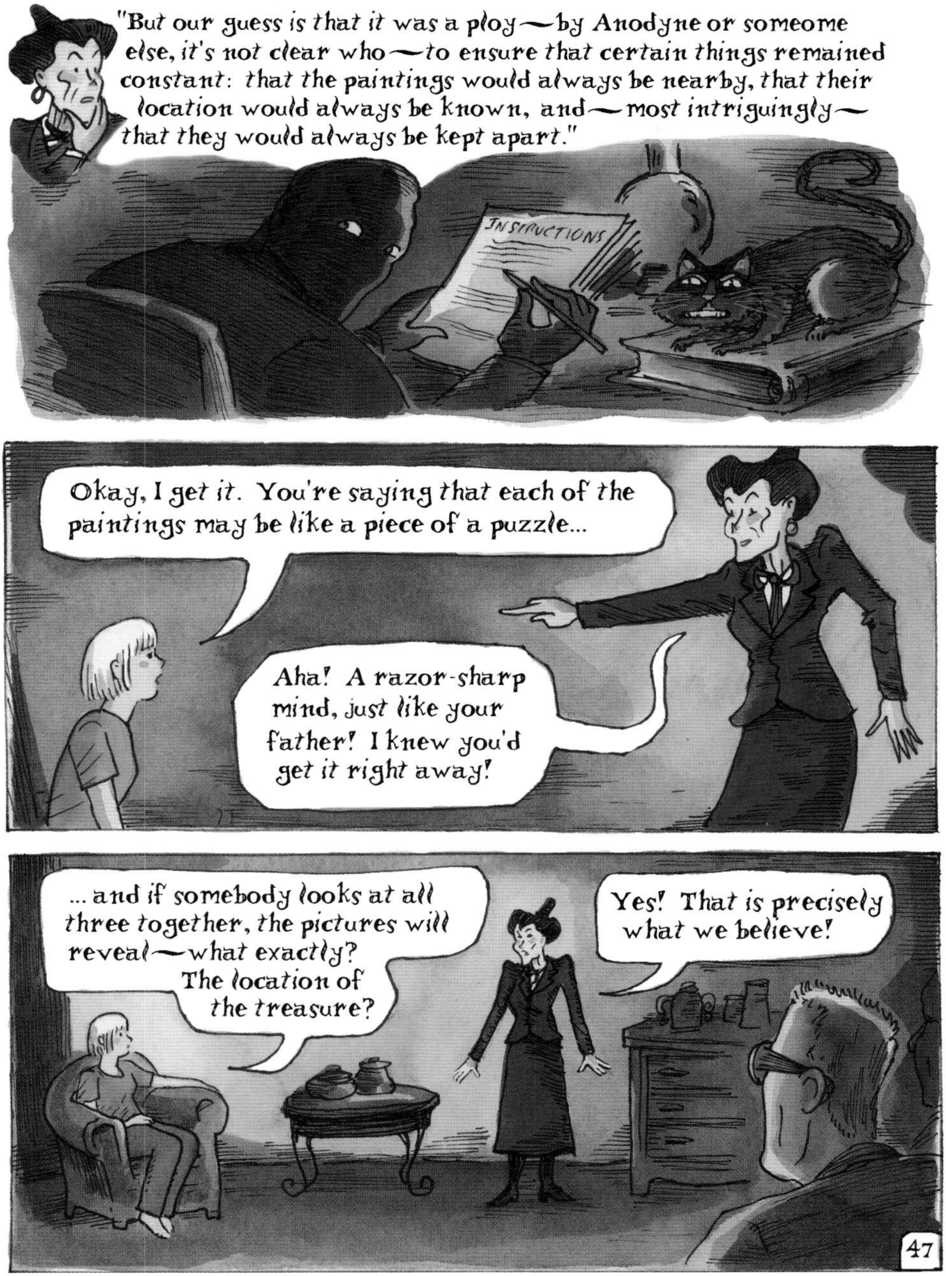
"But our guess is that it was a ploy—by Anodyne or someome else, it's not clear who—to ensure that certain things remained constant: that the paintings would always be nearby, that their location would always be known, and—most intriguingly—that they would always be kept apart."
INSTRUCTIONS
Okay, I get it. You're saying that each of the paintings may be like a piece of a puzzle...
Aha! A razor-sharp mind, just like your father! I knew you'd get it right away!
... and if somebody looks at all three together, the pictures will reveal—what exactly? The location of the treasure?
Yes! That is precisely what we believe!

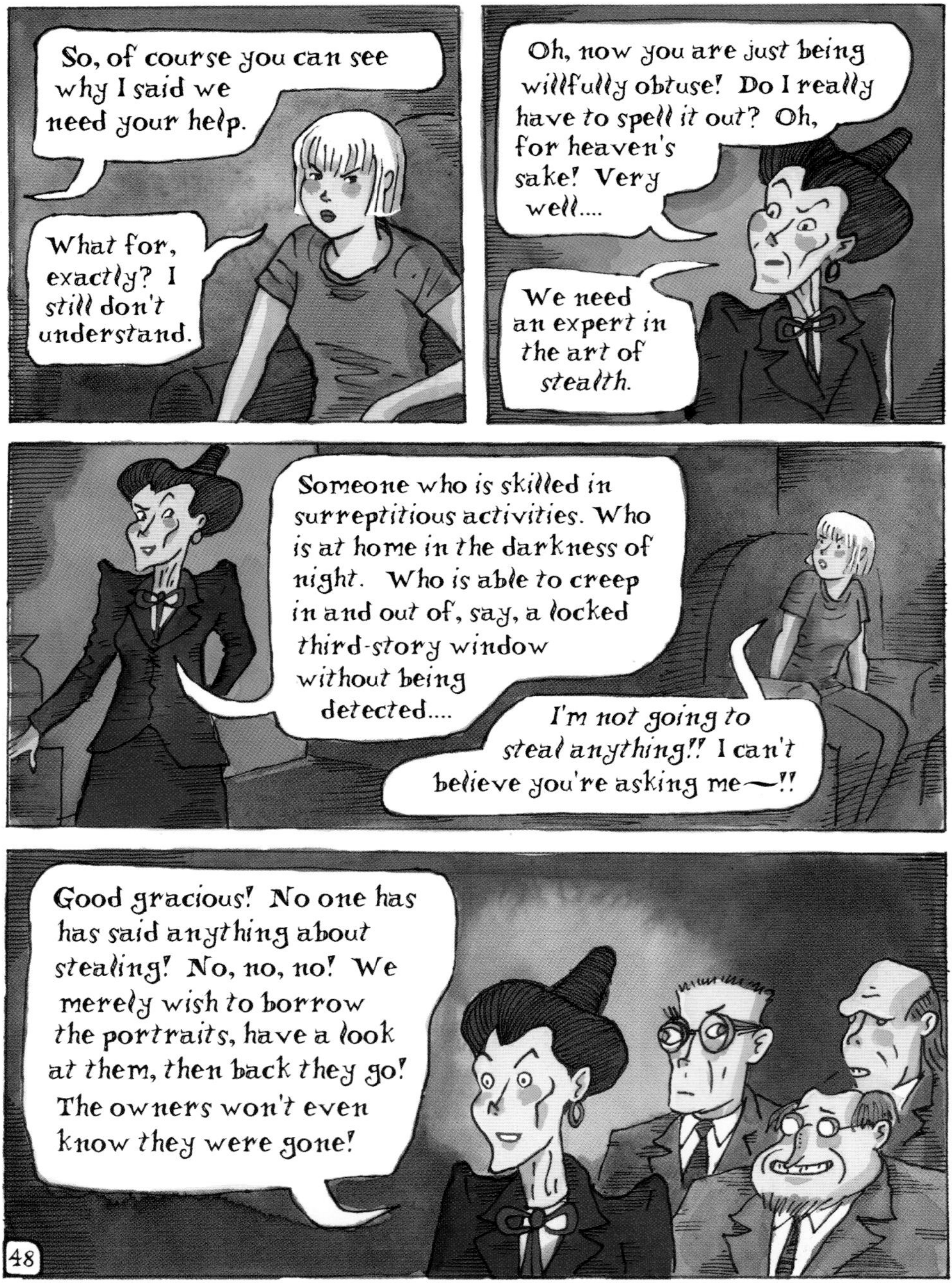
So, of course you can see why I said we need your help.
What for, exactly? I still don't understand.
Oh, now you are just being willfully obtuse! Do I really have to spell it out? Oh, for heaven's sake! Very well....
We need an expert in the art of stealth.
Someone who is skilled in surreptitious activities. Who is at home in the darkness of night. Who is able to creep in and out of, say, a locked third-story window without being detected....
I'm not going to steal anything!! I can't believe you're asking me—!!
Good gracious! No one has has said anything about stealing! No, no, no! We merely wish to borrow the portraits, have a look at them, then back they go! The owners won't even know they were gone!

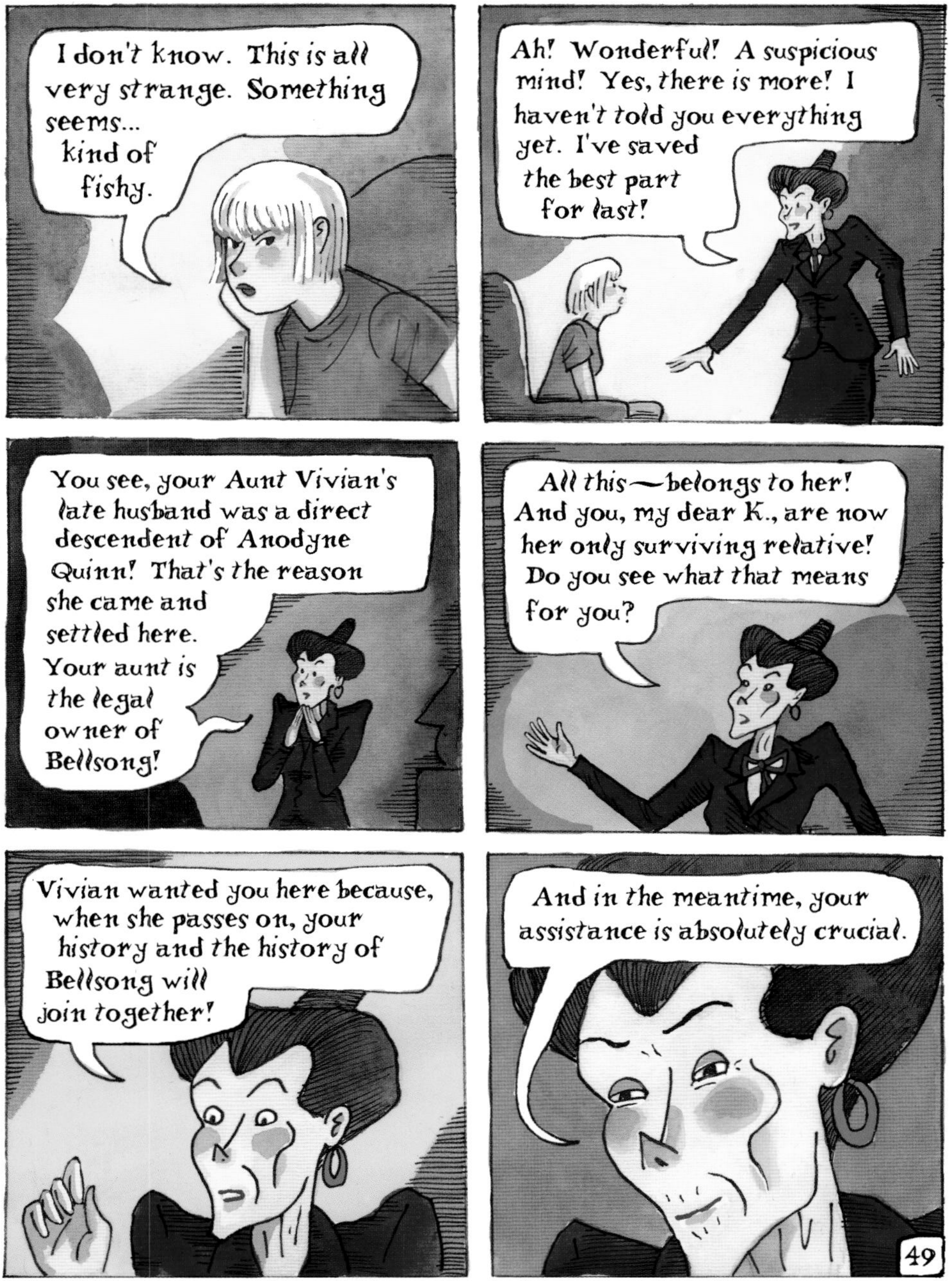

I don't know. This is all very strange. Something seems... kind of fishy.
Ah! Wonderful! A suspicious mind! Yes, there is more! I haven't told you everything yet. I've saved the best part for last!
You see, your Aunt Vivian's late husband was a direct descendent of Anodyne Quinn! That's the reason she came and settled here. Your aunt is the legal owner of Bellsong!
All this—belongs to her! And you, my dear K., are now her only surviving relative! Do you see what that means for you?
Vivian wanted you here because, when she passes on, your history and the history of Bellsong will join together!
And in the meantime, your assistance is absolutely crucial.

CHAPTER TWO

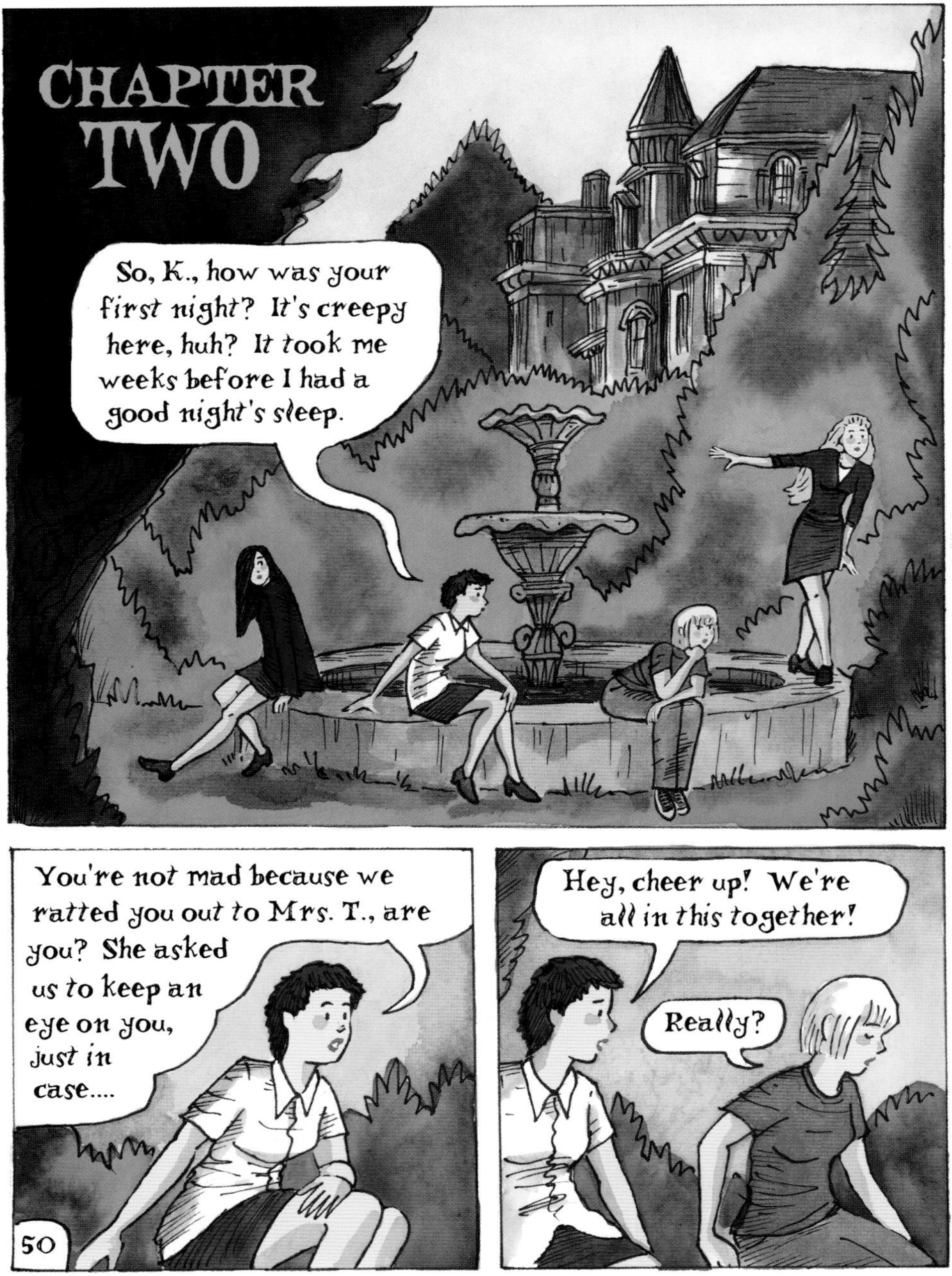

So, K., how was your first night? It's creepy here, huh? It took me weeks before I had a good night's sleep.
You're not mad because we ratted you out to Mrs. T., are you? She asked us to keep an eye on you, just in case....
Hey, cheer up! We're all in this together!
Really?

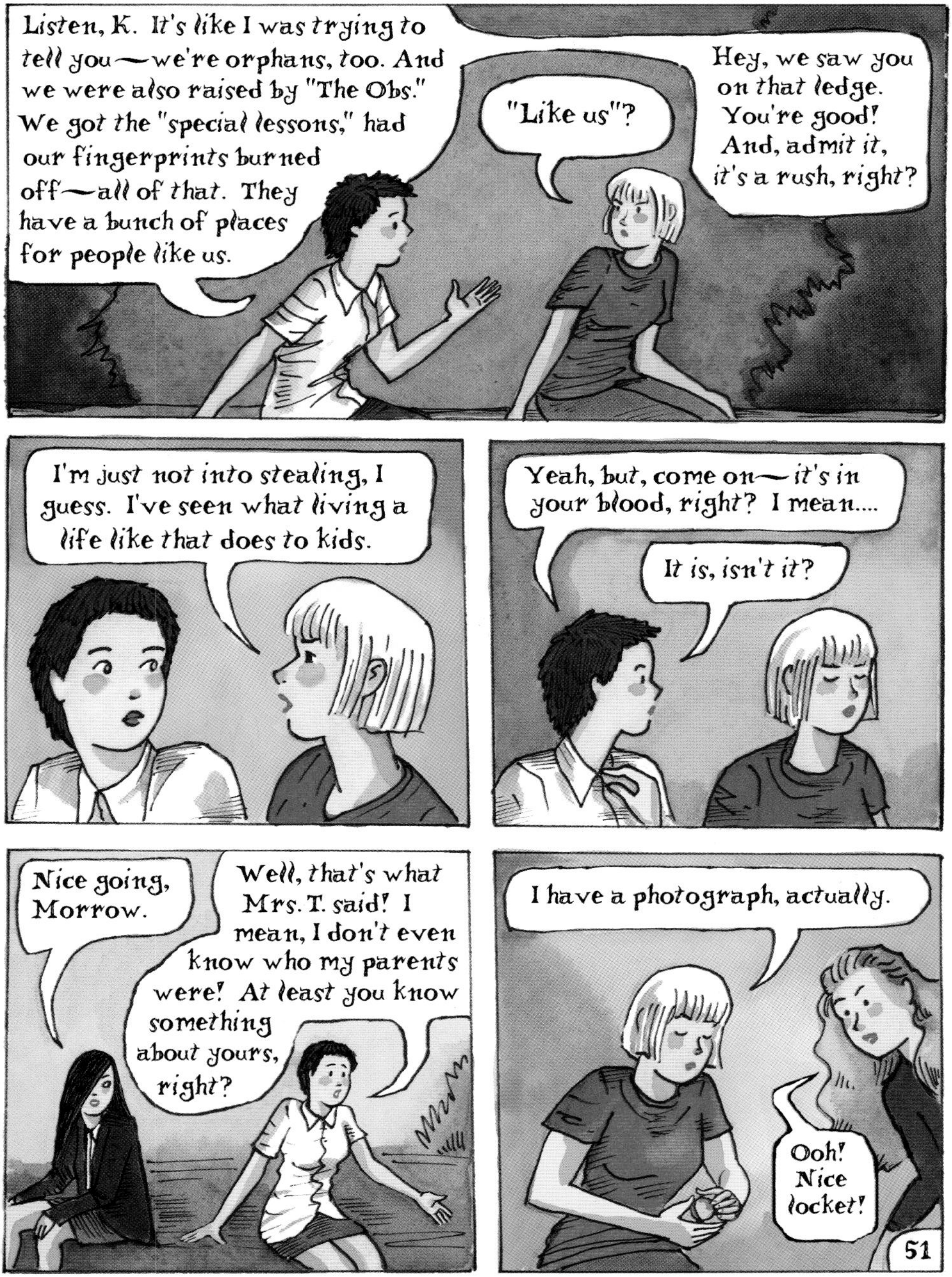
Listen, K. It's like I was trying to tell you—we're orphans, too. And we were also raised by "The Obs." We got the "special lessons," had our fingerprints burned off—all of that. They have a bunch of places for people like us.
"Like us"?
Hey, we saw you on that ledge. You're good! And, admit it, it's a rush, right?
I'm just not into stealing, I guess. I've seen what living a life like that does to kids.
Yeah, but, come on—it's in your blood, right? I mean....
It is, isn't it?
Nice going, Morrow.
Well, that's what Mrs. T. said! I mean, I don't even know who my parents were! At least you know something about yours, right?
I have a photograph, actually.
Ooh! Nice locket!

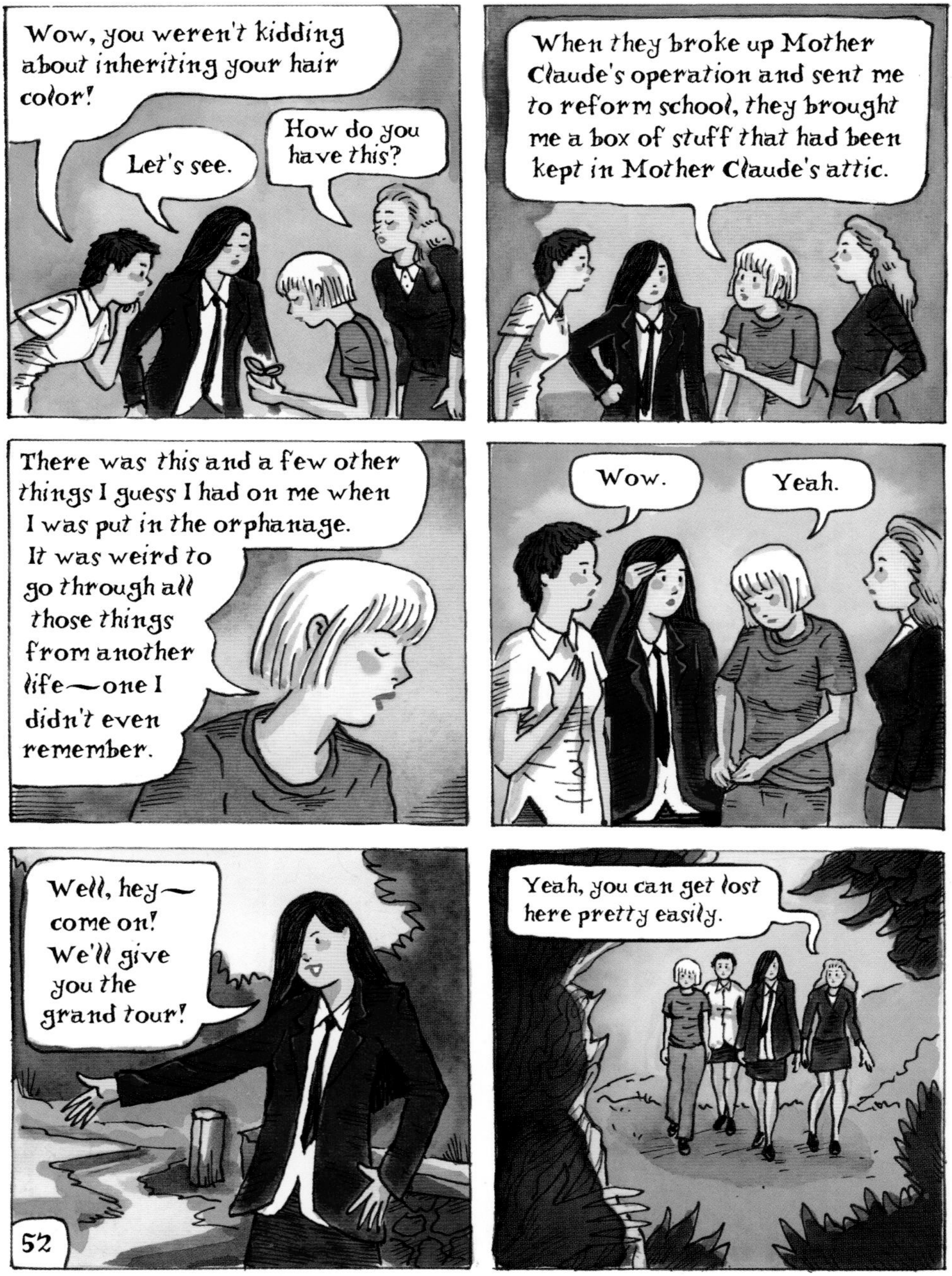
Wow, you weren't kidding about inheriting your hair color!
Let's see.
How do you have this?
When they broke up Mother Claude's operation and sent me to reform school, they brought me a box of stuff that had been kept in Mother Claude's attic.
There was this and a few other things I guess I had on me when I was put in the orphanage. It was weird to go through all those things from another life—one I didn't even remember.
Wow.
Yeah.
Well, hey—come on! We'll give you the grand tour!
Yeah, you can get lost here pretty easily.

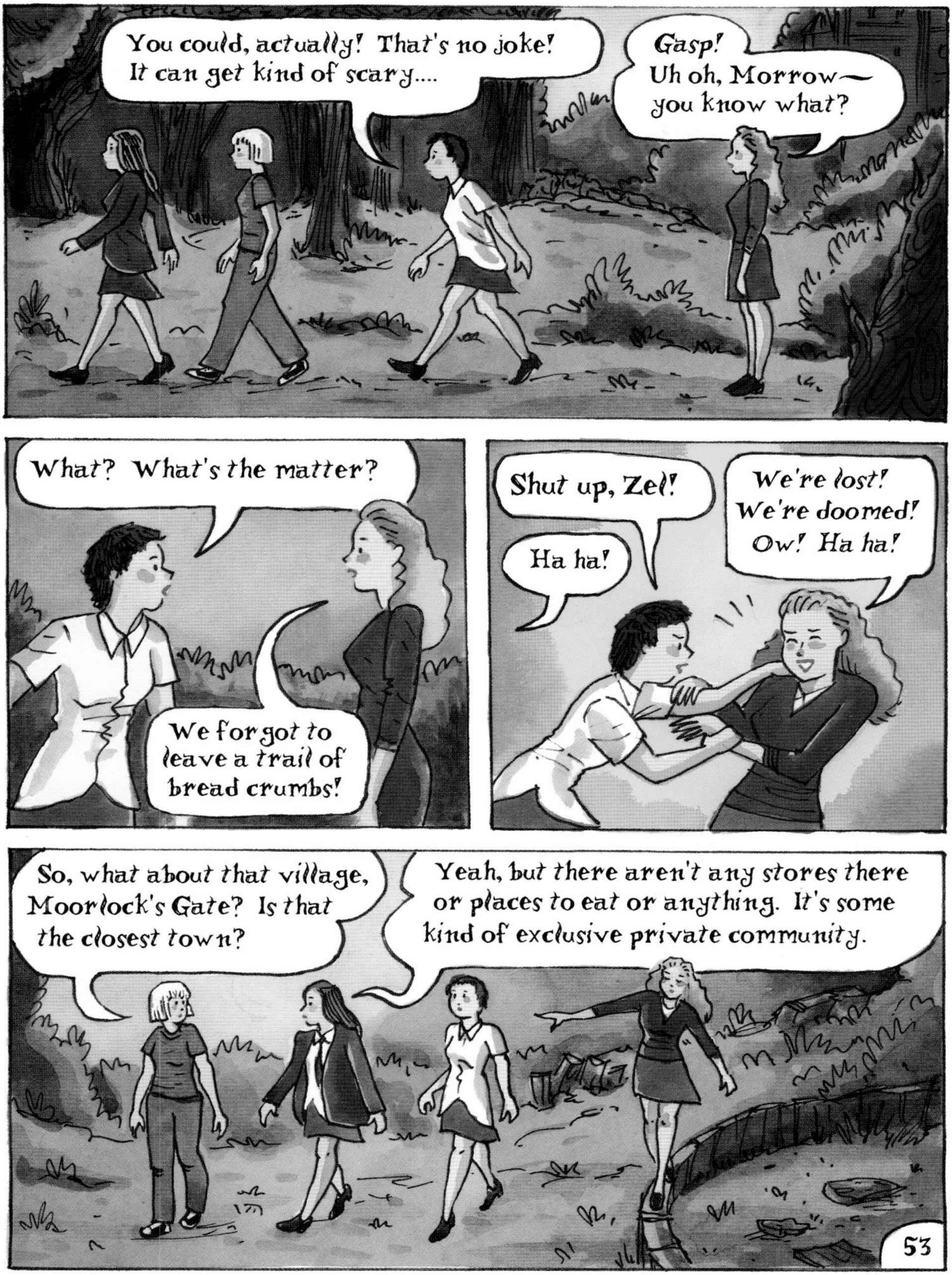
You could, actually! That's no joke! It can get kind of scary....
Gasp! Uh oh, Morrow— you know what?
What? What's the matter?
We forgot to leave a trail of bread crumbs!
Shut up, Zel!
Ha ha!
We're lost! We're doomed! Ow! Ha ha!
So, what about that village, Moorlock's Gate? Is that the closest town?
Yeah, but there aren't any stores there or places to eat or anything. It's some kind of exclusive private community.
53

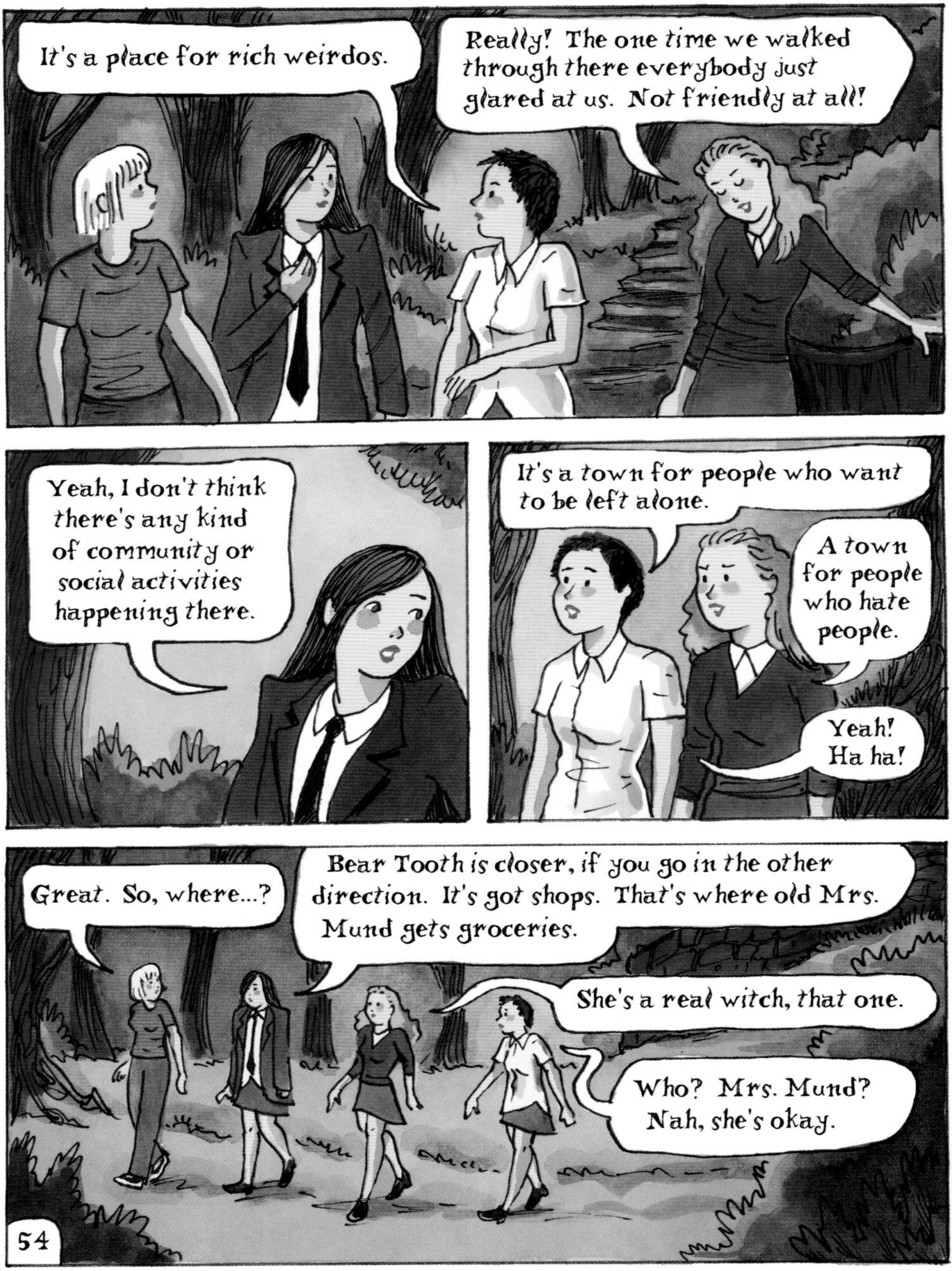
It's a place for rich weirdos.
Really! The one time we walked through there everybody just glared at us. Not friendly at all!
Yeah, I don't think there's any kind of community or social activities happening there.
It's a town for people who want to be left alone.
A town for people who hate people.
Yeah! Ha ha!
Great. So, where...?
Bear Tooth is closer, if you go in the other direction. It's got shops. That's where old Mrs. Mund gets groceries.
She's a real witch, that one.
Who? Mrs. Mund? Nah, she's okay.

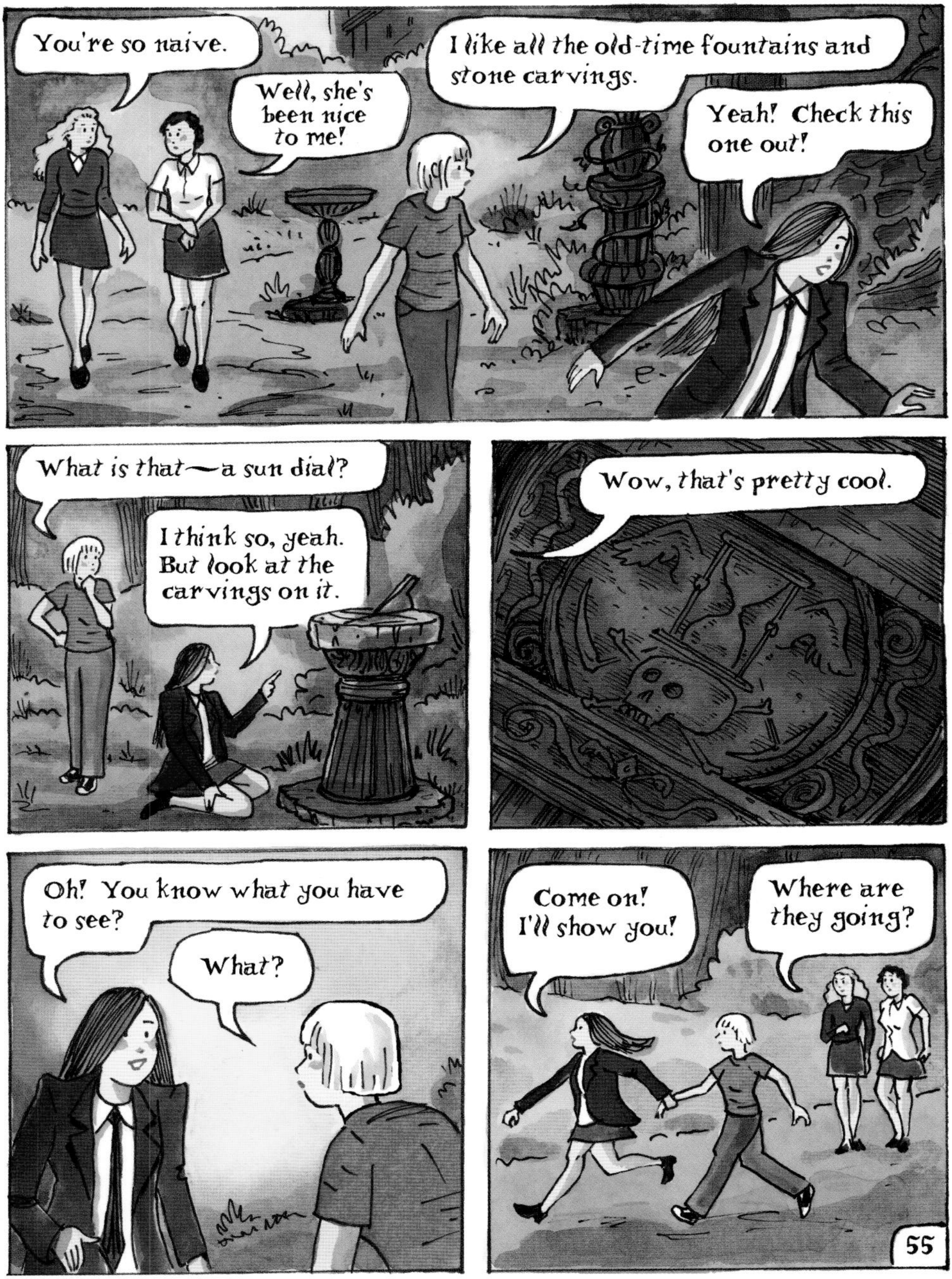
You're so naive.
Well, she's been nice to me!
I like all the old-time fountains and stone carvings.
Yeah! Check this one out!
What is that—a sun dial?
I think so, yeah. But look at the carvings on it.
Wow, that's pretty cool.
Oh! You know what you have to see?
What?
Come on! I'll show you!
Where are they going?

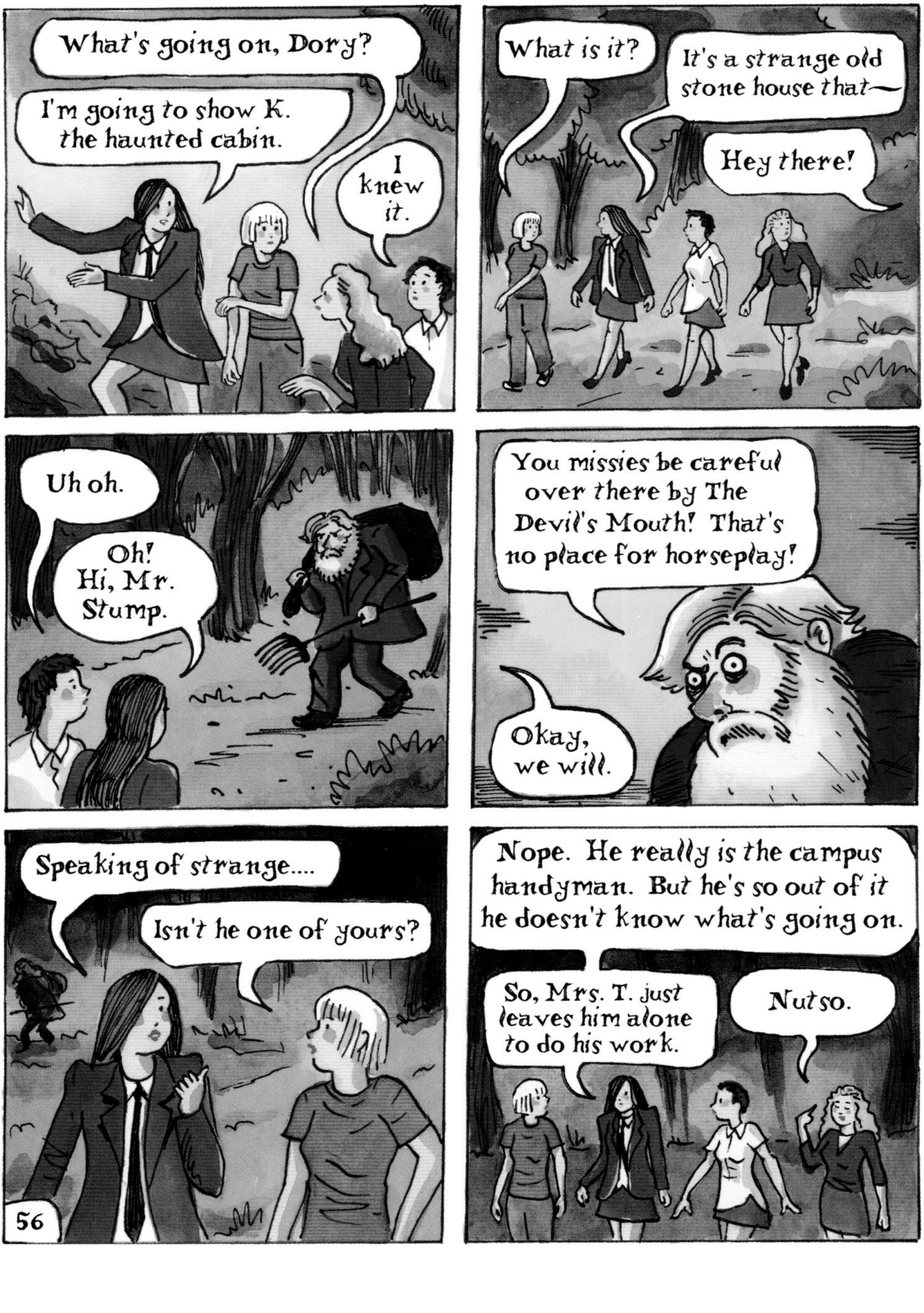
What's going on, Dory?
I'm going to show K. the haunted cabin.
I knew it.
What is it?
It's a strange old stone house that—
Hey there!
Uh oh.
Oh! Hi, Mr. Stump.
You missies be careful over there by The Devil's Mouth! That's no place for horseplay!
Okay, we will.
Speaking of strange....
Isn't he one of yours?
Nope. He really is the campus handyman. But he's so out of it he doesn't know what's going on.
So, Mrs. T. just leaves him alone to do his work.
Nutso.

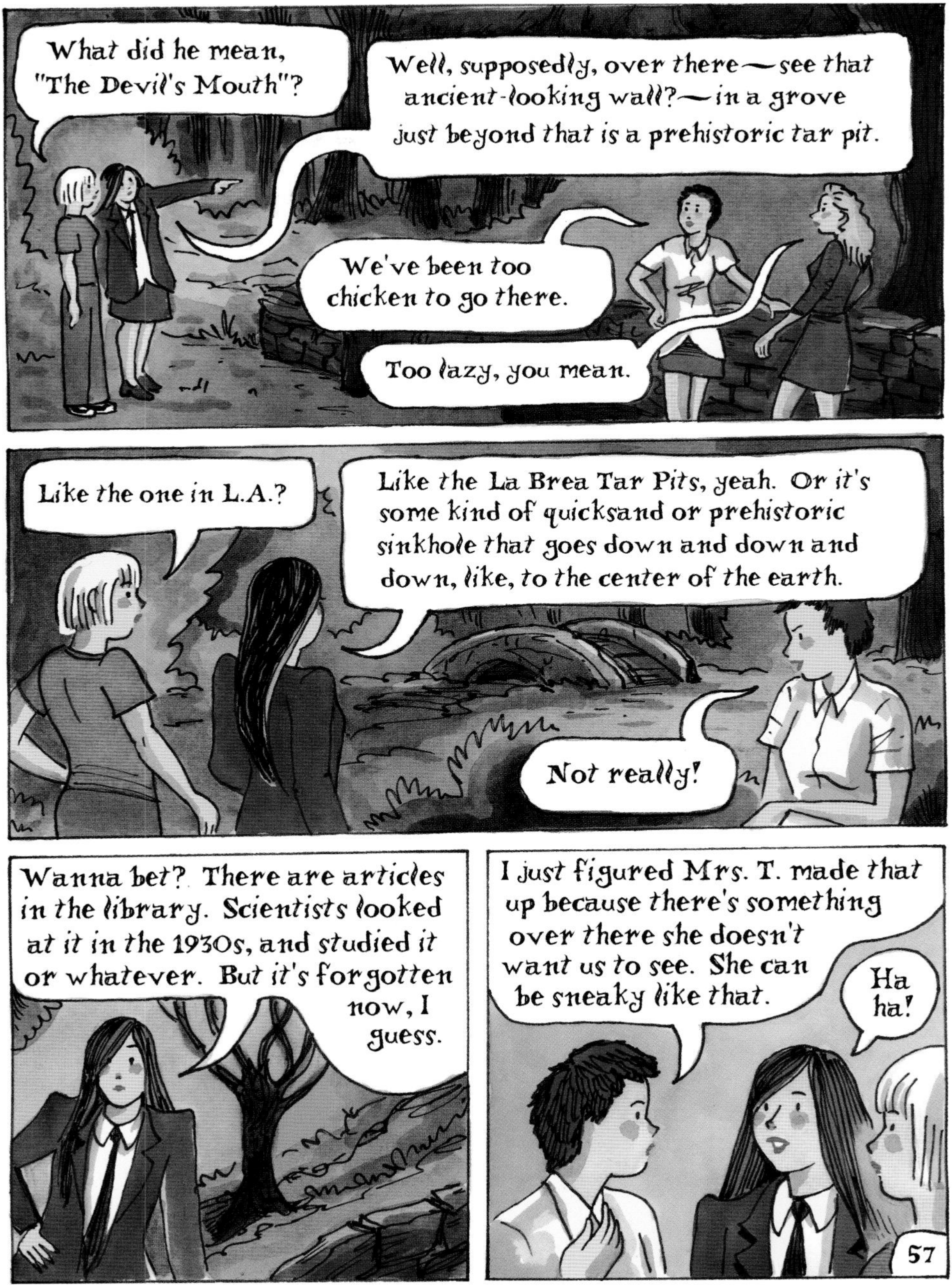
What did he mean, "The Devil's Mouth"?
Well, supposedly, over there—see that ancient-looking wall?—in a grove just beyond that is a prehistoric tar pit.
We've been too chicken to go there.
Too lazy, you mean.
Like the one in L.A.?
Like the La Brea Tar Pits, yeah. Or it's some kind of quicksand or prehistoric sinkhole that goes down and down and down, like, to the center of the earth.
Not really!
Wanna bet? There are articles in the library. Scientists looked at it in the 1930s, and studied it or whatever. But it's forgotten now, I guess.
I just figured Mrs. T. made that up because there's something over there she doesn't want us to see. She can be sneaky like that.
Ha ha!

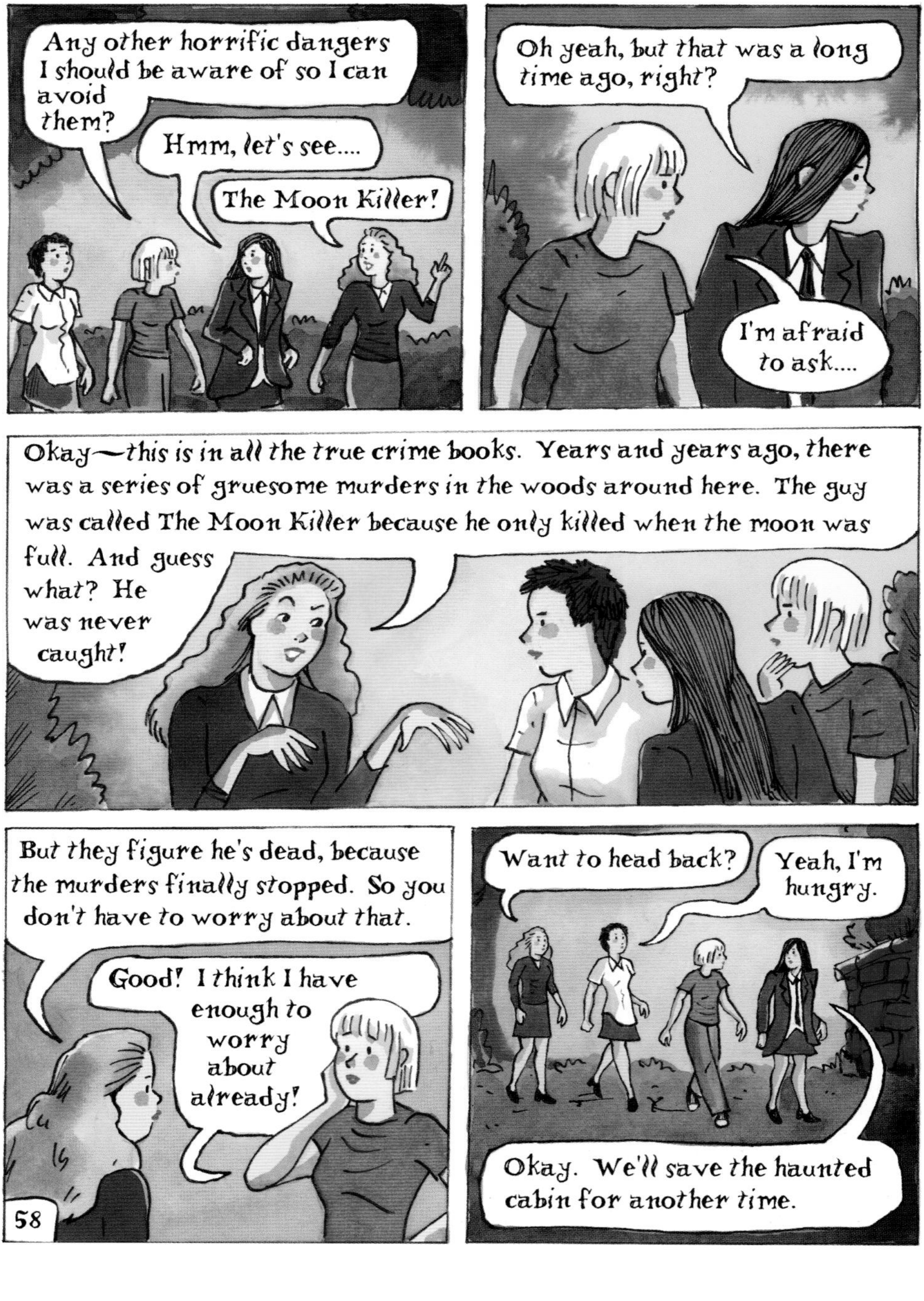
Any other horrific dangers I should be aware of so I can avoid them?
Hmm, let's see....
The Moon Killer!
Oh yeah, but that was a long time ago, right?
I'm afraid to ask....
Okay—this is in all the true crime books. Years and years ago, there was a series of gruesome murders in the woods around here. The guy was called The Moon Killer because he only killed when the moon was full. And guess what? He was never caught!
But they figure he's dead, because the murders finally stopped. So you don't have to worry about that.
Good! I think I have enough to worry about already!
Want to head back?
Yeah, I'm hungry.
Okay. We'll save the haunted cabin for another time.

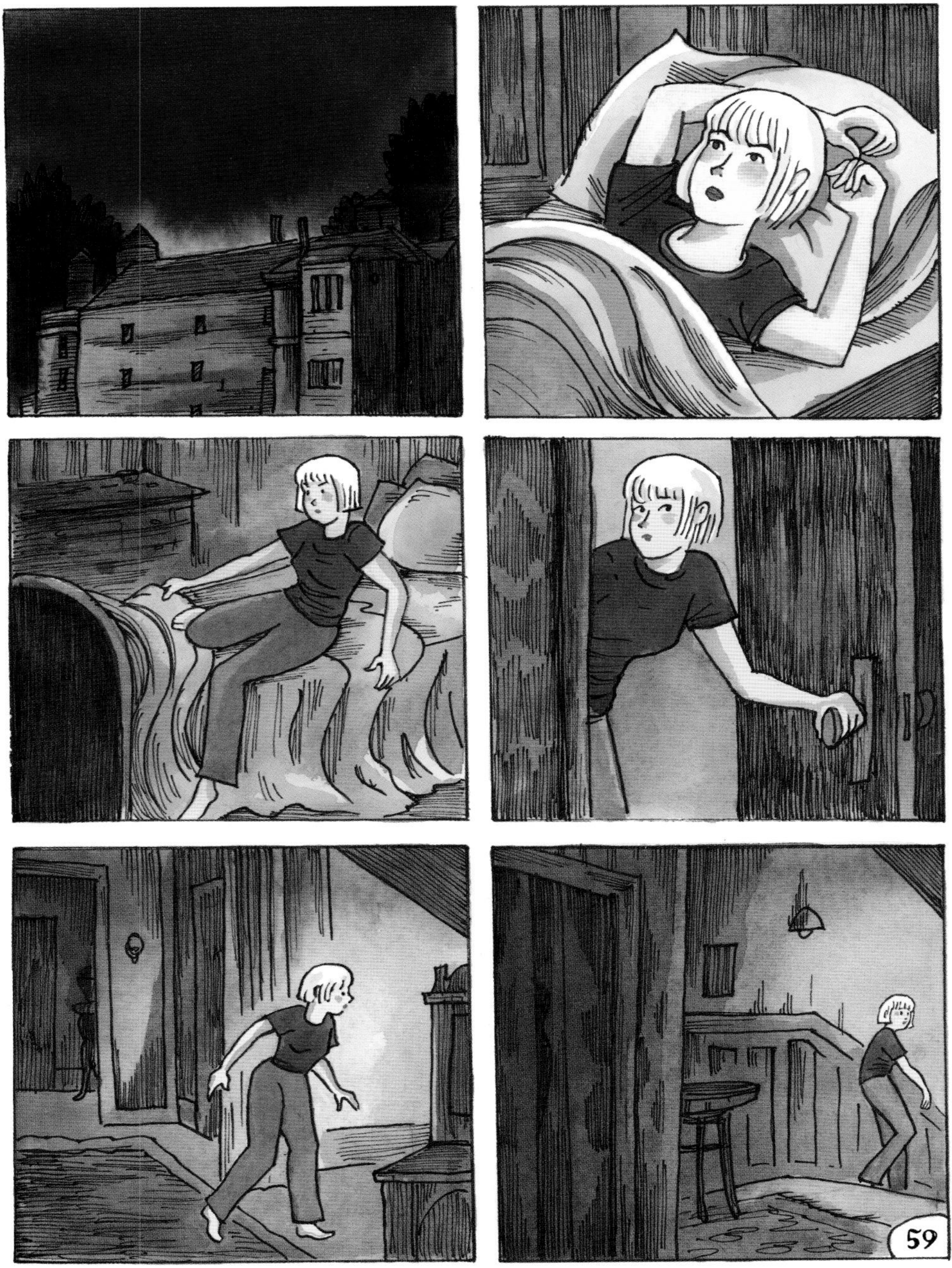

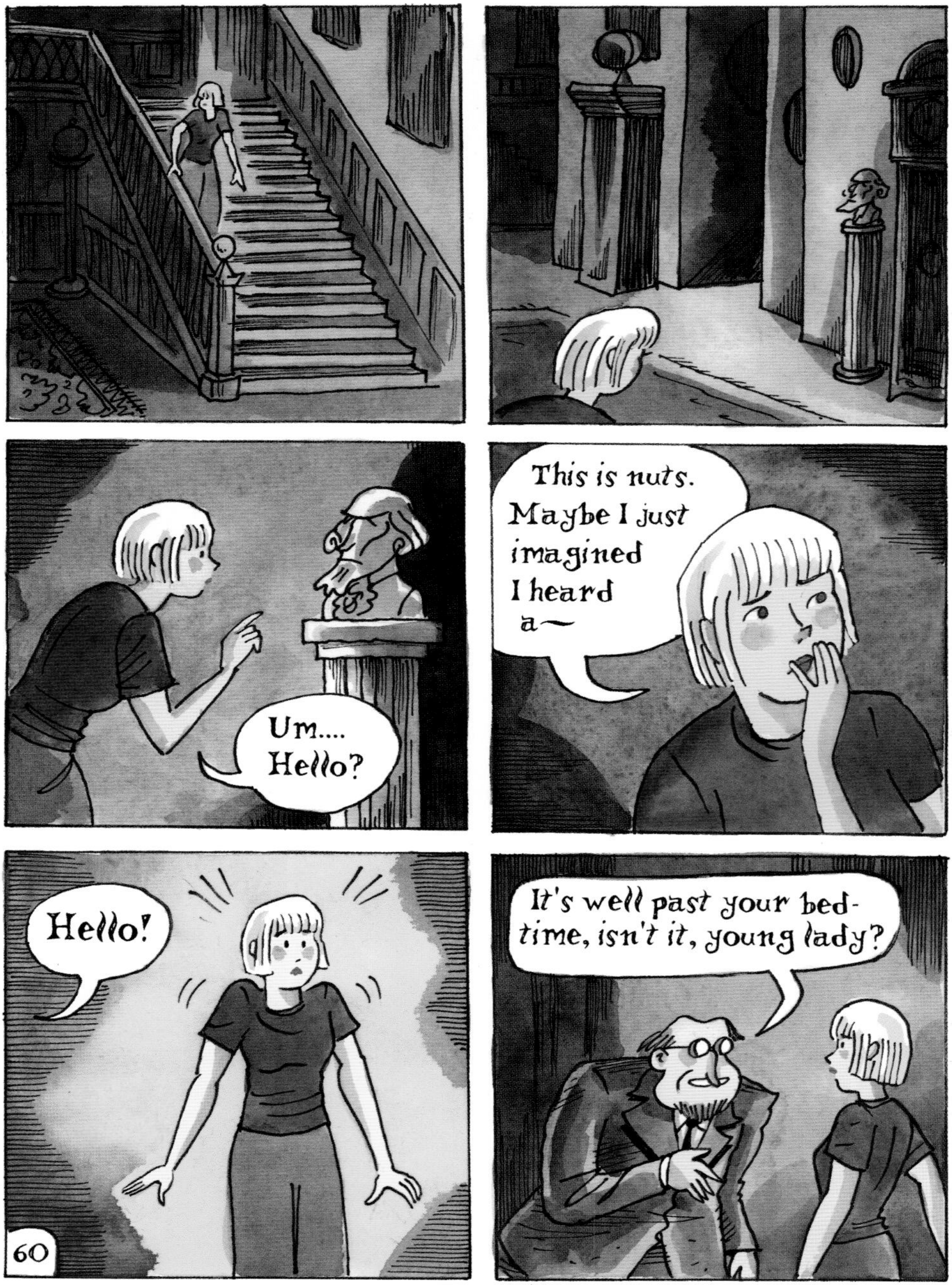
Um....
Hello?
This is nuts. Maybe I just imagined I heard a—
Hello!
It's well past your bed-time, isn't it, young lady?

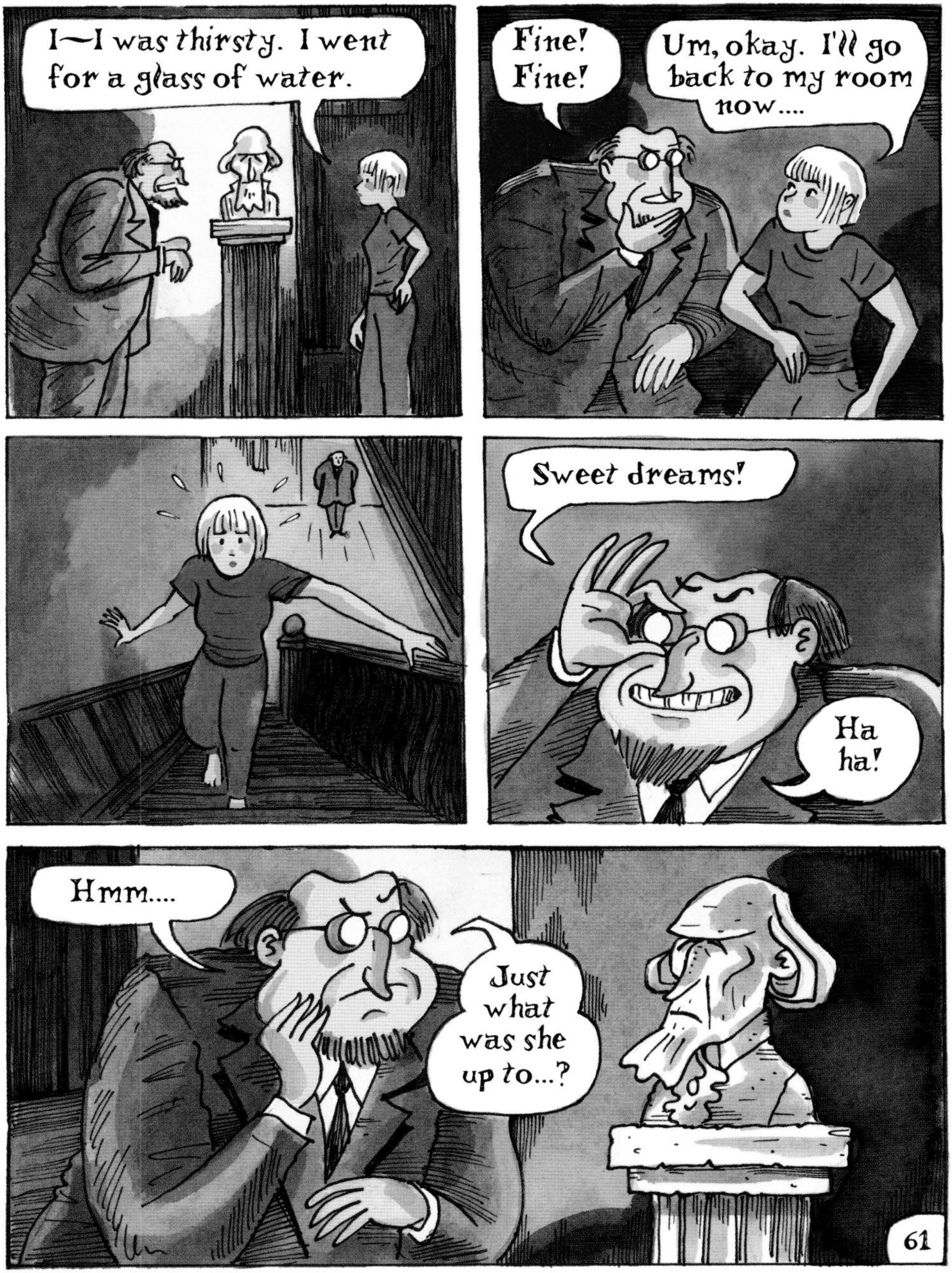
I—I was thirsty. I went for a glass of water.
Fine! Fine!
Um, okay. I'll go back to my room now....
Sweet dreams!
Ha ha!
Hmm....
Just what was she up to...?

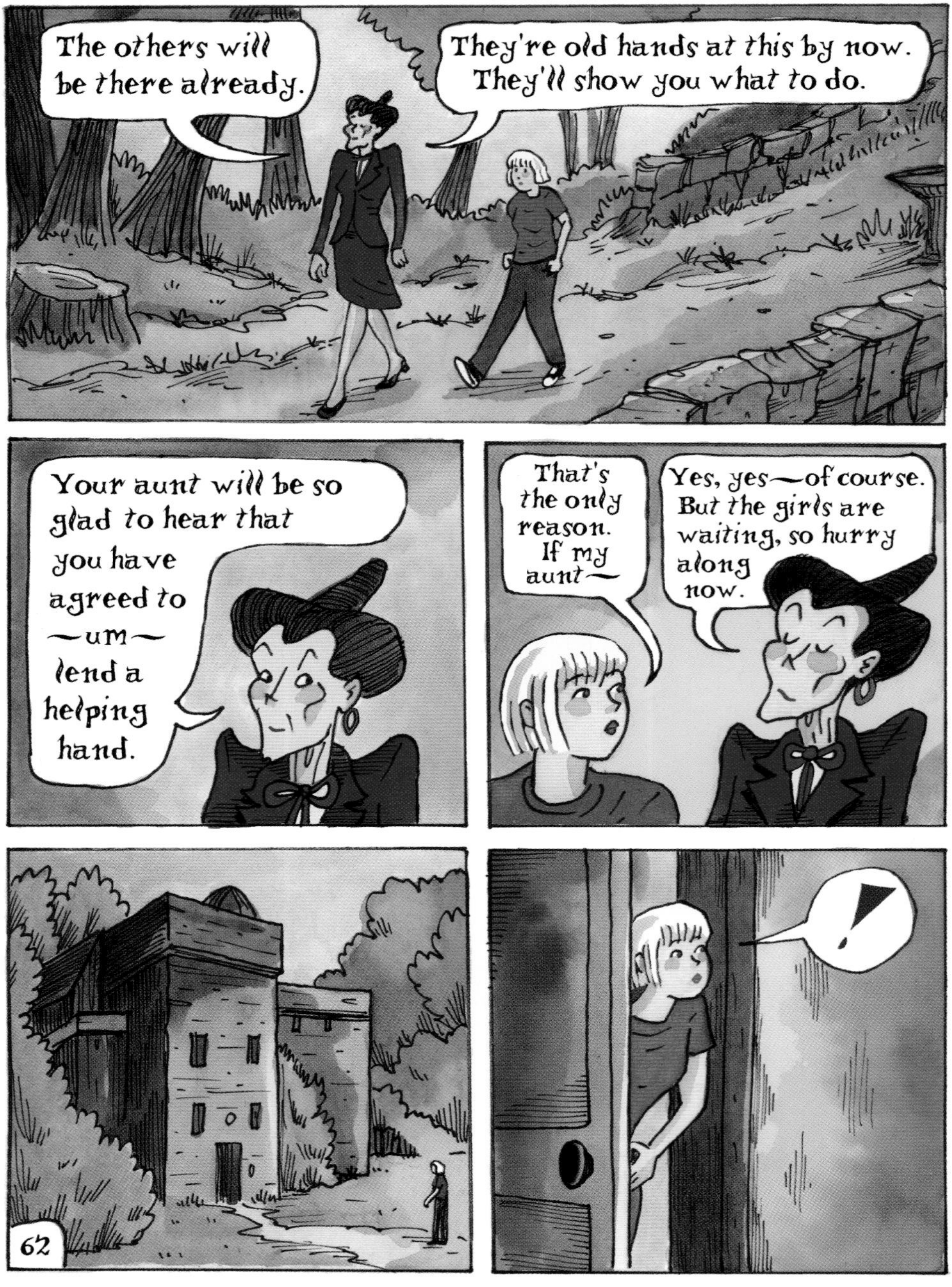
The others will be there already.
They're old hands at this by now. They'll show you what to do.
Your aunt will be so glad to hear that you have agreed to —um— lend a helping hand.
That's the only reason. If my aunt—
Yes, yes—of course. But the girls are waiting, so hurry along now.
!

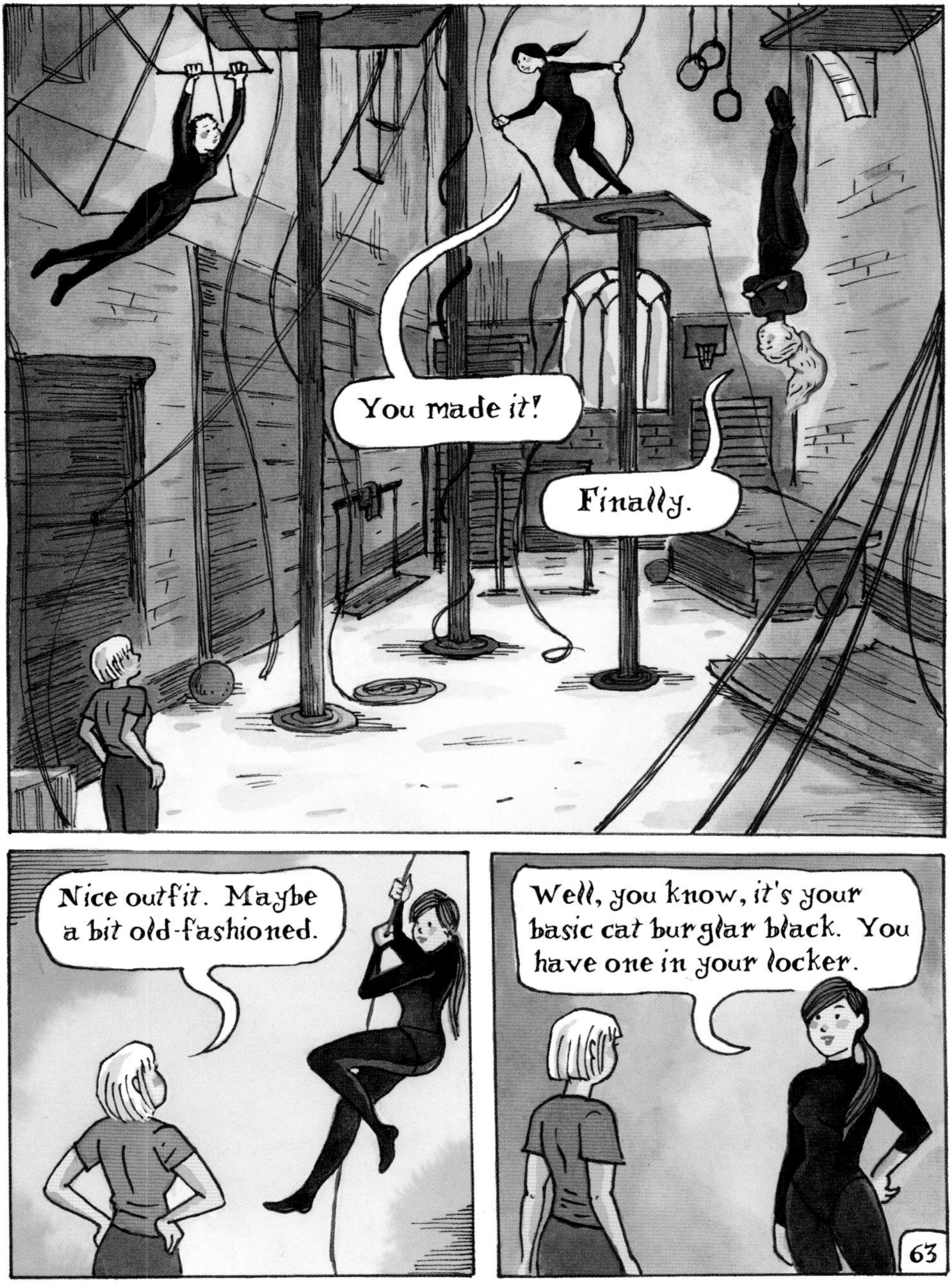
You made it!
Finally.
Nice outfit. Maybe a bit old-fashioned.
Well, you know, it's your basic cat burglar black. You have one in your locker.

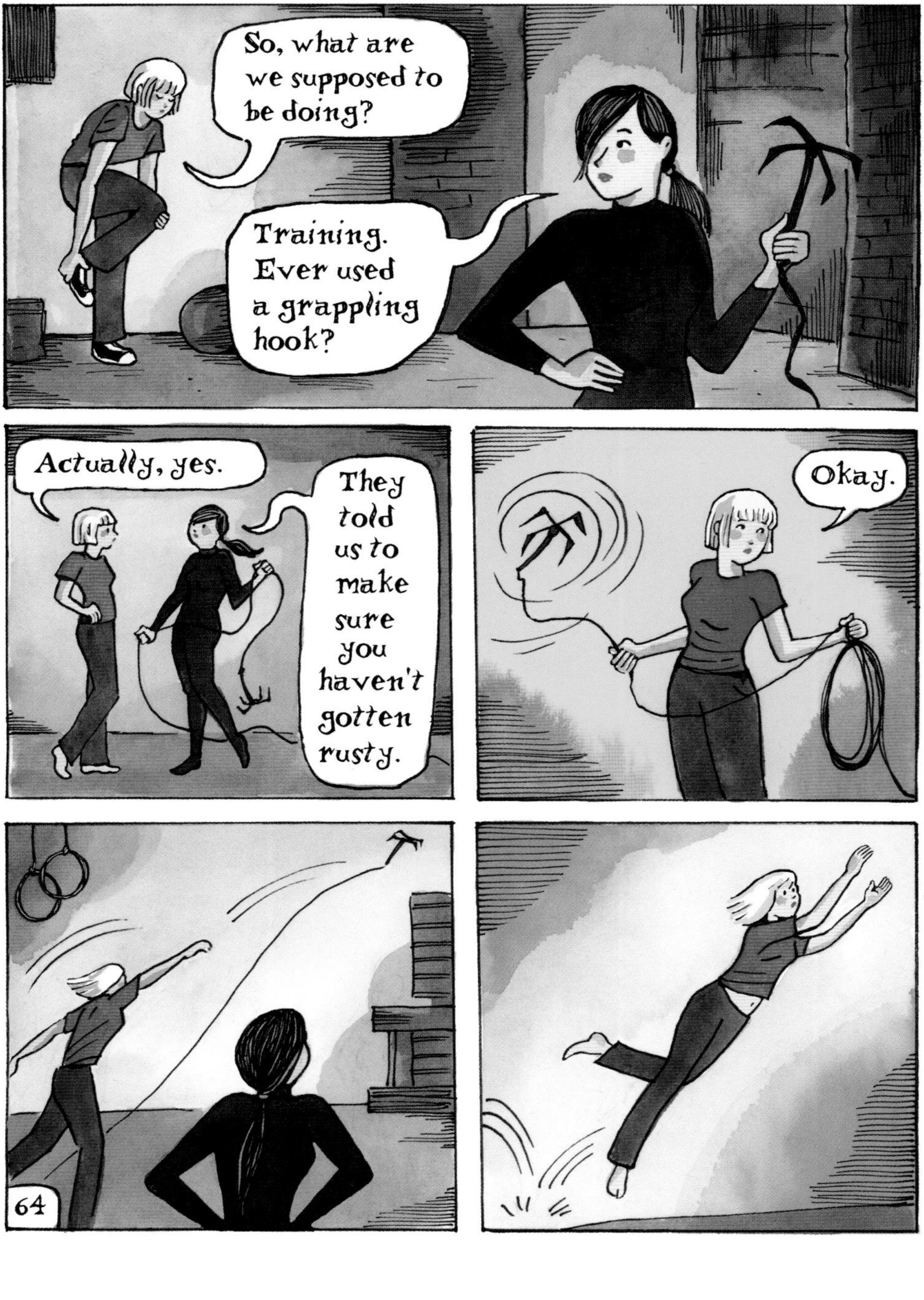
So, what are we supposed to be doing?
Training. Ever used a grappling hook?
Actually, yes.
They told us to make sure you haven't gotten rusty.
Okay.

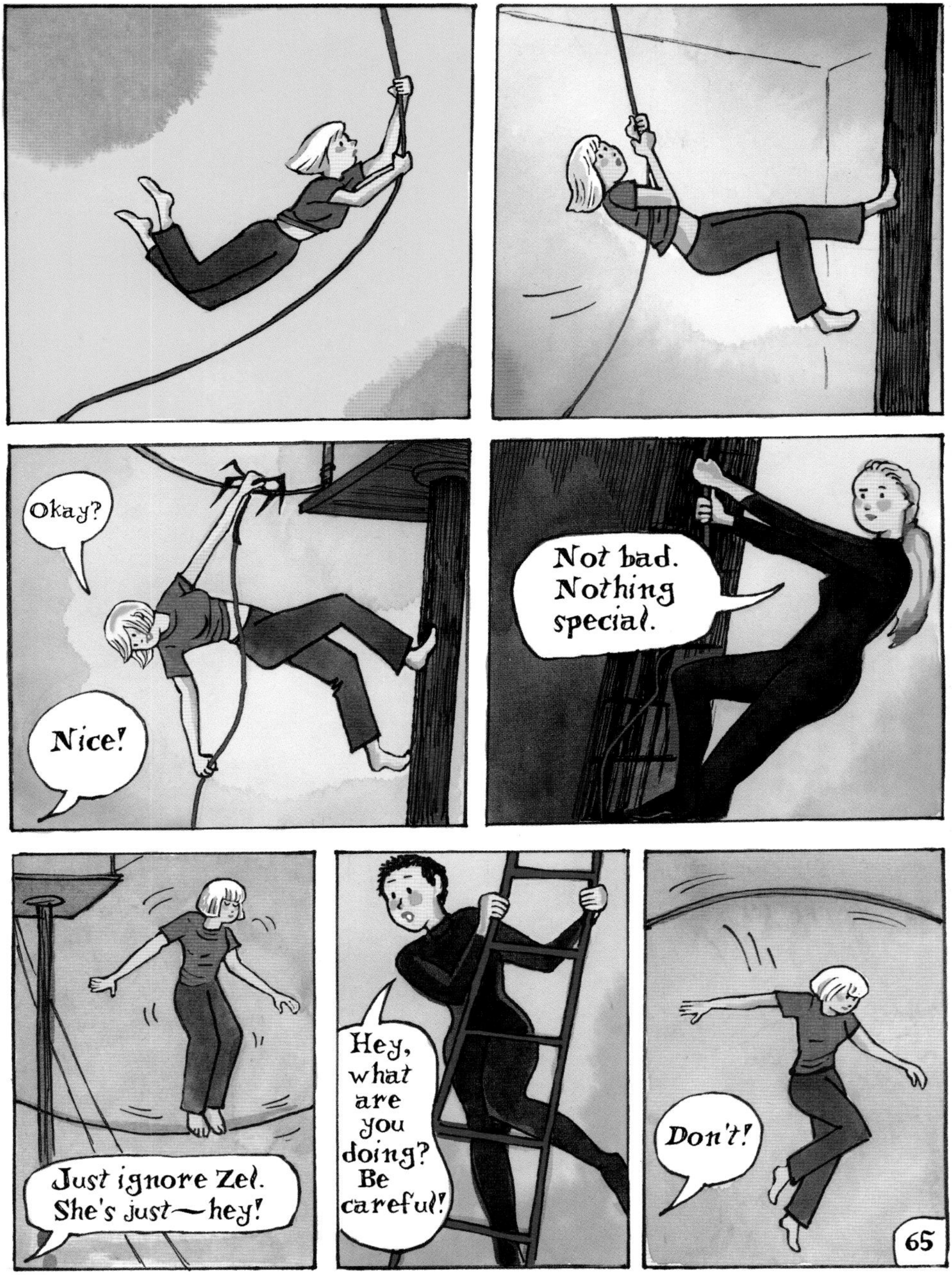
Okay?
Nice!
Not bad. Nothing special.
Just ignore Zel. She's just—hey!
Hey, what are you doing? Be careful!
Don't!

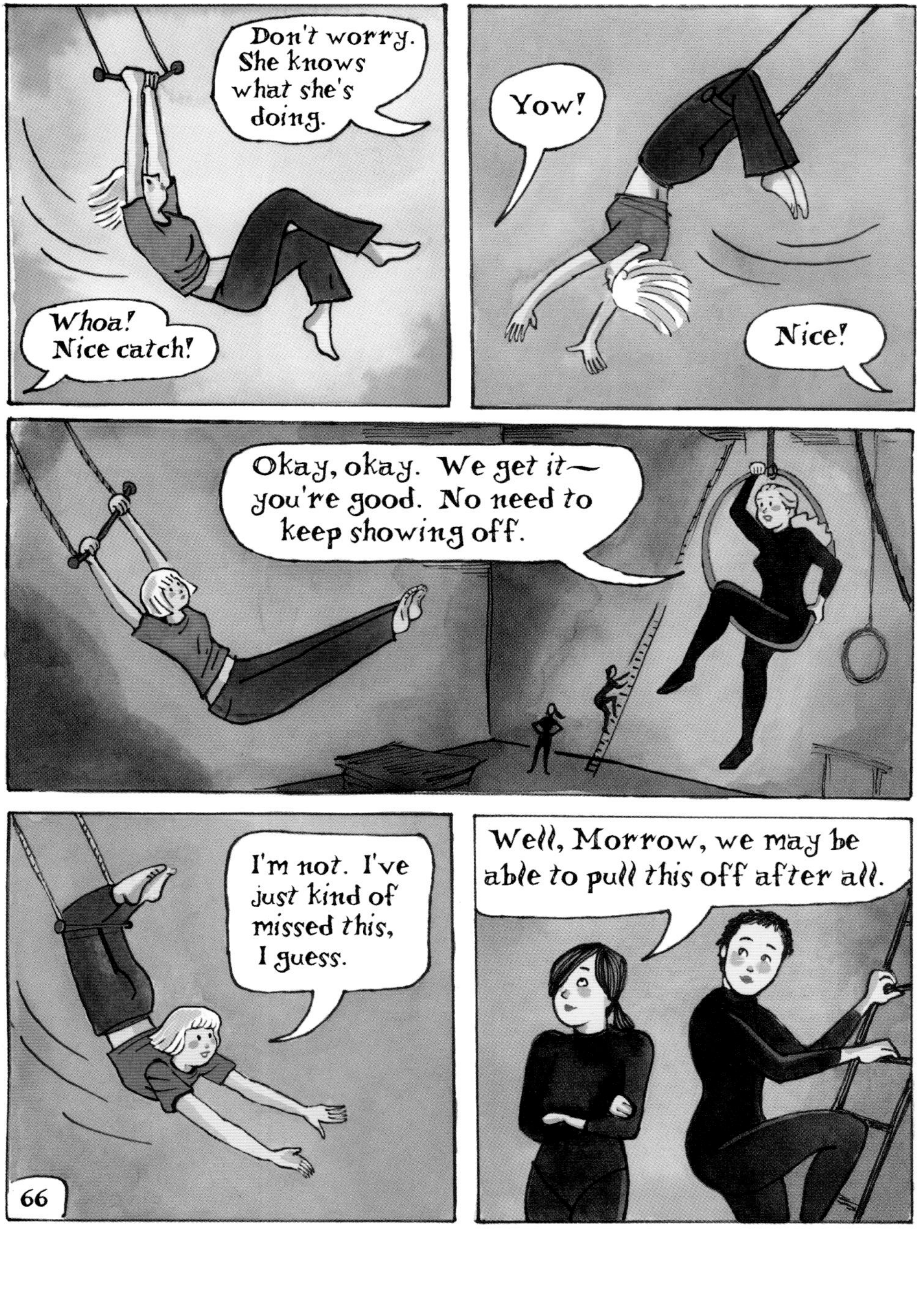
Don't worry. She knows what she's doing.
Whoa! Nice catch!
Yow!
Nice!
Okay, okay. We get it— you're good. No need to keep showing off.
I'm not. I've just kind of missed this, I guess.
Well, Morrow, we may be able to pull this off after all.

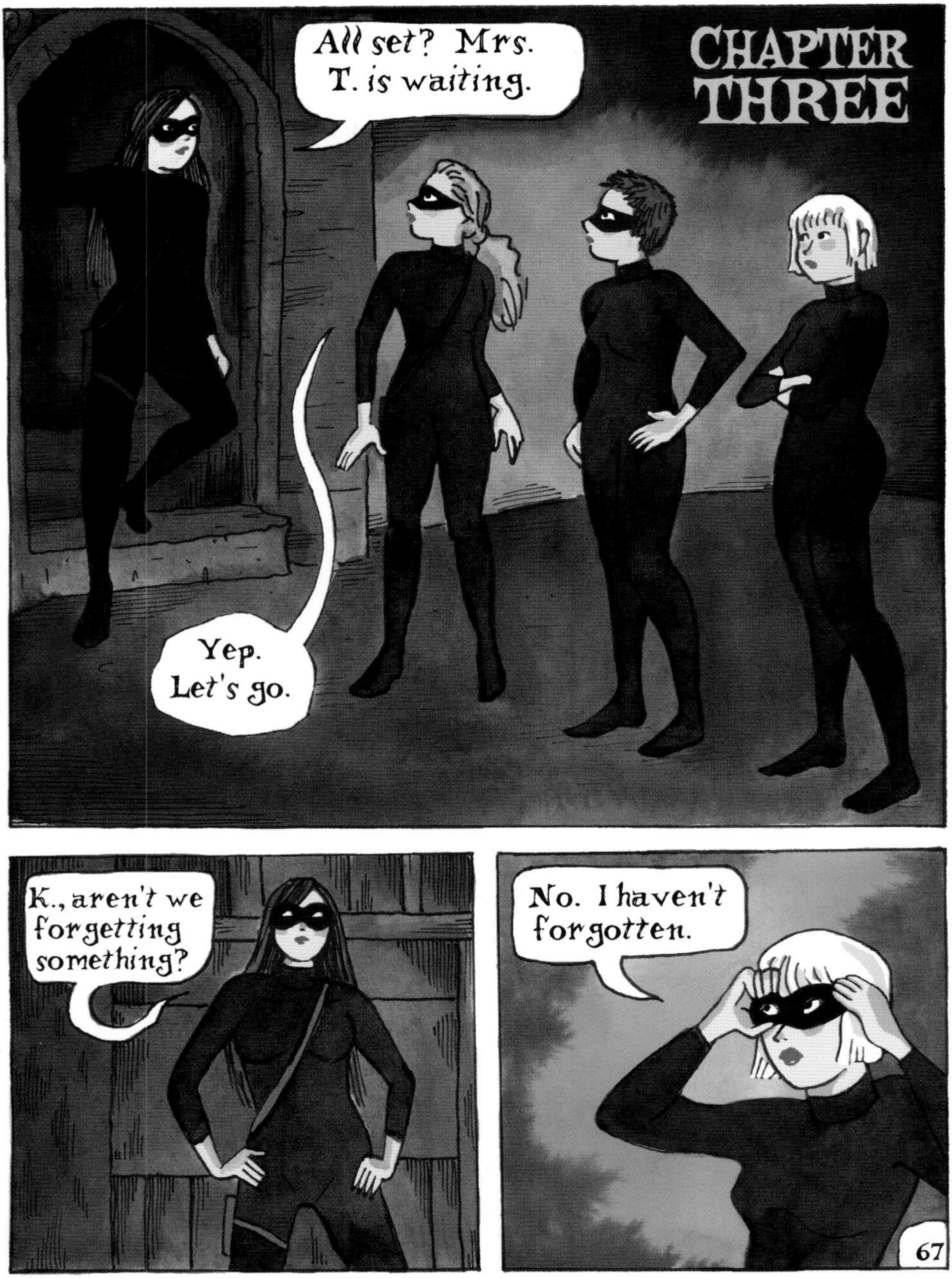
CHAPTER THREE
All set? Mrs. T. is waiting.
Yep. Let's go.
K., aren't we forgetting something?
No. I haven't forgotten.

All right, we've been over this enough times now that you should be fairly familiar with the layout. But that's no reason to feel overly confident. There may always be something unexpected. Remember, our goal is to obtain all three paintings, and this house contains only one.

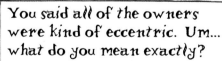

You said all of the owners were kind of eccentric. Um... what do you mean exactly?

I simply meant that each has their own —er— unique habits, lifestyles, and interests. This one, for example, Pierre Voll, is something of an amateur ichthyologist. The man is obsessed with creatures of the sea.

68

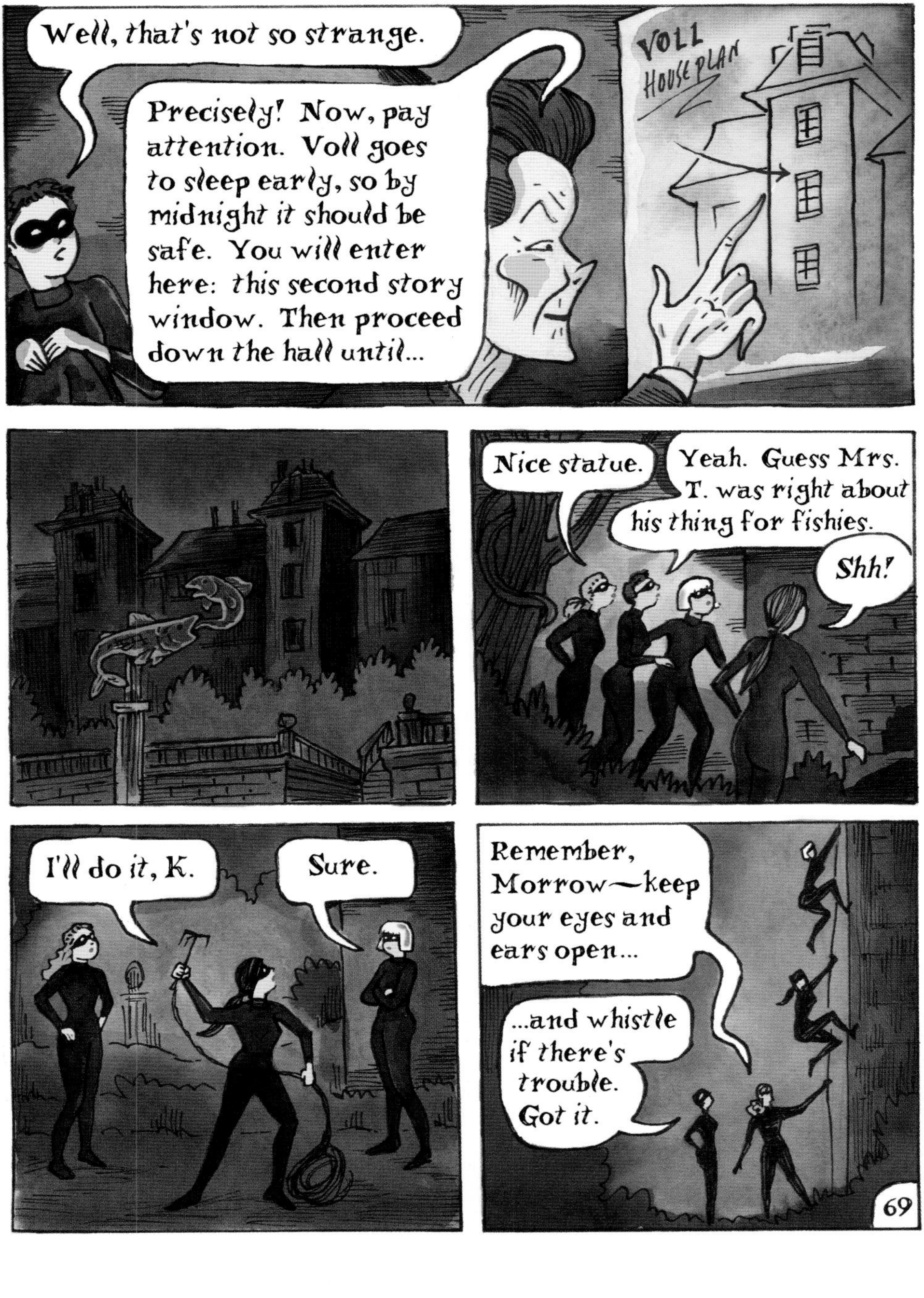
Well, that's not so strange.
Precisely! Now, pay attention. Voll goes to sleep early, so by midnight it should be safe. You will enter here: this second story window. Then proceed down the hall until...
VOLL HOUSE PLAN
Nice statue.
Yeah. Guess Mrs. T. was right about his thing for fishies.
Shh!
I'll do it, K.
Sure.
Remember, Morrow—keep your eyes and ears open...
...and whistle if there's trouble.
Got it.

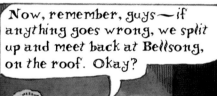

Now, remember, guys — if anything goes wrong, we split up and meet back at Bellsong, on the roof. Okay?

Okay.

Holy...

...mackerel?

Look at all the fishes.

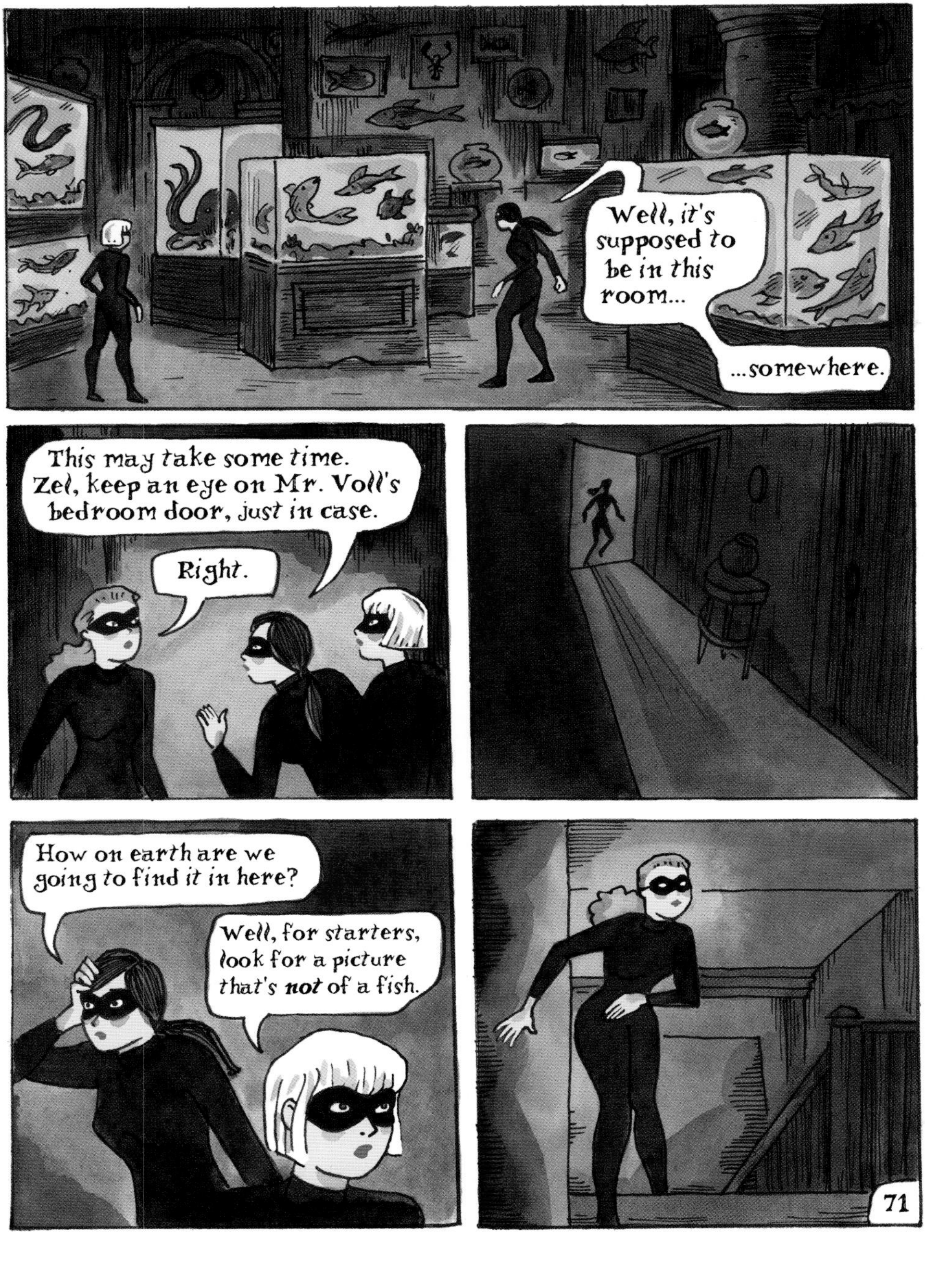
Well, it's supposed to be in this room...
...somewhere.
This may take some time. Zel, keep an eye on Mr. Voll's bedroom door, just in case.
Right.
How on earth are we going to find it in here?
Well, for starters, look for a picture that's not of a fish.
71

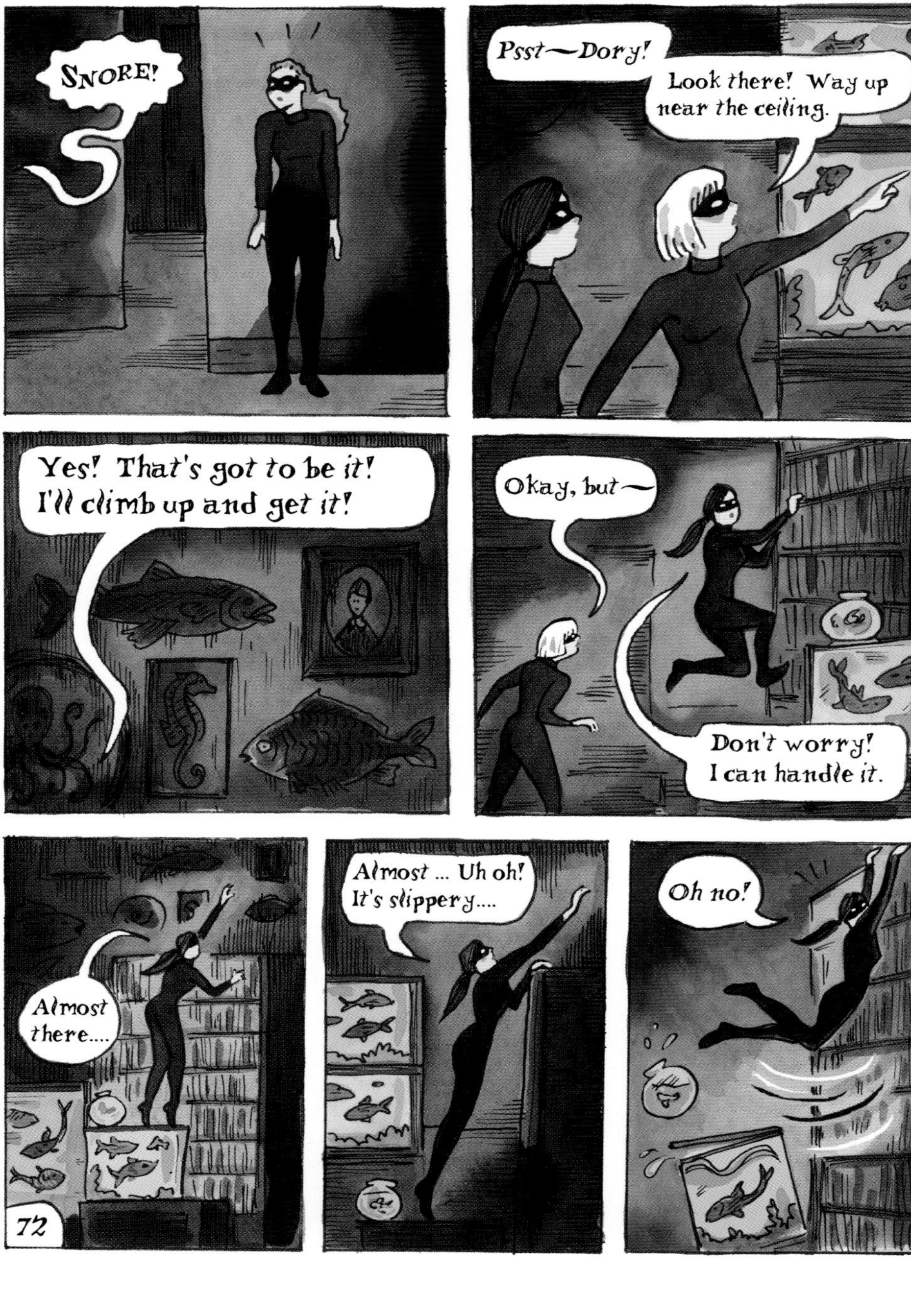
SNORE!
Psst—Dory!
Look there! Way up near the ceiling.
Yes! That's got to be it! I'll climb up and get it!
Okay, but—
Don't worry! I can handle it.
Almost there....
Almost ... Uh oh! It's slippery....
Oh no!

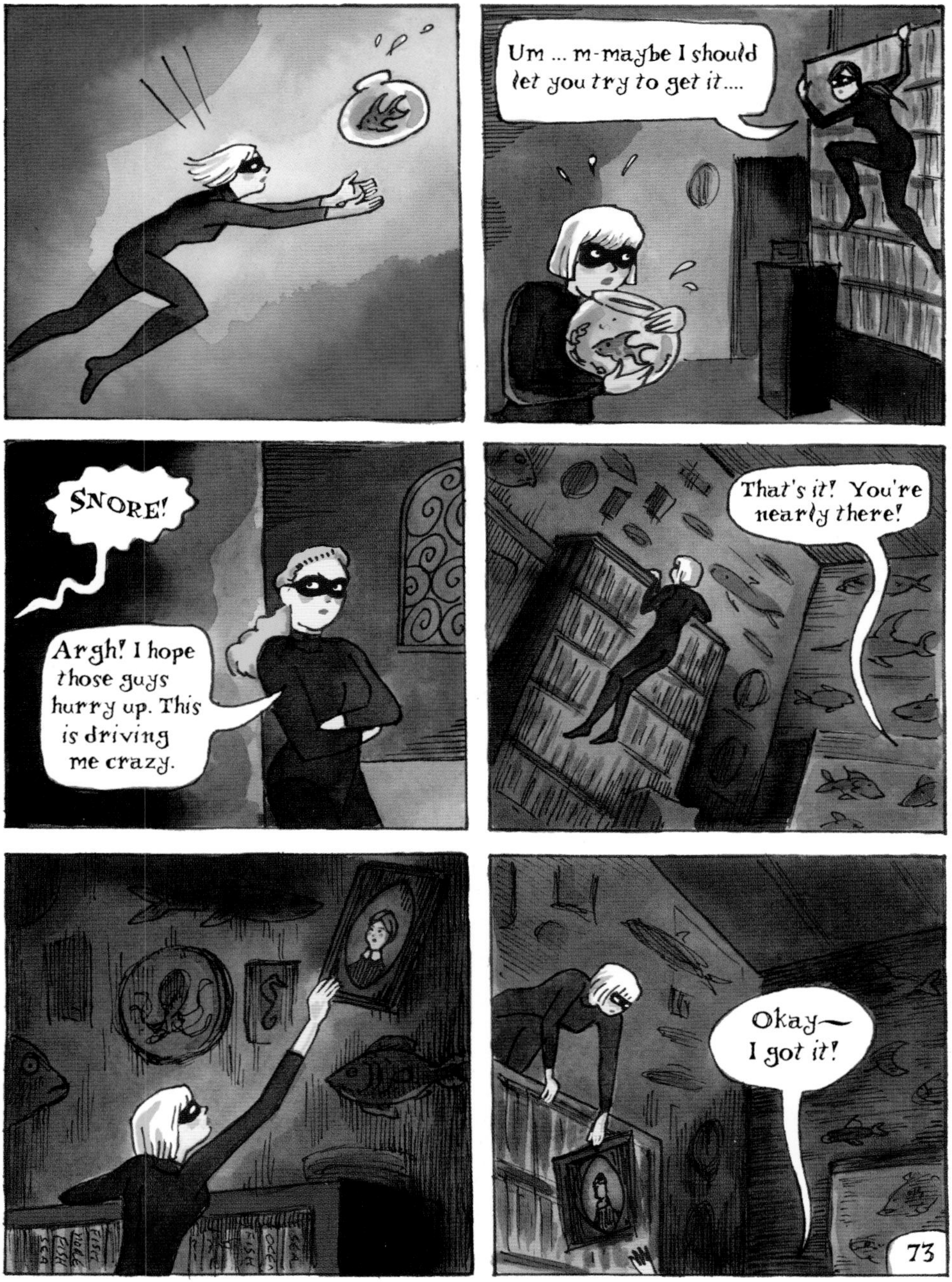
Um ... m-maybe I should let you try to get it....
SNORE!
Argh! I hope those guys hurry up. This is driving me crazy.
That's it! You're nearly there!
Okay— I got it!

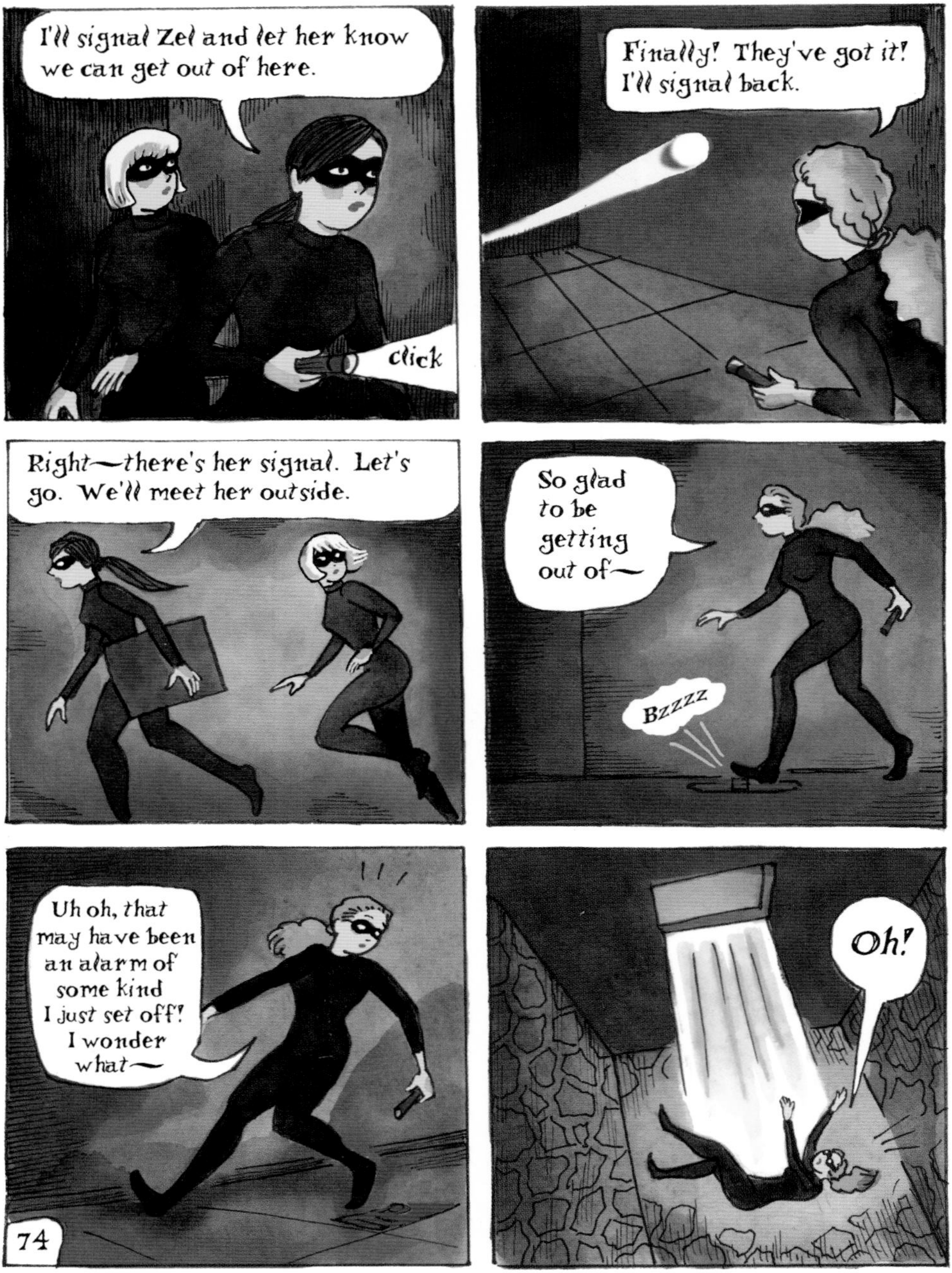

I'll signal Zel and let her know we can get out of here.
click
Finally! They've got it! I'll signal back.
Right—there's her signal. Let's go. We'll meet her outside.
So glad to be getting out of—
Bzzzz
Uh oh, that may have been an alarm of some kind I just set off! I wonder what—
Oh!

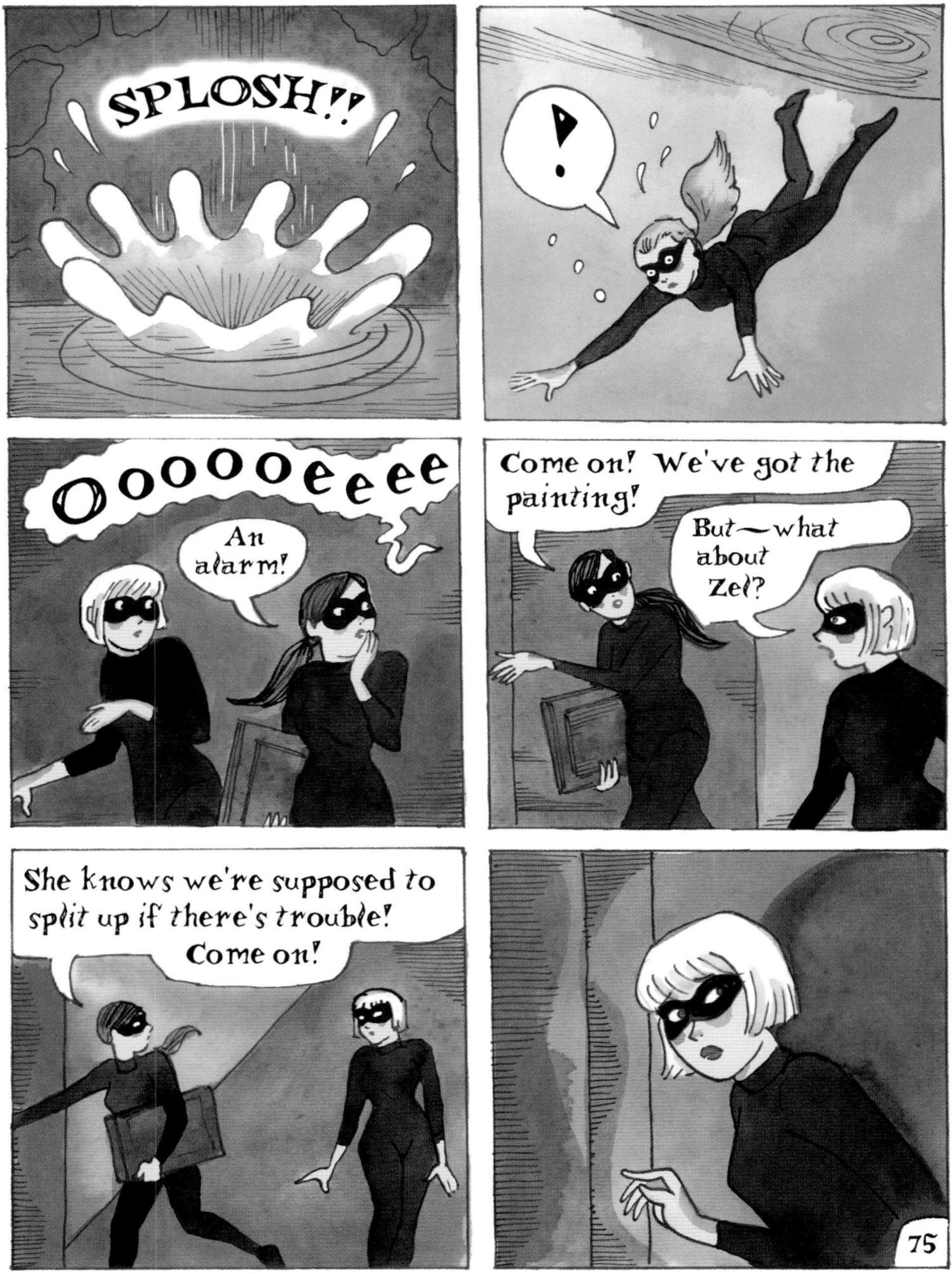
SPLOSH!!
!
Oooooeeee
An alarm!
Come on! We've got the painting!
But—what about Zel?
She knows we're supposed to split up if there's trouble! Come on!
75

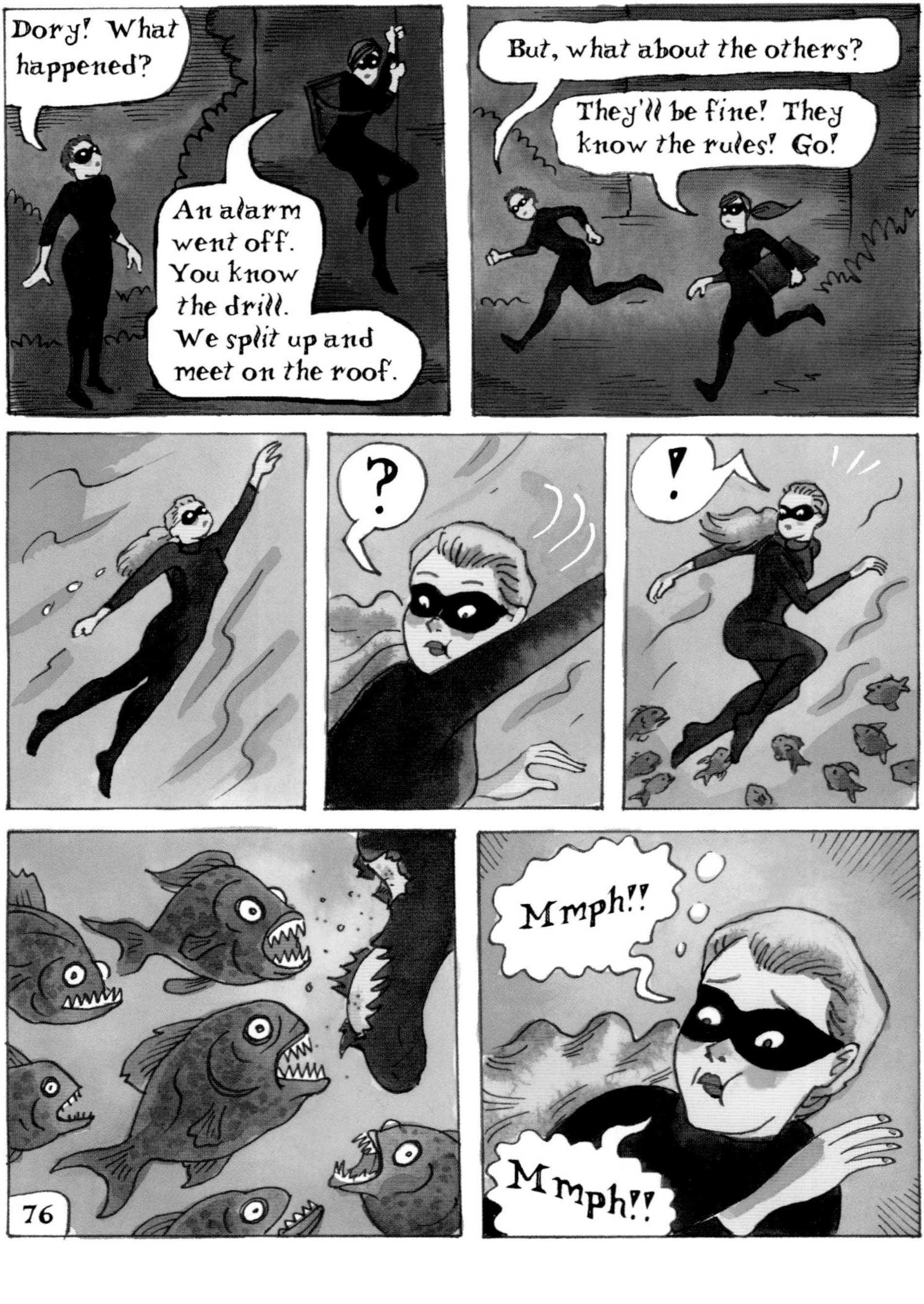
Dory! What happened?
An alarm went off. You know the drill. We split up and meet on the roof.
But, what about the others?
They'll be fine! They know the rules! Go!
?
!
Mmph!!
Mmph!!

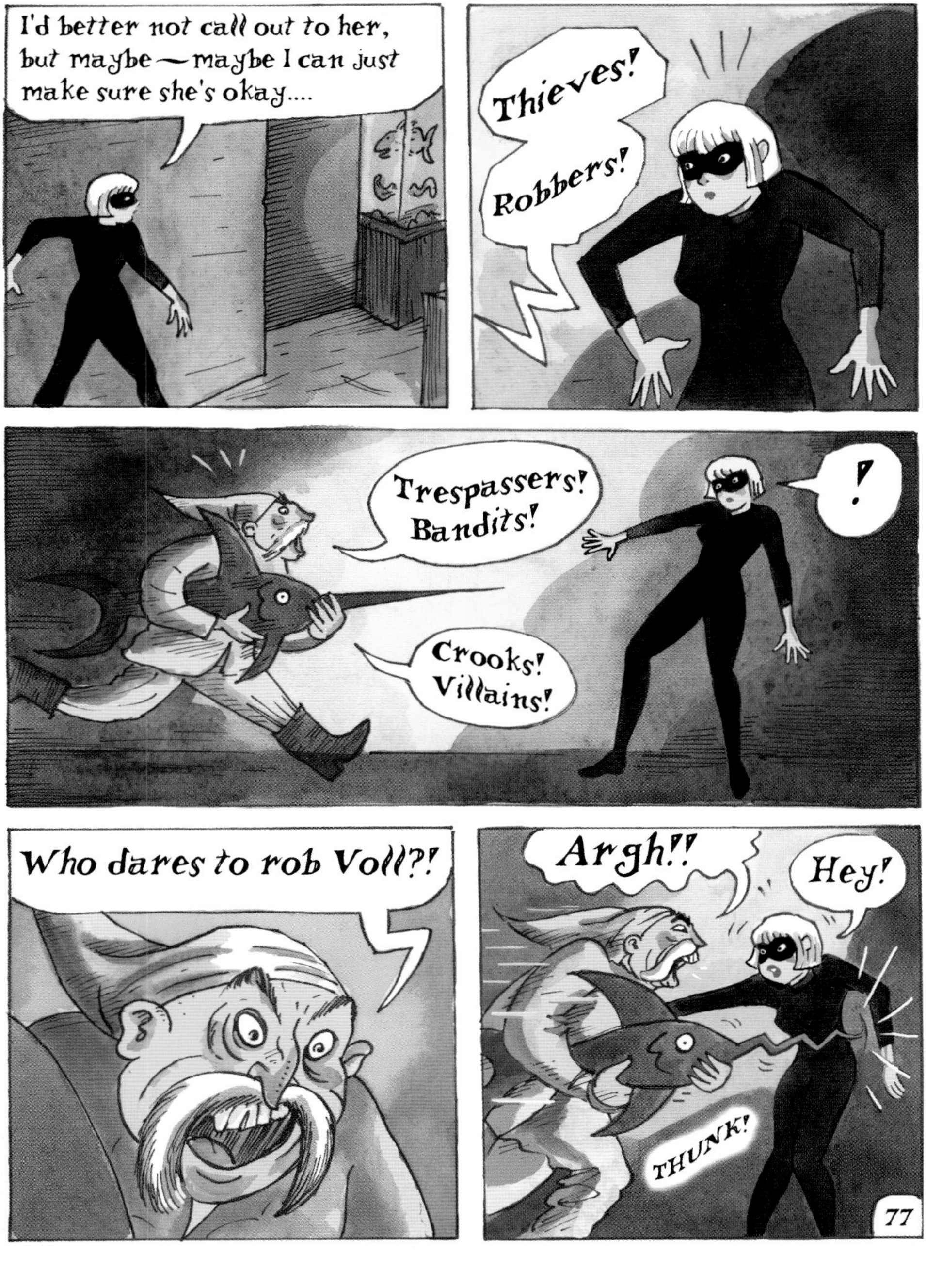
I'd better not call out to her, but maybe—maybe I can just make sure she's okay....
Thieves!
Robbers!
Trespassers! Bandits!
!
Crooks! Villains!
Who dares to rob Voll?!
Argh!!
Hey!
THUNK!

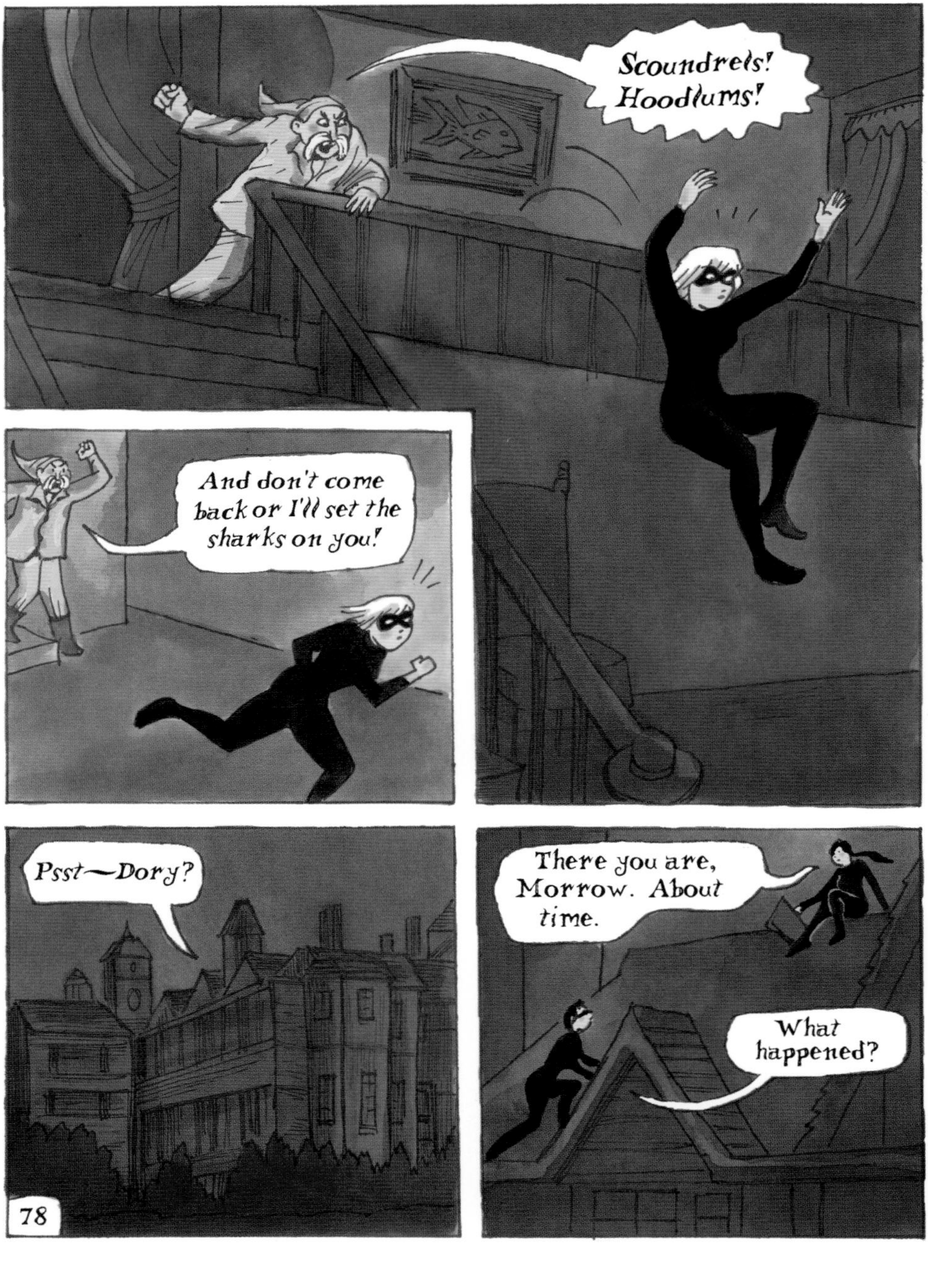

Scoundrels! Hoodlums!
And don't come back or I'll set the sharks on you!
Psst—Dory?
There you are, Morrow. About time.
What happened?

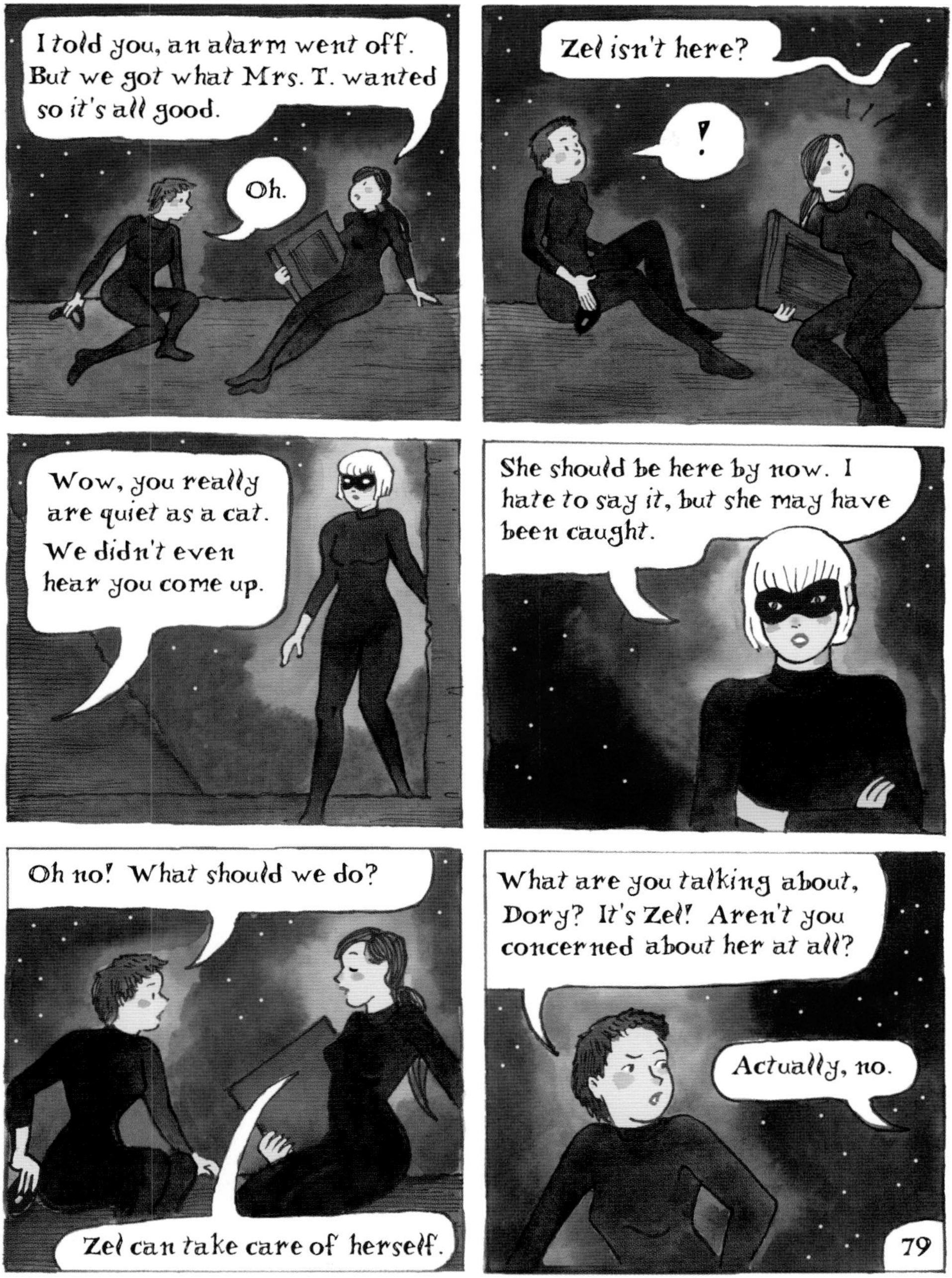

I told you, an alarm went off. But we got what Mrs. T. wanted so it's all good.
Oh.
Zel isn't here?
!
Wow, you really are quiet as a cat. We didn't even hear you come up.
She should be here by now. I hate to say it, but she may have been caught.
Oh no! What should we do?
Zel can take care of herself.
What are you talking about, Dory? It's Zel! Aren't you concerned about her at all?
Actually, no.

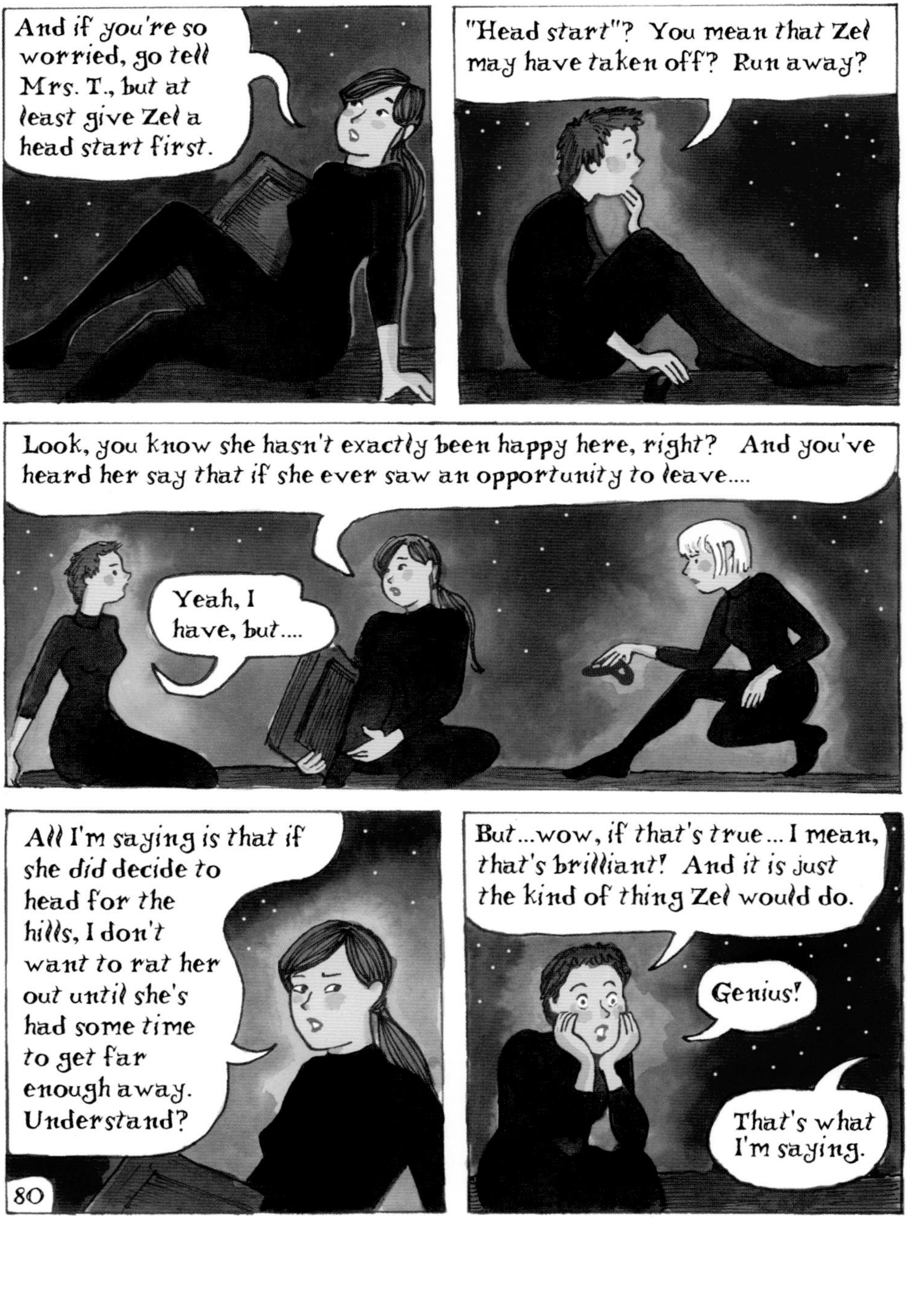
And if you're so worried, go tell Mrs. T., but at least give Zel a head start first.
"Head start"? You mean that Zel may have taken off? Run away?
Look, you know she hasn't exactly been happy here, right? And you've heard her say that if she ever saw an opportunity to leave....
Yeah, I have, but....
All I'm saying is that if she did decide to head for the hills, I don't want to rat her out until she's had some time to get far enough away. Understand?
But...wow, if that's true...I mean, that's brilliant! And it is just the kind of thing Zel would do.
Genius!
That's what I'm saying.

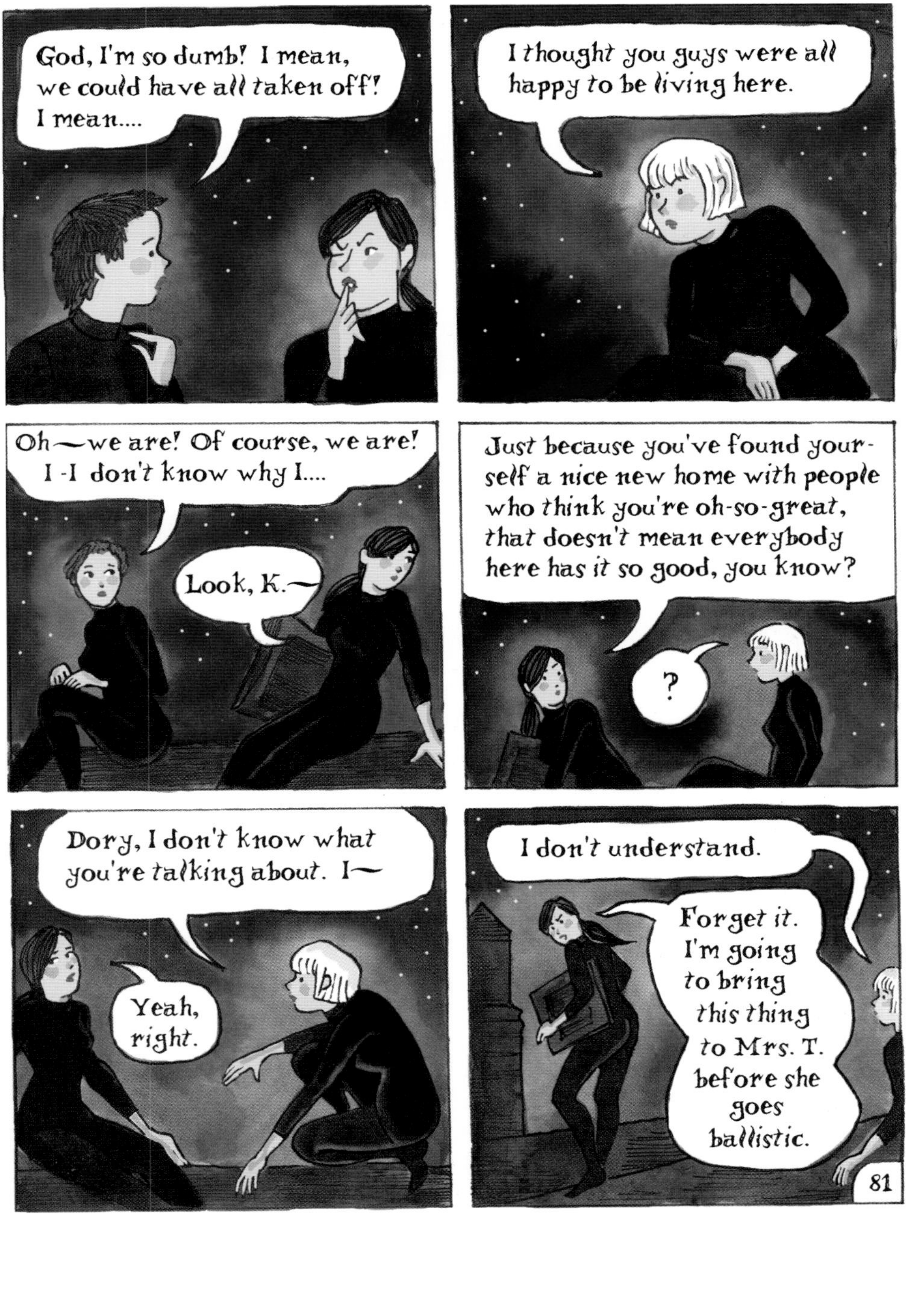
God, I'm so dumb! I mean, we could have all taken off! I mean....
I thought you guys were all happy to be living here.
Oh—we are! Of course, we are! I-I don't know why I....
Look, K.—
Just because you've found yourself a nice new home with people who think you're oh-so-great, that doesn't mean everybody here has it so good, you know?
?
Dory, I don't know what you're talking about. I—
Yeah, right.
I don't understand.
Forget it. I'm going to bring this thing to Mrs. T. before she goes ballistic.
81

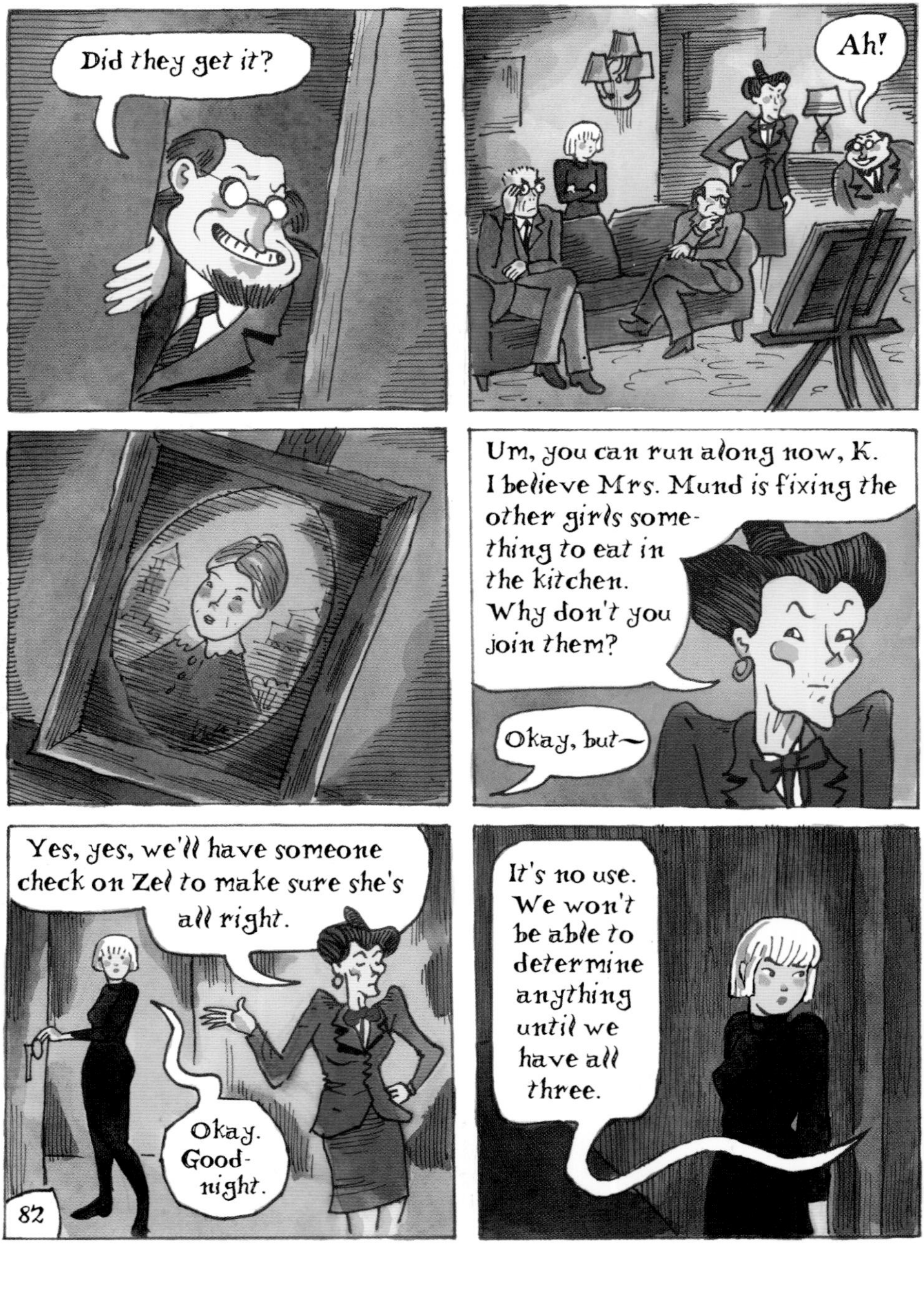
Did they get it?
Ah!
Um, you can run along now, K. I believe Mrs. Mund is fixing the other girls some-thing to eat in the kitchen. Why don't you join them?
Okay, but–
Yes, yes, we'll have someone check on Zel to make sure she's all right.
Okay. Good-night.
82
It's no use. We won't be able to determine anything until we have all three.

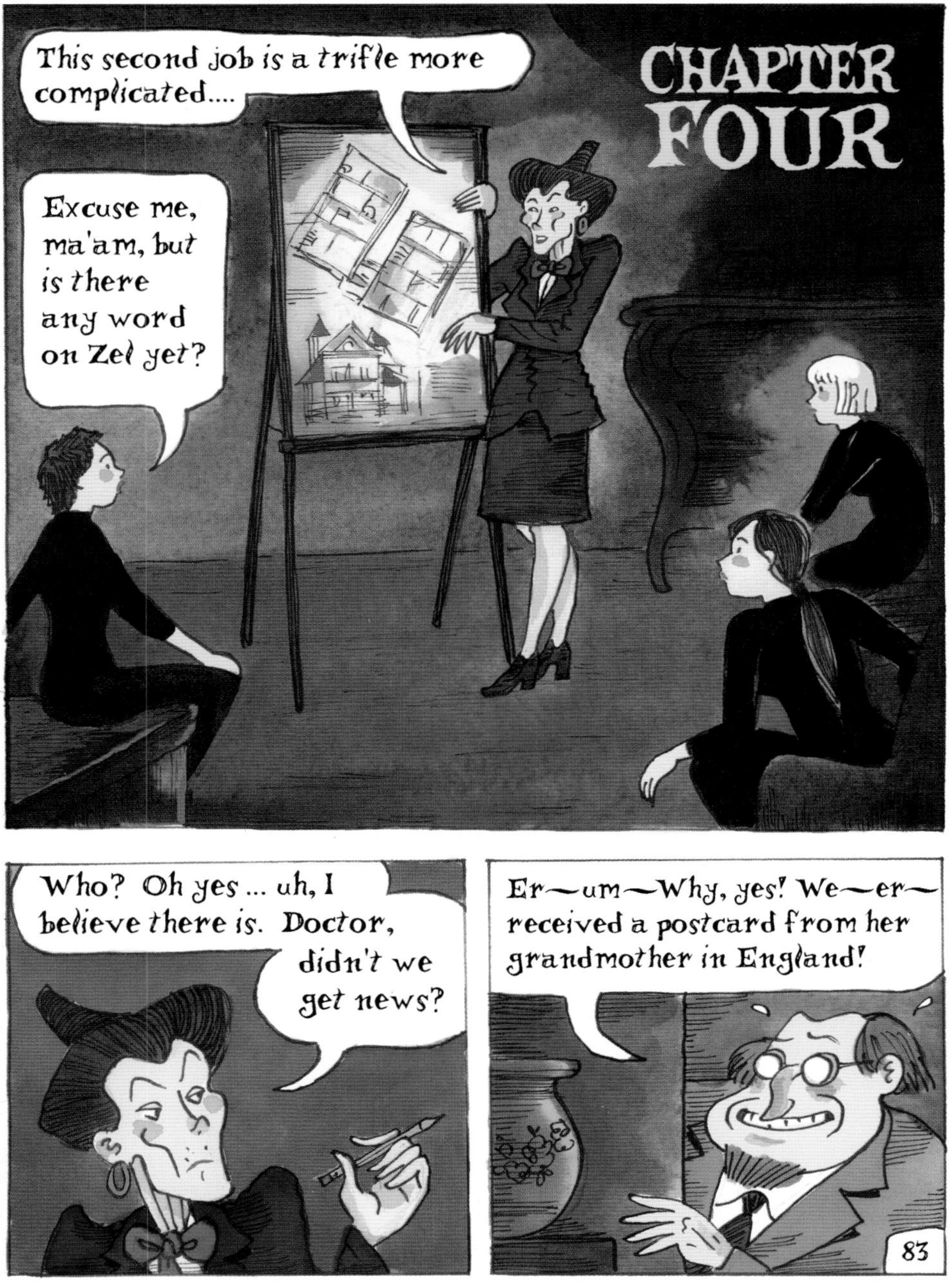
CHAPTER FOUR
This second job is a trifle more complicated....
Excuse me, ma'am, but is there any word on Zel yet?
Who? Oh yes ... uh, I believe there is. Doctor, didn't we get news?
Er—um—Why, yes! We—er—received a postcard from her grandmother in England!
83

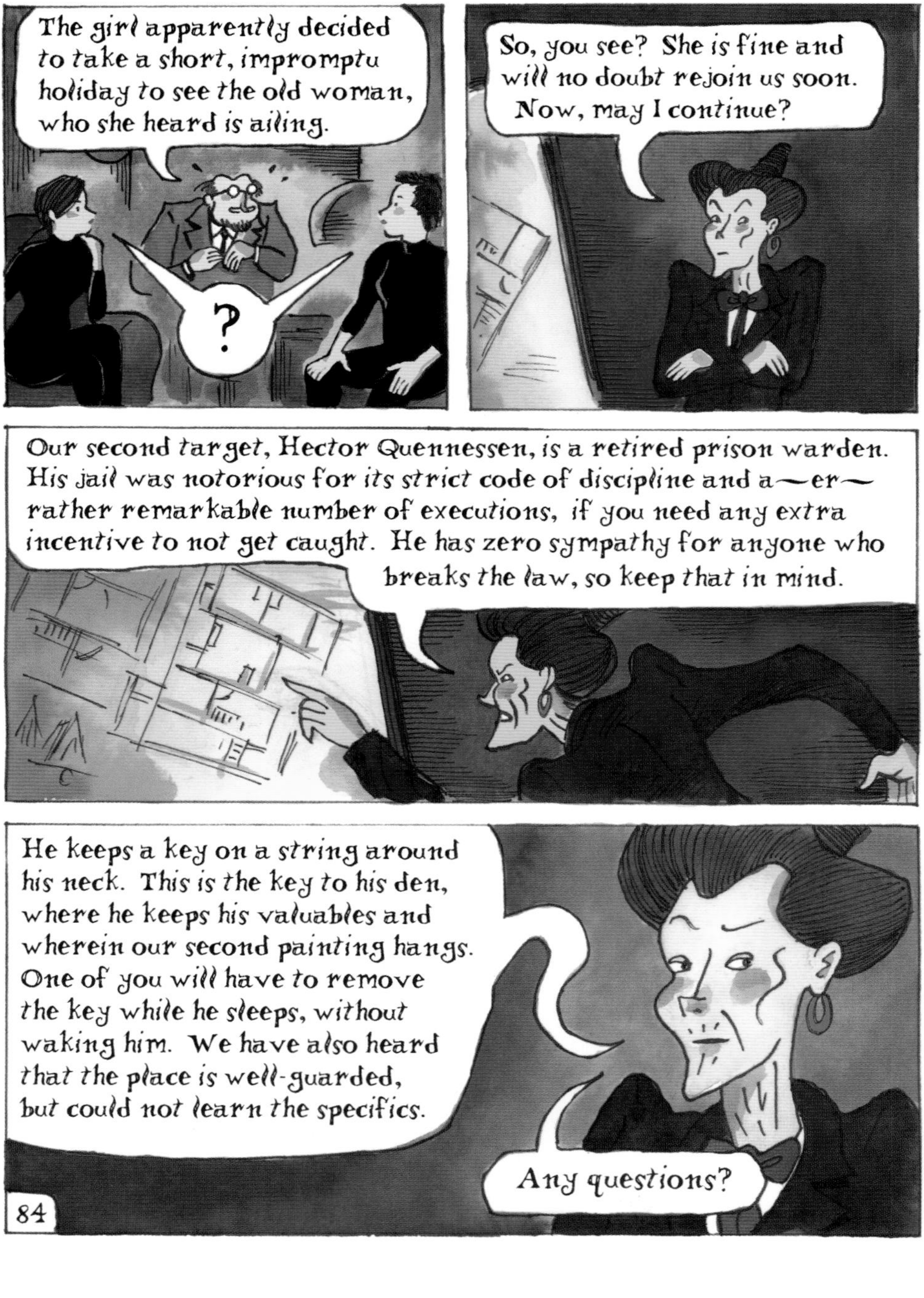
The girl apparently decided to take a short, impromptu holiday to see the old woman, who she heard is ailing.
?
So, you see? She is fine and will no doubt rejoin us soon. Now, may I continue?
Our second target, Hector Quennessen, is a retired prison warden. His jail was notorious for its strict code of discipline and a—er—rather remarkable number of executions, if you need any extra incentive to not get caught. He has zero sympathy for anyone who breaks the law, so keep that in mind.
He keeps a key on a string around his neck. This is the key to his den, where he keeps his valuables and wherein our second painting hangs. One of you will have to remove the key while he sleeps, without waking him. We have also heard that the place is well-guarded, but could not learn the specifics.
Any questions?

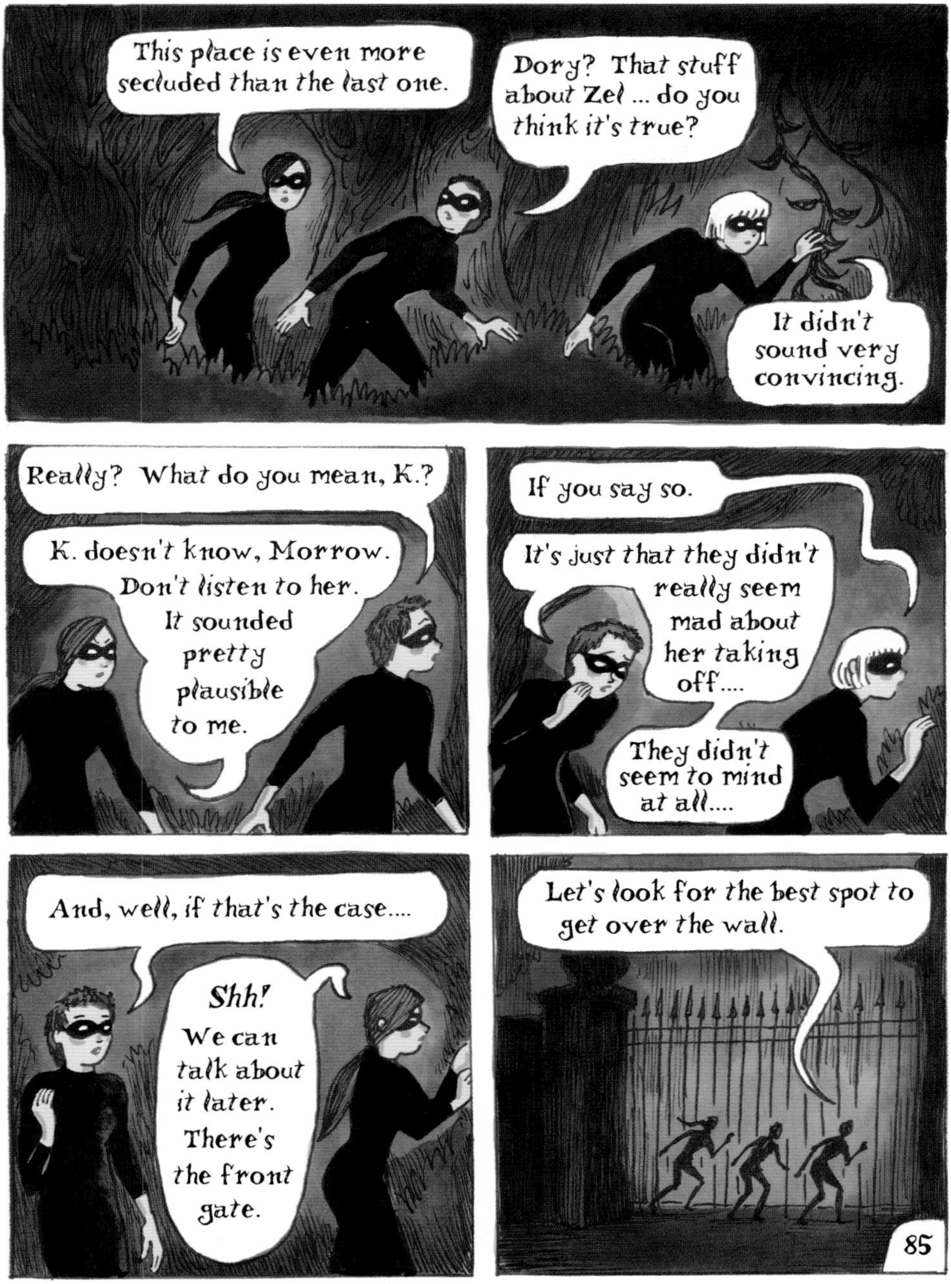
This place is even more secluded than the last one.
Dory? That stuff about Zel ... do you think it's true?
It didn't sound very convincing.
Really? What do you mean, K.?
K. doesn't know, Morrow. Don't listen to her. It sounded pretty plausible to me.
If you say so.
It's just that they didn't really seem mad about her taking off....
They didn't seem to mind at all....
And, well, if that's the case....
Shh! We can talk about it later. There's the front gate.
Let's look for the best spot to get over the wall.

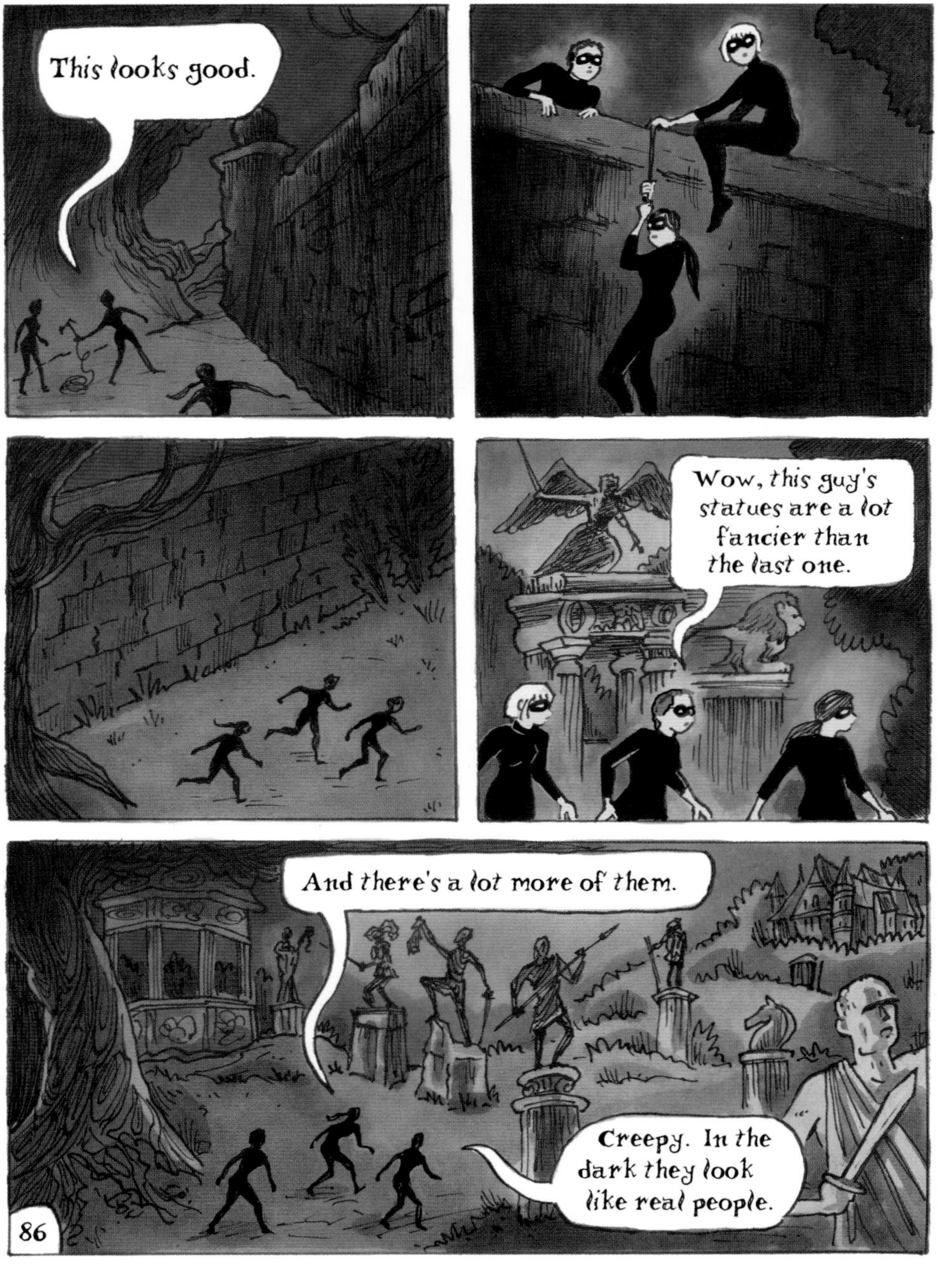
This looks good.
Wow, this guy's statues are a lot fancier than the last one.
And there's a lot more of them.
Creepy. In the dark they look like real people.

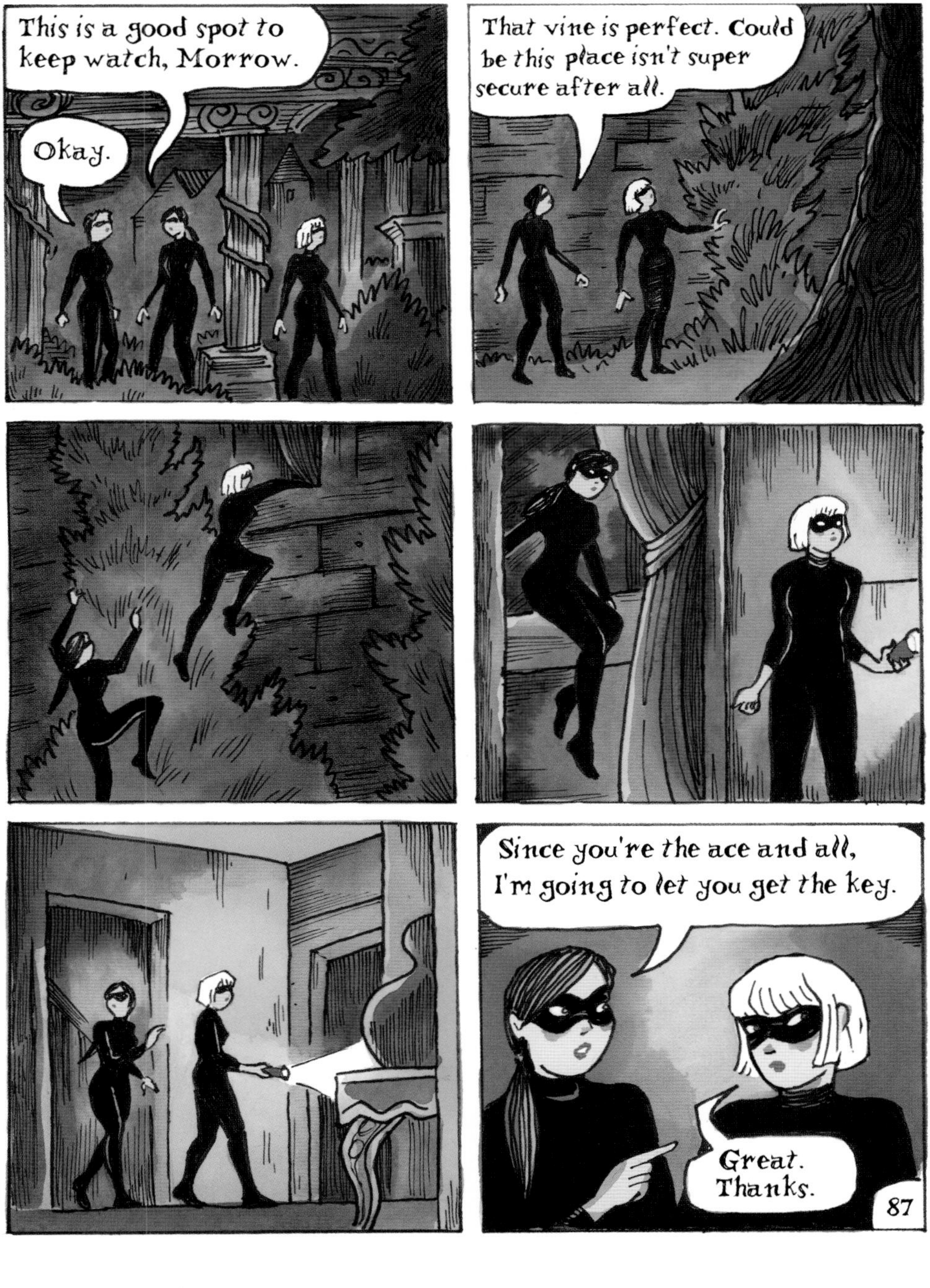
This is a good spot to keep watch, Morrow.
Okay.
That vine is perfect. Could be this place isn't super secure after all.
Since you're the ace and all, I'm going to let you get the key.
Great. Thanks.

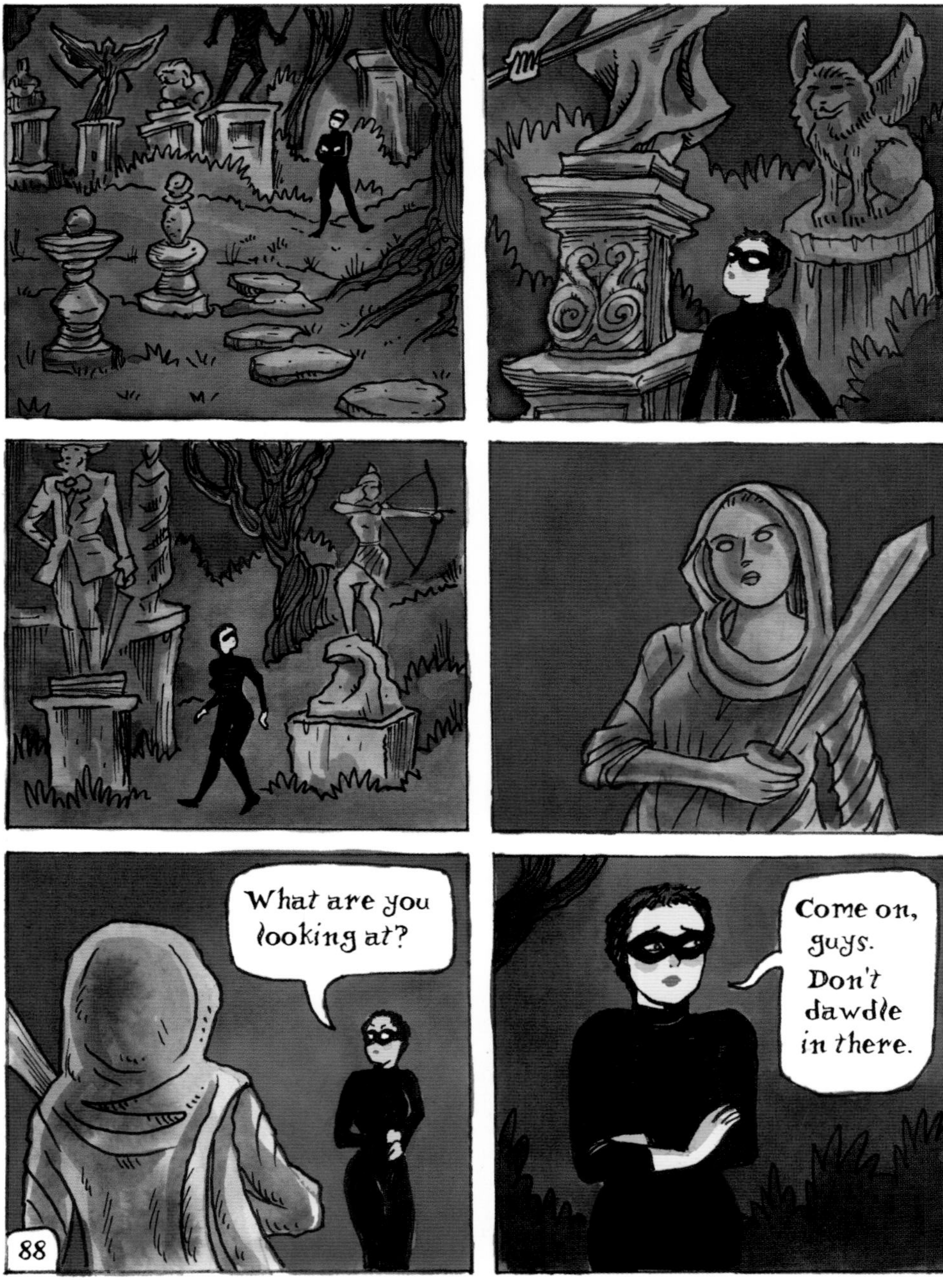
What are you looking at?
Come on, guys. Don't dawdle in there.

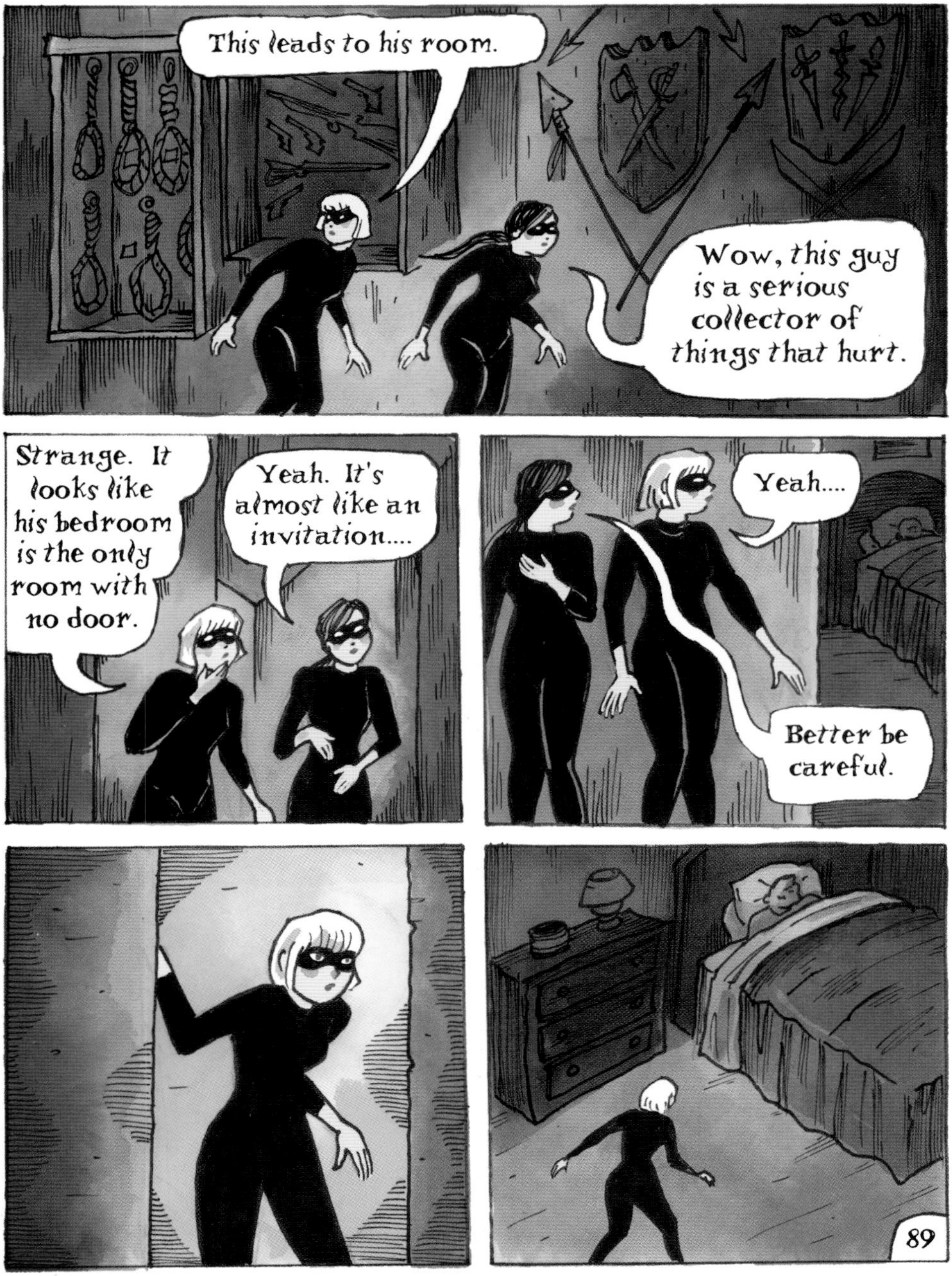
This leads to his room.
Wow, this guy is a serious collector of things that hurt.
Strange. It looks like his bedroom is the only room with no door.
Yeah. It's almost like an invitation....
Yeah....
Better be careful.
89

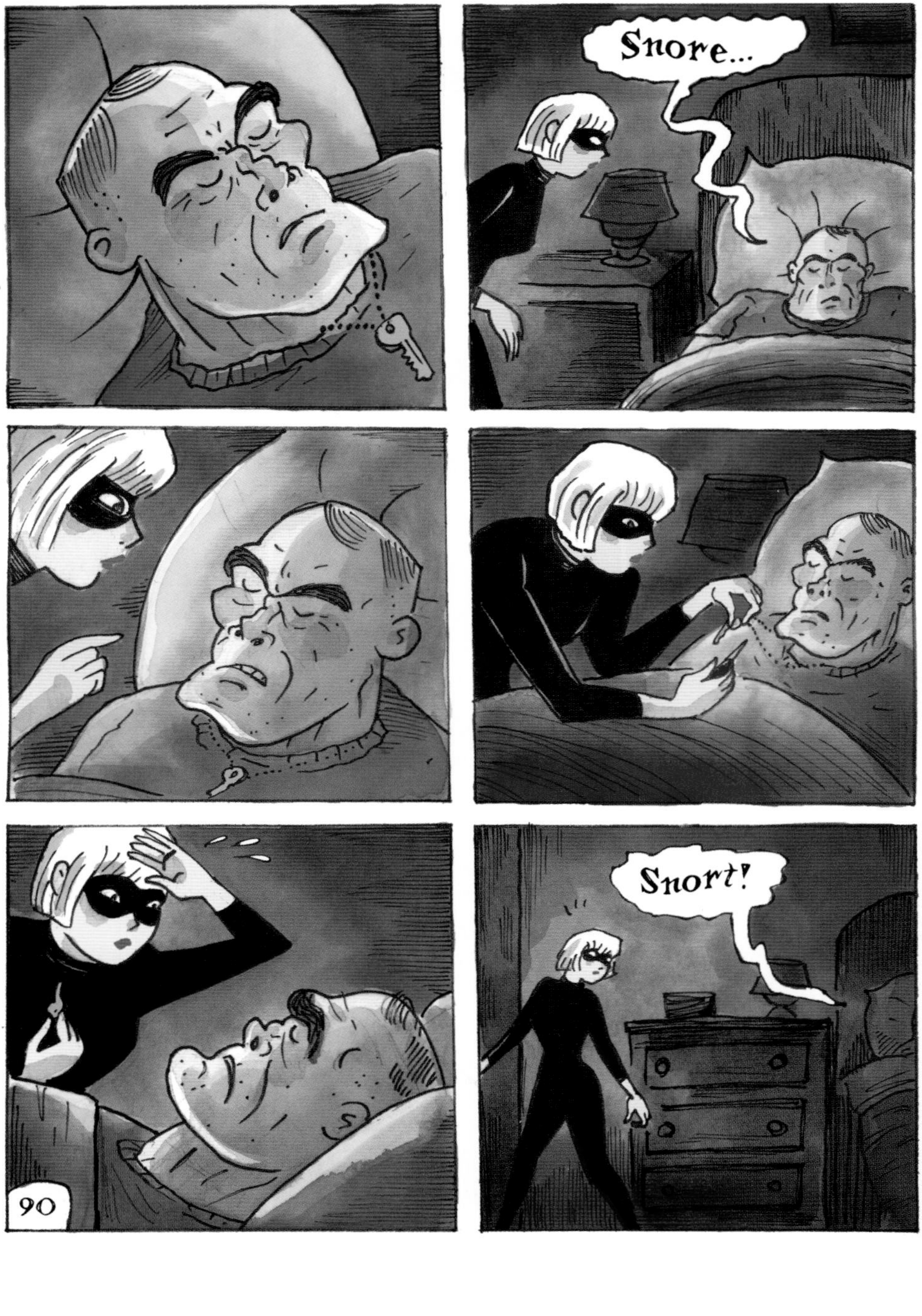
Snore...
Snort!

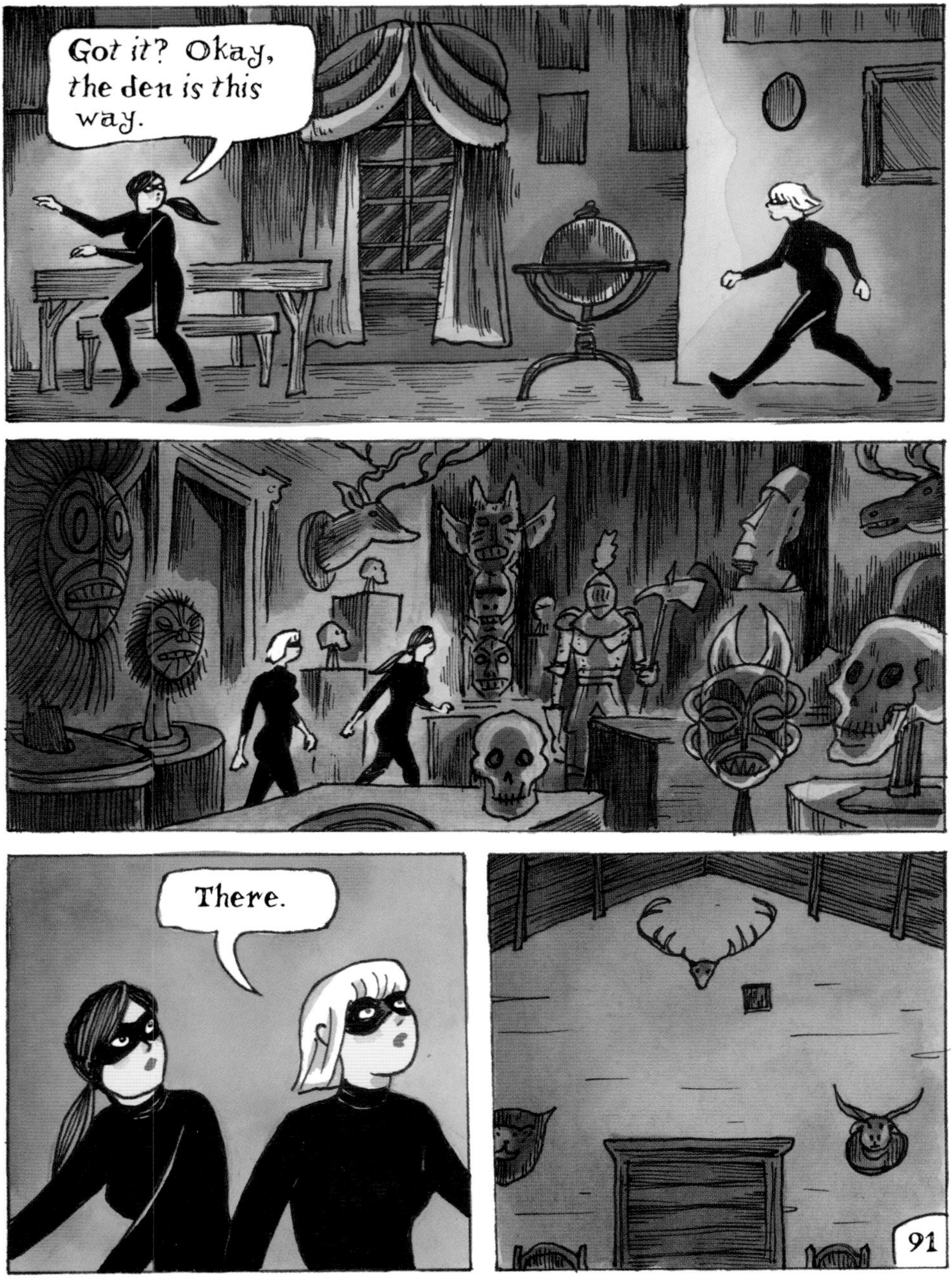

Got it? Okay, the den is this way.
There.

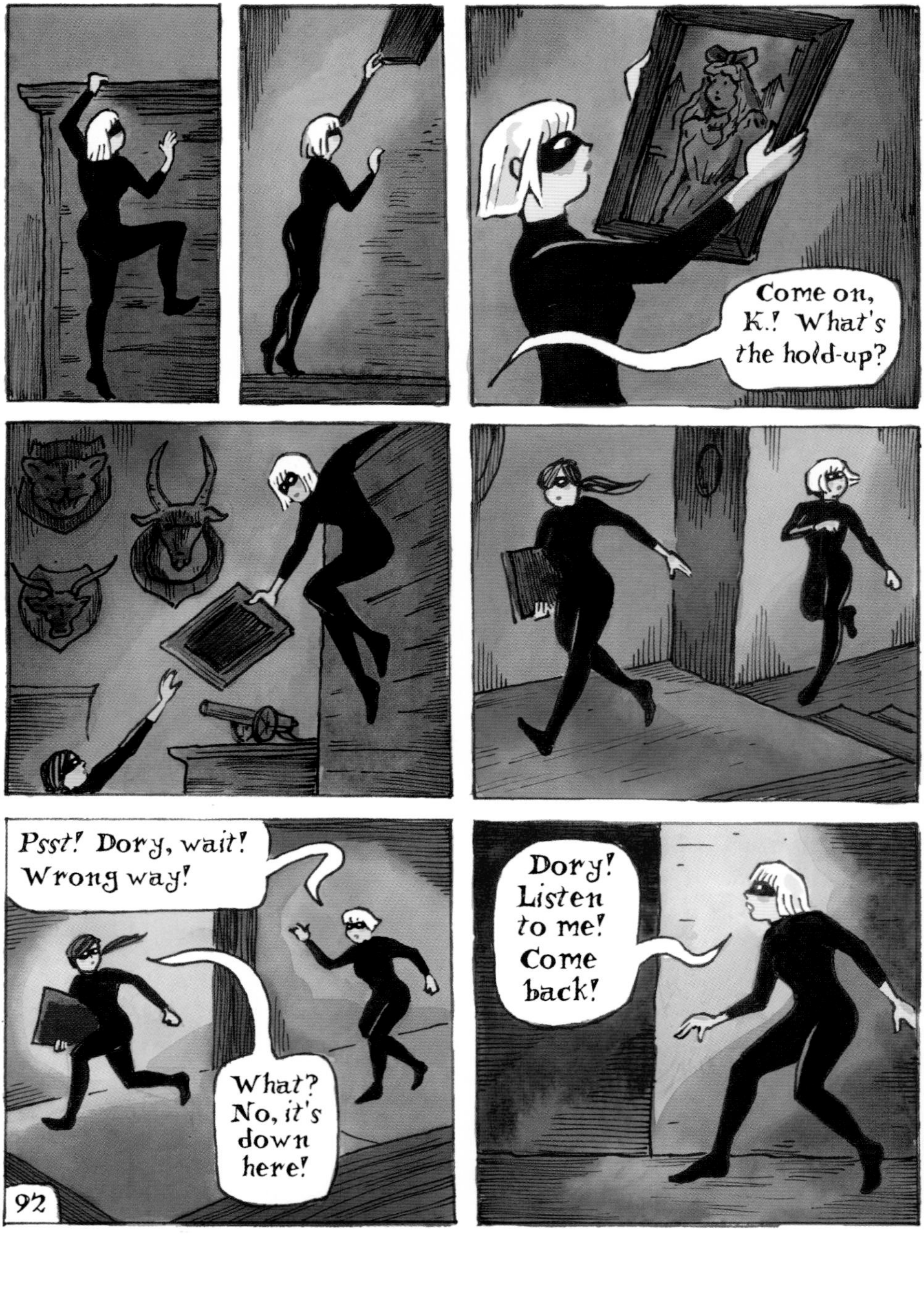
Come on, K.! What's the hold-up?
Psst! Dory, wait! Wrong way!
What? No, it's down here!
Dory! Listen to me! Come back!

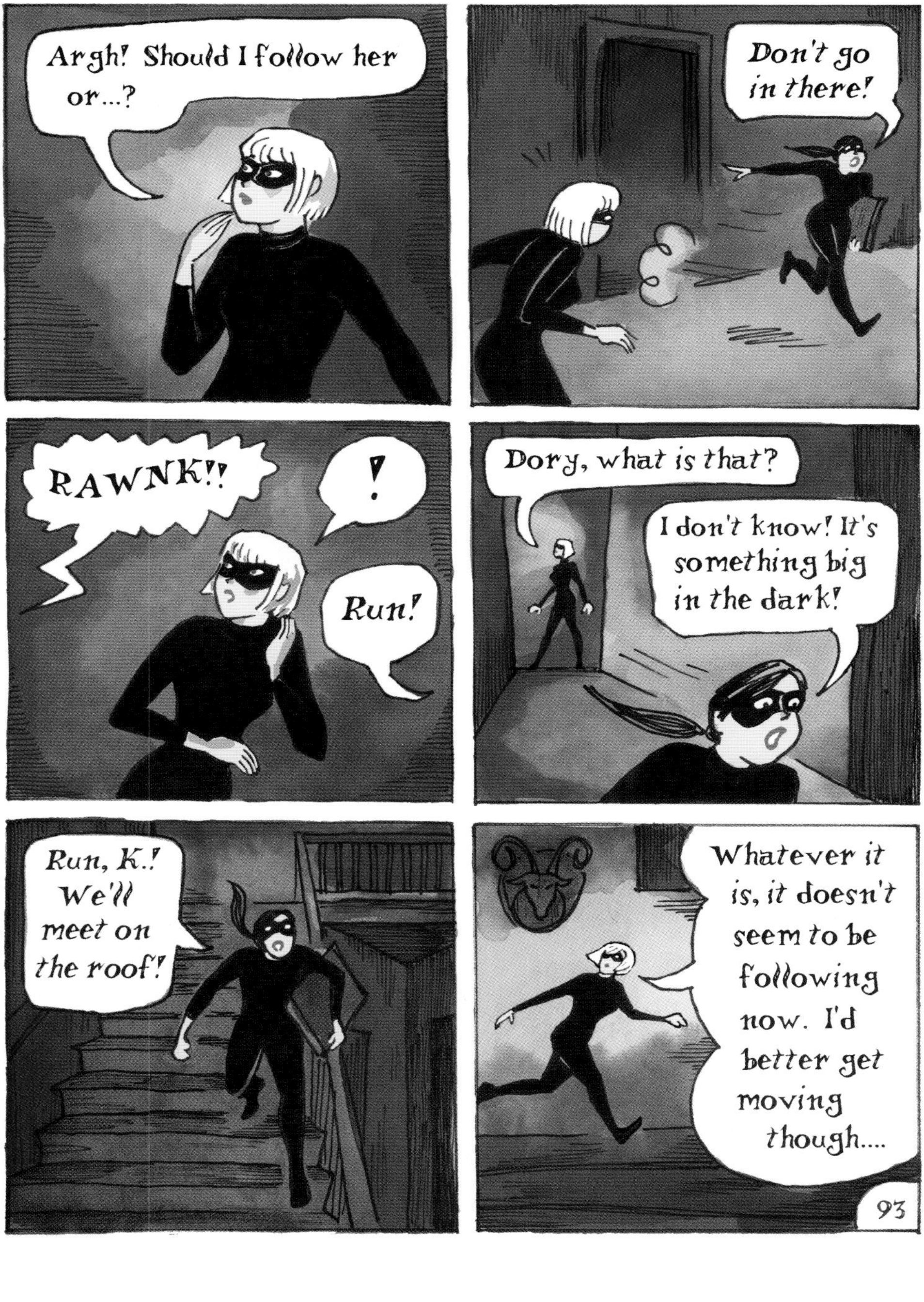
Argh! Should I follow her or...?
Don't go in there!
RAWNK!!
!
Run!
Dory, what is that?
I don't know! It's something big in the dark!
Run, K.! We'll meet on the roof!
Whatever it is, it doesn't seem to be following now. I'd better get moving though....

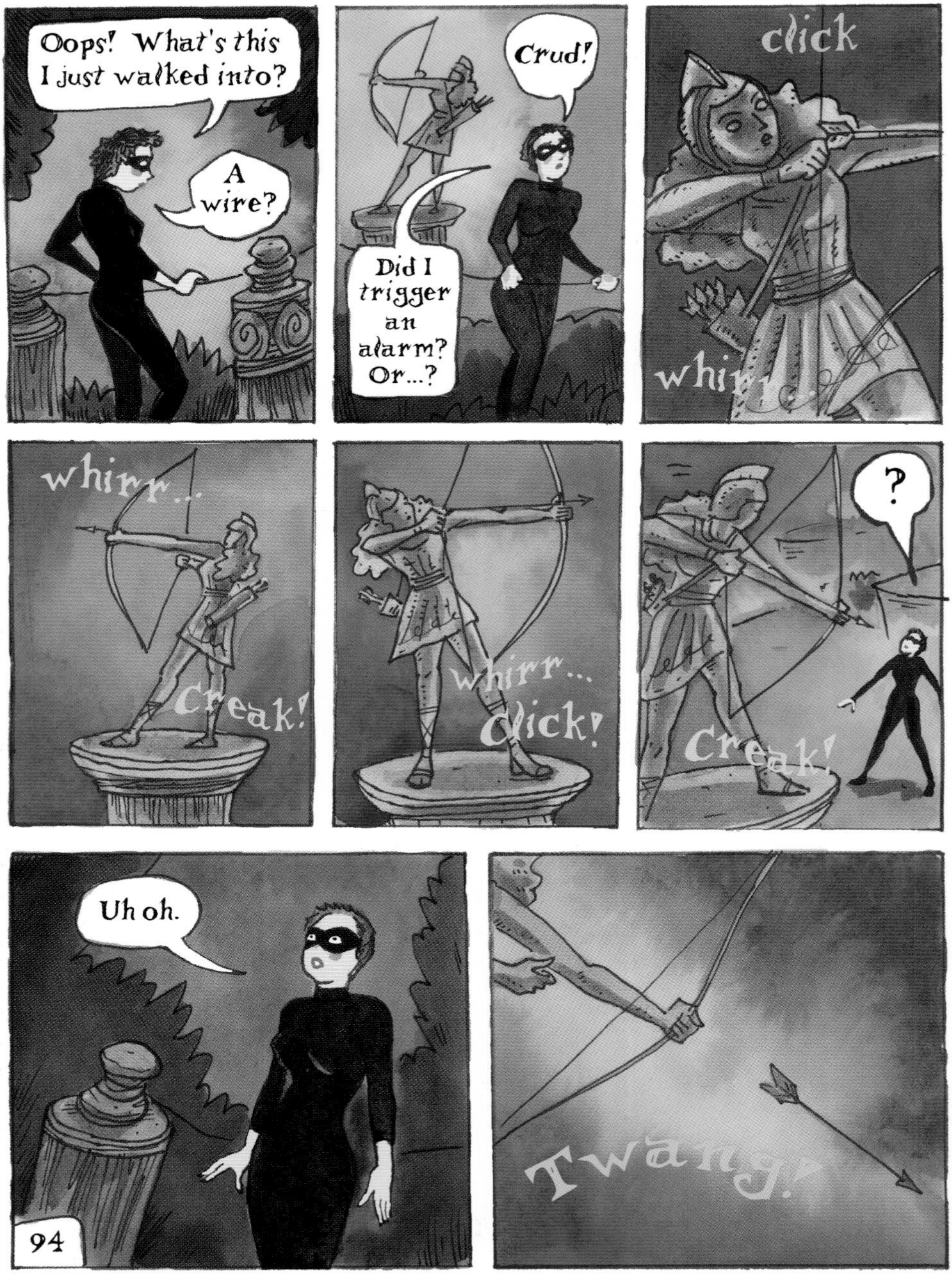

Oops! What's this I just walked into?
A wire?
Crud!
Did I trigger an alarm? Or...?
click
whirr...
whirr...
creak!
whirr...
click!
?
creak!
Uh oh.
Twang!

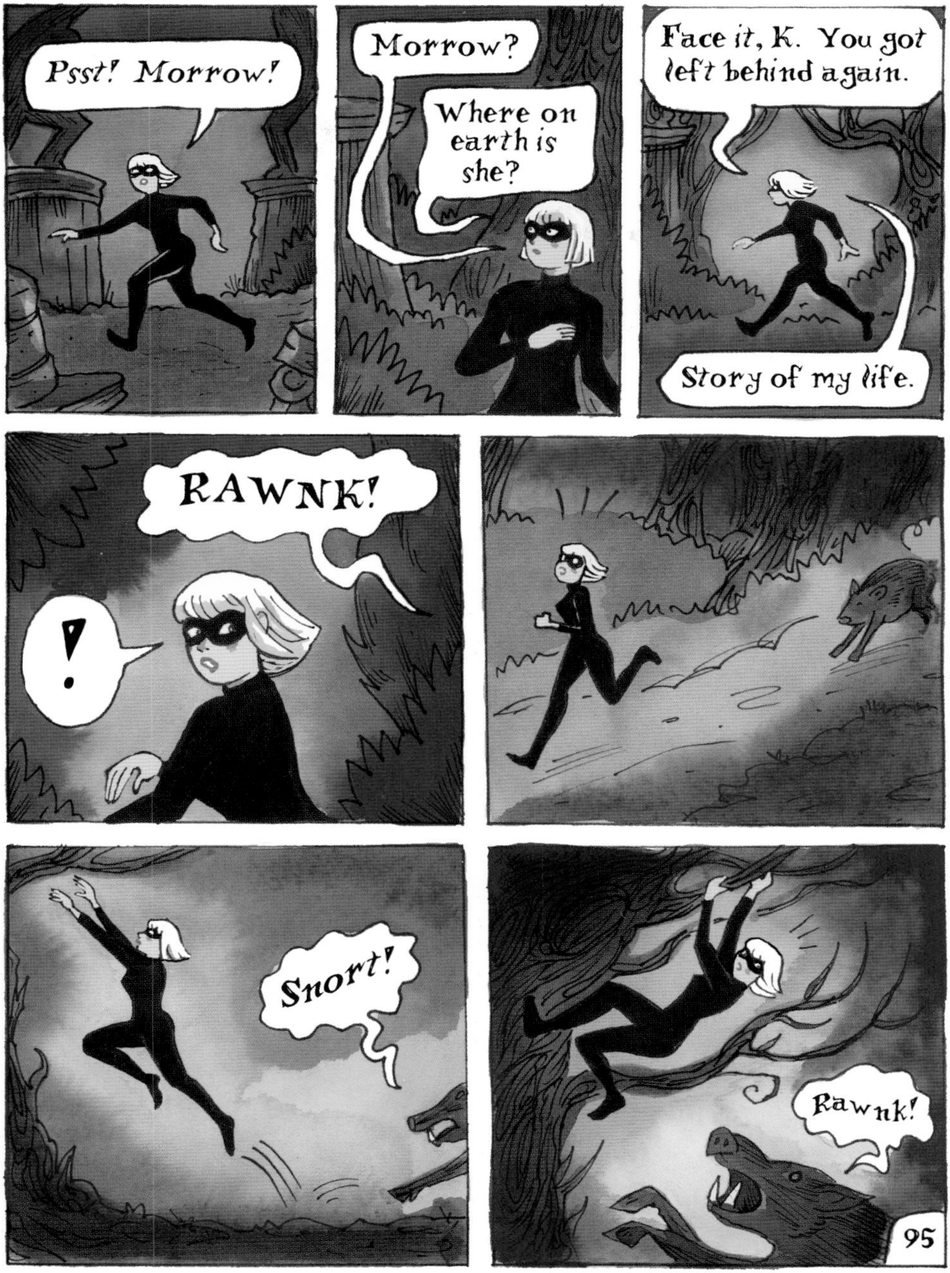
Psst! Morrow!
Morrow?
Where on earth is she?
Face it, K. You got left behind again.
Story of my life.
RAWNK!
!
Snort!
Rawnk!

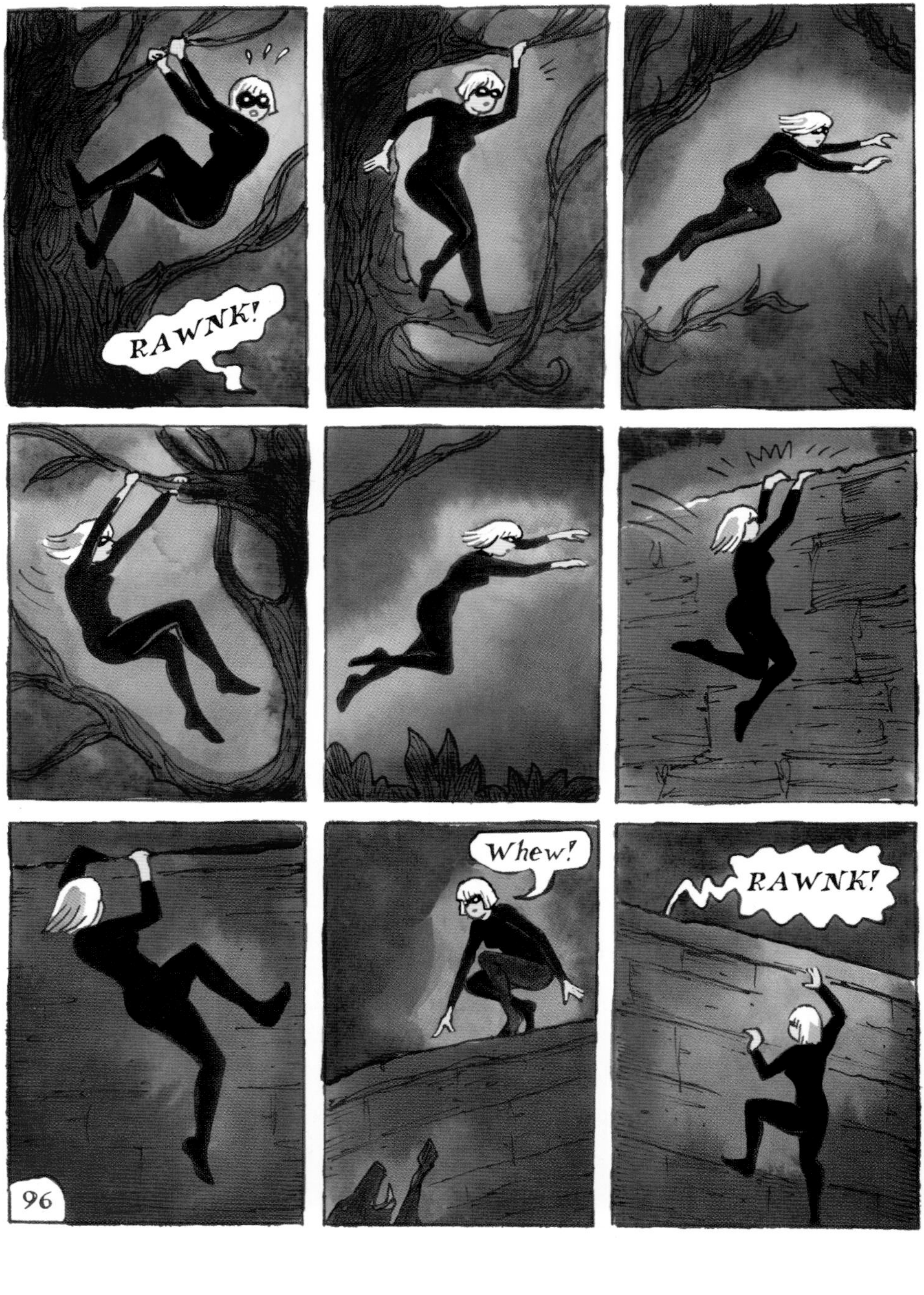
RAWNK!
Whew!
RAWNK!

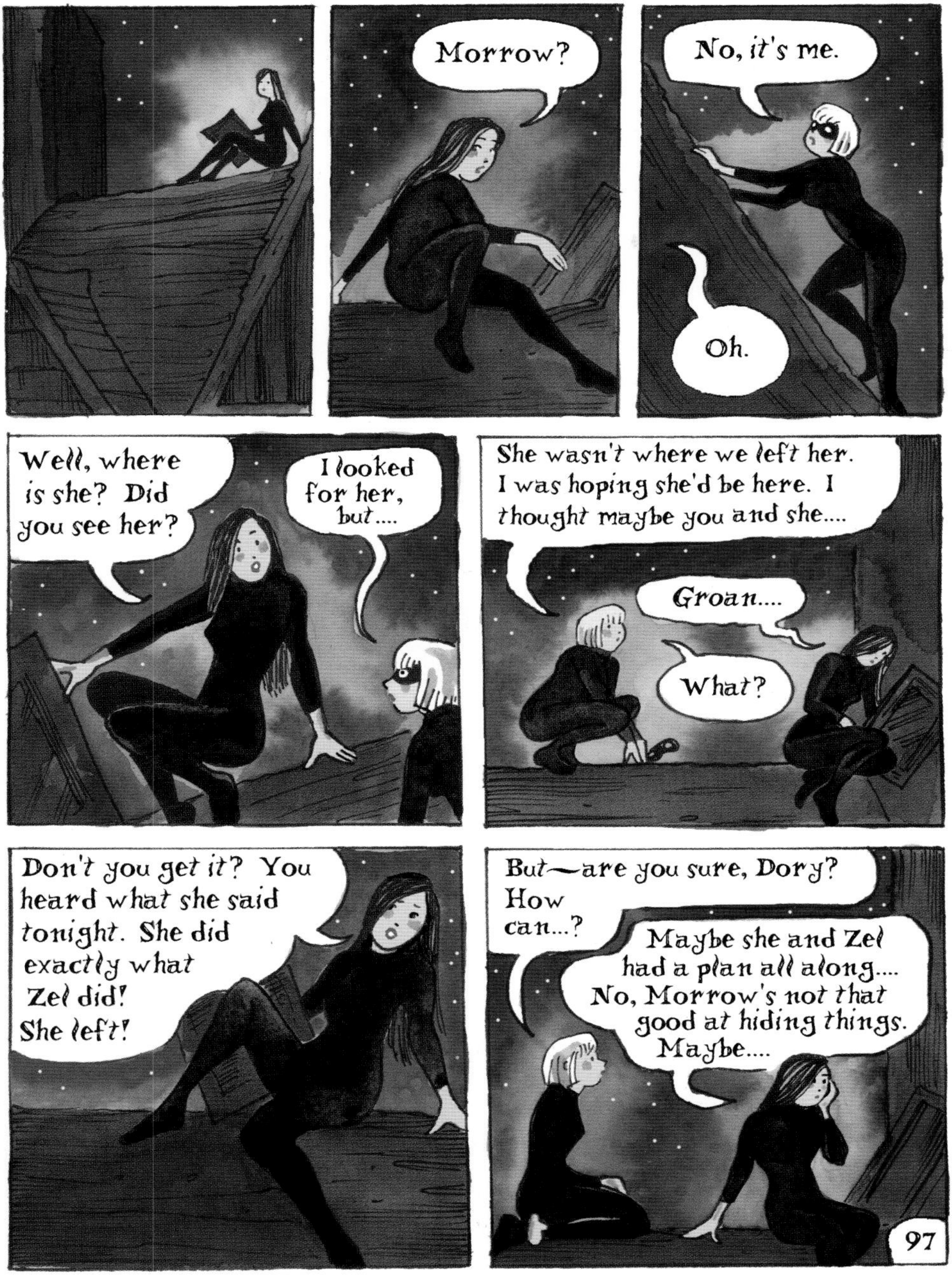
Morrow?
No, it's me.
Oh.
Well, where is she? Did you see her?
I looked for her, but....
She wasn't where we left her. I was hoping she'd be here. I thought maybe you and she....
Groan....
What?
Don't you get it? You heard what she said tonight. She did exactly what Zel did! She left!
But—are you sure, Dory? How can...?
Maybe she and Zel had a plan all along.... No, Morrow's not that good at hiding things. Maybe....

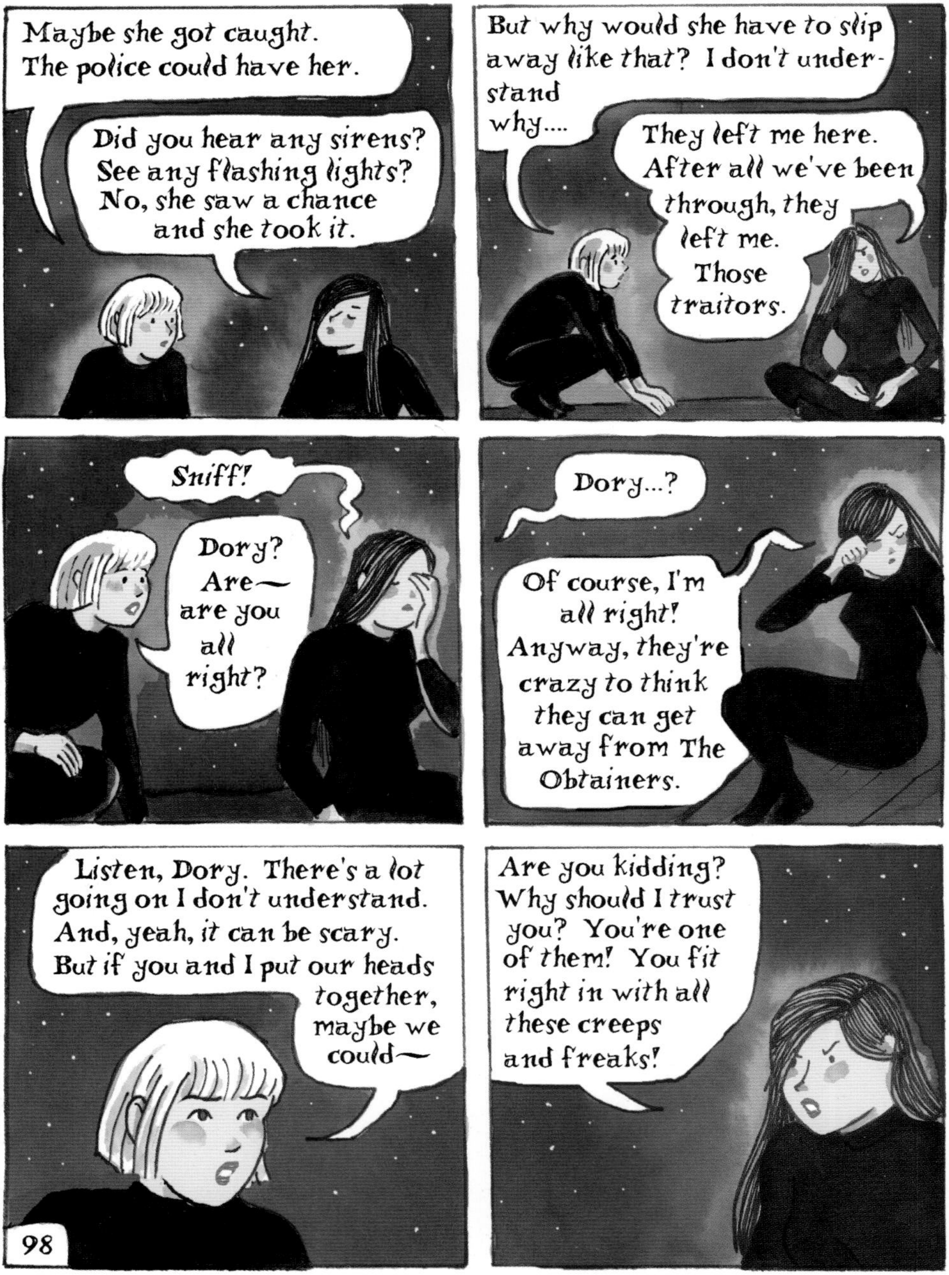
Maybe she got caught. The police could have her.
Did you hear any sirens? See any flashing lights? No, she saw a chance and she took it.
But why would she have to slip away like that? I don't understand why....
They left me here. After all we've been through, they left me. Those traitors.
Sniff!
Dory? Are— are you all right?
Dory...?
Of course, I'm all right! Anyway, they're crazy to think they can get away from The Obtainers.
Listen, Dory. There's a lot going on I don't understand. And, yeah, it can be scary. But if you and I put our heads together, maybe we could—
Are you kidding? Why should I trust you? You're one of them! You fit right in with all these creeps and freaks!

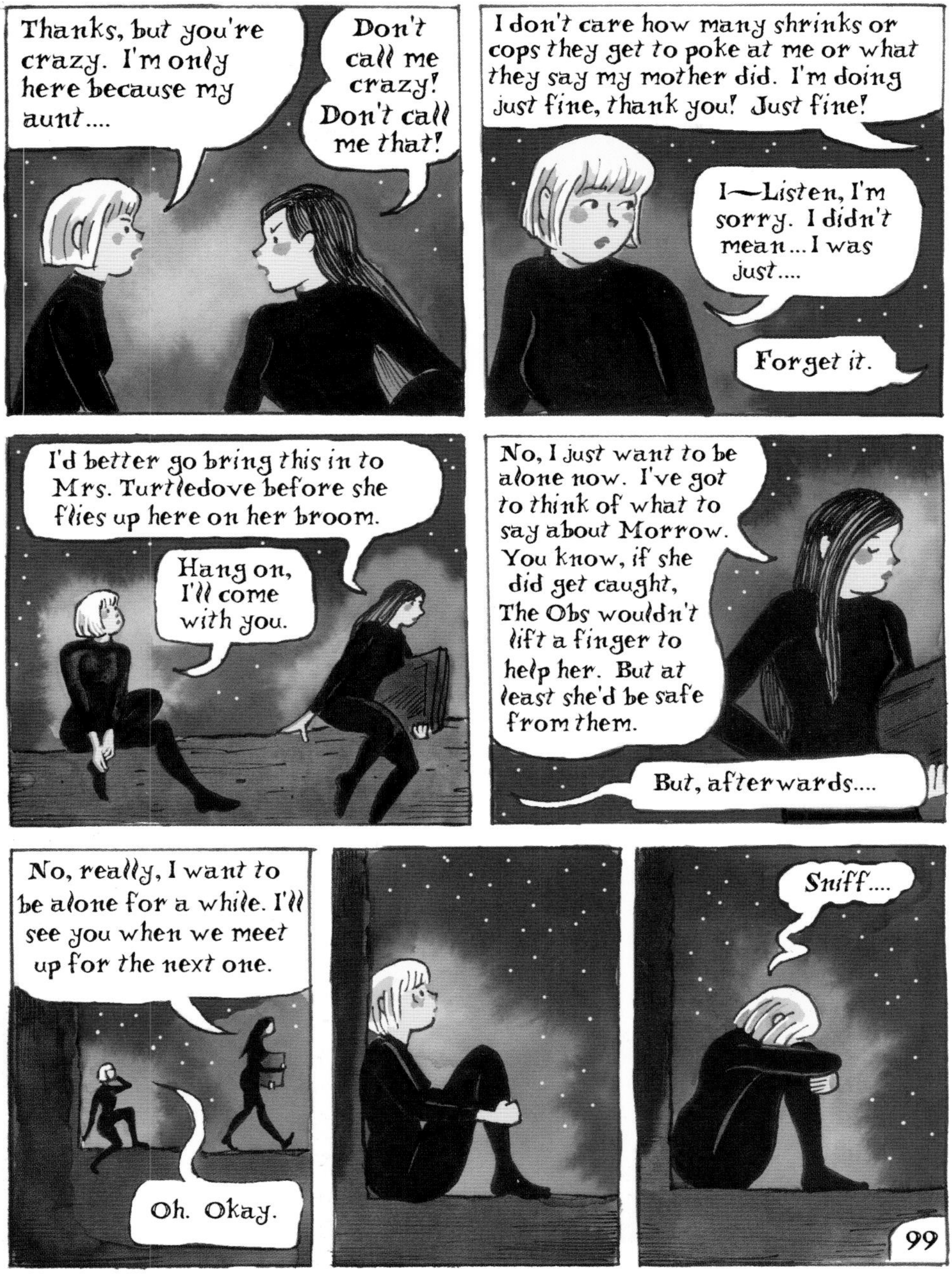
Thanks, but you're crazy. I'm only here because my aunt....
Don't call me crazy! Don't call me that!
I don't care how many shrinks or cops they get to poke at me or what they say my mother did. I'm doing just fine, thank you! Just fine!
I—Listen, I'm sorry. I didn't mean...I was just....
Forget it.
I'd better go bring this in to Mrs. Turtledove before she flies up here on her broom.
Hang on, I'll come with you.
No, I just want to be alone now. I've got to think of what to say about Morrow. You know, if she did get caught, The Obs wouldn't lift a finger to help her. But at least she'd be safe from them.
But, afterwards....
No, really, I want to be alone for a while. I'll see you when we meet up for the next one.
Oh. Okay.
Sniff....
99

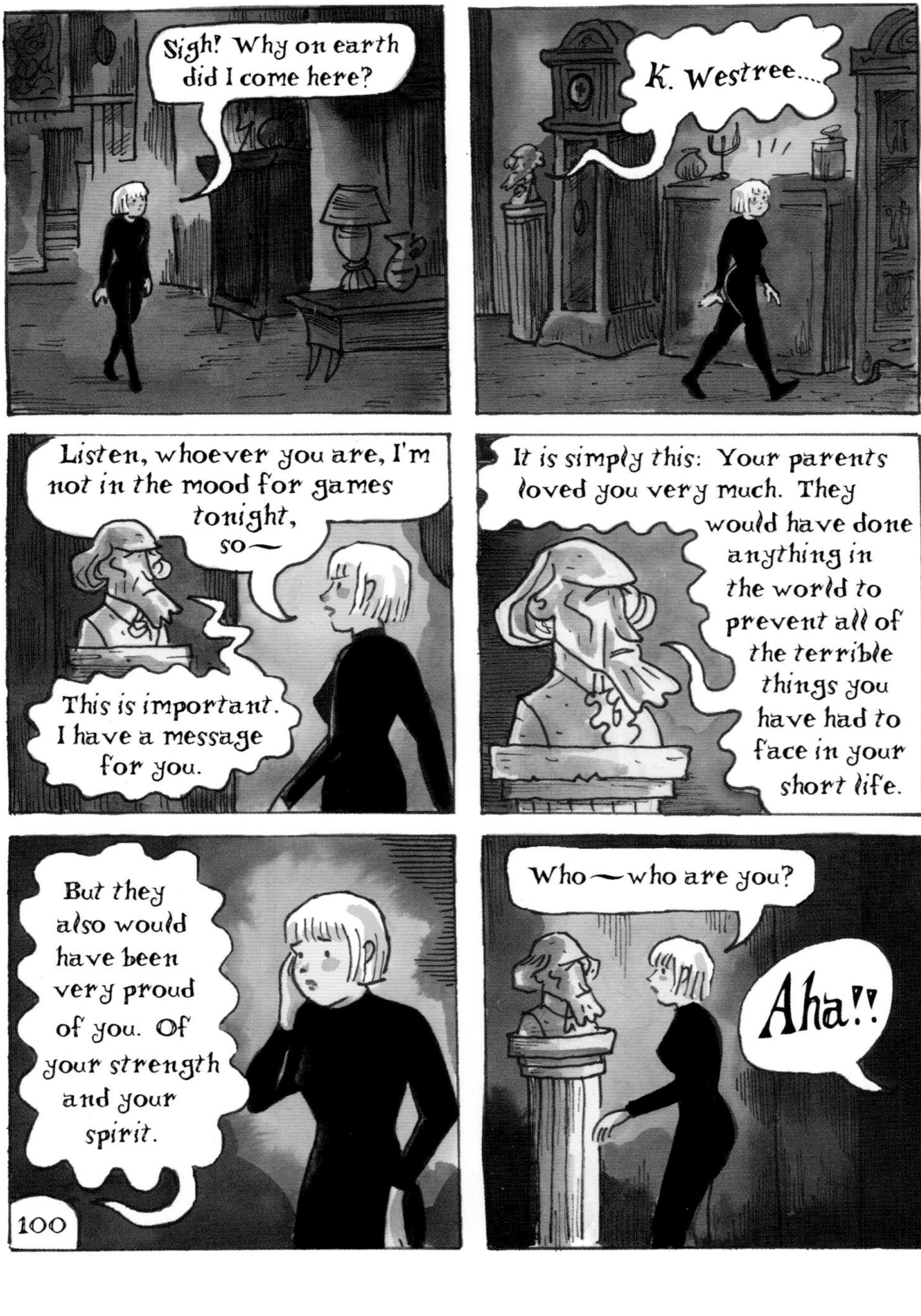

Sigh! Why on earth did I come here?
K. Westree....
Listen, whoever you are, I'm not in the mood for games tonight, so—
This is important. I have a message for you.
It is simply this: Your parents loved you very much. They would have done anything in the world to prevent all of the terrible things you have had to face in your short life.
But they also would have been very proud of you. Of your strength and your spirit.
Who—who are you?
Aha!!

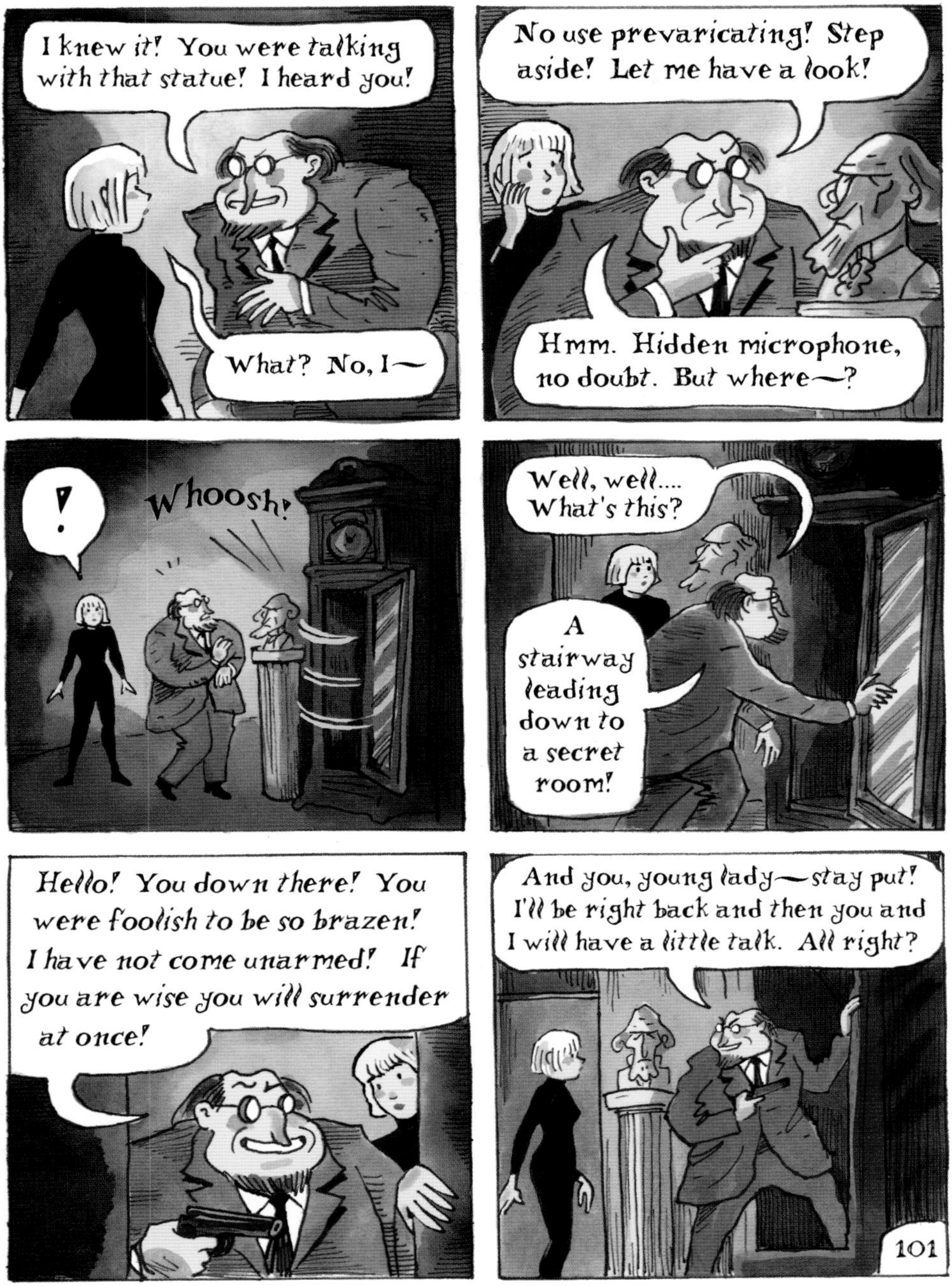
I knew it! You were talking with that statue! I heard you!
What? No, I—
No use prevaricating! Step aside! Let me have a look!
Hmm. Hidden microphone, no doubt. But where—?
!
Whoosh!
Well, well.... What's this?
A stairway leading down to a secret room!
Hello! You down there! You were foolish to be so brazen! I have not come unarmed! If you are wise you will surrender at once!
And you, young lady—stay put! I'll be right back and then you and I will have a little talk. All right?
101

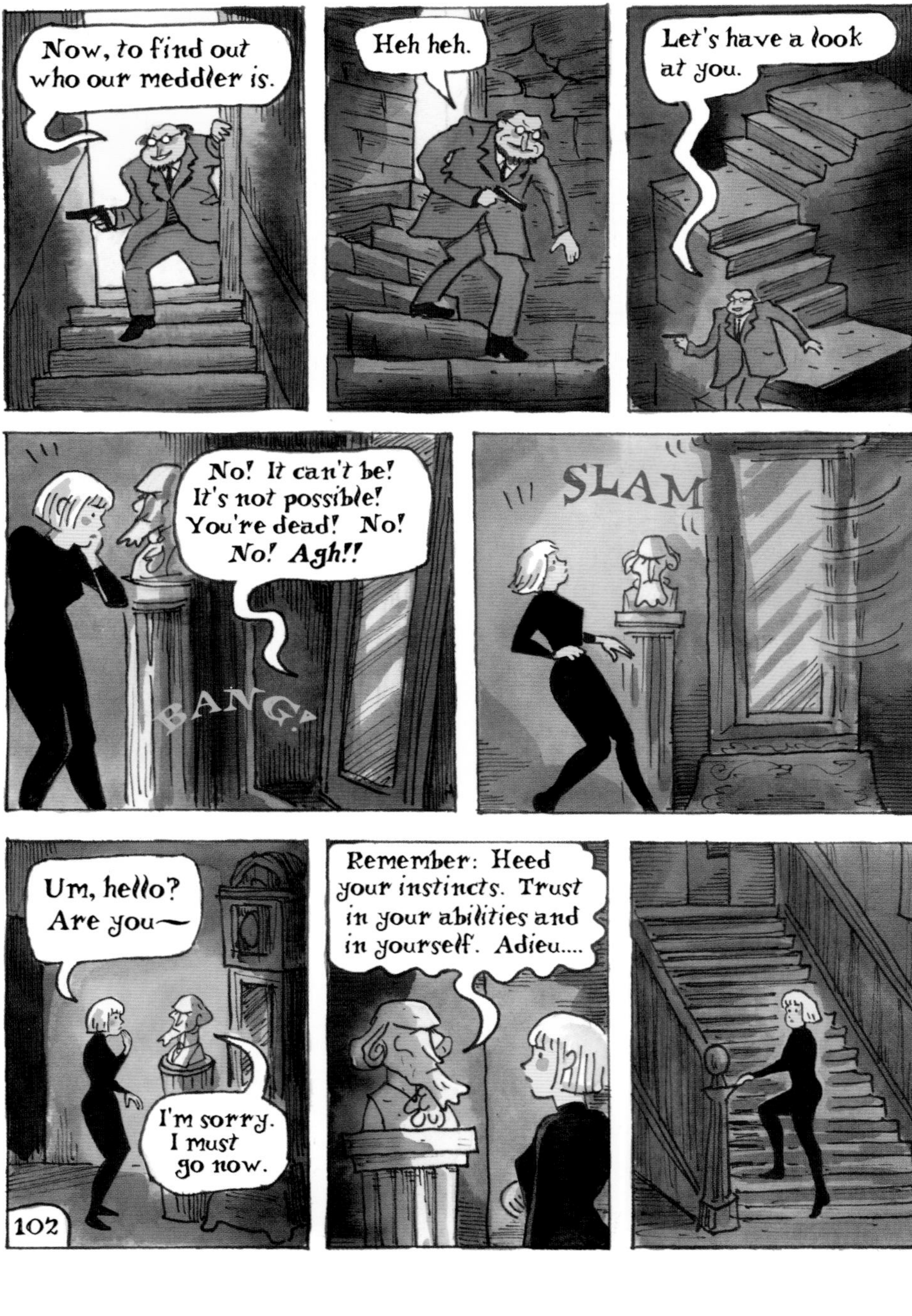
Now, to find out who our meddler is.
Heh heh.
Let's have a look at you.
No! It can't be! It's not possible! You're dead! No! No! Agh!!
BANG!
SLAM
Um, hello? Are you—
I'm sorry. I must go now.
Remember: Heed your instincts. Trust in your abilities and in yourself. Adieu....

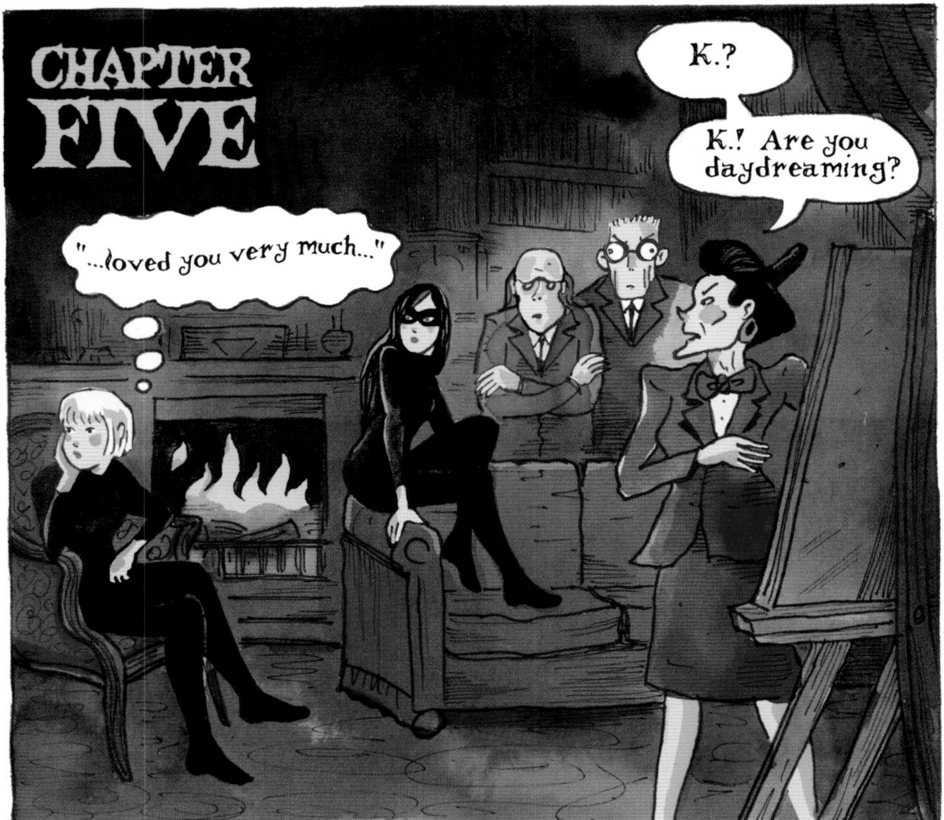
CHAPTER FIVE
K.?
K.! Are you daydreaming?
"...loved you very much..."

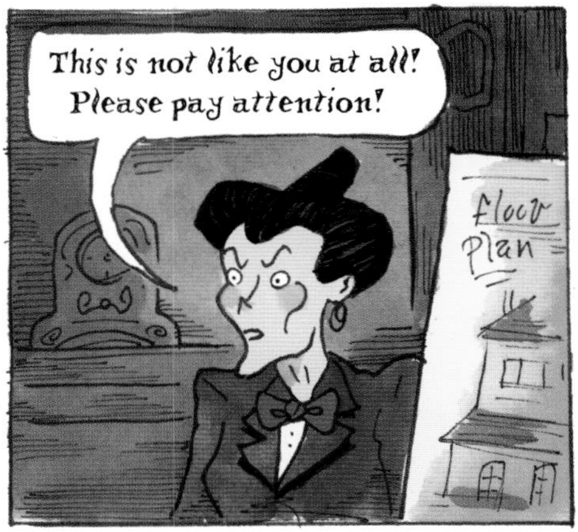
This is not like you at all! Please pay attention!
Floor Plan

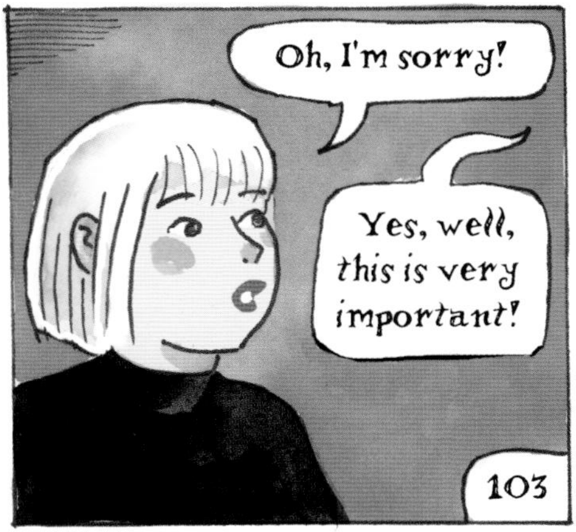
Oh, I'm sorry!
Yes, well, this is very important!

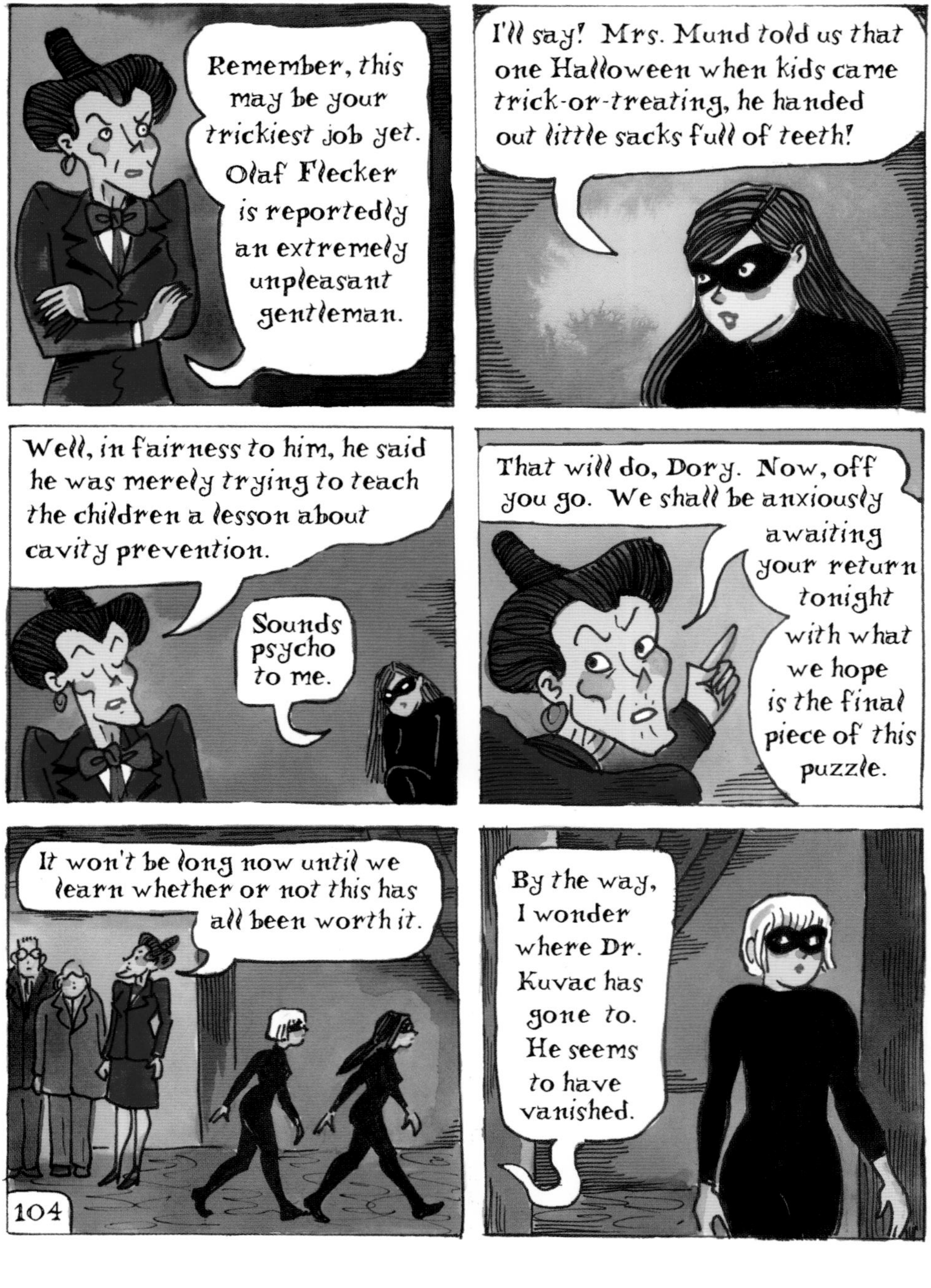
Remember, this may be your trickiest job yet. Olaf Flecker is reportedly an extremely unpleasant gentleman.
I'll say! Mrs. Mund told us that one Halloween when kids came trick-or-treating, he handed out little sacks full of teeth!
Well, in fairness to him, he said he was merely trying to teach the children a lesson about cavity prevention.
Sounds psycho to me.
That will do, Dory. Now, off you go. We shall be anxiously awaiting your return tonight with what we hope is the final piece of this puzzle.
It won't be long now until we learn whether or not this has all been worth it.
By the way, I wonder where Dr. Kuvac has gone to. He seems to have vanished.

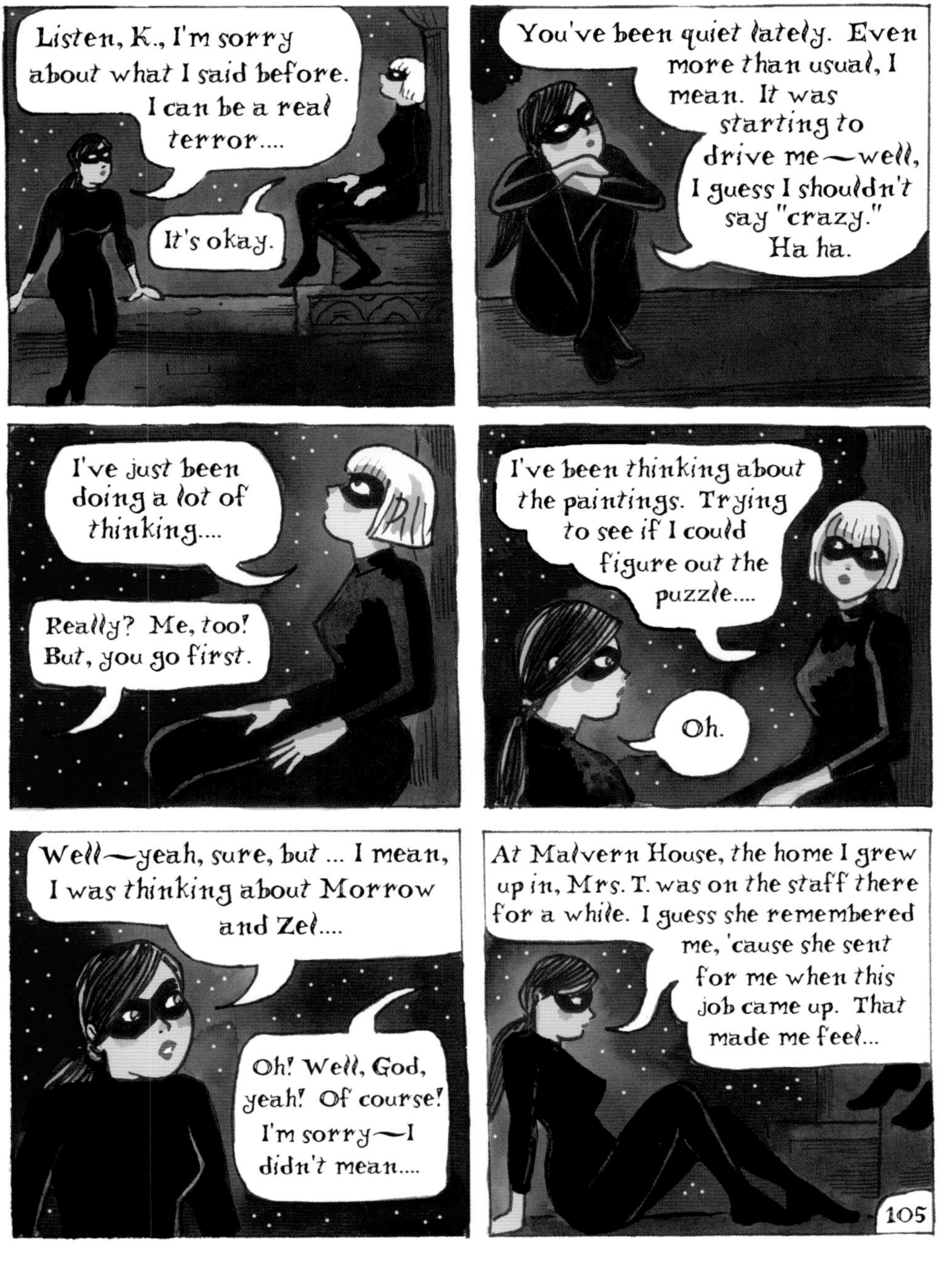
Listen, K., I'm sorry about what I said before. I can be a real terror....
It's okay.
You've been quiet lately. Even more than usual, I mean. It was starting to drive me—well, I guess I shouldn't say "crazy." Ha ha.
I've just been doing a lot of thinking....
Really? Me, too! But, you go first.
I've been thinking about the paintings. Trying to see if I could figure out the puzzle....
Oh.
Well—yeah, sure, but ... I mean, I was thinking about Morrow and Zel....
Oh! Well, God, yeah! Of course! I'm sorry—I didn't mean....
At Malvern House, the home I grew up in, Mrs. T. was on the staff there for a while. I guess she remembered me, 'cause she sent for me when this job came up. That made me feel...

...I don't know. Special, I guess. She picked me 'cause she knew I had real skill, but also because I'm a good soldier. And I wanted to be wanted. I wanted to belong somewhere.

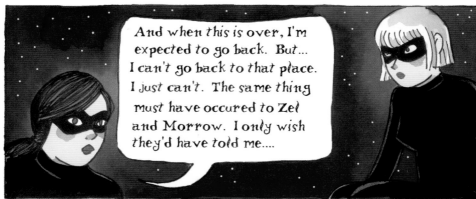

And when *this* is over, I'm expected to go back. But... I can't go back to that place. I *just* can't. The same thing must have occured to Zel and Morrow. I only wish they'd have told me....

Dory, do you suppose there's any chance they might still be in those houses?

What? Like, held prisoner?

No. I mean, in that case why wouldn't Mrs. T. say so?

Why would they make up stories about post-cards and...? Why?

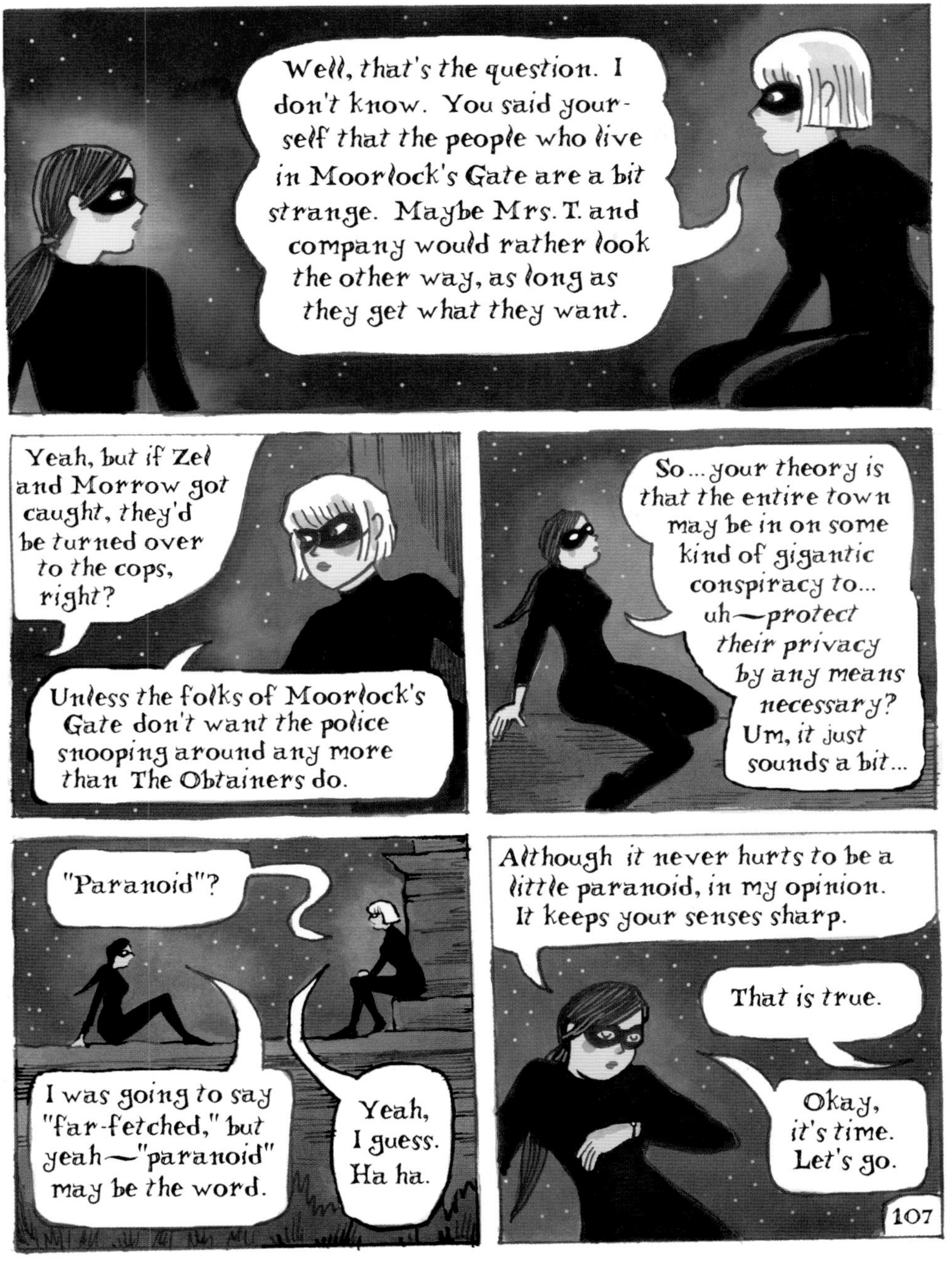

Well, that's the question. I don't know. You said yourself that the people who live in Moorlock's Gate are a bit strange. Maybe Mrs. T. and company would rather look the other way, as long as they get what they want.
Yeah, but if Zel and Morrow got caught, they'd be turned over to the cops, right?
Unless the folks of Moorlock's Gate don't want the police snooping around any more than The Obtainers do.
So... your theory is that the entire town may be in on some kind of gigantic conspiracy to... uh—protect their privacy by any means necessary? Um, it just sounds a bit...
"Paranoid"?
I was going to say "far-fetched," but yeah—"paranoid" may be the word.
Yeah, I guess. Ha ha.
Although it never hurts to be a little paranoid, in my opinion. It keeps your senses sharp.
That is true.
Okay, it's time. Let's go.

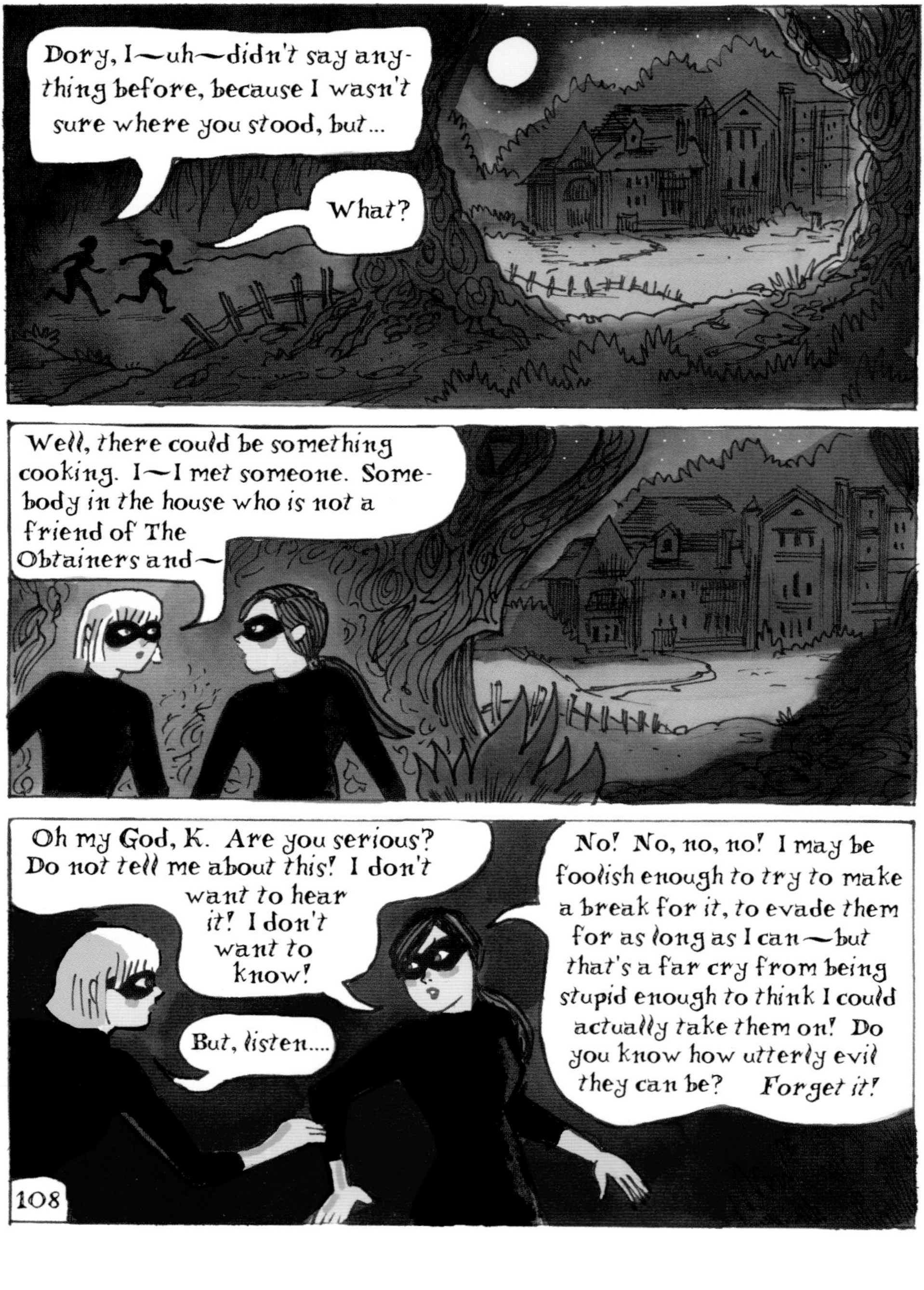

Dory, I—uh—didn't say anything before, because I wasn't sure where you stood, but...
What?
Well, there could be something cooking. I—I met someone. Somebody in the house who is not a friend of The Obtainers and—
Oh my God, K. Are you serious? Do not tell me about this! I don't want to hear it! I don't want to know!
But, listen....
No! No, no, no! I may be foolish enough to try to make a break for it, to evade them for as long as I can—but that's a far cry from being stupid enough to think I could actually take them on! Do you know how utterly evil they can be? Forget it!

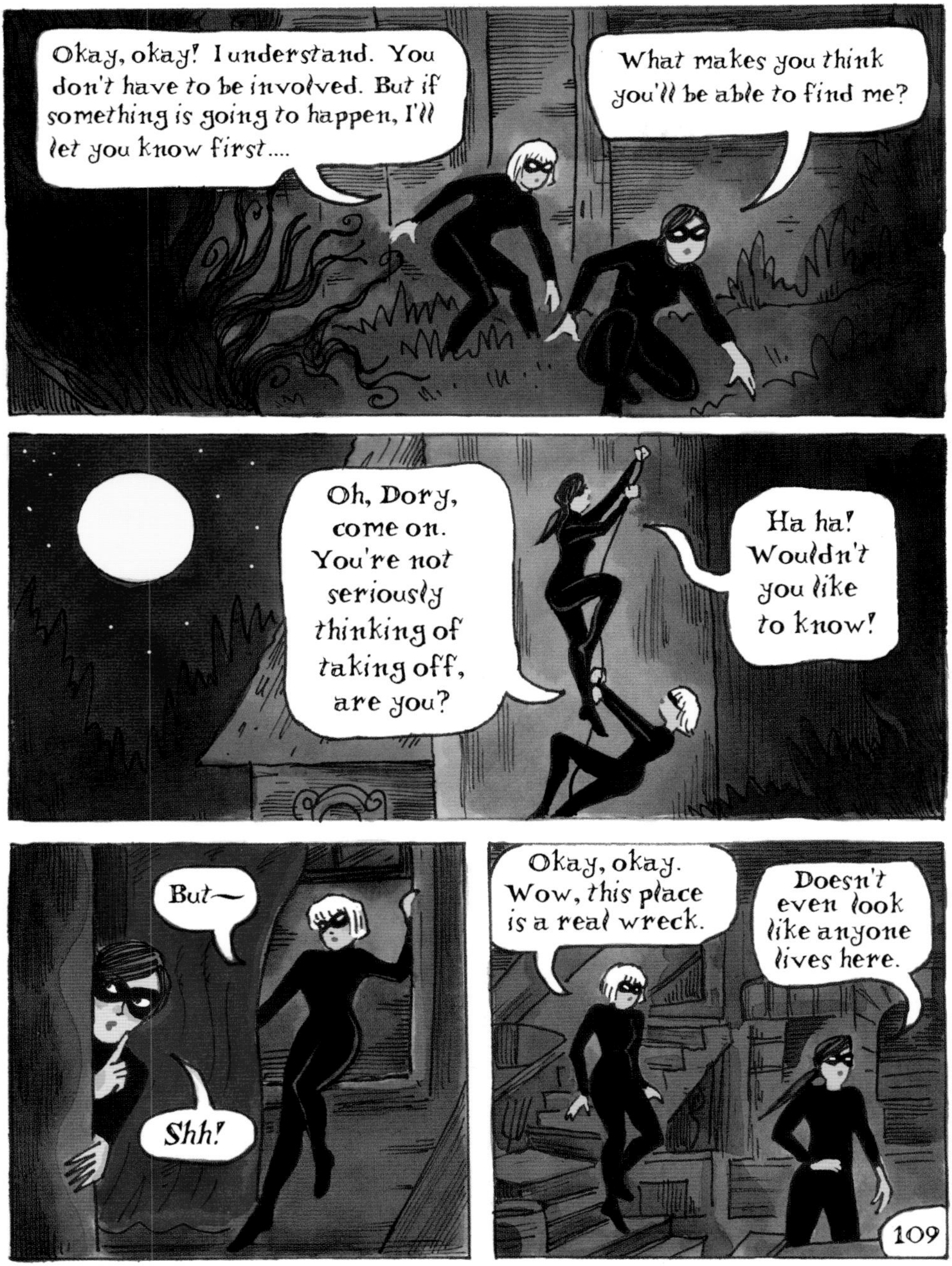

Okay, okay! I understand. You don't have to be involved. But if something is going to happen, I'll let you know first....
What makes you think you'll be able to find me?
Oh, Dory, come on. You're not seriously thinking of taking off, are you?
Ha ha! Wouldn't you like to know!
But—
Shh!
Okay, okay. Wow, this place is a real wreck.
Doesn't even look like anyone lives here.

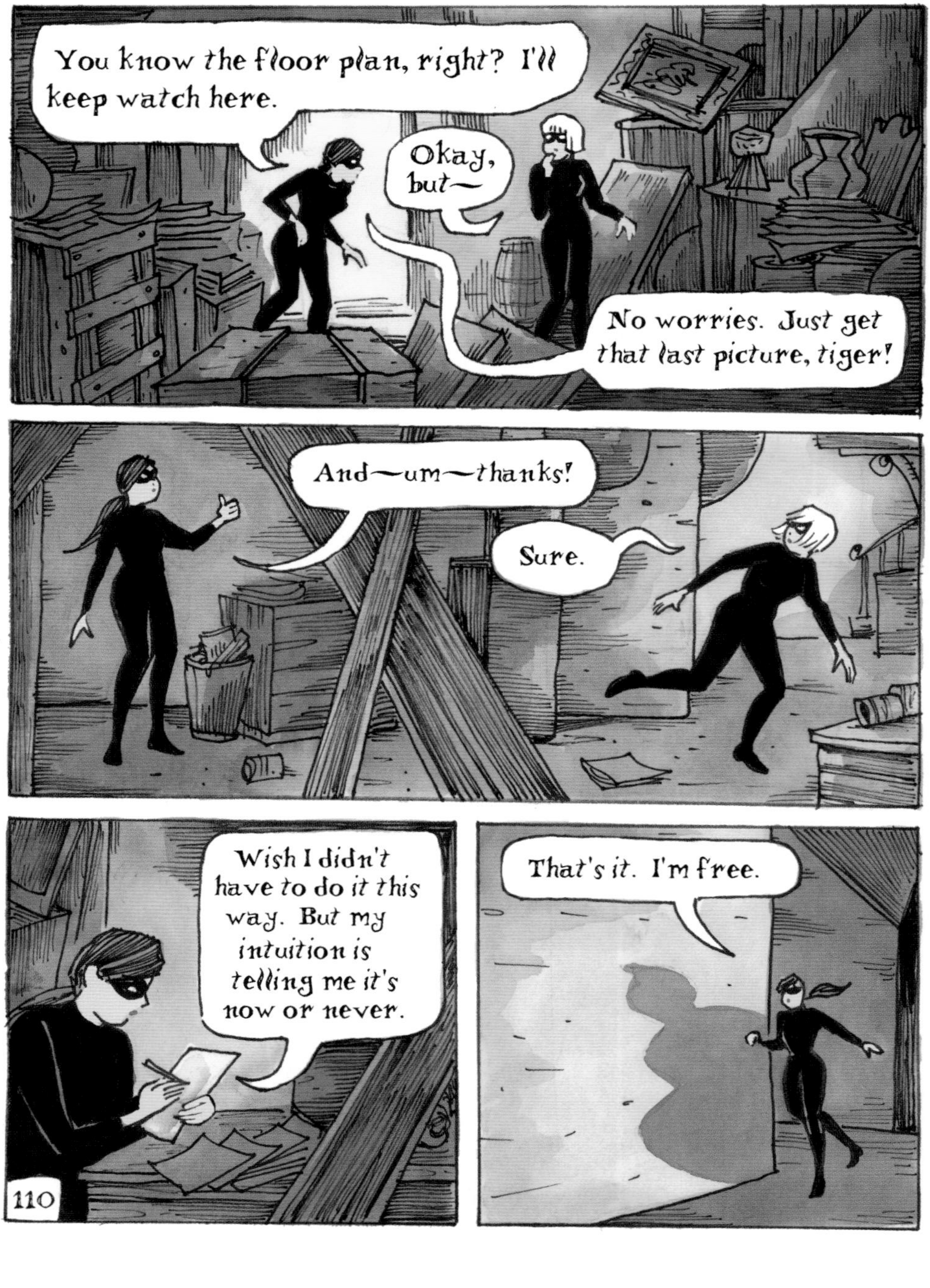
You know the floor plan, right? I'll keep watch here.
Okay, but—
No worries. Just get that last picture, tiger!
And—um—thanks!
Sure.
Wish I didn't have to do it this way. But my intuition is telling me it's now or never.
That's it. I'm free.

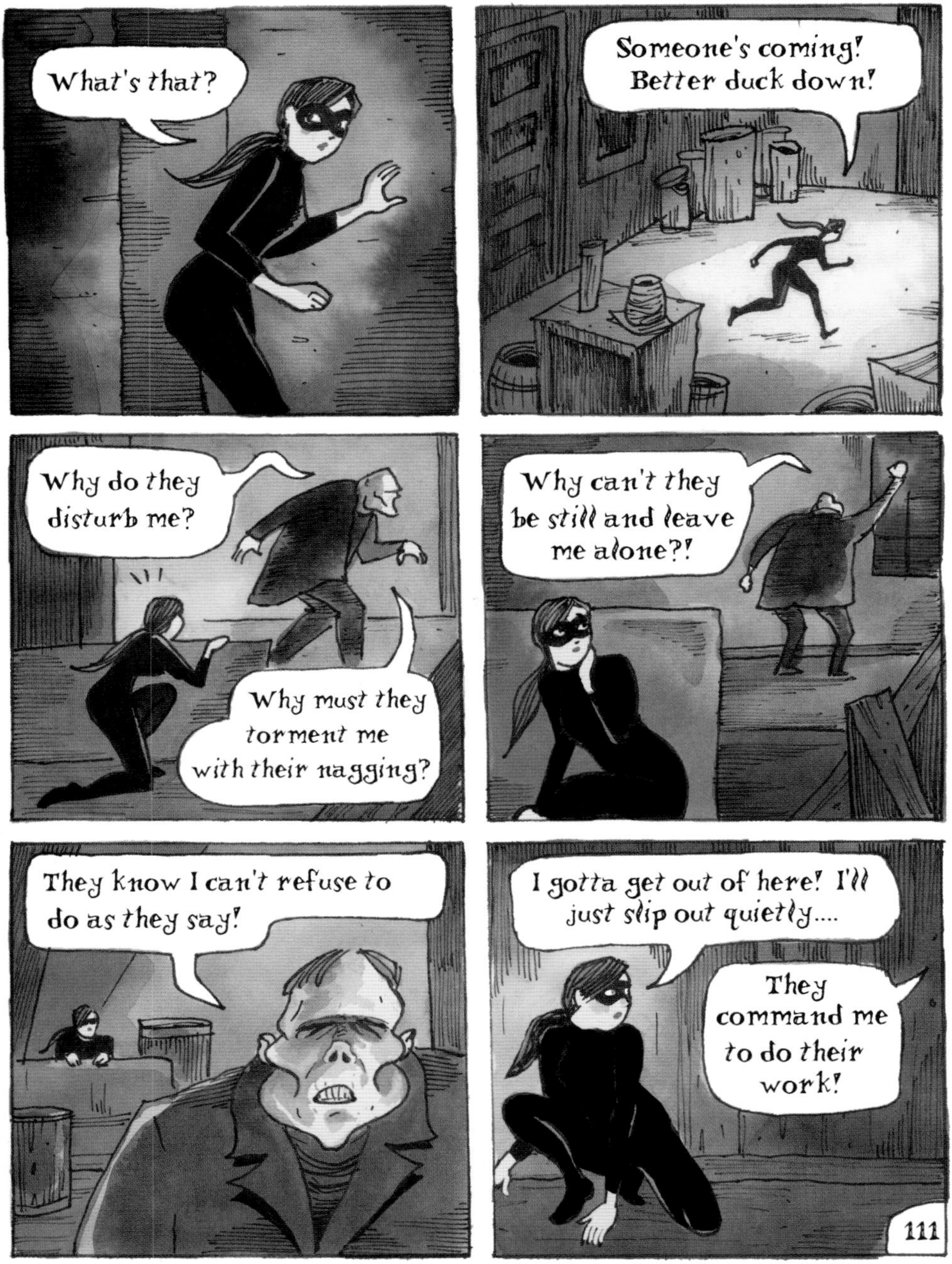
What's that?
Someone's coming! Better duck down!
Why do they disturb me?
Why must they torment me with their nagging?
Why can't they be still and leave me alone?!
They know I can't refuse to do as they say!
I gotta get out of here! I'll just slip out quietly....
They command me to do their work!
111

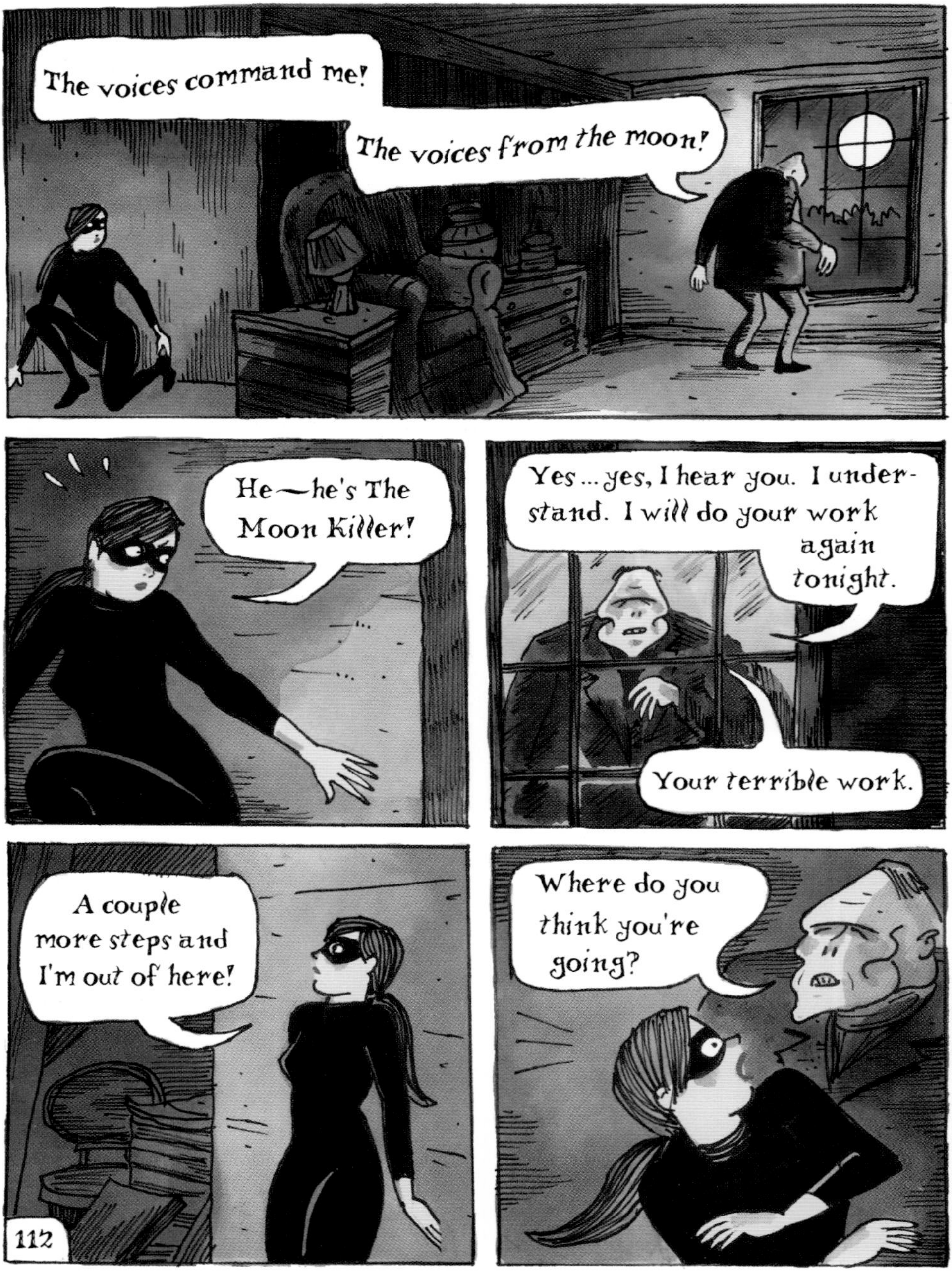
The voices command me!
The voices from the moon!
He—he's The Moon Killer!
Yes ... yes, I hear you. I understand. I will do your work again tonight.
Your terrible work.
A couple more steps and I'm out of here!
Where do you think you're going?

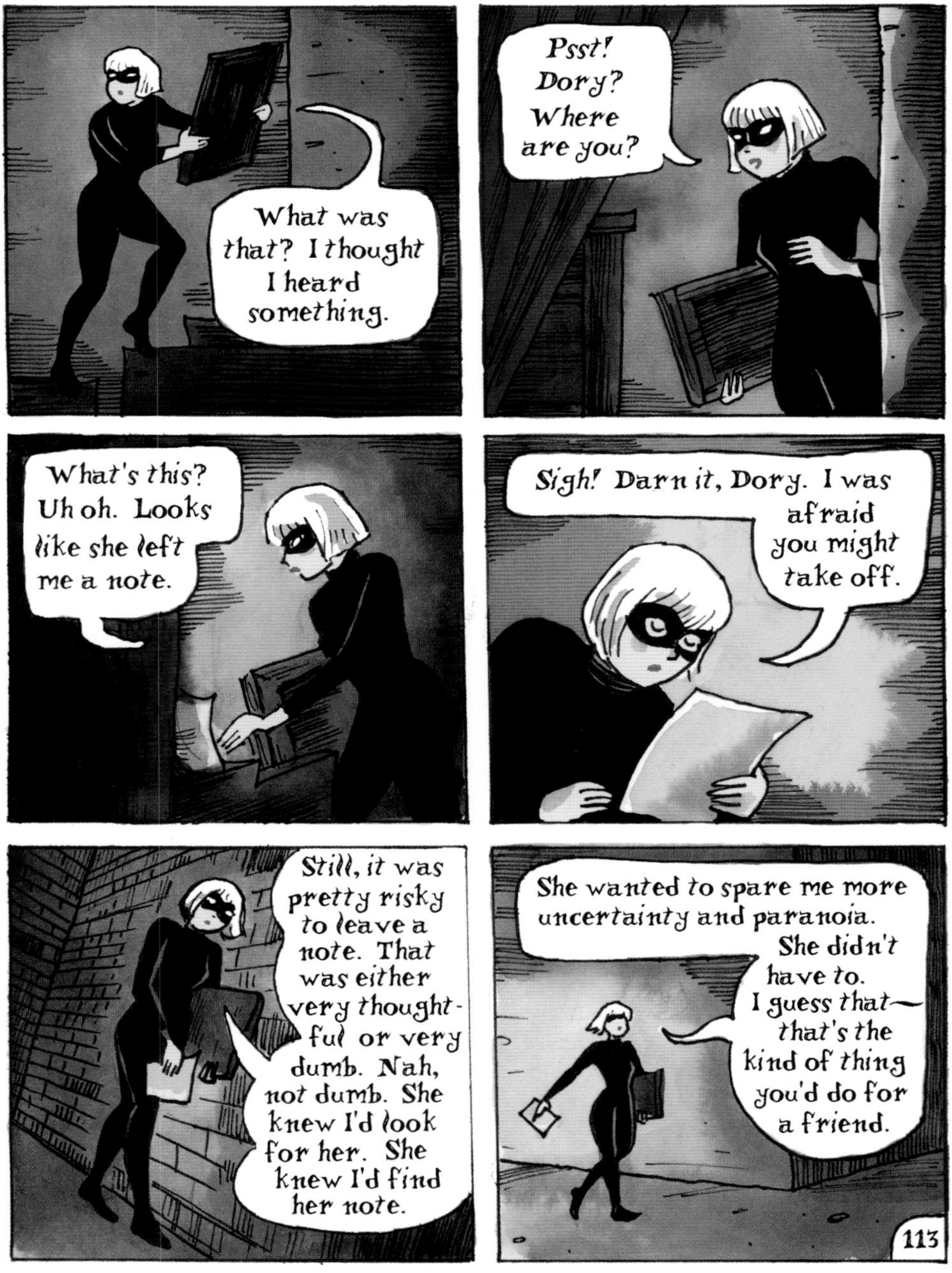
What was that? I thought I heard something.
Psst! Dory? Where are you?
What's this? Uh oh. Looks like she left me a note.
Sigh! Darn it, Dory. I was afraid you might take off.
Still, it was pretty risky to leave a note. That was either very thought-ful or very dumb. Nah, not dumb. She knew I'd look for her. She knew I'd find her note.
She wanted to spare me more uncertainty and paranoia.
She didn't have to. I guess that— that's the kind of thing you'd do for a friend.

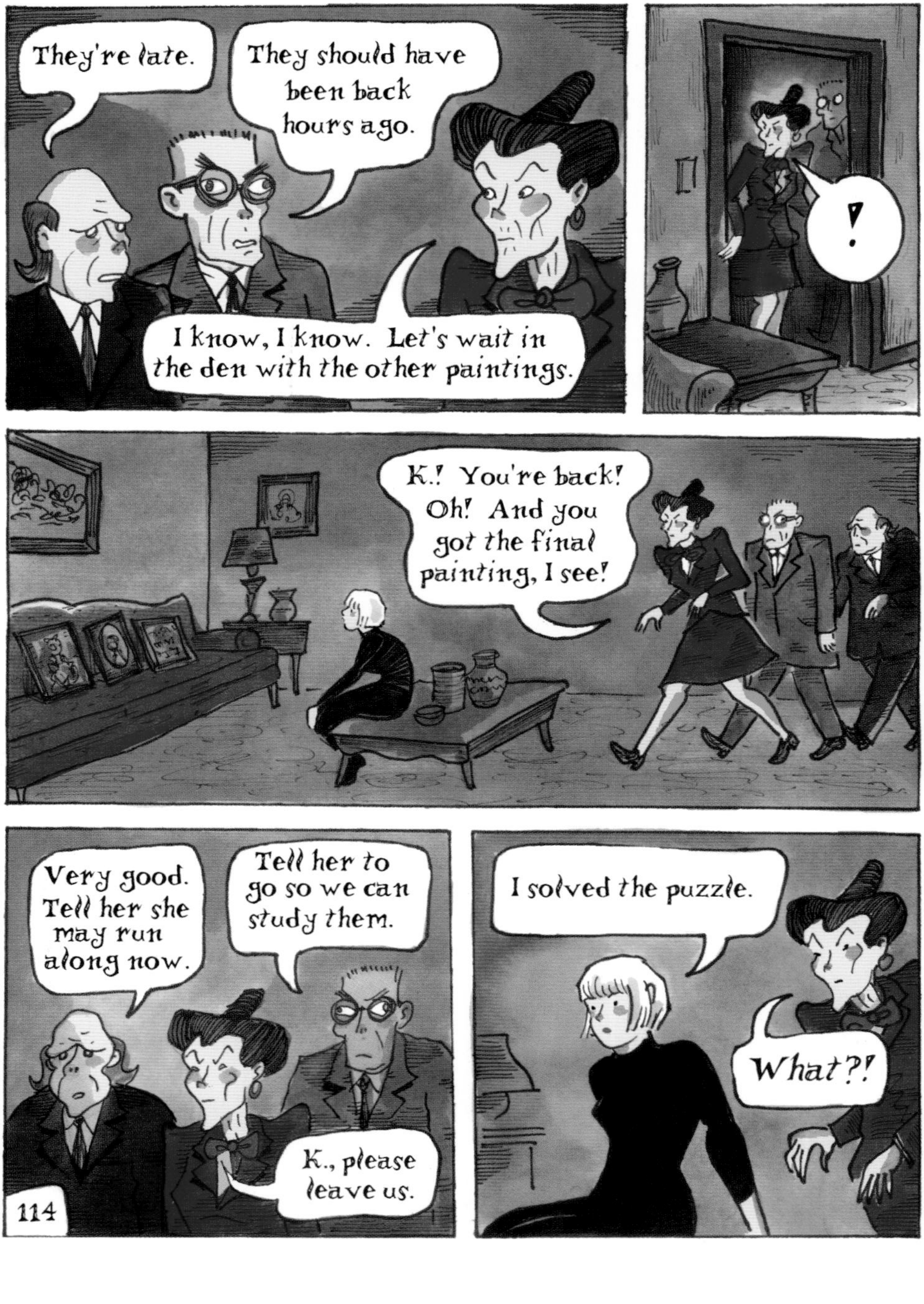
They're late.
They should have been back hours ago.
I know, I know. Let's wait in the den with the other paintings.
!
K.! You're back! Oh! And you got the final painting, I see!
Very good. Tell her she may run along now.
Tell her to go so we can study them.
K., please leave us.
I solved the puzzle.
What?!

Impossible!

Doubtful!

Improbable!

Highly unlikely!

Quiet, you two!

Well, my dear, don't keep us in suspense! Tell us!

It wasn't hard.

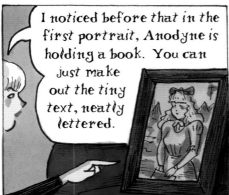

I noticed before that in the first portrait, Anodyne is holding a book. You can just make out the tiny text, neatly lettered.

It's The Riddle Book, published in 1828 by J. Metcalf. There is a copy in the library—here it is. It may even be the same copy.

Interesting, K. Please continue.

Okay. In the second picture there are thirteen roses.

So, I tried looking on page thirteen of The Riddle Book to see what riddle was printed there.

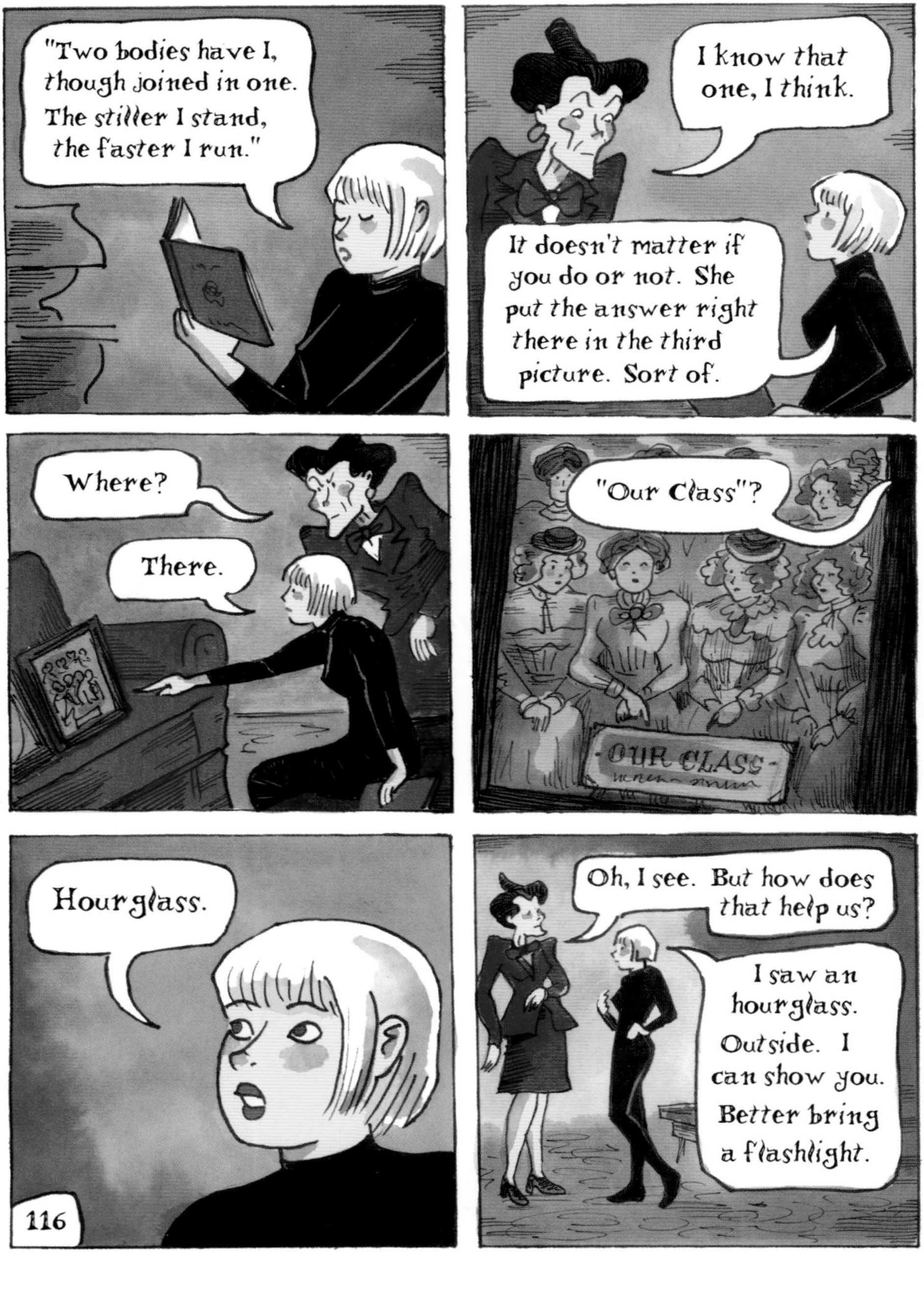
"Two bodies have I, though joined in one. The stiller I stand, the faster I run."
I know that one, I think.
It doesn't matter if you do or not. She put the answer right there in the third picture. Sort of.
Where?
There.
"Our Class"?
OUR CLASS
Hourglass.
Oh, I see. But how does that help us?
I saw an hourglass. Outside. I can show you. Better bring a flashlight.

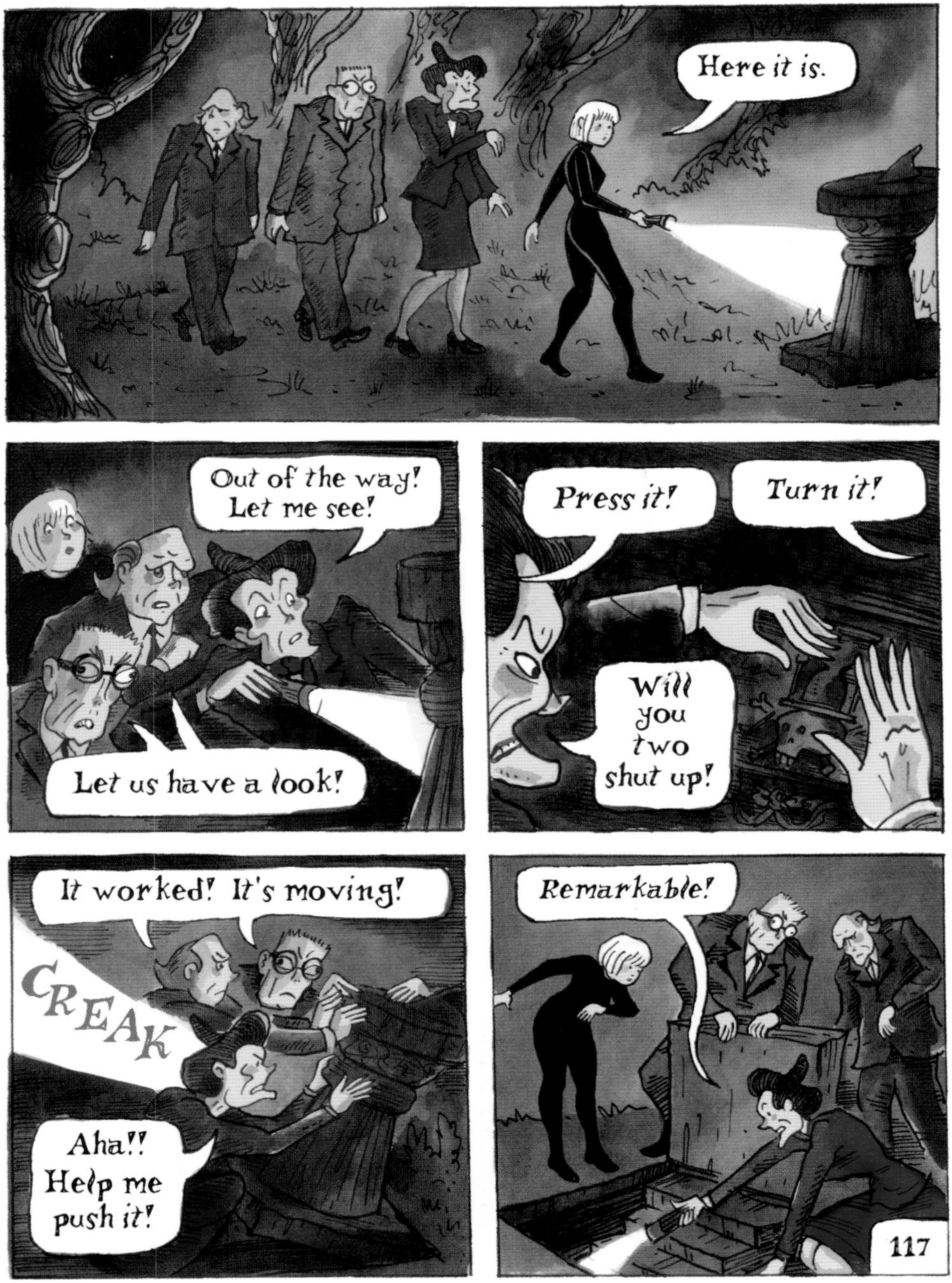
Here it is.
Out of the way! Let me see!
Let us have a look!
Press it!
Turn it!
Will you two shut up!
It worked! It's moving!
CREAK
Aha!! Help me push it!
Remarkable!

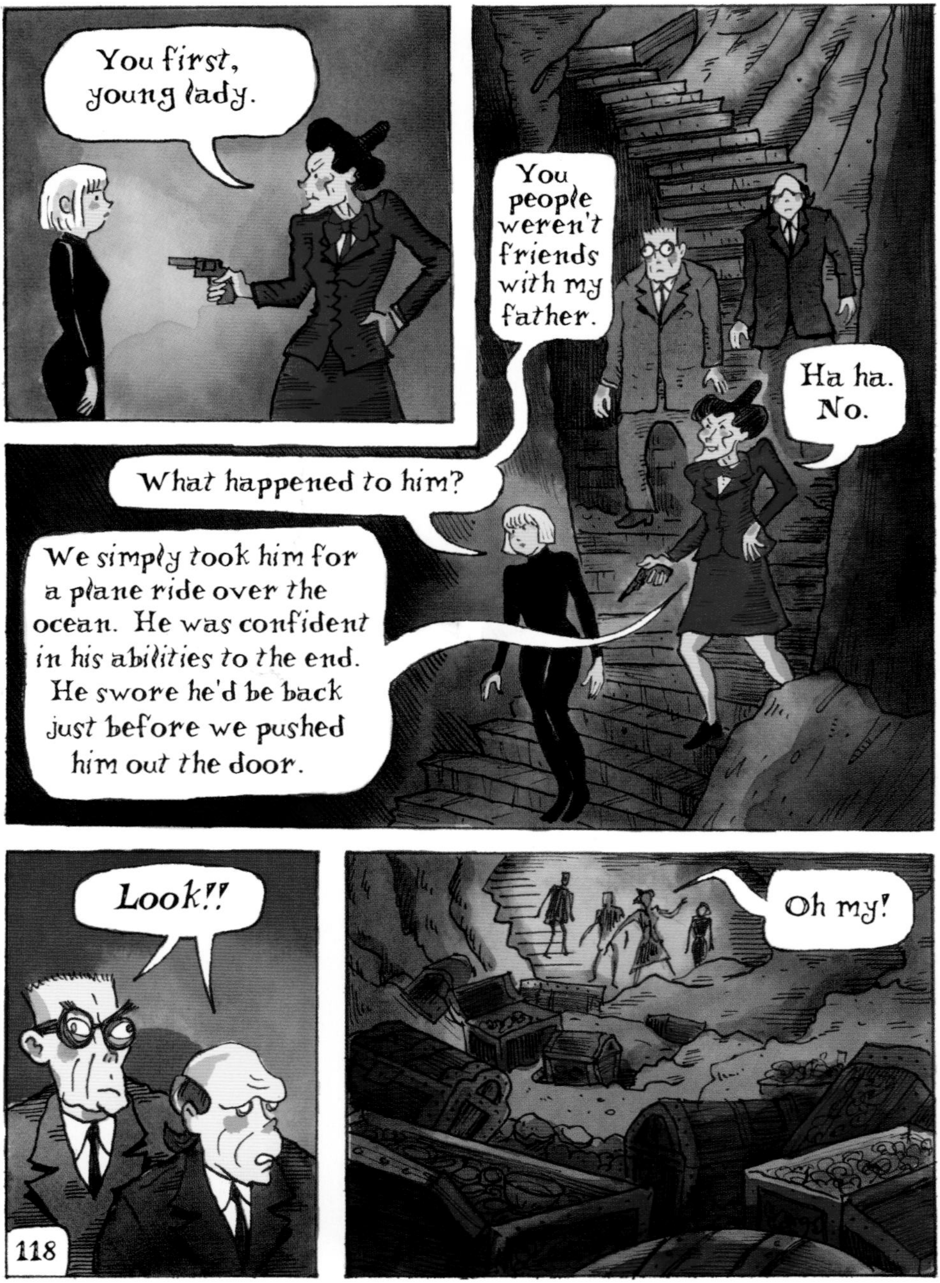
You first, young lady.
You people weren't friends with my father.
Ha ha. No.
What happened to him?
We simply took him for a plane ride over the ocean. He was confident in his abilities to the end. He swore he'd be back just before we pushed him out the door.
Look!!
Oh my!

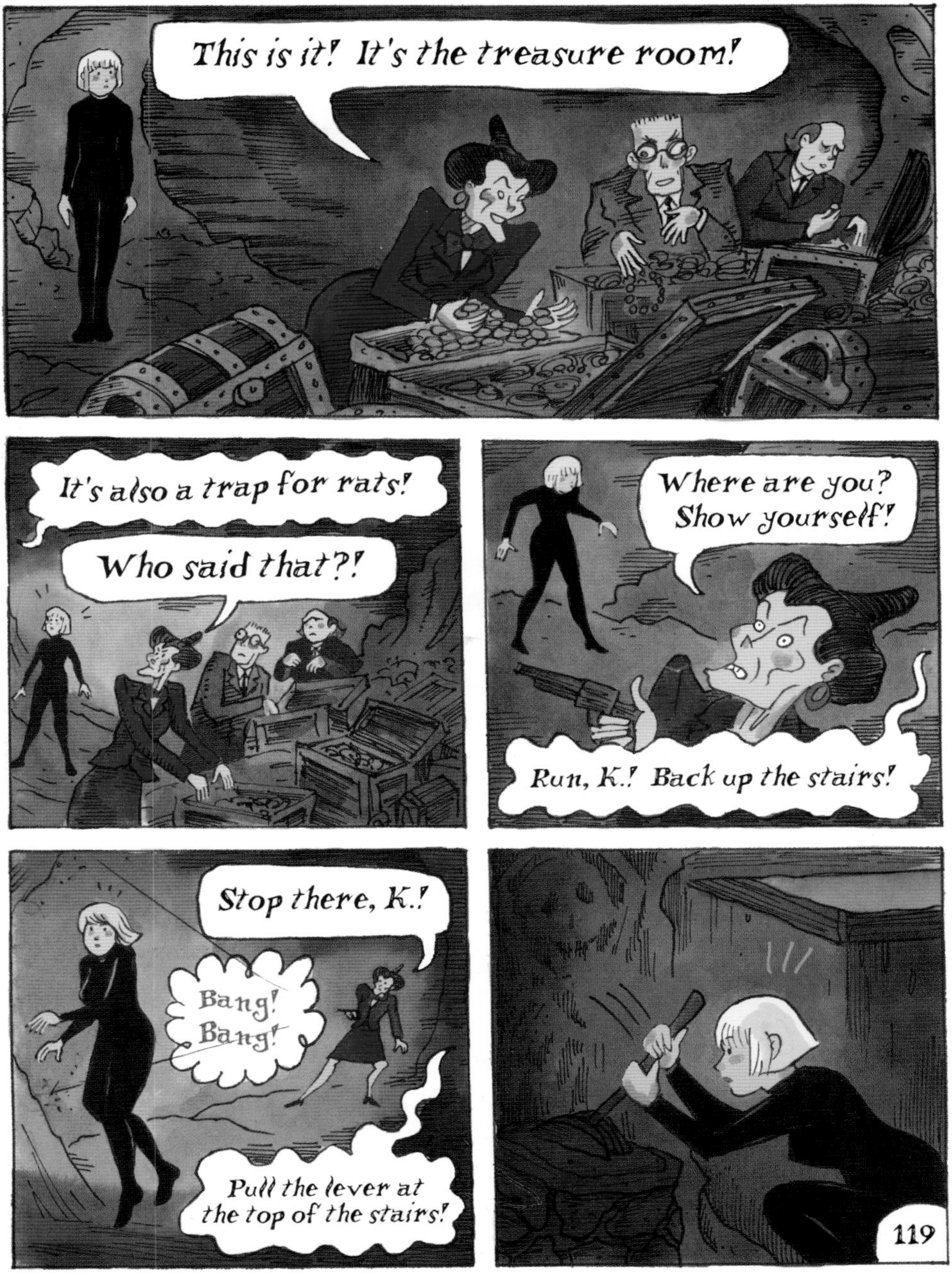
This is it! It's the treasure room!
It's also a trap for rats!
Who said that?!
Where are you? Show yourself!
Run, K.! Back up the stairs!
Stop there, K.!
Bang! Bang!
Pull the lever at the top of the stairs!

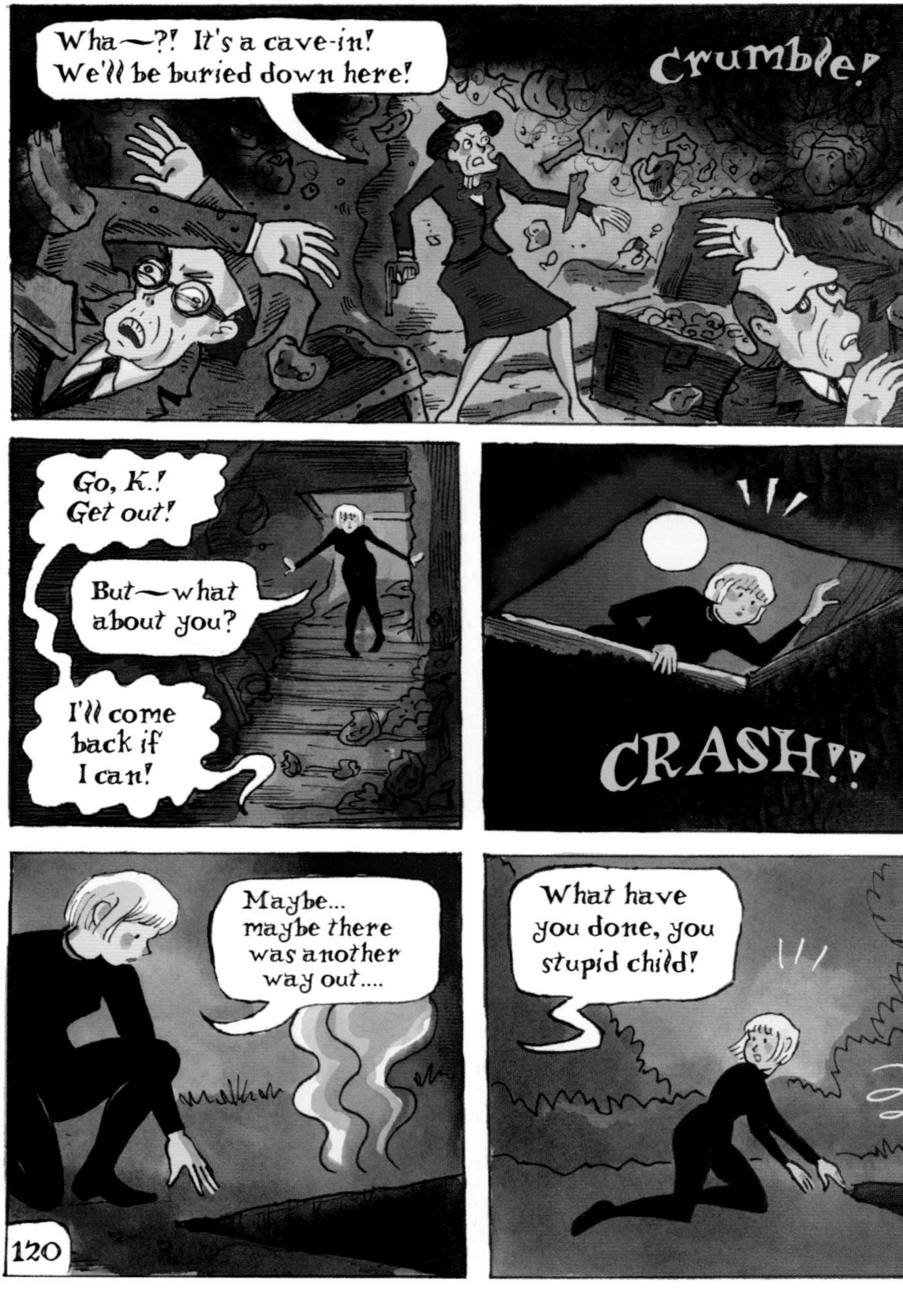

Wha—?! It's a cave-in! We'll be buried down here!
Crumble!
Go, K.! Get out!
But—what about you?
I'll come back if I can!
CRASH!!
Maybe... maybe there was another way out....
What have you done, you stupid child!

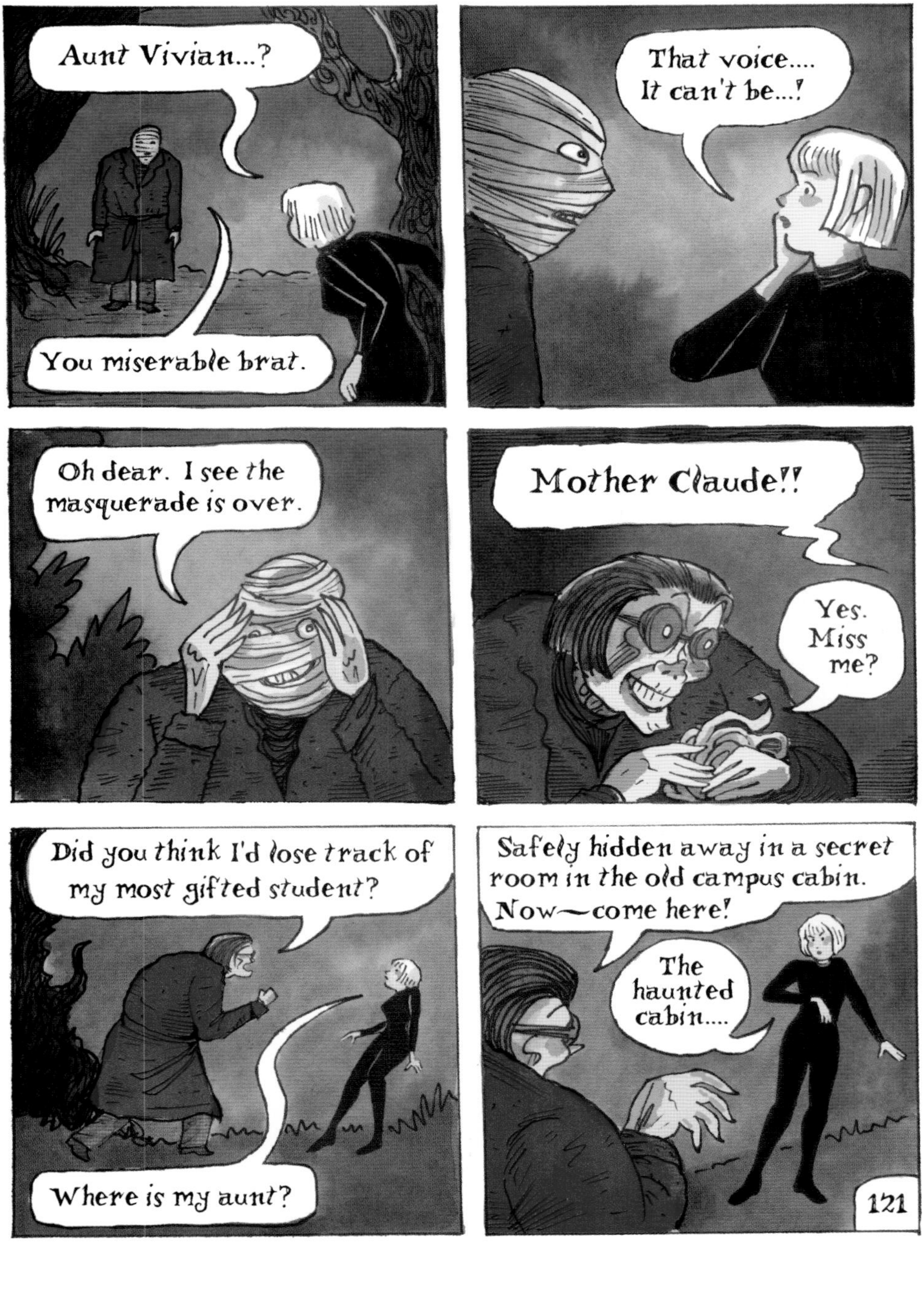
Aunt Vivian...?
You miserable brat.
That voice.... It can't be...!
Oh dear. I see the masquerade is over.
Mother Claude!!
Yes. Miss me?
Did you think I'd lose track of my most gifted student?
Where is my aunt?
Safely hidden away in a secret room in the old campus cabin. Now—come here!
The haunted cabin....

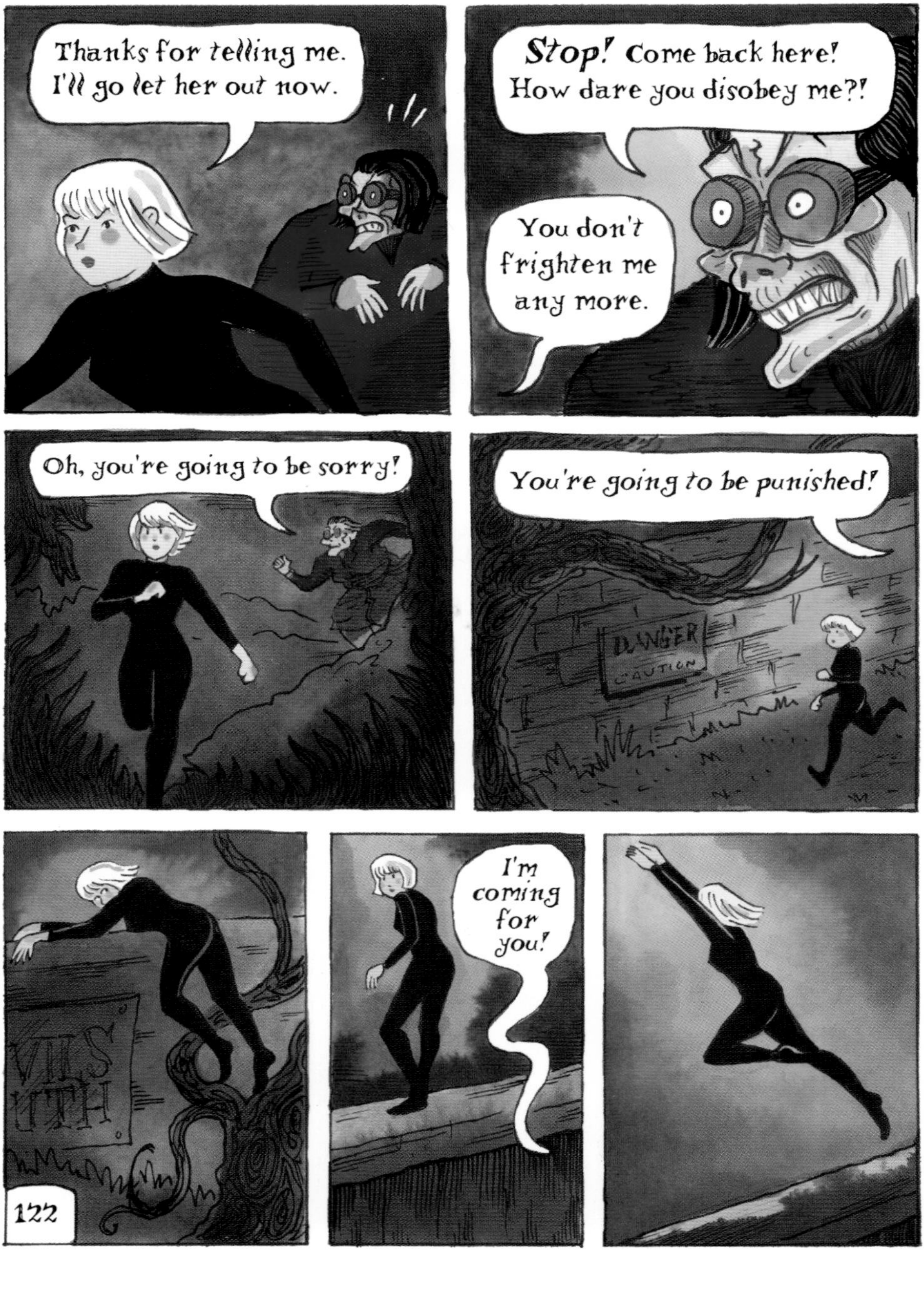
Thanks for telling me. I'll go let her out now.
Stop! Come back here! How dare you disobey me?!
You don't frighten me any more.
Oh, you're going to be sorry!
You're going to be punished!
DANGER
CAUTION
I'm coming for you!

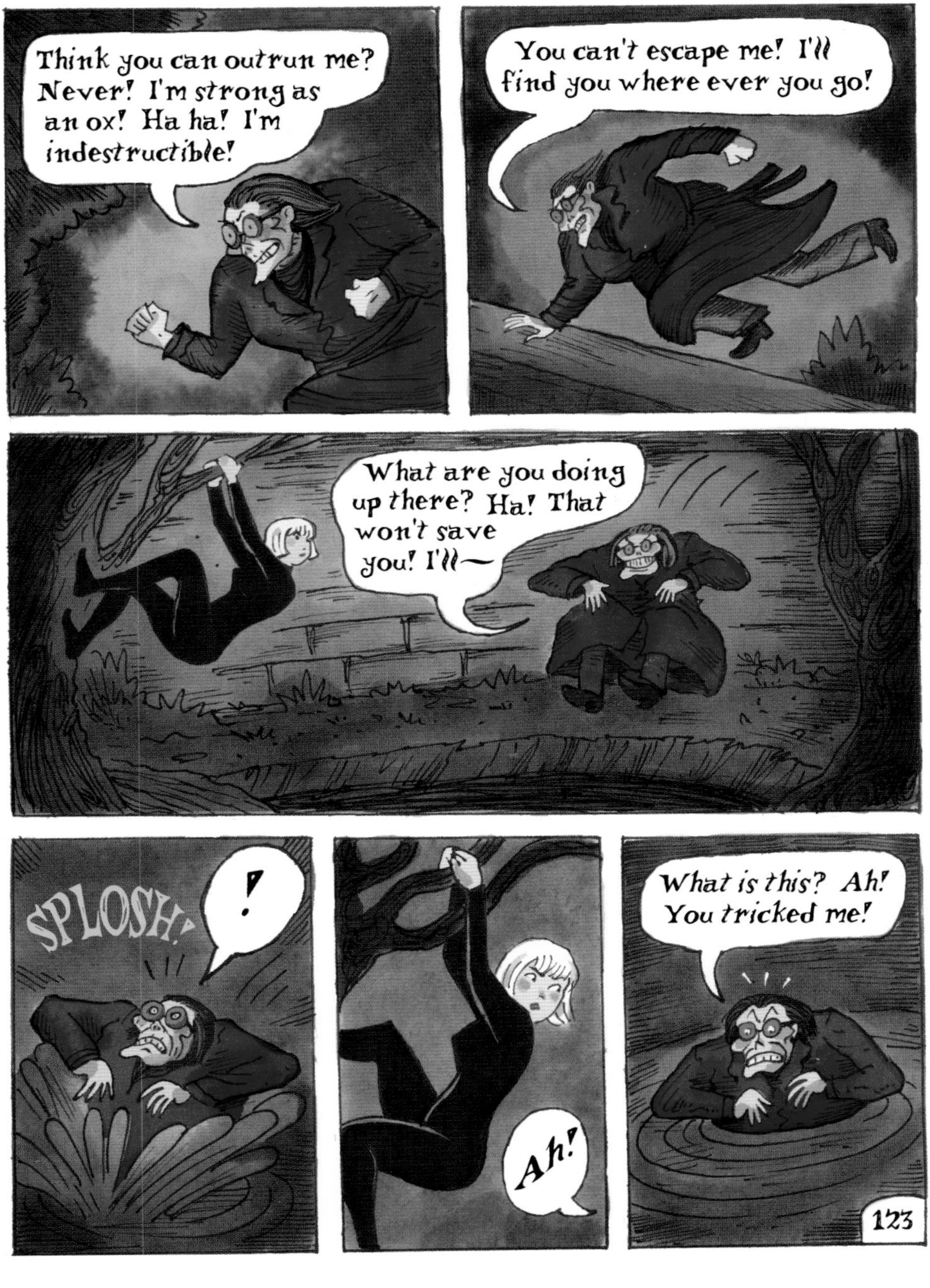
Think you can outrun me? Never! I'm strong as an ox! Ha ha! I'm indestructible!
You can't escape me! I'll find you where ever you go!
What are you doing up there? Ha! That won't save you! I'll—
SPLOSH!
!
Ah!
What is this? Ah! You tricked me!

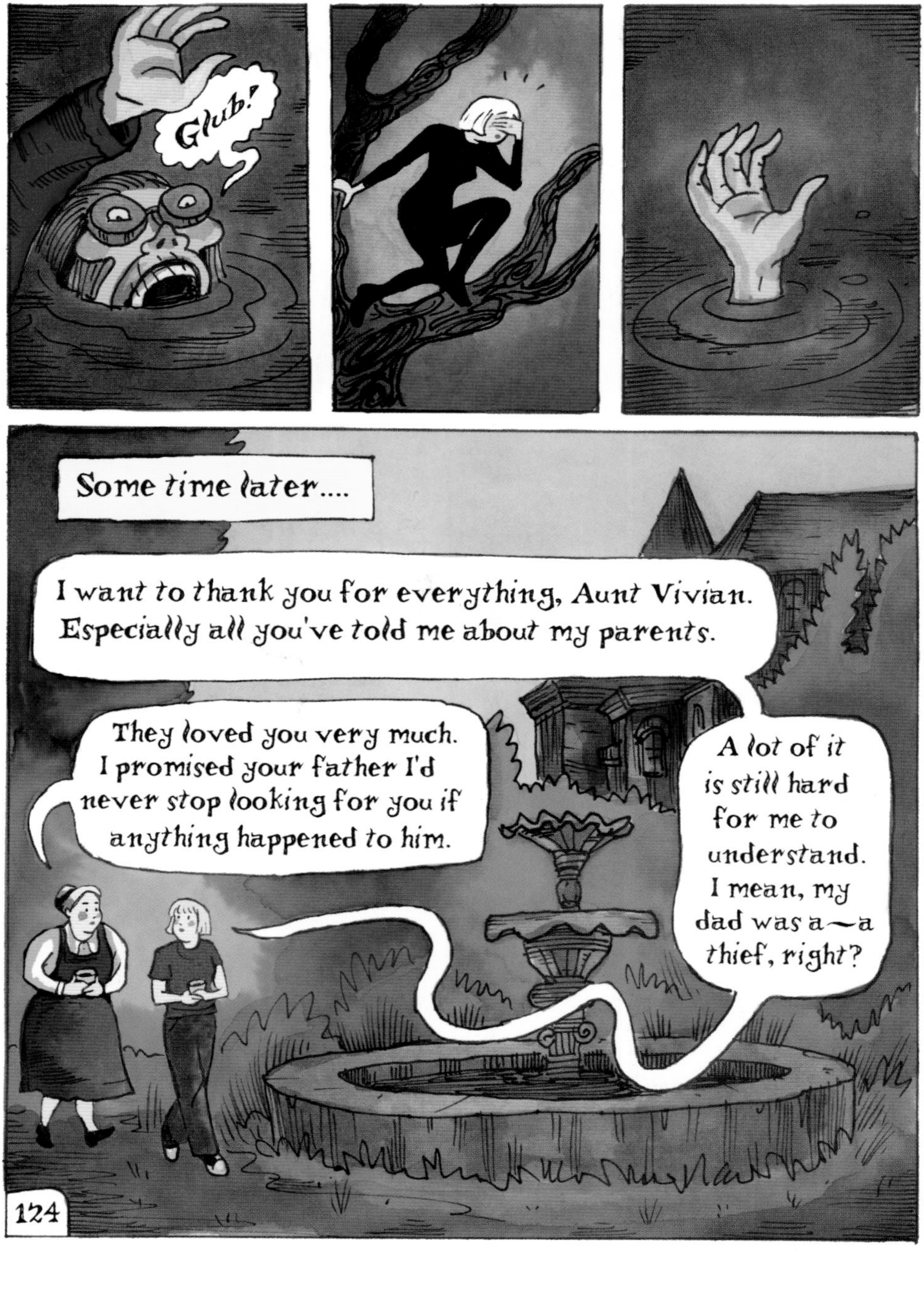
Glub!
Some time later....
I want to thank you for everything, Aunt Vivian. Especially all you've told me about my parents.
They loved you very much. I promised your father I'd never stop looking for you if anything happened to him.
A lot of it is still hard for me to understand. I mean, my dad was a—a thief, right?

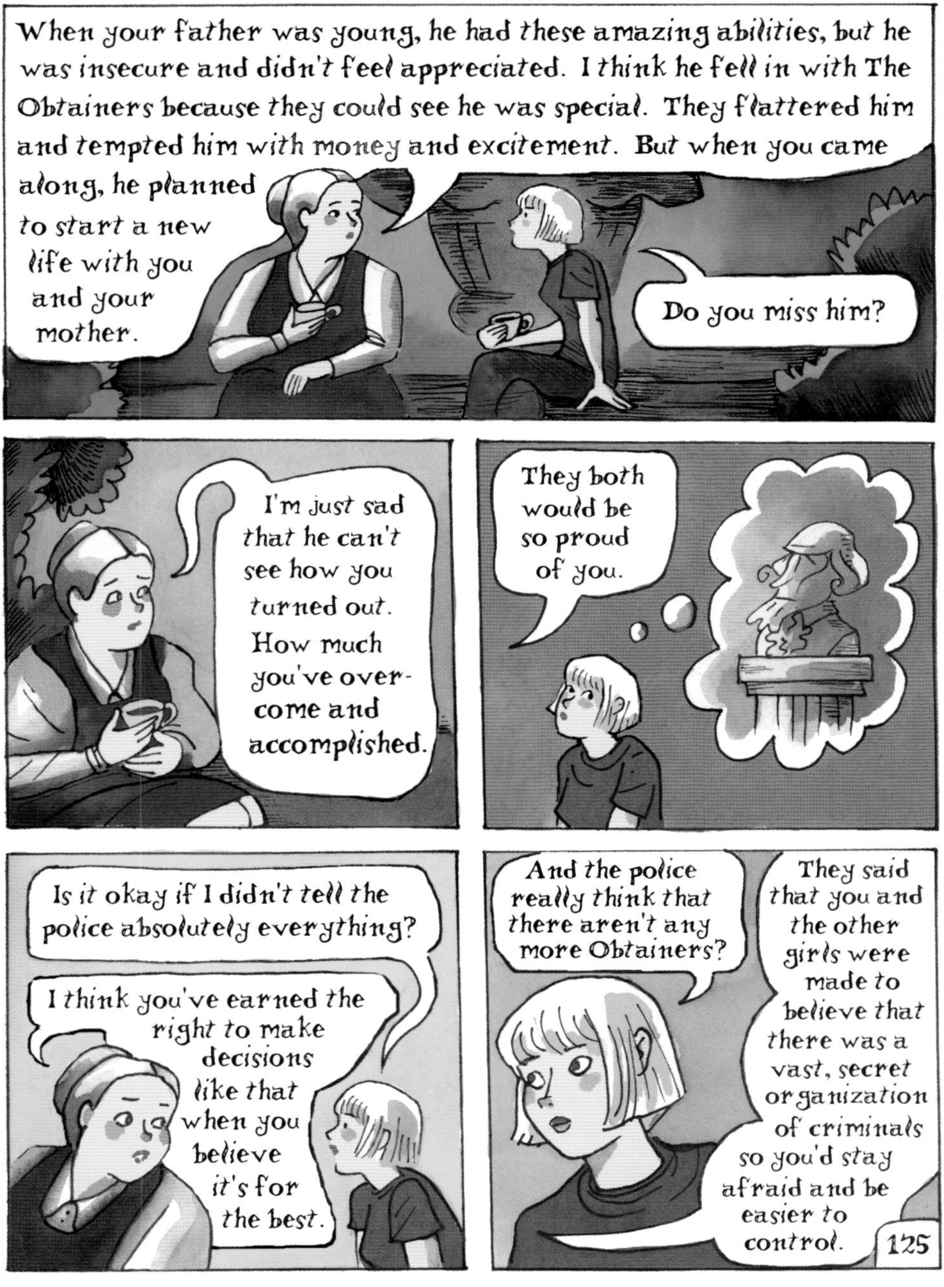

When your father was young, he had these amazing abilities, but he was insecure and didn't feel appreciated. I think he fell in with The Obtainers because they could see he was special. They flattered him and tempted him with money and excitement. But when you came along, he planned to start a new life with you and your mother.
Do you miss him?
I'm just sad that he can't see how you turned out. How much you've over-come and accomplished.
They both would be so proud of you.
Is it okay if I didn't tell the police absolutely everything?
I think you've earned the right to make decisions like that when you believe it's for the best.
And the police really think that there aren't any more Obtainers?
They said that you and the other girls were made to believe that there was a vast, secret organization of criminals so you'd stay afraid and be easier to control.
125

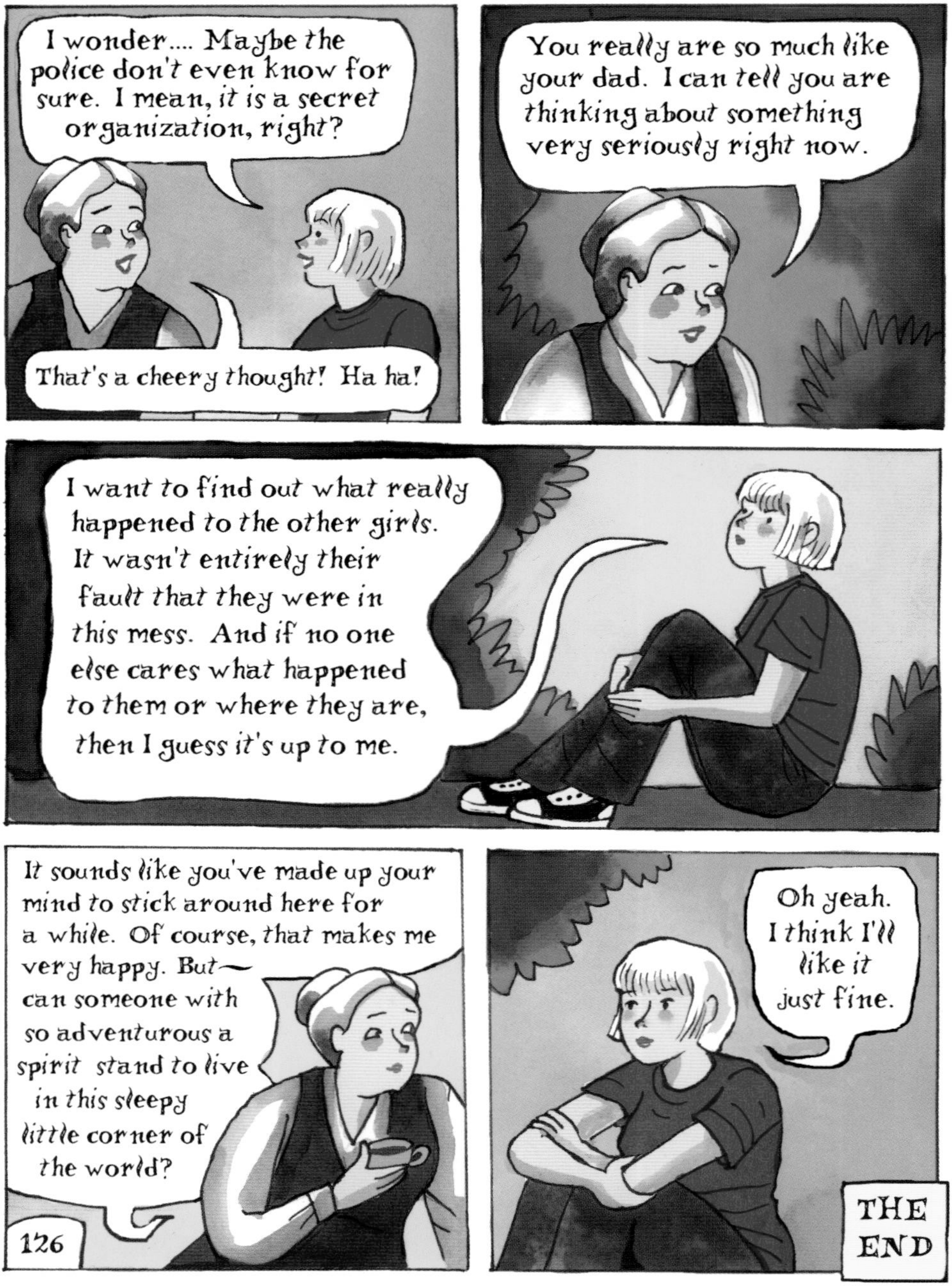
I wonder.... Maybe the police don't even know for sure. I mean, it is a secret organization, right?
That's a cheery thought! Ha ha!
You really are so much like your dad. I can tell you are thinking about something very seriously right now.
I want to find out what really happened to the other girls. It wasn't entirely their fault that they were in this mess. And if no one else cares what happened to them or where they are, then I guess it's up to me.
It sounds like you've made up your mind to stick around here for a while. Of course, that makes me very happy. But— can someone with so adventurous a spirit stand to live in this sleepy little corner of the world?
Oh yeah. I think I'll like it just fine.
THE END

First Second

New York & London

Copyright © 2009 by Richard Sala

Published by First Second
First Second is an imprint of Roaring Brook Press,
a division of Holtzbrinck Publishing Holdings Limited Partnership
175 Fifth Avenue, New York, NY 10010

All rights reserved.

Distributed in Canada by H. B. Fenn and Company Ltd.
Distributed in the United Kingdom by Macmillan Children's Books,
a division of Pan Macmillan.

Interior design by Danica Novgorodoff and Colleen AF Venable
Cover design by Colleen AF Venable

Cataloging-in-Publication Data is on file at the Library of Congress.

ISBN: 978-1-59643-144-7

First Second books are available for special promotions and premiums.
For details, contact: Director of Special Markets, Holtzbrinck Publishers.

First Edition September 2009
Printed in April 2009 in China by South China Printing Company Ltd.,
Dongguan City, Guandong Province.
1 3 5 7 9 10 8 6 4 2